BENEATH HIS WINGS

LIONEL HART

Lionel Hart

Copyright © 2021 by Lionel Hart

All rights reserved.

No portion of this book may be reproduced in any form without written permission from the publisher or author, except as permitted by U.S. copyright law. It is illegal to copy this book, post it to a website, or distribute it by any other means without permission.

Cover design by Midnight Coffee - https://midnightcoffee.co.uk/

Contents

Epigraph	V
Prologue	1
1. Chapter One	5
2. Chapter Two	14
3. Chapter Three	27
4. Chapter Four	36
5. Chapter Five	54
6. Chapter Six	63
7. Chapter Seven	78
8. Chapter Eight	89
9. Chapter Nine	102
10. Chapter Ten	118
11. Chapter Eleven	135
12. Chapter Twelve	148
13. Chapter Thirteen	165

14. Chapter Fourteen	178
15. Chapter Fifteen	187
16. Chapter Sixteen	204
17. Chapter Seventeen	214
18. Chapter Eighteen	225
19. Chapter Nineteen	235
20. Chapter Twenty	246
21. Chapter Twenty-One	263
22. Chapter Twenty-Two	277
23. Chapter Twenty-Three	288
24. Chapter Twenty-Four	298
25. Chapter Twenty-Five	309
26. Chapter Twenty-Six	324
27. Chapter Twenty-Seven	338
28. Chapter Twenty-Eight	349
29. Chapter Twenty-Nine	364
30. Chapter Thirty	374
About the Author	383
Also By Lionel Hart	384

The hunger of a dragon is slow to wake, but hard to sate.
-Ursula K. Le Guin

Prologue

In the days following their surrender to the human rebellion, the dwarven city of Polimnos was razed to the ground. In the midst of the dwarven evacuation and the arrival of human forces, the dragon Zamnes found the city abandoned. Both sides could only bear witness as the city burned, and the dragon fled with his hoard, his black scales hiding him amongst the smoke and ash. A small handful of brave warriors gave chase. None returned.

Zamnes, Scourge of Polimnos, was sighted occasionally in the following weeks and months, flying along the coast to deter any humans from entering the ruins of the city. Even if they had, there was nothing left to scavenge. The dragon had been nothing if not thorough.

After the war between the elven nation of Aefraya and the dwarven dynasty in Robruolor officially ended, and Autreth was granted independence from both, the dragon was not seen again. Eventually, despite whispers and rumors, the city was carefully picked clean, the rubble hauled away, and the beginnings of a new town rose from the ashes.

Some believed Zamnes' lair was deep in distant mountains where labyrinthine tunnels kept the outside world from disturbing him; still others claimed he had taken up residence in a volcano rising up from the ocean, on an island that was weeks away by boat, but surely only hours by flight.

Only a few dared whisper that the Scourge had never left at all: that his lair was deep beneath the very foundation of Polimnos itself, and he slept content on his hoard for now. To rebuild was foolish, they would say, because when Zamnes eventually woke—as all dragons do—he would rise up and level the city once more, taking whatever wealth it had amassed in his absence as his own.

These few were closest to the truth. Zamnes' lair was not directly underneath the city, but nestled underground in a cliff face less than two miles north of the city's remains. There he slumbered after gathering his newly-found spoils. When he eventually woke, he set out to provide his last offerings to his progenitors, a symbol of true independence from his clutch.

His father, Mithantos, had scales black and gleaming as his own, and his lair was far to the south in a mountain made of obsidian. To him, Zamnes offered a chest of uncut gems: they would be worth much, and he had little knowledge of his father's personal likes and dislikes. His mother, Ilrenth, was dark blue, and their only resemblance was their equally blue eyes. Ilrenth had claim to a remote island in the middle of the ocean, where her blue scales camouflaged her against the sight of all sailors, and she supplied her hoard with spoils taken from pirates and merchants alike. To her, Zamnes presented a collection of dwarven vases and urns. He knew she enjoyed the tiny details of pottery, and she thanked him for the gift, before they parted for what was likely the last time. After all, dragons were solitary creatures.

His offerings made, facilitating a clean break, Zamnes returned to his lair and found it undisturbed. Again he slumbered and lived idly, until he decided to investigate what had become of Polimnos in the two years since he had burned it down and carried its riches underground.

He decided to assume the guise of an elven mage. Elves commonly traveled the world, would live far longer than the humans that made up the population of Autreth, and had an innate knack for magic that would ensure his own prowess would be unremarkable. In front of a gleaming silver mirror he transformed, tweaking and adjusting his appearance until it suited his fancy perfectly. Tall, fair skin, a handsome face with hair as black as his scales, and familiar blue eyes.

"Adrissu," he murmured to himself, meeting his own eyes in the mirror. "A good name."

It was the name of a powerful elven wizard from an age long past, a name that promised prosperity for this false identity. Magic interested him more than anything, and now that he had his own hoard, he was free to pursue his interests at his leisure. Perhaps, in time, he could even surpass the original Adrissu.

"A wizard should have a familiar," he decided, and with two of the countless jewels that he had claimed, he performed the summoning rites. The familiar took the form of a small snake with gleaming black scales—fitting, he thought with a laugh, as he extended his hand and watched it slither up into his sleeve, as naturally as if it had always been there.

"Let us see what Polimnos has become in my absence," Adrissu said to it, and left his lair.

Book One
Ruan

Chapter One

A heavy knock thudded at the wooden door of his tower.
"Adrissu!"
From the second floor, Adrissu sighed and gestured toward the stairs.
"Vesper, be a dear and answer the door," he said. With a heavy dragging sound, Vesper uncurled herself from where she dozed at his feet. The snake, far larger now than when Adrissu had first summoned her, made her way down the stairs; and a moment later he heard the thud of her pressing her weight against the door handle to push it open.
"I'll be down in just a moment, Councilor," he called. Distantly, he could hear a slightly startled exclamation—he did not know *why*, as Vesper's presence in his tower should have been common knowledge to anyone who visited him, and the insufferable councilor had made more than a few house calls as of late. Benil Branwood was a skinny, nervous man who sought Adrissu's advice too often and his favors even moreso; much as he tried to avoid the councilor, he had put this lunch meeting off twice already and suspected that the man would not take so kindly to another cancellation.
So with a sigh, Adrissu set down the alchemical ungents he had been mixing, wiped his hands clean, and descended the stairs to find Benil standing nervously in the doorway and eyeing Vesper as she curled up near the bottom step.

"Adrissu!" the man exclaimed as he appeared in the stairway, the nervous expression quickly replaced with an appeasing grin. "Good to see you. Thank you for agreeing to meet with me today."

"Of course," Adrissu replied simply, giving the man a slight nod. "Forgive the delay, Councilor Branwood. I received a new shipment of sebran leaves last week and have been experimenting."

"Is that what I'm smelling?" Benil said. "And please, please, we're friends, aren't we? You can always just call me Benil."

Adrissu managed a tight smile. The human reminded him every time: he was starting to suspect that he was either too stupid to get the hint that they were *not* friends, or being purposely bullheaded. Knowing him, it truly could go either way.

"Shall we go?" Adrissu said, gesturing for the door.

Saltspire Tower, his home, sat on the northernmost edge of Polimnos' borders near a cliff face that dropped into the ocean. Most days he could hear the soft sounds of the waves crashing far below, particularly during high tide. As they stepped out of his tower now, he could not hear the sea, but the smell of the ocean air was as thick as ever. The morning mist had burned off by now, a warm spring day well underway.

"Have you eaten?" Benil chattered, as they began to walk down the hill where his tower stood and along the path that led directly into town. The first few feet leading up to his tower were marked with stepping-stones; beyond those, the path was only packed dirt. "Margo, the baker, she's started making these delicious meat pies. I'd be happy to get you one, my treat."

"Certainly," Adrissu agreed idly, looking out to where the land dropped off into a sheer cliff—the sky was deep blue and covered with huge, fluffy clouds. It had been a long time since he'd flown. Maybe he would sneak away one of these nights for a flight.

Polimnos had grown significantly in the twenty-odd years since it was destroyed, quicker than he had expected when he first arrived. Granted, it was an appealing location; and humans with their newfound freedom had flocked there in droves. Humans were nothing if not industrious, he had learned, and had quickly rebuilt the city to suit their own tastes. Whatever lingering dwarven aesthetic or motif that might have survived the city's past destruction had long since been built over. The city had become completely and utterly human, for better and worse.

Most of the town's populace was crammed around the central avenue that followed the shape of the cliffs for a time, then veered west to become the main footpath that supplied the city's trade and commerce. The buildings now were mostly wood with only a few made of stone—none crafted out of large slabs of rock, the way dwarves constructed their buildings. It only served to show that they no longer feared the return of Zamnes, nor any dragon that might try to burn their city down again. In the end, for all that effort, its riches were a fraction of what it had once been and of no appeal to dragons anymore. And of course, Adrissu's presence would deter any other dragons from the area—not that the townsfolk would know that.

The city's exports of fish, stone, and pottery served as their lone connection to the other human city-states that had emerged since Autreth had overthrown their dwarven conquerors and driven away the elf forces that had sought to seize it in the power vacuum that remained. For now, a tentative peace had emerged between the independent city-states in the landmass that made up Autreth; young as he was, Adrissu knew enough of the cycles of time that their independence was bound to come under fire once again. Until then, he would enjoy the relative isolation of Polimnos and its scenery.

He realized Benil had asked him something while his mind was occupied with the sky. "I beg your pardon?"

"Oh, well, I was only asking—" the man stuttered, wringing his hands in front of him. Much as he tried to feign confidence, his nervous tics were far too apparent to fool anyone with even remote powers of observation. "I had only wondered, well, if you might be willing to sign on to the project. I know we don't have the workforce for it just *yet,* but if the quarry were expanded, the workers would surely come."

"Ah," Adrissu said. The man had been spearheading an effort to expand the quarry outside of Polimnos. The stone there was its primary export, and the Branwood family was one of the three founding members who had begun a mine in the first years of Polimnos' independence. Much as Adrissu had kept his head down, the townspeople had come to respect him—or perhaps fear him, though he supposed it functioned the same way. His magical ability was known to most; and even to those who weren't familiar with the arcane, he was the only elf in a town of humans, who lived in a tower just outside of town and didn't socialize much. Humans were prone to fits of romanticism, he had learned, so this had cultivated an air of mystery that they found appealing, rather than off-putting. If he were to sign on to the proposed project of increasing the quarry's allotted budget, which the town had remained quite divided on since the proposal was first made earlier this year, those on the fence might be swayed.

Adrissu stifled a sigh. While it was better than being hounded about coming to dinner at the Branwood residence—where he knew Benil would try to orchestrate a situation in which he and his daughter would be alone together—it was still an irritant. He did not particularly care whether or not the quarry was expanded; if anything, he would almost rather the town stay small, so that he would not draw any undue attention to himself. None of the town's residents had ever pried into his past or tried to get into his tower—he hosted the occasional visitor on the ground floor to appease the curious and deter that very behavior—outsiders might not be so courteous.

"I... shall consider it," he finally settled on as Benil beamed up at him, and forced himself to return a tight smile.

"I knew you would," the man said. The moment he turned away, the smile fell from Adrissu's face.

When they arrived in the bustling center of town, a few of the townsfolk called out to them, waving to each of them in turn. Adrissu was not so reclusive that most townsfolk didn't know him on sight; his elven ears, coiffed dark hair, and loose, cool-toned robes in the most fashionable styles all made him quickly recognizable. Benil, of course, was far more inclined to stop and talk with each of them. Adrissu took a polite step away until their conversation came to an end so they could take a few steps further into town, before Benil would start another conversation, and the cycle began anew.

Eventually, when it seemed Benil had spoken to just about every person in town, they made it to the baker's stand. The smell of warm, fresh bread filled the air around them, comforting and homey. He had not been particularly hungry when Benil had arrived in his tower, but now the thought of fresh meat pies did sound appealing. Benil was good for the occasional free meal, at least.

True to his word, Benil bought two meat pies from Margo, the woman running the stand, and handed one to Adrissu. The pie was steaming and hot as he bit into it: the outer crust was crispy and flaky, the inside warm and savory. The chunk of mutton inside was coated in a small bit of gravy that dripped down his chin. For all that Benil irritated him, he did have a knack for getting ahold of the best food in town, despite his scrawny figure.

"So tell me more about this quarry proposal," Adrissu said idly, as Benil swiped gravy off his mustache and licked his fingers clean. He did not particularly care, but feigning interest would be best.

"Shall we walk and talk?" the human offered, and Adrissu nodded. So they set back out again, still following the main road. Their pace remained leisurely, but once Benil started talking, he was less inclined to stop and converse with the others they passed.

"The mine could be expanded to nearly double its current capacity with just the workforce we have now," Benil explained as they walked. "We've done a few exploratory surveys of the outer edges, and there should be plenty of good rock to mine for years to come. I know some folks are concerned that it will divert workers from other necessary tasks, but I don't think that will be the case. Rather, it will help encourage new residents to come to Polimnos to work in the quarry as well as the mines. An abundance of work never hurt anyone, I'm sure."

"And is the infrastructure in place to accommodate all these new workers coming to Polimnos?" Adrissu asked, and Benil's smile became more strained.

"Not as yet," he admitted. "But Polimnos grows by the day. We would be able to house young workers without families on-site, where the barracks could be expanded without much issue. As for in town, well, building more houses would only bring more business to everyone else, no? More jobs for the carpenters and all that. I mean, look at this!"

He gestured at one of the newest buildings as they passed. The large guild hall had only been finished a few months prior, and a small organization that trained and organized mercenaries was now stationed there. The building housed recruits and had two spacious courtyards for training: one hidden in the back, and one in front visible over a low stone fence. "If something like this was approved, I don't see why an expansion of the quarry would be any worse."

Adrissu looked out toward the guild hall. In the front courtyard, a group of young men were practicing fighting drills, and an instructor called out directions as they swung wooden swords and lifted shields—the swords were practice, but the shields looked real.

"I think it is safe to say Polimnos values fighters and protectors more than mine-workers at this stage of its growth, Benil," he remarked. He could hear Benil start to protest, but in the yard the instructor had called for a rest, and the men were breaking out of their orderly lines and into smaller groups, chatting and passing waterskins between them.

One of the trainees turned around to face his companion, reddish-brown hair glinting in the sun, and the world around them stopped.

Adrissu's breath hitched. Something in him snapped at the sight of the man, all of his senses honing in to focus entirely on him as everything else became blurry and distant. Was this someone else's magic? Had he been put under a spell? Panic rose in his throat, but he couldn't tear his eyes away from the man. He could focus on nothing else; the visage of the man had become the entire world.

The trainee was young, hardly more than a boy, with suntanned skin and auburn hair that he was pushing out of his face. He was not even particularly handsome, though his features were narrow and his cheekbones high for someone so obviously born of common human stock. He smiled at the man passing him a waterskin, as if he had not felt the earthquake that had so shaken Adrissu.

He hadn't felt it at all, Adrissu realized—no one else had felt it.

"Adrissu? Are you all right?"

Benil's voice reached him, distant at first, but it was the anchor that he needed to snap himself out of whatever fugue state had overtaken him. He shook his head, raising one hand to press against his chest where his heart still thundered.

"I—" he stammered, unable to form words. Though he had come back to himself, his eyes were still locked onto the man in the courtyard, watching as he drank deeply from the waterskin, rivulets overflowing from his mouth and trickling along his jaw, down his neck until it dampened his tunic. Adrissu squeezed his eyes shut and forced himself to turn his head away from the radiant sight, back toward the droll human next to him. "I... I apologize, Benil, what were you saying?"

"Are you ill? Perhaps the pie isn't sitting well with you?" Benil fretted, his eyebrows knitting together. "I mean, mine seemed fine, but I suppose a bad one could have snuck in the batch. I feel alright. Perhaps something else, then?"

Finally, an emotion broke through the awe and terror that had overtaken Adrissu—*irritation*. Benil Branwood was one of the most pathetically anxious men that he had ever met. Why had he agreed to get lunch with the slimy little human?

"I am feeling rather unwell, actually," Adrissu muttered before Benil could get too far into his increasingly nervous rambling. Every instinct in him was desperate to look back at the guild hall, to catch sight of the man again, to drink him in and never look away—but he forced himself to keep his focus on Benil Branwood's dark, beady eyes, his patchy goatee, and his slicked-back black hair. "I beg your pardon, Benil, but I think we may have to discuss this some other time."

"Of course, of course," Benil said quickly, lifting his hands in a placating gesture even as he took a fearful step away from Adrissu, as if he were somehow contagious. If he could focus, Adrissu would have hated him all the more; but as it was, everything felt so far away that he couldn't bring himself to care.

Against his better judgment, he risked a glance back toward the training yard. As if sensing his attention, the man glanced in his direction—their eyes met, and Adrissu could have wept. The man blinked, a hint of a smile on his face. It was an expression he had seen a hundred times over written on the face of those who did not know him, but recognized who he was all the same. Whatever pull Adrissu felt toward him, it was clearly not reciprocated. He looked away quickly, before his crumbling resolve failed him, and he marched up to the man to—to do what? Introduce himself? The very notion was absurd.

"Goodbye," he said abruptly, spinning on his heel to walk back the way they came without waiting for a response from Benil. His pace was rapid, eyes downcast, and he was sure that he must have been a sight nearly running out of town. But he didn't care, *couldn't* care, about anything but getting away. His heart was still pounding, and his breath came out hard, by the time he arrived back at his tower, flinging the heavy wooden door open and stumbling inside to safety.

As Adrissu slumped down to the floor, he heard Vesper stir from her usual spot, sunning herself underneath a window. He felt her gaze find him, partly curious and partly concerned.

"Come here," he breathed, and when he held out his hand, Adrissu could see that his fingers were trembling. He scowled down at the sight of them. Vesper approached, her jet black body a stark contrast to the pale stone floor beneath them. Though familiars were not able to utilize spoken language, the magic that had summoned her to his service allowed for some rudimentary communication between them. As she pressed her cool head into his hand, before slithering up the length of his arm to settle within the sleeve of his robe, he had the distinct feeling that she was trying to comfort him.

Absently, Adrissu folded his hands into his sleeves so he could feel the cold weight of her, grounding him. He was unsure of what had happened in town—even now the thought of it made his vision start to swim, remembering the warmed bronze of the man's skin, the way his hair was cast with a reddish glow in the light, his teeth flashing as he smiled—

He shook his head, stamping down the part of him that yearned to go find him. What was happening? What sort of trick was this? Had a spell been cast upon him without his knowledge?

"We'll get to the bottom of this," he murmured as he got to his feet, more to himself than to Vesper. While his own library was nothing impressive as of yet, still he was bound to find something—anything similar to what had happened to him today. Whatever the man had done to him, he would find out.

Chapter Two

Adrissu had never truly believed in the existence of fated mates.

They were said to exist to help further the lineage of dragonkind. As beings that were effectively immortal, that did not die due to the passage of time, but who could be killed by outside forces, dragons were naturally leery of each other and often would avoid the company of other dragons unless absolutely necessary. After all, every dragon knew through base instinct that another dragon was one of the few things in the world capable of ending its life.

Even dragons that held to the belief in fated pairs acknowledged that they were rare. It was true that some dragons did live in pairs, but it was more common that two dragons of relatively nearby territories would come together just long enough to procreate and raise their hatchling until it could survive on its own, as had been the case with his own parents. Adrissu did not know any dragons firsthand who believed themselves to be part of a fated pair or had constant companionship with another dragon.

The idea of fated mates had always seemed absurd to him—the idea of fate itself was entirely debatable, so the existence of some magical connection between two beings that had been written in the stars long before either had even been born... It was laughable.

And yet, despite his disbelief, what Adrissu had felt that day could only be the pull of the fated bond, unmistakable and irresistible.

It made no *sense*. He kept turning the idea over and over in his head as he sequestered himself for days in his tower. Fated mates should not exist; but if they did, it certainly should not apply to a human. Their tiny lifespans, their weak innate magic, their fragile, breakable bodies—he hated the very idea of it, but there was no other sufficient answer. The more he resisted, the more some small part deep within him knew it was the truth.

The man he had seen in the mercenary guild's courtyard was his fated mate.

When he could finally bring himself to accept the idea as the truth, he hated it all the more. He raged against this fate, digging through his hoard for the few draconic tomes that he did own, desperately searching for some way to sever this unwanted, intolerable connection. But the draconic texts did not speak of breaking a fated bond, only of the suffering and grief one dragon might face if their mate were to meet their demise.

"I am cursed," he muttered under his breath, late in the night after days spent secluded in his lair deep within the cliffside of Polimnos. Vesper was coiled on his desk; her black, beady eyes peeked through the folds of her body and fixed on him as she tilted her head in curiosity.

"There is no record of a dragon and a human ever being a fated pair," he spat, gesturing toward the pile of papers that he had been rifling through. "As far as I can tell, I am cursed, either to suffer intolerably while apart from this man, or to put off my suffering until he dies in a few short years. This is a curse."

Vesper's narrow tongue darted out briefly, and he felt an inkling of sympathy from the spot in his chest where his awareness of her was centered.

With a groan, he gathered her in one arm and brought her with him into his sleeping chamber. It had been dug in his dragon form—the perfect size to curl up snugly and be surrounded by his wealth—in this moment, it felt expansive and hollow. He was tempted, briefly, to drop his disguise and indulge in the primal part of him that wanted to lounge amidst his spoils; but the longer he thought on it, the more he did not want to be a dragon. At that moment, he didn't want to be anything at all. He only wanted to forget.

After three days of seclusion, Adrissu ventured back out into town again. It was not unusual for him to remain in his tower for long stretches of time, yet he felt as self-conscious in the streets of Polimnos as if he had been away for months and every eye was watching him with the utmost curiosity. In truth he knew that the townsfolk took little notice of his comings and goings, and they went about their business like it was any other day. Still, he could not bring himself to make his usual rounds to the grocer, the butcher, and the apothecary. Instead, he found himself standing in front of the mercenary hall once more, cursing himself for having walked here.

This time the front courtyard was empty, but he could hear the sounds of sparring echoing from the yard behind the building. There was a low stone fence surrounding the property, but the gate that guarded the entrance was unlocked and propped open.

Adrissu glanced around. Though still on the main avenue, the sprawling compound was far from the central part of Polimnos. As such, there were a few passers-by, and foot traffic was quite leisurely here. The buildings opposite the mercenary hall were largely residential homes, though a little ways away was a forge that had been abandoned for nearly a decade, but that the mercenary guild was currently in the process of refurbishing. All in all, there were few here to see him, and none that might question him.

Against his better judgment, he stepped through the gate and onto the grounds. He had promised himself that he would avoid this man, but already his resolution had given way to raw want. The urge to see him again was entirely instinct. Adrissu hated that he could not ignore it, no matter his best efforts; but still that did not stop him from continuing up to the wide double doors of the guild hall and testing the handle. It too was unlocked, so he strode inside.

The entry hall was sparse, its wooden walls unadorned, but it opened almost immediately to a larger room into which he peered. The room seemed to be a central meeting area: it held several benches and tables throughout with a clear spot toward the far wall where an instructor might stand and give a lecture to the gathered students. As it was, the room was largely empty save for a young human man who looked to be no more than eighteen, who was pushing chairs out of his way as he swept the floor. He had glanced up briefly when the doors swung open, and Adrissu watched his head whip up in a double-take, as he stepped into the meeting room.

"Oh," the boy said, straightening. "You're, ah, Lord Adrissu, correct?"

"You flatter me," Adrissu answered quickly, his eyes flickering across the room and barely lingering on the boy. The room was filled with the scent of fresh wood—the building was new enough that much of it had a similar bright, herbal smell—and was as sparsely decorated as the entryway, aside from the various chairs and benches. "I am no lord. But I am called Adrissu, yes."

"My mistake," the boy stammered. He was not the man Adrissu was looking for, but he gave the human an appraising look all the same. He was too young to truly be a fighter; and if he was here cleaning when the rest were sparring, Adrissu guessed he was perhaps the younger relative of a recruit, or maybe the son of one of the instructors or guild attendants. "Is, um, is there some way I can help you? Are you perhaps looking for the guildmaster?"

He was not, but he couldn't very well ask to go appraise the troops and pick one out, as he would a batch of fruit or a cut of meat at the market, so meeting the guildmaster would have to suffice.

"I am," Adrissu replied. "Would you take me to him?"

"Her," the boy corrected, then added quickly, "Of course." He set down his broom and led Adrissu back into the entryway.

Adrissu followed him up a flight of stairs and through the first door on the second floor. Inside, a stern-looking woman was sitting at a desk with a pile of papers in front of her and a quill in one hand. She glanced up as they entered, a slight frown on her face. Adrissu looked her over quickly: she was an older woman with graying hair pulled into a tight bun. A hooked-shape scar curved from her lower left eyelid across the bridge of her nose, and the frown remained on her lips even as her gaze flickered from the boy toward Adrissu.

"Lord—er, that is, the mage Adrissu asked to see you, ma'am," the boy said, gesturing toward Adrissu.

"I see," the woman said, looking him over. Between her stern face and no-nonsense clothing, Adrissu guessed that she was a retired soldier or seasoned warrior in her own right—past her prime, maybe, but still more than capable of training up others. She stood as they appraised each other. "I have heard of you, Adrissu. Your presence here honors us. I'm Maya Graylight, the guildmaster of Polimnos' branch of the mercenaries' guild. How can I help you?"

"Thank you for speaking with me," Adrissu said, bowing his head slightly. She gestured for him to sit across from her desk. He stepped closer, but remained standing, one hand hovering anxiously over the chair. The boy who had led him here quietly backed out, his footsteps echoing back down the stairs. "I've recently considered hiring a personal guard to keep an eye on my tower, and thought your organization would be a good place to start looking."

The lie came easily. A sorcerer needed no guardian, and a dragon less so, but there was a sense to it. After all, he was the only mage in Polimnos, and he was sure the humans assumed that he had all sorts of rare and powerful items and ingredients that would need safeguarding, especially as the town expanded and the population grew with it.

"A guard, eh?" Maya mused, setting down her quill. "I'm sure some of our recruits would be up for the job. If you want to leave your information, I can pass it to our instructors."

"I was wondering if I might have a look at your current crop of recruits," Adrissu said quickly, before she could continue. "I am rather... particular about those I would allow in my tower. I'm sure you can understand why I would prefer to select someone myself and extend the offer in person."

At first, the woman was silent, eyeing him suspiciously. After a tense moment, though, she shrugged and stood.

"I think that should be fine," she said, stepping around her desk. "We have a class going on right now. I'll take you to the training ground."

Adrissu nodded and followed her back out of the room, stifling the self-satisfied smile that threatened to spread across his face. His lie had worked. He would meet his mate.

He shook the thought from his head as they descended the stairs, regret bubbling up inside him once more. What was he going to say to the man when he arrived? What if he didn't want to come guard Adrissu's tower at all? His chest filled with dread, even as he followed Maya outside and into the back courtyard. But he kept the same neutral expression, while Maya went on about the guild's activities since its founding the year prior.

She opened the door to the courtyard ahead of him, flooding the walkway with light. The sounds of shouting and the clash of wooden swords filled the air as they stepped out. Although the group gathered in the courtyard must have been around thirty people, Adrissu's gaze was immediately drawn to him—his fated mate.

The man was swinging his sword, focusing on the instructor near the center of the yard. He wore a sleeveless tunic over tight breeches, and his exposed arms glistened with sweat in the sunlight, as did his short auburn hair.

"Here," Maya said, gesturing toward one of the instructors. "I'll let you talk to Ederick here. He should be able to help you."

The man was noticeably older than the recruits, closer in age to Maya herself. Ederick wore a short beard, the same dark gray as the rest of his short-cropped hair; and although he seemed to notice Maya's attention, he only glanced briefly in their direction before looking back at the trainees. He was observing, rather than instructing.

"Ederick," she repeated in a louder tone, and this time the man turned to face them. "This is Adrissu, the resident mage. He's looking for a personal guard. Will you point out some of the more promising recruits to him? Anyone that might be interested in taking the job."

"Sure," Ederick said gruffly, nodding to both.

"Thank you," Adrissu said smoothly, as Maya stepped away. "Hello, sir."

"Hello, Adrissu," he answered, looking him up and down. "I don't believe we've met, but I've heard of you. Good to finally meet you."

Adrissu smiled. "I'm afraid you have me at a disadvantage, then, as I'm not aware of you."

The man laughed. "Ederick Shay," he said, gesturing toward himself. "I'm a retired mercenary and one of the lead instructors here at the guild. I've worked with most of these recruits one-on-one at least once. You say you're looking for a bodyguard?"

"Not quite, although I suppose that would be part of it," Adrissu said. "I'm considering hiring a personal guard, more for my tower than my own person. I have no concerns about my own ability to protect myself, but my... supply of arcane items and ingredients has grown enough that a second set of eyes might be better to have sooner rather than later."

"Understandable," Ederick agreed, and he started to look out toward the group of recruits. "Hmm. You'd want someone responsible, who you could trust not to go through your things themselves. I have a few in mind." He pointed at a few in turn— none of them were the man who kept Adrissu's focus. "Let's see. There's Seta, Glenn, and Hostus... Those would probably be my first choice. Not top of their class, so they're not going to consider themselves above a guard job, but more than capable of what you need."

"Hmm," Adrissu said, pretending to look around the field. The people he had pointed out did appear capable and strong: it was unfortunate for them that he had no interest in their ability. "What of her?" He gestured toward the only woman that he had spotted on the field.

"That's Ketlin. She can hold her own, certainly, but I don't think she's well-suited to guard work. She's better with ranged weapons, and frankly, Adrissu, she's too ambitious by far to accept a guard position. I don't think she'd be interested, unfortunately," the other man replied, scratching his beard.

"What about that one, over there?" He pointed at the auburn-haired man, trying to sound casual. The man hadn't seemed to notice him at all, his focus still on the instructor who was guiding them through different stances.

"Ah," Ederick said, a chagrined expression crossing his face. Adrissu watched him closely, noting the change as he spoke. "That's Ruan. To be honest, he's probably too mischevious for something like guard duty. He'd get restless and bored, and that's not something you'd want to deal with."

"Is that so?" Adrissu asked, hoping his feigned disinterest seemed convincing. His heart was pounding in his chest: he knew his mate's name, Ruan. *Ru-an.* He repeated the syllables over and over in his head, anxious to try them on his tongue. Ederick's comment was as infuriating as it was intriguing; of course the first thing that he learned about his mate was how irritating he was. "I take it he's a problem student of yours, then?"

"Well..." Ederick started, only to pause, tapping his chin with one finger. "I wouldn't say that, necessarily. He's a fast learner and good at what he does. He'll make a fine warrior someday. But he's an orphan, grew up basically on the streets. He really only joined for the roof over his head and regular meals, so he's a bit... rowdy, compared to some of our other trainees. He'll need some more work before he's ready to take on any kind of job, I think."

"I see," Adrissu repeated slowly, looking back over at the man. *Ruan*. Everything Ederick said about him had ignited his frustration all over again. *Mischievous, rowdy...* He sounded utterly human, everything Adrissu was not. What was he even doing here? It had been a mistake to even entertain the thought of meeting the man. *Ruan*. He wished he could forget his name.

"I mean, if you have your eye on him, I could float the idea," Ederick offered. Adrissu flushed with shame at the thought that this human could read his interest so easily—that he was so obvious despite his usually guarded nature. "No need to make a decision now, sir, unless you really need someone immediately."

"Nothing so urgent," Adrissu said quickly, clasping his hands behind his back and straightening his spine. If he was going to stand here like a fool, he would at least maintain his composure. "I will consider your other recommendations, sir; but if you would, as you say, float the idea both with them and with this... Ruan." The name on his lips was intoxicating, and the world seemed to tremble around him as he said it. *His* Ruan. He shoved the thought away again. "Well, sometimes I do enjoy a challenge. Perhaps he would do well with a strong hand." The words left him unbidden, more out of instinct than anything else, so he forced himself to smile up at the taller man as he spoke. He grinned, baring his teeth in a way he knew would often leave humans unsettled. He liked to think it was some part of his draconic nature flashing through for just an instant—a hint of power that humans would detect on an instinctual level, but could never articulate to themselves.

"Perhaps," Ederick agreed after an uncertain beat of silence.

"As you said, I need not make a decision at this moment," Adrissu continued briskly. He had remained here too long already. "Perhaps I can return at a more opportune time to discuss this further with you?"

"Certainly," Ederick said. "I oversee most practices, but usually the recruits break for the hotter parts of the day. Come again around midday, and you should find most of us available to speak with you."

"Excellent," Adrissu said, nodding once. "In that case, I bid you good day." He spun on his heel and headed for the door without waiting for a response.

Despite his own self-flagellation over how poorly his conversation with Ederick had gone, Adrissu could only hold out against the urge to see Ruan again for a few days. The next time he made his way to the guild hall, he brought Vesper with him, who stayed coiled in the sleeve of his robe. It was midday this time, and the heat of the day was at its peak. But Vesper was cool against his skin, making up for the extra layer that he wore to carry her comfortably. She did enjoy sometimes peeking out as they walked, but for the most part she remained in her hiding place.

He had brought her with the instruction to bite him if he began to make too much of a fool of himself. Though lacking venom, Adrissu hoped that the unpleasant sensation would snap him out of the horrible state that overtook him whenever he caught sight of that man, Ruan. But today was about following up with Ederick—and maybe introducing himself to Ruan. Possibly. Perhaps. Vesper's expression remained the same as he explained; but he had the distinct sense that if she could, she would be rolling her eyes at him.

As he walked along the main road and the guild hall came into view, it seemed most of the recruits were sitting in small groups within the front courtyard eating lunch together. Ruan's auburn hair was like a beacon, glistening a warm reddish-brown in the midday sun, and Adrissu's eyes found him instantly.

Adrissu hesitated at the gate. He had meant to speak with Ederick, but Ruan was right there. How far was he really going to go with this ruse, when he knew that he only wanted to talk to Ruan? In his sleeve, Vesper shifted. He tensed, expecting to feel the prick of her fangs, but it never came. She only seemed curious for now.

He sighed, stepped through the gate, and veered to the left where the recruits sat. As he navigated between the pockets of space that formed around the groups of four or five, those that noticed him gave him quick, curt nods of greeting, seemingly aware of who he was. Ruan was facing away from him as he approached. The man sitting across from him, however, met Adrissu's gaze and bowed his head slightly, prompting the man to turn and look toward him.

Their eyes met, and Adrissu nearly stumbled as he closed the distance between them. Ruan's eyes were a honeyed brown, warm and bright where the sun caught them. Everything about him seemed kissed by the sun, from his hair to his skin to his eyes. The human blinked, bowing his head slightly in the same way, though a slight grin started to spread across his lips as he did so. This close, Adrissu could see the beginnings of stubble had formed over his upper lip and along his chin.

"Hello," Adrissu said, ignoring the thudding of his heart. Hopefully his voice sounded stronger than he felt. "You're Ruan, yes?"

"I am," the man said, standing to his feet. "And you're Adrissu."

It was the first time that he had heard Ruan speak, and hearing his own name in Ruan's voice sent a chill racing up his spine. Even as he longed to hear his name come from Ruan's lips again, he hated how much power the human instantly had over him with absolutely no awareness of it.

"Yes," Adrissu said, forcing himself to focus. "I came by a few days ago and spoke with Ederick about a potential job. Did he speak of this to you?"

"He mentioned it, yeah," Ruan said, lifting one hand to push his hair out of his eyes. "I might be interested. What's the pay?"

Adrissu paused, pursing his lips in thought. He hadn't considered the pay; he did not even know what was reasonable to offer. But he *did* want Ruan to take the job, if he was considering it...

"A gold per day," he said, and Ruan's eyebrows flew up his face in surprise. The men who were sitting nearby watching spluttered, and several of the recruits who were a little further off swung their heads to look in their direction, also obviously shocked.

"Done," Ruan said quickly, starting to laugh. "If you haven't filled the position yet, that is. I'll take it."

"Excellent. It is yours," Adrissu said, bowing his head. "Do arrangements need to be made with your guildmaster?"

"They'll just need to read over the contract," Ruan laughed. "Just bring me whatever I need to sign, and I'll be off the hook with them for whatever hours you give me. Since it's through the guild they'll take a percentage, but at a gold a day, I'm more than happy to give them their share. A pleasure doing business with you, Lord Adrissu." He held out his hand.

Adrissu breathed in deeply to brace himself, then extended his hand as well. They shook. Ruan's hand was rough against his own, but warm.

"I am not a lord," he said, as Ruan released him from his grasp. He was tempted to let his fingers linger for a moment longer; but he knew Vesper would bite him if he did, and the last thing he wanted was to embarrass himself now of all times. "You may simply call me Adrissu."

"Adrissu," Ruan repeated. Another shiver shot up Adrissu's spine.

"How soon can you start?" he asked, glancing down at his hand.

"Whenever," Ruan said, and Adrissu looked back up at him to see him shrug, a self-satisfied grin still on his face. "I can start tomorrow if that's what you'd like."

Adrissu couldn't quite stop the smile that spread across his face, showing his teeth. He *was* a dragon, after all, and he always got what he wanted. Even if he hated that he wanted it.

"In that case, I will have the contract written up now," he said, looking toward the guild hall. Ruan only laughed, following him as he turned to go.

"See you all later," he called out to his companions, sounding insufferably smug. The humans he had been sitting with grumbled a reply that Adrissu only half-heard.

He had done it. Somehow, his lie had worked.

Chapter Three

It only took a week of their new arrangement before Adrissu began to dearly wish that he could bring himself to hate the insufferable human.

Exactly as Ederick had warned him, Ruan was too loud, too restless, too terribly *human*. Despite how eager he had been to take the job, he clearly hated being idle. Though Adrissu had invited him into the sitting room on the ground floor when he'd shown up for his first day of duty, the human's constant humming and tapping and muttering to himself was so distracting that Adrissu couldn't get any work done. Not that he would have gotten much done anyway: not with how distracting his mere presence was, as it took every ounce of willpower to ignore what his body instinctively wanted to do now that he'd gotten his mate alone in his den. He offered Ruan a book to read, but the human declined. He showed Ruan around his tower—at least, the parts of the tower that were safe for him to know about—but he seemed mostly disinterested.

He told the man to guard the door from the outside on the second day, which was only marginally better. At the very least, Adrissu got a bit of work done in the morning, when he could pretend that the human was *not* only a few steps away from him. Ruan had asked to eat his lunch inside, though, complaining of the heat. Adrissu agreed, only to instantly regret it as he loudly chewed the bread and cheese that he had brought, and *belched* just as audibly, as if he had no manners at all.

Even the knowledge that Ruan was *his*—and the primal urge to be around him and claim him as his own—did not ease the constant vexation of his presence. Adrissu had hoped that a bit of time spent around each other would soothe some of the irritation away, and that he might even be able to enjoy Ruan's presence eventually; but so far he was only miserable, and he was sure Ruan knew it.

The only good thing about him was that he was not afraid of Vesper, and they even seemed to like each other. Ruan had been stunned at her appearance on his first day, and apprehensive at first; but Vesper was curious and probably too friendly for her own good, which won him over easily.

"I'm glad he gets along with one of us," Adrissu muttered sourly that evening, after Ruan had left for the day. Vesper had only answered by tilting her head to one side, her tongue flicking in and out.

Sometimes Ruan would make small talk with him, when he was eating in the sitting-room.

"So did you get robbed recently or something?" he asked through a mouthful of food one afternoon, peering curiously over to the opposite side of the room where Adrissu sat, reading.

"No," Adrissu answered primly, not looking up from his book. He hated seeing humans speak with their mouths full.

"So why hire a guard?"

"A preventative measure, if you will."

"Hm." He did not sound convinced. "I guess you do have a lot worth stealing, though."

At that, Adrissu glanced over his book toward him, an eyebrow raised. "I hope you aren't getting any ideas."

Ruan laughed: much as he hated himself for it, Adrissu did dearly enjoy hearing him laugh. "Not at all. I wouldn't know what to do with any of this stuff, I assure you." He glanced around the room before speaking again, this time blessedly with his mouth empty of food. "I guess you must make a pretty decent living doing all this? Do you sell potions or something?"

Adrissu managed a dry chuckle. "Not at all. Most of my work is the study of magic, which earns very little."

Ruan's eyebrows raised in surprise. "Then how can you afford a gold a day for a guard you don't even need?"

Adrissu's smile grew cold at the pointed question. "I was lucky enough to receive a sizable inheritance from a relative," he said, returning his attention to his book. "That is what allows me the time and resources to pursue the mysteries of magic without having to worry about such trivial matters as food and housing."

He could feel Ruan rolling his eyes even without looking up at him.

"What mysteries of magic?" the human asked after a moment of silence. Adrissu sighed and closed his book, setting it in his lap. Getting any work done while Ruan was there was going to be impossible.

"Much of magic is a mystery," he said with a shrug. "Though its usage is widespread, we actually know very little about how it truly works. It seems to be a force of nature, but is it a limited resource that one day might run out? Is it truly some force of will created by its wielder?"

"I don't know," Ruan shrugged in return. "I suppose that seems interesting, though."

"Very," Adrissu agreed dryly. Ruan did not ask any further questions, and when he looked back down at his book, the man tidied up the table where he'd been eating and went back to his post outside.

Their stilted conversations did not get any easier, and Adrissu was trapped in the constant state of limbo: wanting the human to like him, while simultaneously being frustrated and irritated with nearly every interaction that they had. It would have been so much easier to hate him; it would have been best if he had never spoken to the man at all.

He was already on edge, so when Ruan had some friends join him for part of the day at the beginning of his second week, he stormed out of his tower in a rage and demanded they leave.

"Why?" Ruan scowled. And even though his two companions, boys who looked even younger than Ruan, shrunk away with obvious remorse, the man remained seemingly unaffected by Adrissu's anger. "We can be quieter if we're bothering you. But they shouldn't have to leave."

"Because I hired you, not them," Adrissu growled. Vesper was in his sleeve and poked her head out curiously; one of the boys yelped in surprise as she appeared, but Ruan was still unmoved.

"I'm not asking you to *pay* them," he said, rolling his eyes. "And they're not stopping me from doing my job. Gods forbid I have a way to pass the time while minding your tower."

"The *gods* aren't paying you. I *am*," Adrissu spat. Still Ruan seemed undeterred, meeting his eyes with equal parts frustration and expectation, waiting for his verdict. Vesper's hold around his forearm tightened, and Adrissu scoffed in irritation, turning back in the doorway. "Be quieter. If I hear them again, I won't give them a second chance." He slammed the heavy wooden door closed behind him, so if Ruan thanked him for his accommodation, he did not hear it.

At the end of the second week, Ruan approached him before he left for the day and said abruptly, "I won't be returning next week. Sorry."

Adrissu scowled, but was not entirely surprised. "Is that so?"

"Yes. I..." To his surprise, the human at least had the decency to look embarrassed. "Well, I appreciate the opportunity to work with you, and to save up a little bit of money. But the guild just got a contract for a hunting expedition, and I'd like to do that, so..."

"I see," Adrissu sighed, and looked back down at his desk. "Well, I wish you luck on your expedition, then."

"Sorry it didn't work out," Ruan said, and turned to go.

Adrissu bit his lip, hesitating, then stood before Ruan made it to the door. "You're welcome to return when you get back," he called, then added, "If you'd like, that is."

Ruan paused, looking back over at him. The door was half-open, and he was haloed in the late afternoon light with his rucksack slung over one shoulder. A slight grin started to play at his lips, and Adrissu's heart ached all over again. Why was he doing this to himself? What was the purpose of prolonging his suffering this way? It would be better to let him go and make a clean break of it all, wouldn't it?

"Sure. I'll let you know when I'm back in town," Ruan laughed. "If you haven't already filled the position again by then."

Adrissu nodded, then Ruan stepped through the door and was gone.

———⊖✦⊖———

Mercifully, he did not see Ruan again for well over a month. Without the knowledge that the man was just a short walk away at any given moment, it was easier to ignore the ache in the pit of his stomach that Adrissu felt in his absence. There were even days that he could avoid ruminating on his disastrous luck and pretend that he had never felt that accursed connection to the human—that he had never felt his bones ache and blood sing out for a man with whom he had only ever shook hands. It never lasted long, but it was nice while it did.

If he had learned anything from this botched venture, it was that he worked best alone, so he did not even consider hiring on another guard, and the mercenary guild did not reach out to him about it. He had gotten away with his ruse, though he wondered if the instructor—Ederick—was more perceptive about it all than he had seemed at first glance.

Whenever he ruminated on it too long, though, Vesper would look at him with her black pearl eyes, and he would feel something like sympathy emanating from her. The last thing he needed was a *snake* feeling *sorry* for him, so he would throw himself into his work whenever it happened, and eventually the feeling would fade until he dwelled on it too long again.

Benil Branwood kept pestering him about the quarry. He almost welcomed the irritation: at least it was something different to be frustrated over. He was tempted to give into the man's supplication, if only to settle the matter once and for all; but agreeing to this would likely embolden the human to start pestering him again about his damned daughter with renewed fervor. Of a lesser concern were Adrissu's own misgivings about the expansion of the mine without first expanding the town. Though certainly a problem for Polimnos, it would affect him little, if at all; since his life had settled back into a semblance of a normal routine, he was far more interested in keeping his interactions with Benil and his brood to a bare minimum.

Then Ruan returned. The moment the knock sounded against the heavy wooden door, Adrissu knew it was him. Normally he would have Vesper answer the door, but with his heart leaping up into his throat, he descended from his private upper floors to answer it himself.

Ruan grinned up at him when the door swung open; his skin was a few shades darker from working in the sun, and Adrissu could see a healing wound on his shoulder, but the man didn't look too terribly worse for wear.

"You're back," he said dryly, forcing down the elation that swelled in his fickle, foolish heart at the sight of him. He had been perfectly fine without him: why now did seeing him whole and hale feel like such a breath of relief?

"Missed me?" Ruan laughed. Just as traitorous as his heart, Vesper came up behind Adrissu as quickly as she could slither, radiating excitement as she rose up to greet him. He smiled, sunlight emanating from his grin, and crouched to meet her. He gave a light stroke under her chin with two fingers, before glancing back up at Adrissu through his eyelashes. "I noticed you haven't hired a new guard."

Adrissu sighed. "I have not."

For a moment, Ruan was silent. It was only the span of a heartbeat, maybe two, but it seemed to go on for much longer. His warm eyes flickered from Adrissu's face down the length of his body only to flash up to meet his eyes again, and for the first time something like recognition—like *heat*—stirred in the human's expression. Adrissu kept his face as stony as he could. Let the human suspect whatever he wanted; Adrissu would never admit to anything.

"Should I come by the usual time tomorrow morning?" Ruan finally asked as he straightened back up, and Vesper slid back toward Adrissu. His tone was light, but that lingering heat was still in his eyes.

"I thought the job was too boring for you," Adrissu retorted, and Ruan laughed again.

"I may not be as smart as you, Adrissu, but I know better than to turn down being paid to do nothing," he said, shaking his head. Despite himself, a small, amused grin twitched at the corners of Adrissu's mouth, and his cheeks ached with the effort of forcing it back down. He knew he should deny Ruan—he should send him away so he would never have to see his face again.

"You may resume your post at the same time tomorrow, then," he said with a nod.

Adrissu did his best to ignore Ruan when the human arrived the next morning and took up his usual post outside the door of his tower. But he was acutely aware of his presence, even as he attended to his morning chores and settled in with a book. Predictably, he ended up reading the same paragraph over and over with no memory of what the words said.

Ruan came inside for his lunch as casually as if he'd never left. Adrissu pretended to ignore him, watching him sit down at the low table and unwrap his small bundle of bread and cheese.

"So what are you reading?" Ruan asked, peering over at him as he took a huge bite of bread. Adrissu hid his scowl in his book: he hated when humans spoke while eating.

"This is a text on the magical properties of plants native to Aefraya," he said, keeping his tone as dry as he could manage.

"Hmm," Ruan replied through a mouthful of cheese. "Sounds boring."

"Perhaps."

"Don't you ever read anything for fun?"

Adrissu raised an eyebrow at the provocation. "Would you like something to read? My library is extensive. I'm sure there's something even you might tolerate."

To his surprise, Ruan's face flushed a deep red, and he looked away quickly rather than make some quip the way he usually would.

"No," he said, his attention suddenly consumed by the mundane task of slicing the block of cheese in his hand. Adrissu's gaze lingered on him for a moment, noting the red that crept all the way to the tops of his ears, and the twist of his lips into an uncomfortable frown.

"You can't read," he said just as the thought occurred to him, and Ruan's scowl deepened. "Is that it?"

But he knew the truth; it seemed obvious now. Ederick said that he'd grown up as an orphan; of course he had received no formal education. While Polimnos did have a single schoolhouse for the basic education of children, if he had had no parents to enforce his attendance, who else would have brought him to school? No one would have cared, especially if he were as rowdy and unruly as Ederick had claimed; and immediately, Adrissu imagined an even younger, more immature Ruan.

"No, I can't," Ruan finally muttered, still looking down at his food. For the first time Adrissu could recall, he didn't have the same arrogant, brash air about him. Now, he was a child again: jealous of what he did not have and too embarrassed to admit it.

Adrissu opened his mouth to speak, then snapped it shut. The small part of him that he had been trying unsuccessfully to squash wanted to comfort Ruan, to offer the chance to learn how to read, and to teach him everything he knew. The rest of him balked at the very idea of it, and he raged that magic beyond his understanding had linked him so inextricably to someone so completely unsuited to him. A tiny lifespan and a tiny brain to match—he bit his lip and looked back down at his book.

After a moment, he could feel Ruan's eyes flicker back over to him, watching him—waiting. He *wanted* Adrissu to offer to teach him, he knew. He would not give the human the satisfaction of thinking Adrissu *cared* about him. He would not give in to that part of himself. After a moment, he felt Ruan's gaze slide off him; and after another beat of silence, the young man gathered his things in silence and stepped back outside.

He did not come back til sunset, when his obligation was at an end. Ruan opened the door; but instead of coming inside, he stood in the doorway and called out to Adrissu, "I'm going home."

With a sigh, Adrissu reached across his desk for the gold piece that he had set aside for Ruan, tossing it across the room to him. Ruan caught it easily in his free hand. Their eyes met. Ruan's face was suddenly inscrutable, but he didn't look away. Heat rose in Adrissu's face, and quickly he looked back down to his work. And without saying goodbye, he heard Ruan close the door behind him as he left.

Chapter Four

They settled into a strange routine after that. Eager for adventure, Ruan would take jobs through the mercenary guild whenever they were offered, so he often left Polimnos for extended stretches of time. When he was gone, usually for two or three weeks at a time, Adrissu pretended that he had never existed; and he could typically ignore the ache in his chest that always sprung up when he was absent. Once, however, Ruan was away for two months, and Adrissu wondered and worried over his absence. But then he was back with a new scar and a story to tell.

He always came back, though he never announced his return to Adrissu: he would simply show up the morning after he'd returned to town to take up his usual post. He would come inside for lunch, and at the end of the day Adrissu would toss him his gold piece. And so their routine would continue, until a different job came up, and Ruan left again.

Once—only once—he mentioned hunting dragons.

"The man who submitted the job to the guild claims to have killed three dragons," he said over lunch, his first day back, after having been gone for a five-week excursion. "The guild doesn't take jobs like that, but I gave him my information for if he ever hunts down another. Imagine being able to say I'd helped slay a dragon!"

Despite the way his heart had leapt anxiously into his throat, Adrissu could not stop a snort of derision at Ruan's eagerness. The human scowled, but Adrissu only shook his head.

"What? You think I couldn't do it?" he pressed.

"No," Adrissu replied. He glanced away. It was a dangerous topic. "And I don't think that man is being truthful with you, either."

"What? Why?"

"Because it takes much to kill a dragon," he said. "Much more than a handful of humans with swords or spears."

"He did say he usually has a mage with him to help," Ruan muttered, folding his arms across his chest.

"Hm," Adrissu said. He forced his voice to ooze disinterest. "I'm sure that helps, then."

"Do you think you could do that?" Ruan asked after a moment. "Use your magic to kill a dragon?"

Adrissu was silent for a long moment, considering the question. His heartbeat must have been audible in the silence between them; but human senses were dull, and Ruan only kept peering at him with the same half-curious, half-goading expression.

"Yes," he finally answered. "But I will not help you kill a dragon, Ruan."

"Name your price," Ruan said.

"More than you could afford. More than your supposed dragon slayer could afford."

"Hmph," Ruan sighed, but he did not bring it up again.

———⊰✦⊱———

Ruan had been working for him on and off for a year, when the council finally came to a decision regarding the quarry expansion. Much to Benil Branwood's dismay, the plans to expand the mine were halted. Instead, city funds would be allocated to improving the main road and creating six new residential streets. Once more housing was in place, the city council would reconsider the Branwood proposal.

"I'm buying one of those new houses they're building off the main road," Ruan told him, the next time he arrived to take up his post outside of Adrissu's tower.

"Is that so?" Adrissu replied, his tone disinterested despite the slight smile that twitched at the corners of his lips. He remained turned away from Ruan, looking down at the tome that he was reading. "You've saved up that much, then?"

"Thanks to you, yes," Ruan replied. Adrissu could sense him watching him, waiting for his response, but he remained silent. "Adrissu, I..."

Something inside him thrummed at the softer tone of Ruan's voice, and he couldn't help but glance up, their eyes meeting from across the room. Adrissu could feel the heat rising in his face—first desire, then shame as he recognized the emotion—but there was enough distance between them that he hoped Ruan could not tell.

"Adrissu," Ruan started over, his voice rough. "I do want to thank you. I don't know why you took such interest in me that day, but... I appreciate you hiring me. I really wouldn't have been able to do it without this job. Maybe once I'm settled into the new place, I can have you over for once."

Adrissu turned away. He wanted to scoff at the admission—wanted to respond with scorn and derision the way he had a hundred times before. But Ruan had never been so... *soft* toward him, and his mind had gone completely blank. No words came to him.

His throat suddenly felt very dry.

"You're welcome," he managed to get out without his voice breaking. He did not risk looking back, but he could feel the heat of Ruan's eyes on him for a long moment. Finally, the human turned away, and he heard the door swing open and close once more. His lunch break was over.

Adrissu could barely string together a coherent thought for the remainder of the evening. Was that really all it took to undo his self-control? A few words of thanks, and all his carefully constructed walls had come down?

His body ached with the knowledge that he was helpless to the damned fated bond. He'd had a hundred chances to cut Ruan out of his life, yet he had continued to keep him around, if only at arm's length. But clearly Ruan did not want to be held at arm's length any more, and of all he had learned about Ruan so far, he could be certain that the human was almost as stubborn as he was.

The thought was so consuming that he did not realize when Ruan had returned at the end of the afternoon.

"Are you alright?" Ruan's voice came, only a few feet behind him, and Adrissu nearly jumped. "Ah—sorry, I didn't mean to startle you."

"You didn't," Adrissu said quickly, reaching out for the gold piece that he kept on his desk each day. Normally, he would toss it to Ruan from the other end of the room. Now, with only a few feet between them, he held it out for the other man to take.

Ruan eyed him for a moment, his expression somewhere between confused and appraising, then he took the gold piece from Adrissu's hand. His fingers brushed against Adrissu's palm and lingered there for a beat longer than necessary.

"I'll see you tomorrow," he said, then turned to go.

"Goodbye," Adrissu said faintly, watching him leave with wide eyes.

It had been many years since he'd taken his elven form; though it was not constant, he had spent the better part of the past twenty-seven years inhabiting this humanoid body. In that time he had rarely experienced any kind of sexual urge: he was quite sure that he had not felt any such base desire until after that cursed day, when he first spotted Ruan across the courtyard of the mercenary guild. But *now*—something about the contact of Ruan's fingers on his palm, brief as it was, set his blood ablaze. His cock strained shamelessly against the layers of his robes and trousers. Hating himself for it, he reached into the folds of his clothing to take it in his hand, sending shivers up his spine at the tentative touch.

Instinct immediately took over, and his body yearned for relief—it would have been embarrassing if he had not wanted it to be over quickly. A few hard strokes was all it took for his muscles to tense and his cock to shoot its release, making a mess of the underside of his desk.

Panting, he leaned back in his chair and closed his eyes. Shame flooded him the moment it was over, and his blood still boiled with unmet need.

"Damn it," he growled, covering his face with his clean hand. "Damn him. Damn it!"

When Ruan moved into his new house, a few months later, he invited Adrissu to have dinner with him. Adrissu declined.

Around the same time, Benil Branwood and one of the other council members, a human woman named Ellisa Tanner, invited him to attend a small dinner party that the Tanner family was hosting for some other prominent community members. This time, Adrissu accepted.

The council of Polimnos, which acted as a governing body of the small city-state, consisted of only five members. Polimnos had only flourished and grown in the decades that Adrissu had lived there; he was certain the council was poised to expand very soon, and strongly suspected that they were going to ask him to join them.

Part of him wanted to decline. Elves were quite long-lived, but not the way dragons were. While he might be able to get away with living in Polimnos for an indeterminate length of time without raising suspicion, eventually official documentation with his name on it could start to raise questions. But on the other hand, Polimnos had changed so much in the twenty-five years that he had lived there: things were bound to change again, the method of governance included, and his name would be lost among outdated records.

Adrissu had little lust for social power; the knowledge that he had already brought the city to the ground, and could do so again any time he wished, was more than enough for him. But to be able to officially guide the town in the direction that he wanted had a certain appeal. After all, he was arguably the most permanent resident of Polimnos, so why shouldn't he have the most say? But until they offered him the position, it was only conjecture. So he went to the dinner to see if that was, in fact, the ulterior motive behind the invitation.

He arrived promptly at six in the evening; he had never understood the human custom of purposely arriving late. He had been to the Branwood estate a few times, but not the Tanner family home. It was smaller than the former, but closer to the center of the city. He knew Ellisa Tanner was a widow who had several grown children, lived with only her adult daughter, and owned a flower shop in town. He was not entirely sure what Ellisa Tanner had done in her life to earn a spot on the small council of Polimnos, and their interactions over the years had been few, but he liked the woman well enough. She was far more tolerable than Benil Branwood, at the least.

When he arrived, Ellisa's daughter answered the door.

"Welcome, welcome," she said, grinning up at him and stepping aside as she opened the door. The woman was of a shorter stature and full-figured with brown hair pulled back in a tight bun. Her dress was fine, but not at all ostentatious—very much suitable for a daughter of a government official, even in a small city like Polimnos.

He bowed his head to her in greeting, but she had already turned away to call down the hallway, "Mother! Mr. Branwood! Adrissu has arrived." She turned back to look at him with the same smile and gestured once more for him to come inside.

"Thank you," he murmured, stepping past her. He could see the entry hall open up into a large sitting room about ten feet away.

"Adrissu, welcome," Benil Branwood called out to him. Adrissu stepped into the doorway and glanced quickly around the room before fully entering. Benil was getting up from a plush armchair to greet him; Elissa Tanner sat up a little straighter without leaving an identical armchair opposite him.

The human woman must have been around sixty, perhaps a little older. Her hair was mostly gray and pulled back in a bun, similar to her daughter's hairstyle, and her weathered face was littered with lines. She smiled warmly at him, and he bowed his head.

"Thank you for so graciously inviting me into your home, Mrs. Tanner," Adrissu said, and when he glanced back at the woman, she waved one hand dismissively. He had never known her late husband, but she still wore a ring on one of her fingers that humans adorned to signify their marriage.

"We're pleased to have you join us, Adrissu," she replied.

"It's good to see you, my friend," Benil said briskly as he stepped up to him. Adrissu forced himself to smile for a brief moment down at the human. He did not like to consider Benil his *friend,* but it was unfortunately undeniable that of all the humans in Polimnos, Benil Branwood was the one who made the most effort to maintain a relationship with him. "Come, sit, have a glass of wine. I brought a lovely bottle from a vineyard up in Gennemont. Claire and I went there over the summer and have just a few bottles left. I thought this would be the perfect opportunity to open one up, maybe even two."

Adrissu nodded and allowed himself to be led to the corner where a small side table stood with a bottle of wine and a few goblets; and he took a seat on the other side of Ellisa.

"Dinner will be ready in about half an hour," the Tanner daughter called, peeking into the room with a smile before heading back into the hallway.

"I must thank you again for joining us," Ellisa said, shifting in her chair to face him.

"I'm honored to be here," he replied, smiling dryly. "Forgive me, could you remind me of your daughter's name?"

"Oh, that's my Luelle," Ellisa laughed, hiding her grin behind one hand. "Don't worry, sir, I won't tell if you won't."

"Here you are," Benil interrupted, handing Adrissu a goblet. Carefully, he pushed back the sleeves of his robe, before accepting it and taking a sip. It *was* a good wine, he thought begrudgingly.

"We're expecting just a few more guests," Ellisa continued, as Benil reclaimed his seat on her other side. "I would imagine you would know them. Maya Graylight from the mercenary's guild, Yue Lang the blacksmith, and our fellow council members Cyrus, Abe, and Shefali."

"I see," Adrissu replied, taking another sip of his wine. The two not already on the council were prominent community members in their own rights. He had met Maya Graylight only the one time, but knew she was well-respected for training up the members of the mercenary's guild, and for the role she took in the safety and security of Polimnos. Yue Lang owned and operated the largest of the three forges in town—the other two were so much smaller in comparison that they may as well have been hobbyists. He had only met Yue a handful of times; but Ruan had often spoken of how he armed anyone worth their salt in the guild, and how he had eagerly saved up to have a new sword and armor custom made by him, bragging about it constantly to Adrissu when he had finally procured the items.

He took a breath and pushed all thoughts of Ruan from his mind.

"Yes, I am familiar with everyone," he continued abruptly, realizing Ellisa had been waiting expectantly for him to continue. "You honor me by including me in their presence. These are all upstanding citizens of Polimnos, as I am sure you know."

"Well, don't sell yourself short," she replied warmly. "You've made quite a name for yourself, Adrissu. Everyone in town knows you, and not only because you're an elf in a sea of humans. Your skill in magic hasn't gone unnoticed."

"Thank you," he replied, nodding.

The list of names only solidified his suspicion that they were going to offer him a place on the council, along with Maya

Graylight and Yue Lang. Although he already considered himself well above them all, there was a quiet satisfaction to being recognized as a key member of the community.

Another knock sounded at the door, followed by Luelle's voice calling out, "Coming!"

Benil started chattering about something or other, but Adrissu focused on what he could hear from the hallway. The creak of the door opening, Luelle's voice again, then another voice—Maya Graylight had arrived.

A moment later the stern-looking woman appeared in the doorway of the sitting room. The one time Adrissu had met her, he vaguely recalled her wearing a practical outfit, what looked like a man's shirt and trousers. Now, she wore similar attire. In place of a dress like Ellisa's or Luelle's, she was dressed in a smart, finely made set of black leather breeches and a gray silken shirt, buttoned in the front like a man's tunic, but cut to be more form-fitting. A deep red shawl slung over her shoulders and falling past her hips was the only part of her outfit that wasn't obviously practical and plain.

"Good evening," she said briskly, and as both Benil and Ellisa responded eagerly, Adrissu noted that she too carried a bottle of wine in her arms. Hopefully, they had not been expecting him to bring something as well.

"And this is Adrissu, who I'm sure you recognize as our local mage," Benil said, as he led Maya to their corner of the sitting room, pulling Adrissu from his rumination.

"We've met," Maya replied, and Adrissu nodded.

"We have," he agreed, standing to greet her and bowing his head. "My pleasure to see you again."

"And you as well," she said, nodding curtly as she set her bottle of wine on the table with the other.

Adrissu listened idly as Benil and Ellisa went through the same conversation with Maya, thanking her for coming and telling her who else would arrive.

The next two visitors, the councilors Abe and Shefali, arrived together. Luelle guided them in as well, and they headed straight for Benil and Ellisa, greeting each of them in turn.

Maya sat down next to him as the four councilors became absorbed in their own conversation, folding her red shawl around her as she did.

"Any idea what this dinner's all about?" she asked, though her gaze lingered on the councilors. Adrissu took a sip of his wine before answering.

"I have my suspicions," he said, looking her over. She sat in the chair next to him comfortably, almost idly, with her legs crossed and her chin resting on one hand; but her eyes were trained on the councilors like a hawk.

"Which are?" she asked.

"I suspect we're here to be offered seats on an expanded council," he replied, and finally she looked away from the four councilors to smirk up at him.

"Good. That means I'm not thinking too highly of myself for suspecting the same," she chuckled, and he gave her a wry smile in return.

"No, I don't think so," he said. "If anything, I'm surprised they've grouped us together. Running the mercenary's guild has been a boon to Polimnos. My magical study is largely for my own gain."

"Well, most of us can't do much magic at all, which makes yours all the more impressive," she said with a shrug. "That translates to power, so of course the city council would be eager to have that power on their side."

The woman was as shrewd as she looked. His smile widened, his teeth showing.

"I suppose I must agree with you," he said. "And here I was thinking I had gone unnoticed all this time."

"Not at all," Maya chuckled, shaking her head. "Not at all."

She took a sip of her wine, and they were both silent for a moment. The four councilors were still speaking with each other. Clearly, they were not trying to exclude them, with their loud voices and boisterous gestures; but Adrissu had little interest in whatever they were saying, and Maya seemed to feel the same.

The fifth counselor, Cyrus, arrived then. The human was probably about the same age as Ellisa, perhaps a bit older; he was rather portly with a full, well-groomed beard the same gray as the hair that had receded far back on his head. What hair he did have was long and tied back in a neat, low ponytail with a short black ribbon. When he stepped into the room, he greeted them warmly in turn, before joining the other councilors in their conversation.

After a moment, Maya turned to him again.

"I take it things went well with Ruan," she said, and Adrissu paused with his goblet halfway to his lips. Every time that he tried to get the damned human out of his thoughts!

"And how is that?" he replied primly, looking down at his wine.

"Well, you came looking to hire a guard that day," she said, shrugging. "And since then Ruan's bought his own weapons and armor, and even moved into his own home. He takes plenty of jobs, of course, but no one in his age bracket has made those kinds of strides yet."

"Ah. Yes, in that case, you could say things have gone well," he replied, and this time he did take a long, deep drink of his wine, nearly emptying the goblet.

"Knowing him, he hasn't said it to you, so I'll thank you on his behalf," Maya said, her eyes still on Adrissu's face. Her expression was unchanging, but somehow Adrissu sensed she suspected him of *something*. "Ruan has been rude and thoughtless as long as I've known him. Though his attitude has been... *tempered* somewhat in the past several months. Maybe he's finally maturing a bit."

"He has thanked me, yes," Adrissu said quickly, squashing the feeling of indignation that her words elicited in them the moment they arose. Why should he care if she thought he was rude and thoughtless? She wasn't *wrong*—to feel the need to defend him was laughable.

"Oh, good. Maybe that boy will make something of himself yet," she sighed, finally glancing away. "He's a great fighter, I'll give him that. He'll always be cut out for mercenary work. I'm glad to hear you've been a good influence on him, too. He's always talking about you."

He was briefly thankful that he had already drained his wine glass, or else he would have choked on his drink when she said it.

"Is that so?" he asked. He was sure his carefully disinterested tone had broken at the question, but he couldn't bring himself to regret it. Ruan thought about him, talked about him—that had to mean something, didn't it?

"Oh, yes. Other recruits are always asking if you're hiring on anyone else," she said, meeting his eyes. "He always says he'll tell them if you do, but apparently you never hire anyone else."

"No," Adrissu said. "I have no need for multiple guards."

"Even when Ruan is on other jobs?"

He was silent for a long moment. He had no excuse for that, other than the truth: that he wanted a reason to keep Ruan nearby. It was not out of some sort of benefactory instinct that he had offered the job, and he couldn't give less of a fuck about the other mercenaries or their guild. He only cared about Ruan.

But he could not say as much.

"Not even when Ruan is on other jobs," he agreed simply.

"Hmm," was all Maya murmured in reply; but sneaking a glance at her again, there was something like a self-satisfied smile on her stern features. The thought that his favor might be so obvious to an outsider was mortifying, but if he tried to defend himself it would only solidify her opinion, so he remained silent.

Luckily, the final guest Yue Lang arrived at that moment; and when they were all ushered into the kitchen, Adrissu was seated on the opposite end of the long table as Maya, far enough away that they could not easily converse. Even if she had tried, Benil seemed eager to make up for their lack of conversation earlier in the evening, chatting incessantly at him through the first two courses of the meal.

By the time dessert was being set out, there was palpable anticipation in the air. Benil, Ellisa, and Shefali kept glancing surreptitiously over at Cyrus, the most senior member of the council, who sat next to Ellisa at the head of the long table. Adrissu was sure that they would soon learn the reason for this dinner invitation.

When the servant had quietly left the dining room, but before anyone started on the dish—a simple dessert of cold cream and fresh berries dusted with sugar—Cyrus finally stood, wineglass still in hand.

"Thank you all so much for joining us tonight," the man said, his voice a deep and resonant bass tone that effortlessly filled the room. "Adrissu, Maya, and Yue, I'm sure I can speak for the whole council when I say that we all admire you deeply and recognize the positive impact you've had on Polimnos and its citizens."

The other council members murmured their assent. Maya nodded curtly. Yue, who Adrissu only vaguely knew, lifted a placating hand in a gesture of modesty. Adrissu managed a tight-lipped smile as he looked back at Cyrus who was surveying them all, his expression largely inscrutable beneath his facial hair. He always had a more difficult time reading humans with beards.

"It is because we've recognized your positive influence that the Polimnos council and myself would like to extend an offer of councilorship to each of you," Cyrus said, when the other members quieted down. The tension in the room broke as Adrissu leaned back in his chair, watching the slightly relieved expressions on both Maya and Yue's faces: this was exactly what they had been expecting as well.

"As Polimnos has grown, we've decided expanding the council is the most logical next step," Ellisa explained, interjecting before Cyrus could continue. "Of course, you can decline if you'd prefer; but the five of us decided that the three of you are among the best Polimnos has to offer, and can help guide the city to an even brighter future."

"Precisely," Cyrus agreed. Across from him Benil Branwood was nodding eagerly, his beady eyes darting rapidly between Cyrus and Adrissu. "You needn't give us a decision immediately, but if you're unsure, one of us will reach back out to you in three day's time."

"No need for that," Yue Lang said quickly, smiling. "I'm honored you'd consider me, and I'll gladly accept."

"Excellent, excellent," Cyrus said, nodding, as the other council members clapped their hands enthusiastically.

"I'm flattered as well," Maya said around a tight-lipped smile. Her expressions were nearly inscrutable—if anything, her face was not expressive at all, Adrissu thought. "My duty to the guild will always come first, but if that won't cause problems, I'd be happy to accept a position on the council."

"Oh, of course," Cyrus agreed, nodding. "We wouldn't want it any other way. We believe the mercenary's guild could potentially become one of the supporting pillars of Polimnos itself, so cultivating it will become a priority of ours, as well."

An expectant silence settled over the room, as each set of human eyes flickered over to Adrissu. He sighed, swirling the wine in his goblet for a moment before speaking.

"I must thank you for your consideration," he started slowly, unsure which one he wanted to look at as he spoke. Finally, his eyes flickered up to Maya and stayed trained on her. "I will certainly consider this, but... I'm afraid I can't give as definitive of an answer as Maya or Yue at this time."

There was another beat of silence, and he risked a glance over to the councilors. Cyrus looked utterly unfazed. Ellisa and Shefali looked mildly surprised, and both were glancing over at Benil, whose grin had faltered into a nervous grimace.

"I completely understand," Cyrus said smoothly, as if he did not notice Benil's blanched face. The thought that the others ignored Benil as much as did gave Adrissu a tiny hint of satisfaction—maybe being on the council wouldn't be too terrible. "Are there any particular concerns you might have that perhaps we could address for you?"

"Well," Adrissu sighed, taking a sip of his wine to collect his thoughts. There were *many* reasons as to why he shouldn't accept a position on the Polimnos council, but which were reasonable to share? "I suppose that while I'm flattered at your consideration, I don't entirely see why you might choose me amongst these community leaders." He gestured further down the table to where Maya and Yue sat. "They are proprietors of thriving businesses that have had huge impacts on the culture of Polimnos: its exports and trade, its taxes and funding... And I am only an outcast elf, playing around with magic in an isolated tower."

He smiled as he said it, eliciting a few nervous chuckles from the others.

"You're much more than that, of course, Adrissu," Benil stammered, and this time it was Adrissu's smile that faltered.

"Of course," he agreed. "I only mean that... Polimnos is a human city. I appreciate your apparent fondness of me, but I doubt that the city's residents might be as... amenable to my own non-human sensibilities and instincts. They might question why the only resident elf gets an entire council seat to himself."

"Why, that's—" Benil sputtered, but Cyrus raised a placating hand to silence him.

"If I may," the older man said evenly, keeping his eyes trained on Adrissu. He was liking the man more and more, now. "I understand your concerns, Adrissu; and frankly that they are a concern at all to you only speaks to your character. *That* is the kind of admirable quality we'd like to keep on the council. You have lived in Polimnos nearly since its inception, and as an elf, you will more than likely see its progress far longer than anyone at this table."

"Of course," Adrissu agreed. If they only knew how true it was!

"And why shouldn't we strive to be a bit more like elves, anyway?" Ellisa said, laughing. "I mean, Aefraya has a much nicer track record than Autreth, as far as wars and conquerors."

"Aefraya and the orcish tribes have been at war for centuries," Adrissu pointed out, and the older woman waved her hand dismissively.

"Anyone bordering the orc tribes would war with them. They refuse to acknowledge borders. That's hardly their fault," she said, shaking her head. "No, Aefraya has been a stable, prosperous nation for just as many centuries. We could take a page or two from their book. I know I'm not the only human who thinks so, Adrissu."

"And in the end, humans respect power," Maya said, speaking up for the first time. Several pairs of eyes swung to look at her, but her gaze was firmly on Adrissu. "I'm loath to admit it, Adrissu, but you're probably the most powerful one in the room anywhere you go. I've trained to fight all my life, but to me magic is something else entirely. You could kill me right now if you wanted to."

Adrissu met her eyes, his mind racing. It was completely *impossible* for the human woman to have even any inkling of his secret; yet her statement implied some level of knowledge that she knew, or at least suspected, he was not what he appeared. He had never harmed anyone with his magic—not for as long as he'd lived in Polimnos as Adrissu. He had given no one any reason to believe he was dangerous. Was his persona of an eccentric, studious mage truly so flimsy?

"Not that we think you *would*, of course, Adrissu," Cyrus said, a hint of nervousness in his voice for the first time. Adrissu blinked and finally tore his gaze away from Maya to glance back over at him. "What Maya is trying to say, I think, is that magic is its own power. Even your purely academic study of magic could benefit the city in hundreds of ways."

"Of course," Adrissu said slowly, nodding. "I understand. You've given me much to think over." He did not look at Maya again, instead taking a deep drink of his wine. "Well, I will still give it some thought, but I am feeling rather more open to the idea now."

"I'm glad to hear it," Cyrus said. Next to him, Benil's shoulders visibly sagged; but whether it was in relief or disappointment, Adrissu could not discern and did not entirely care.

The tension in the room had drained, and now the humans had started on their dessert. Absently, Adrissu spooned the sweet concoction into his mouth, turning everything over in his mind. What could Maya possibly know that could have made her say such a thing? Or was it more innocuous, an opinion born from a lack of understanding of magic, rather than any true suspicion on her part? He felt quite sure he had not given any resident of Polimnos reason to suspect him of anything, yet...

"Adrissu," Maya's voice snapped him out of his thoughts, and he looked up quickly to see her standing next to him. The group had started making their way back to the sitting room, Yue Lang speaking animatedly with the councilors as they walked and keeping a slow pace to accommodate Ellisa's bad hip.

"Maya," he replied evenly, hoping his tone sounded less shaken than he felt.

"I apologize if I said anything untoward," she said gruffly, her lips pursed in an uncomfortable but resolute expression. "I didn't mean to offend you."

Adrissu nodded slowly, considering. If she was perturbed by his reaction, maybe it had truly been an innocuous statement—at the very least, she didn't suspect him of anything, which was a relief.

"No offense taken," he replied evenly. "Rather, I was... unsettled, I suppose. I had never quite seen it that way before, but I admit you were correct in your assessment."

"I only meant that I recognize your power," she continued curtly. Though her face and posture were the perfect image of stony aloofness, as she held her wine goblet in one hand, her thumb rubbed up and down the stem of it—a nervous gesture that she seemed entirely unaware of. "And other humans would recognize it, too. Even the strongest human mages are only on the level of an average elf, and from what I can tell, your ability is well above average. Some might be wary of you, but that kind of power commands respect. I would know."

He smirked at that. His worry was mostly assuaged now: whatever she did think of him, it wasn't anywhere near the truth.

"I understand entirely," he said, then stood. "Shall we join the others, then?"

He remained for only a little while longer, excusing himself with a short goodbye. He wanted to clear his head, to stretch his wings. It was late that night when Zamnes, Scourge of Polimnos, departed his lair from the cliffside outside of the town. Disguised under the shield of night, he flew silently and aimlessly over the dark ocean for miles. The cold spray of it on his scales, the salt that lingered in his nostrils—Polimnos was his home. If they wanted him to help guide it, why shouldn't he?

Chapter Five

When it was announced that the council of Polimnos was to expand, and Adrissu was to occupy one of its new seats, Ruan was out of town on a job. Adrissu absolutely did not care that Ruan was not there when the town crier made the announcement—that the first one to congratulate him was, of course, the insufferable Benil Branwood. None of it mattered to him at all.

But he did have a faint sense of satisfaction when Ruan arrived at his tower on his first day back nearly two weeks later, and he called out to the human from the second floor,

"Have you heard the news?"

"What news?" Ruan shouted back. Adrissu huffed, wishing he weren't so damned loud, and stepped up to the railing to look down on Ruan in the doorway.

"I have been offered a place on the city council," he said, not bothering to stifle the prideful grin that he could feel spreading across his face, revealing all his teeth. "And I have accepted."

Ruan blinked, clearly taken aback. A surprised smile spread across his face as well, the sun beaming out from behind a cloud. Adrissu's heart stuttered. Every time Ruan was gone, he forgot how radiant the man's face was, and with each return, he was struck anew by his smile.

"Adrissu!" he exclaimed, taking a step toward the stairs. "That's incredible news. I'm happy for you. What an honor!"

"Yes," Adrissu agreed, allowing himself a moment to preen. "It was only myself and two others who were approached. Your guildmaster Maya Graylight, and the smith Yue Lang."

"Yue too? Seems I've been rubbing elbows with all the right people," Ruan said, laughing. Sometimes Adrissu hated his laugh, loud and unreserved like the braying of a donkey. But when he laughed now, it was a warm, intimate sound. "This news calls for a celebration. Maybe now you'll finally agree to come to my home for dinner?"

Adrissu opened his mouth to decline, but the words that escaped him were, "Yes, I think I will."

For a moment they were both silent, surprise obvious on Ruan's face—it must have been just as obvious on his own face, as well. Why had he said that?

"Tomorrow, then?" Ruan said brightly, a slow smile creeping onto his lips again, as if he, too, could not believe Adrissu had finally agreed.

Adrissu licked his lips anxiously, looking away. He hadn't meant to, but what would it hurt now?

"Tomorrow," he agreed.

And so he ended up standing in front of Ruan's house the following evening, only a few hours after the young man had left his tower for the day.

He had not changed from the clothes that he'd already worn that day: the idea that Ruan might think he was trying to impress him was intenable. The fact that he put on one of his nicer robes when he got dressed this morning meant nothing at all.

The human's home was a tall, narrow domicile on one of the new streets: just one amongst many others that had been crammed into the residential area to make room for Polimnos' rapidly growing population. But its stone was still a gleaming, bright gray—almost silvery in its appearance—a testament to the bright future of the town.

He could still turn back. If he didn't show up, Ruan would surely be disappointed—he might even decide to no longer work for him, gold piece or no. Maybe if he left now, he would be rid of the human once and for all—rid of the curse that had plagued him the moment that he set eyes on him, now almost two years ago.

He considered it, then stepped up to the door and knocked.

It took only a moment for Ruan to open the door, as if he had been sitting and waiting for Adrissu to arrive.

"Hello, Adrissu," he said, a wide grin spreading across his face as he leaned in the doorway. The human seemed irritatingly aware of how his smile dazzled him. Adrissu pressed his lips together in a frown, heat rising in his face. Ruan's clean, fresh outfit did not help either: rather than the plain work clothes Adrissu had typically seen him in, now he was wearing a tailored black shirt with loose sleeves and a low collar barely laced closed, tucked into form-fitting breeches. The human knew exactly what he did to him, Adrissu thought with no small amount of irritation.

"Hello," he replied stiffly, pushing past Ruan without waiting to be invited in.

The man's home didn't look especially lived-in: the walkway was mostly bare and opened into a large sitting room with a table, two plush chairs, and a small kitchen off to the side of it. Hung on one wall was a weapons rack where Ruan's armor was displayed alongside his swords; other than that, his home seemed unadorned. The room was warm, and the smell of food wafted from the kitchen.

"I hope you like chicken," Ruan laughed, stepping past him to check the oven. "I can't cook much, but I can roast a chicken."

"I do," Adrissu said, pulling his arms out from his sleeves. He had considered bringing Vesper with him, but she had been unwilling to get into his sleeve when he was leaving, so in a huff he had left her behind. Instead, he pulled a bottle of wine from his sleeve. "I brought this, as well."

"Ah, lovely," Ruan said, waggling his eyebrows. "Needed some liquid courage to get through the evening, eh?"

Adrissu started to scowl again, but this time his lips twitched upward into a tiny smile. Quickly, he hid it behind one hand before Ruan could see him laugh.

"I need to not be sober to deal with you one-on-one," he muttered, but Ruan only laughed, as he pulled two goblets from a small rack hanging in the kitchen. The wine bottle came uncorked with a *pop*, and Ruan poured him a generous amount, before handing the goblet over to him and pouring some for himself.

"To the newest member of the Polimnos council," Ruan said, smiling warmly at him and taking a drink.

"Indeed," Adrissu said hoarsely, lifting the goblet to his lips.

"Food will be ready soon," Ruan said, glancing back at the oven. "I tried to time it just right, but well, what can you do?"

"It's fine," Adrissu said stiffly, taking a seat in one of the armchairs. He took a deep drink of his wine before glancing back over at Ruan: heat crept up his neck and face when he saw that the human was simply standing and looking at him with a soft smile.

He had been so consumed with hiding his desire for Ruan that—for all the human's teasing and joking—it had never quite occurred to him that Ruan might *actually* be attracted to him. The thought struck him now, seeing the soft affection in Ruan's gaze. Why? For all that he had tried to push the stubborn human away, why did Ruan still vye for his attention? Why had he agreed to any of this?

He had become weak, he thought as he took another nervous sip. One moment of weakness, in hiring Ruan so he could see him every day, had grown into more and more moments of weakness that had led to this: to Adrissu sitting alone in Ruan's home, only the premise of wine and food keeping them apart.

He would not, *could* not, be the one to approach Ruan. Whatever resolve he still had left in him, he would not be the first to break.

"Here we are," Ruan said, breaking him from his thoughts. He pulled a roasting tray from the wood-burning oven, setting it on the stone countertop. A perfectly roasted chicken surrounded by root vegetables—turnips and carrots from the smell of it. "Come, sit at the table, Adrissu."

Ruan served him a plate first, and in another moment, they were eating quietly across from each other. Adrissu mechanically cut a piece, placed it in his mouth, chewed, swallowed, and repeated the cycle without letting his eyes stray from his plate. He only risked a glance over at Ruan once, catching his warm brown eyes lingering on him, and did not look in his direction again until his plate was cleared.

"Well, what's the verdict?" Ruan asked when he was done. Adrissu blinked. He had barely tasted any of it.

"It's good," he said simply. The wine had warmed his belly, but hadn't dulled the edge of his nerves.

"I'm glad," Ruan said, grinning across the table at him. "Are you still hungry? I can get you more."

Adrissu shook his head and allowed Ruan to take his plate, watching as he set it in the wash basin. From there he reached into a small icebox, revealing a bowl filled with fruits—cherries, blackberries, grapes, and figs.

"Come, join me for dessert," Ruan said cheerfully, stepping past him back into the sitting room to settle in one of the armchairs.

Silently, Adrissu followed, carefully arranging his robe around him to avoid wrinkling it or accidently sitting on one of his sleeves. Ruan watched him, making him flush under the scrutiny.

"Help yourself," Ruan said, offering the bowl to Adrissu as he took a handful of cherries for himself. Adrissu carefully took a bunch of grapes—trying not to watch too closely as Ruan tossed a few cherries in his mouth and chewed indulgently for a moment, before lifting his now-empty goblet to his lips and spitting out the pits.

"I tried to get ahold of a sweetcake to go with the fruit," he continued, leaning back in his chair. "But the bakery was sold out by the time I got there. This is still good, though, don't you think?"

Adrissu nodded absently. A smear of red cherry juice was still on Ruan's bottom lip.

"You haven't even eaten any," Ruan said, gesturing to the bunch of grapes in Adrissu's hand. "Here."

And before Adrissu could even think to react, Ruan had leaned forward, plucked a grape from the bunch, and held it to Adrissu's lips.

"Ruan," Adrissu hissed in protest, his face immediately starting to burn. The utterance was more than enough for Ruan to press the fruit into his mouth, along with his fingertip. His lips closed around the soft flesh, and the faint whimper that escaped him would have been nothing short of shameful, if not for the similar sound Ruan made at the same time, consuming Adrissu's attention.

"Good?" Ruan asked, barely above a whisper. As he slowly pulled away, his finger dragged along Adrissu's bottom lip. His mind had gone completely blank. He caught himself following the movement with his head, his skin craving the contact, as he bit down into the fruit. "Another?"

"Stop this," Adrissu hissed, seizing the human's wrist before he could pluck another grape.

"Why?" Ruan said, leaning closer to him. Adrissu pushed his hand away, but this time it was Ruan who grabbed his wrist. Only the fabric of Adrissu's robe kept their skin from touching. "I know you want me. I see how you look at me. If I want you, too, what's to stop us?"

"You presume," Adrissu breathed, though he could barely speak over Ruan's voice echoing in his head—*if I want you, too...*

"Don't try to deny it," Ruan said, and his lips split into a smile as he laughed. "You are not nearly as subtle as you think you are, Adrissu, not anymore."

"I am far too old for you," he continued. The protest was weak to his own ears. For all his refusal, he was rock-hard under his robes. If Ruan looked down, the evidence of his arousal would be damning; but the human was only looking at his eyes, his face.

"For the gods' sakes, you're an elf. You're too old for *anyone* in this city," Ruan laughed, shaking his head. "I don't care about any of that, not at all. We're both adults. Why dance around it? Why not just have what we both want?"

Adrissu's voice caught in his throat, silencing his protest. Every cell in his body, every primal instinct he had, was screaming to leap at him now, to take the human's heart and body as his own, to devour him whole. Ruan was offering himself to him—but he couldn't. He had to keep him away, or he risked being found out. For all the animalistic need surging through his body, he clung to the one rational thought he could form. He could not let his secret be known, not even by Ruan; and the closer they were, the more he could find out.

"Because," he managed to choke out, squeezing his eyes shut. If Ruan thought he were being vulnerable, afraid, maybe then he would relent. "Because I will not care for a human. I *cannot*. I will not carry that grief with me for so long, for centuries, Ruan. I will *not*."

His voice broke at the end. For a long moment Ruan was perfectly still, then slowly he exhaled, releasing Adrissu's wrist before leaning back in his chair.

"I..." he started, then shook his head. His brows had drawn together, and his intense gaze had fallen away. Clearly the thought had never occurred to him. Why would it? *He* would not be the one to be left behind—to live so many lifetimes over without his mate. Finally, he sputtered out, "I... I suppose I can't argue with that."

Adrissu was silent, as he looked down at the grapes still in his hand. It was entirely too personal of an admission, now that he could think enough to consider it, but it seemed to have done the job. For a long moment neither of them spoke, only the sound of their breathing between them. With his heart still pounding the way it was, his breath was coming in short, rapid bursts, but so was Ruan's. Adrissu kept his gaze firmly downcast. He would not be the first one to break.

"Adrissu," Ruan said abruptly, and he glanced up at the human once more. "I don't mean to be presumptuous, and... Maybe I'm overstepping. But... You can't stay alone forever, can you? Isn't that worse?"

Part of Adrissu bristled in irritation at that; but a quieter part of him wanted to agree, wanted to beg Ruan to forget what he said, and wanted to finally, *finally* take the other man in his arms and never let go.

"I don't know," he replied quietly. Ruan sighed and rubbed his forehead with one hand, his shoulders sagging in defeat.

"All right," he said. "I can't force you to do anything, of course, Adrissu, but... I hope maybe with some thought you'll change your mind. My..." His cheeks took on a warmer color, and he cleared his throat before continuing in a smaller voice, "My feelings for you won't change."

"*Feelings,*" Adrissu repeated, scowling at the words, that the human would presume to know anything about *feelings*. "You only want me in your bed."

"That isn't true," Ruan snapped, anger flashing in his eyes as he looked back up at Adrissu. For a moment they glared at each other, eyes heated, until finally Adrissu looked away and started to stand up.

"I should go," he muttered.

"Adrissu, wait," Ruan said, but Adrissu had already turned to leave. Ruan's fingers barely caught the edge of his sleeve; he yanked it away, pulling it free almost effortlessly. Ruan did not follow him as he strode out of the room, through the entryway, and out the door.

He had no memory of his walk back to his tower, only returning to his senses as the heavy wooden door closed behind it. He leaned against it heavily, pressing one hand to his chest, as if it might calm his hammering heart. He lifted his other hand to his chest as well, only to realize that he was still holding the bunch of grapes. Like a fool. He glared down at them in his palm.

The sight of them brought back the memory of Ruan's finger in his mouth, and he bit back a whimper at the lingering sensation of the human's warm skin, the rough drag of his calloused finger on his lips, the taste of him—

His cock ached to be touched, so urgently it was nearly painful. Right now, he could have been fucking the human, could have buried his cock deep inside of him; but instead he was here, alone. Hating himself, hating Ruan, he took himself in one hand and stroked—hard and rough—the way he imagined Ruan would touch him with his battle-scarred hands. He lifted the bunch of grapes to his mouth, breathing in the scent deeply, remembering. He imagined taking the rest of Ruan's fingers into his mouth, the feel of them, the taste of his cock—

Adrissu shuddered, crushing a grape between his teeth as he came and letting its sticky juice drip down his chin. He would never have more, he told himself, as his labored breathing finally started to slow. This was all he would have of Ruan. He would never, ever let himself have more.

Chapter Six

Adrissu almost expected Ruan to not show up the next day. The human didn't always check in with him in the morning; sometimes he would just take up his post outside, and Adrissu would not see him until they had lunch. But this time, when Ruan did not greet him in the morning, he silently resigned himself: he had finally driven the human away once and for all.

He should be relieved, he told himself. The whole reason that he was trying to avoid Ruan was to spare himself the heartbreak of his mate dying in just a few short decades, if not sooner. So why was he so miserable now? Why did he still want to be near the human, to see his face and hear his voice?

It was midmorning when the thought of Ruan never sitting outside his tower again became intolerable. Adrissu hadn't been able to focus on any of his work that morning anyway, so he pulled his shoes on and stepped outside—nearly hitting Ruan with the door as he shoved it open.

"Gods!" Ruan hissed, startled. His wide eyes flew up to Adrissu's surprised face, who quickly reigned in his expression, attempting something more neutral. But the tension between his brows remained.

"I didn't realize..." Adrissu started, unsure of what to even say. He was going to plan out what to say on the way to Ruan's home; but now that the man was here he had to say *something*. "I thought maybe you wouldn't come."

Ruan sighed and looked away. "A gold's a gold," he said, his voice so carefully neutral that Adrissu could clearly see through the excuse that Ruan must have practiced in the mirror that morning.

"Come inside," Adrissu said. Ruan glanced up at him, but after a moment, he nodded and straightened up from the wooden stool where he often sat.

When they were both inside, Adrissu closed the heavy wooden door behind them, fiddling with the handle for a moment, before turning to face the human.

"Ruan," he said slowly, forcing himself to meet his eyes. "I... apologize for what I said to you last night."

Ruan blinked, then nodded slowly.

"Thank you," he said, his voice rasping. He cleared his throat before continuing. "I, um... I don't really know what to say. But I meant what I said last night, Adrissu."

"I understand," Adrissu said. "And, Ruan, I hope you can understand me as well. I... am attracted to you, yes." The words seemed woefully inadequate to describe how his very blood seemed to flow toward the human—how his vision swam with Ruan's visage every time they were near each other. "But to be involved this way with a human... Maybe if things were different. But I cannot promise you anything."

"Listen," Ruan interrupted, shaking his head. "I understand, Adrissu, I truly do. I had not considered this before, but once you said it, I... it makes perfect sense, of course. But, Adrissu, half elves *exist*. You can't be the only elf who has dealt with a lifespan difference. You don't even want to try?"

"It isn't that simple," he hissed.

"Why?" Ruan pressed, brows furrowed; and it struck Adrissu that he looked truly grieved. He had been blinded by his own feelings and not seen Ruan's growing affection for him, but it was painfully obvious now.

"I..." Adrissu started, then sighed, pressing his hand to his forehead. "I cannot explain it."

"Fine," Ruan huffed, scrubbing a hand through his hair.

"But," Adrissu said. "But I... I don't want to be apart from you, either."

"You just said—"

"I know what I said," he growled. "I hate that I feel this way. I wish I could just tell you not to come back and be done with it. But I want to be around you, more than I want to be alone."

For a long moment Ruan was silent, staring at him with a blank expression.

"Adrissu," he finally sighed. "I don't understand you at all."

Adrissu scowled, looking away. He hated that he had said anything at all, hated that he was too weak to push the human away, hated that he had ever seen him in the courtyard in the first place.

"But if that's what you want, we can try," Ruan continued, pulling him from his frustrated thoughts. "Despite everything, I do like you, Adrissu. I like being around you. And I like the job, of course. Maybe we don't have to put a label on..." He gestured between them. "On this. If things staying how they've been is enough for you... Well, I can learn to be okay with that, too, I suppose."

Adrissu knew it was a doomed effort even before Ruan was done speaking. Eventually, being around Ruan enough would cause his resolve to fully break. *This* could only go on for so long.

"Yes," he agreed, his voice barely above a whisper. "Let's stay like... Like this."

Ruan was silent for a long moment, eyes on the ground. When he finally looked back up at Adrissu, he managed a tiny smile; but it was forced, stilted—it had none of the radiance that his smile usually did, and a deep thrum of sadness coursed through Adrissu at the sight.

"Alright," he said, a hollowly cheerful tone to his voice. "We'll stay like this, then."

Adrissu nodded, not trusting himself to speak.

"I guess I'd better get back to work," Ruan sighed, and Adrissu sidestepped him, as he moved for the door. "I'll see you for lunch, then?"

Adrissu watched him go silently, until the human paused in the doorway and glanced back at him. His smile, though wavering, was still on his face.

"Yes," Adrissu replied slowly, nodding once. "I'll see you for lunch."

And so, somehow, things gradually started going back to the way they were, and eventually the events of that evening felt like a distant dream. Adrissu would have wondered whether or not it all had happened—the dinner, the arguments, the next morning—if he did not still have such a visceral reaction to the smell and taste of grapes. He stopped eating them entirely.

The only thing that really felt different was Ruan seemed to take more jobs, keeping him away more often than not. Adrissu knew that he was steadily rising through the ranks of the mercenary guild and taking on more difficult assignments, so it only made sense.

Adrissu kept himself busy, as well. His new position on the Polimnos council meant that the meetings and discussions, which had only previously been known to him through Benil Branwood's endless complaints, were now his responsibility to attend. Even though he had no particular speciality in town politics, unlike the rest of the council members, they seemed to value his opinion on how the town should be handled; thus most of his time was spent with the other council members and occasionally other townsfolk.

He saw Ruan less and less; but when they were together, Ruan was always polite and friendly to him. Though their interactions had largely gone back to how they once were, Adrissu was finding it more and more difficult to be distant toward the human. It was exactly as he had feared: his resolve could only last so long, and over time what was once a cool indifference in their interactions became a reluctant affection.

When he *was* cold to him, he would always feel guilty afterward, even though it never seemed to phase Ruan in the slightest.

He knew it was only a matter of time before his will fully broke, until Ruan pushed too far, and he could not stop himself. Still, it took him by surprise when it did finally happen.

When Ruan would go on a job, especially if it were to be something longer than normal, he would tell Adrissu a few days before, then remind him once more the day before, even though Adrissu always remembered. This time, he explained that he would be guarding a trade caravan and would likely be gone for around three months—longer than he'd ever been away before

"I see," Adrissu murmured, and he tried not to think about it for the rest of the week.

At the end of the week, Ruan said to him over lunch,

"I'm leaving tomorrow."

"I know," Adrissu replied, glancing up at him from across the table. They often ate together, and Adrissu had made it a point to hover around him more frequently in the days leading up to his departure.

"Aren't you going to miss me?" Ruan said, a teasing grin spreading across his face. Adrissu huffed, looking away as a flush of warmth rose in his face.

"Perhaps," he replied, and Ruan laughed, shaking his head.

For a moment both were silent, Adrissu glancing over at Ruan as the human swirled the cup of water in his hand and looked down with a suddenly pensive expression.

"Adrissu," he said abruptly, looking up to catch him staring. "I... I must tell you something."

Already his heart had started to quicken. Adrissu swallowed and replied, "What is it?"

Ruan gestured between them. "I can't do... *this* anymore. I don't want to keep pretending to only be your employee. My feelings haven't changed, not at all."

"Ruan..." Adrissu started, but the human was standing, a determined expression coming over his face.

"And I don't think you truly want that either," he continued, taking a step toward Adrissu. "If you didn't, you would have told me not to come back a long time ago."

"Ruan," he said again—his tone more stern now—but he couldn't find anything else to say. Despite all his efforts to keep Ruan at arm's length, lying to the human felt impossible.

"Tell me no, then," Ruan said, closing the distance between them. "If you don't want me, tell me no."

He couldn't. Ruan eyed him for only a moment, then leaned down and kissed him.

Adrissu's hands clenched so hard around the arms of his chair that he thought he might splinter them to pieces. His back stiffened, tension coiling in every muscle, but despite himself his eyes slipped closed. His mate was kissing him, his mouth hot and hungry, and everything in the world seemed to slip into its correct place—the way it had when Adrissu had first seen him across the courtyard. Ruan's tongue swiped against his lips. He groaned and pressed his own tongue against him, and with a faint noise Ruan's lips parted to let him in. He wanted to bite, to claw, to *devour*; but he only let his tongue glide against Ruan's, relishing in the soft moan of pleasure that escaped from the back of his throat.

Everything in him was screaming for more, but Adrissu forced himself to pull away.

"Adrissu," Ruan protested, tilting his head to follow; but with every ounce of restraint that he had left, Adrissu turned his face away, so the human's lips only brushed against his cheek.

"Ruan," he said, his voice barely above a whisper. He sounded as strained and tense as he felt, his fingers dug painfully into the wooden arms of his chair. "If you do this again—I will not stop. I will not be able to stop."

"I don't want you to stop," Ruan murmured, before he leaned in closer. He had pushed himself between Adrissu's legs, but now moved to straddle his waist, sitting in his lap. He pressed his lips to Adrissu's neck; with an involuntary gasp, Adrissu tilted his head so more of his skin was exposed. Ruan started near the crook of his shoulder, mouthing and biting and licking upward until he was pressing kisses to his jaw, his cheek, the corner of his mouth.

When their lips touched again, Adrissu knew it was over. He surged forward—all but leaping to his feet and taking Ruan with him—pushing him up against the table as they kissed, making the human gasp and moan. Adrissu pressed forward until Ruan's back was flush against the table, bent almost painfully at the waist as he leaned over him, first biting the human's lower lip and then soothing it with his tongue. The human had gone entirely limp against him, helpless to the onslaught, but his erection strained against his trousers where they were pressed together.

One of Ruan's hands came up, first cupping his cheek then trailing upward to feel along his ear. Adrissu gasped at the little thrill of unexpected pleasure it sent shooting down his spine.

Their lips finally apart, Ruan grinned up at him through heavy-lidded eyes.

"You like this?" he murmured, as he trailed his fingers along Adrissu's ear again, pressing harder near the lobe and softly at the pointed tip.

Adrissu did not reply. He bit his lip, squeezing his eyes shut. It was not too late; he could still stop this. Couldn't he?

Abruptly, he straightened and took a step back, forcing his way out of Ruan's arms. The human pushed himself back up to his feet, looking suddenly worried.

"Adrissu?" he asked, his voice soft.

He could not stop this. He was sure of it now. He would bury himself in his mate, get it out of his system, then send Ruan away and never invite him in again. He could do that.

"Go upstairs," Adrissu said, his voice rough and gravelly. He couldn't bring himself to look Ruan in the face as he said it. "My bedroom is to the right. I will follow you shortly."

Ruan blinked, then grinned widely at him.

"Good idea. I'll see you there," he said, winking at Adrissu as he moved to the stairs.

Adrissu watched him go, breathing as deeply and evenly as he could manage. He would have him once and never again, he told himself.

After a moment of composing himself, he followed Ruan up the stairs, but veered toward his study instead of the bedroom. He did not have lubricant specifically for sexual purposes, but some of the oils that he kept in his alchemical supply would work just as well. He retrieved the smallest bottle that he could find and brought it with him to his bedroom.

Ruan, shameless as ever, had already undressed and was waiting for him—laying atop his sheets as effortlessly as if he had been there a hundred times before. Adrissu's breath hitched at the sight of him, all sinew and muscle and scars. Ruan's skin was naturally a darker, warmer tone than Adrissu's; his arms and legs were a deeper tan than his torso and thighs, which must have often been shielded from the sun under his armor. He had very little chest hair, and only a light dusting along his stomach and down his groin. His cock jutted up proudly from between his legs where his body hair was thickest.

"Took you long enough," Ruan goaded, only to gasp as Adrissu lunged for him, pressing his lips to the side of the human's neck and trailing his hands down the length of his body. He gasped as Adrissu's fingers found his nipples, and moaned when they trailed further down to touch his cock. The tip of it was already slick with precome. "Gods, Adrissu..."

"Shut up," Adrissu growled, but his voice was muffled against Ruan's skin.

"You know," Ruan panted when Adrissu released his cock. "When I imagined this, I always managed to get you naked first."

Adrissu scoffed, but moved to start pulling off his robe.

"You'll have to get at least some of this off if I'm to fuck you," Ruan continued, laughing, but this time Adrissu scowled and pushed himself up to glare down at the human.

"You will *not* fuck me," he said, and Ruan blinked, surprise crossing his face.

"No?" he asked. "But—aren't elves—?"

Whatever he was going to say was cut off, as Adrissu pushed his legs up and flipped him over. On instinct Ruan started to push himself up onto his hands and knees, but with one hand Adrissu pressed against his back, right between his shoulder blades, forcing his head down with his firm ass still raised.

"Gods, I didn't realize how strong you—ah, fuck!"

Again he was cut off. Adrissu had uncorked the bottle of oil and poured it down the cleft of his ass, watching it stream down until it clung to the insides of the human's thighs, and dripped from the underside of his testicles to the sheets below. Adrissu caught some of the slick liquid with his fingers to rub against the tight ring of Ruan's entrance.

"Adrissu," Ruan said, his voice hitching. "I really didn't—I thought—can we talk about this first?"

"No," Adrissu snapped, pulling his hand away only long enough to let his robe fall away. With his other hand he undid his trousers and kicked them aside. "I told you exactly what would happen. Do you want me or not?"

As he said it, he pushed one finger into Ruan. The human groaned, his eyes squeezing shut.

"Do you want this?" he repeated, waiting. He watched as Ruan bit his lip, eyes fluttering open and glancing back at Adrissu nervously—he barely even seemed to register that Adrissu was now just as naked as he was.

"Yes," he finally rasped, eyes flickering shut again as he said it. He sounded like he was on the verge of tears. "Okay. Yes."

Adrissu made quick work of him, doing his best to ignore the faint sounds Ruan made as he began by fucking him with only one finger, moving in and out until the tight muscle began to relax against him. He added a second, and Ruan yelped; but he did not slow, working him open relentlessly until he could fit a third.

"Adrissu!" Ruan cried, as the third finger was pushed into him. "You're—you're hurting me."

"Relax," he said. The world had narrowed down to the heat and tightness of the channel surrounding his fingers: Ruan's voice was distant in comparison, easy to ignore. His mate was nearly ready to take him, and his blood burned with anticipation. There was nothing that could have distracted him from the task at hand.

He knew when he'd found the most sensitive place, a tight bundle of nerves, when a ragged cry burst from Ruan's mouth —hips bucking and his swollen cock twitching in time with the movement of Adrissu's fingers.

He whimpered as Adrissu pushed in and out of him against that spot, again and again, until he was sure that the human was nearly about to come. Only then did he relent, pulling his fingers out of Ruan's tight hole with a wet sliding sound.

"You're ready for me now," Adrissu said, his voice rough and gravelly. Ruan only nodded, his back heaving as he panted for breath beneath him.

His own cock was hard and twitching with eager anticipation. He coated himself with the lingering oil on his fingers, before he pressed the head of his cock to Ruan's entrance, making the human groan with equal parts anticipation and fear.

Mercilessly, Adrissu pushed himself inside, ignoring Ruan's frantic cry, until he was buried to the base. A low, rumbling breath escaped him as the soft flesh of the human's ass pressed against his hips. He belonged here, more than anywhere else in the world. Why had he denied himself for so long?

"Adrissu," Ruan panted, lifting his head slightly to look back at him. "I don't—I don't think I can—"

"You can," he growled, as he slowly began to pull back, reveling in the keening whimper it elicited from Ruan, until only the head of his cock was still enveloped in his tight heat. He lingered there for only an instant, then pushed himself back in hard. Stars filled his vision—nothing else mattered but *this*, his mate's flesh tight around his cock, submitting entirely to his will.

He could not have stopped himself even if he had wanted, setting a rapid pace to chase after the waves of relief and pleasure that would soothe his burning blood. Adrissu's fingers pressed hard into Ruan's hips, leaving bruises in their wake.

He was nearly on the cusp of orgasm when he realized Ruan had gone entirely soft, his limp cock dangling weakly between his legs. The sounds escaping the human were not those of pleasure, but groans of pain, and the skin under his eyes glistened with tears. His rough, calloused hands were clenched tight in Adrissu's sheets.

Adrissu stopped, his breathing still rapid and shallow as he scowled. He did not *want* to feel guilty—he did not want to care about Ruan's pleasure at all. He only wanted to come inside him, to fill his mate with his seed and mark him forever as his own.

But he did feel guilty, his chest aching at the sight of Ruan's tense brow and the tears glistening beneath his eyes. As much as he had told himself that he wanted to drive Ruan away, to do this once and get it out of his system, to ensure Ruan never pursued anything with him again—the thought that he might actually shatter Ruan's affection toward him felt like a stab in the chest. Maybe he did not want Ruan to part from him after all.

"Ruan," he murmured. One of his hands trailed upward along Ruan's sweat-dampened back until he brushed through the dark auburn strands at the nape of his neck, making him hiss with unexpected pleasure. "I'm going to pull out of you now."

"What?" Ruan mumbled, eyes flickering as he seemed to not quite process what Adrissu was saying to him. He whimpered as Adrissu leaned back, his cock sliding out easily with the movement. Before he could say anything else, Adrissu had flipped him over onto his back and pressed their hips together, leaning over with his hands under Ruan's arms to press his face into the human's neck.

"Adrissu," Ruan breathed, still sounding unsure.

"I have been selfish," Adrissu murmured against his ear. Their weight settled; and he pulled one hand away to swipe his fingers through the oil still slick on the cleft of the human's ass, then grasped his softened cock and stroked it gently, making him moan. "I'm sorry."

"I..." Ruan panted, his hands moving uncertainly at his sides, as if he could not decide whether to hold Adrissu or push him away. "I didn't realize—how strong you are."

A wicked grin crossed Adrissu's face at that—if the human only knew how strong he *truly* was—but he hid it by pressing kisses along the human's collarbone. Ruan's cock had come back to life with the gentle coaxing of his hand, growing hard once again. He kept stroking until a long, low moan escaped the human's lips, then he pushed himself back up to look down on him.

"I'm going to enter you again now," he said, his eyes traveling down the length of Ruan's body. He had not realized at first, but one of his nipples was pierced: a golden barbell through the bud of brown flesh on his left side. He was tempted to touch it, but he was impatient. He kept stroking Ruan's cock, and with the other hand held his own to line it up with Ruan's tight opening. "I'll keep touching you here, but touch yourself instead if that helps."

Weakly Ruan nodded, letting out a gasp as Adrissu pushed into him again, slower this time. His walls twitched and clenched around Adrissu's length, but soon his faint noises of discomfort became moans of pleasure as Adrissu continued to touch him in long, tight strokes.

"You've been so good for me," Adrissu murmured, and Ruan's cock all but jumped in his hand in response. "You've done so well—you feel so good around me. You've been so good, haven't you?"

"Yes," Ruan whimpered, and all the tension in his body seemed to drain out at Adrissu's praise. His cock was steadily weeping droplets of precome now, the head flushed and swollen where it peeked out from under his foreskin.

"Because you've been so good," Adrissu murmured, squeezing his cock harder as he stroked—his own cock twitched eagerly against Ruan's inner walls in response to his moans. "I'm going to make you come around my cock, and then I'm going to come inside you."

"Please," Ruan groaned, nodding rapidly. He had utterly surrendered to Adrissu, and all it had taken was a few words of praise. Adrissu rocked his hips gingerly, barely moving inside him even as he continued to stroke his cock.

"You've been so good," he continued to murmur. "You've waited so long for me, and you've done so well."

"Gods," Ruan moaned, his cries reaching a fever pitch. "Adrissu—I'm—"

Ruan clenched hard around Adrissu's cock, nearly breaking his tenuous self-control, and he moaned wordlessly as he came. His cock pulsed and strained against Adrissu's grip, sending thick lines of come shooting up the length of his torso. His cries became a frantic whine as Adrissu continued to stroke him, squeezing hard at the tip with the end of each stroke. One of his hands flew down to grab at Adrissu's wrist, but his grip had no strength behind it, so he kept stroking.

"I want every drop," Adrissu growled, heat overtaking him. "I want everything you have for me here on your chest."

Ruan's eyes rolled back in his head, and he whimpered faintly. A few more weak spurts escaped him, but Adrissu did not stop until he was sure that he had thoroughly squeezed out everything Ruan could give him. Only then did he release the human's cock, grab him by his hips, and rut into him hard and fast.

"Fuck," Ruan whimpered, pressing one hand to his mouth. "Gods, Adrissu, yes—!"

Whatever else he uttered was entirely lost to his ears. Only the burning heat of Ruan's tight channel around his cock existed; all pretense of self control was gone now, and he thrust like a beast into his tight hole until his orgasm thundered through him.

"Ruan," he growled as he came, eyes squeezing shut. "Ruan!"

"Fuck," Ruan whimpered, as Adrissu thrust hard into him only two, three more times. "Gods, Adrissu, you're—it's so hot—I feel it, Adrissu, fuck, I feel you—"

When he finally came down from the soaring heights, his face was pressed into Ruan's sweaty shoulder, and the human's legs were wrapped around his waist. They were both breathing hard, and Adrissu could feel Ruan's heart thudding rapidly against his own chest. He closed his eyes, listening to its incessant beat, imagining that it beat only for him, his fated one.

"Adrissu," Ruan finally whispered, lifting a hand to run his fingers through Adrissu's dark hair. "I think this is the longest lunch break you've ever allowed me."

Adrissu scoffed, hoping his ridiculous grin was imperceptible from where his face was buried in Ruan's shoulder. After a moment longer, he pushed himself back up and carefully eased his softening cock out of Ruan, both gasping at the sensation. His release leaked steadily out of him, oozing from between his legs onto his sheets.

"Wait here," Adrissu said, leaning out of his doorway to peek into his study. Vesper was coiled on his desk, peering curiously in their direction—he rolled his eyes and, ignoring her, flicked his wrist to send the clean cloths that were stacked neatly on one of his work tables sailing through the air across the hall and into his hand.

When they were both cleaned up, and the mess magicked out of his sheets, Ruan moved to gather his clothes from the floor.

"I suppose I should get back to work," he said, a smile slowly returning to his face. Before he could get far, though, Adrissu had grabbed him by the waist and hauled him back to bed. Together they tumbled onto the clean mattress, and Adrissu pushed himself against his back and enveloped him as much as his elven body would allow, as if he were in his draconic form and curling around his hoard.

"I think you're done for the day," he murmured. Ruan settled against him as he laughed. The sound was sweet and clear, more pleasing than any music Adrissu had ever heard.

Chapter Seven

Several hours later, after Ruan left to prepare for his imminent journey, Adrissu was left with the cold, sinking realization of what he'd done.

For nearly three years he had fought against every instinct to be with the human. He had promised himself that he would never allow the weakness of indulging in his base instincts, of letting Ruan get even the tiniest foothold in his heart. Now he sat miserably at the edge of his bed in nothing but his dressing robe, alone with the knowledge that he had finally broken against the unfair, unfathomable magic that had drawn him to Ruan in the first place.

"One more day!" he muttered to himself, shaking his head. "You only had to hold out one more *day*."

Vesper had made her way across the hallway and was now peering up at him curiously, her black eyes gleaming. She was concerned about him. He ignored her, but she slithered up into his lap anyway.

There was nothing to be done. He knew that when Ruan returned he could not hide behind the pretense of trying to keep the human away, or pretend that their fated connection did not exist. All he could do was resign himself to it, and wait.

Why did it have to be *Ruan*? It could have been any other dragon on the face of the planet, and Adrissu would have been able to accept it eventually. It only made sense for dragons to be drawn to their own kind. But a human? *This* human? Half the time he couldn't say he even liked the man; but whatever damned magic allowed fated mates to exist in the first place kept drawing him back, over and over again, no matter how rationally he had tried to convince himself that it would never work out—that there was no *reason* to want to be around Ruan.

The dark thoughts rattled around in his head until well past sunset, when his tower had gone pitch black in the night. Finally he roused himself enough to bring a flickering orb of flame into his hand, deciding that he needed to clear his head the best way he knew how. He descended to the first floor, where his trap door to his cliffside lair was hidden, and threw himself down it.

It was a sheer drop only another flying beast could traverse: it would be impossible to climb up from below, and a fatal fall for anyone coming from above. The tunnel went straight down and was narrow at first, allowing him to step off and free fall for a moment in his elven form; but through his own painstaking design, it began to widen into chasm, so that as he finished his transformation into his natural, true form, it was wide enough for him to spread his wings and slow his descent enough to safely land within the confines of his lair.

The drop was familiar to him and had no sense of novelty anymore; but it always sent a thrill of excitement through Vesper that he felt in his own chest. Stretching all of his limbs, he carefully opened his claws where he had been holding her, and deposited her on the stone floor. She slithered over to one of the many marble dwarven statues that he had set up in this chamber, curled around the arms of her favorite—a dwarven king with a hammer held out like an executioner's ax—and blinked up at him.

I'll return, he said to her, and her tiny serpentine head nodded once. On all fours he moved through this chamber, lingering for a moment in the chamber where his stores of gold were piled, then headed for the opening.

It was just wide and tall enough for him to move through, leading out to a cave mouth hidden near the midpoint of the cliff face that could only be seen from dead-on. Travelers on the road above could not see it, even if they peered down from the very edge of the cliff, and no ships out at sea would have any reason to come close enough to the towering cliffs to spot it. Until mortals developed better means of flight, he had no concern that he might be spotted entering or leaving his lair, especially in the dead of night.

The sheer drop down the cliffside was always his favorite part: the cold ocean air against his scales, the smell of salt filling his nose, the snap that shook him to his core when he finally opened his wings after so long of being crammed into his tiny humanoid form. To stretch his wings as he plummeted down to the ocean was incandescent.

Just before he could plunge beneath the surface, he gave a powerful flap of his wings and began to ascend once more. The wind whistled across his body as he lifted himself higher and higher, until he was far above the cliff. When the trees of the land below were impossible to pick out as individuals, only large shapes of greenish color in the darkness, he began to fly out over the sea.

There was something primal about flying, about being out in the open sky like this. Dragons were intelligent, of course, and some of the most powerful beings in existence—but something about the lives of mortals seemed so much more complicated than dragons ever seemed to be. Here, there was nothing but the stars above him and the sea below. Adrissu was *not* a beast, but here he felt like he could be one: a simple creature with simple desires and a simple life. He could forget, or at least pretend to.

He flew aimlessly, sometimes dropping down enough to let his wings skim the surface of the water, and sometimes soaring so high it became hard to breathe. There was nothing but the pure instinctual pleasure of flight: the adrenaline of nothing at all around him, nothing supporting him but the strength of his own wings.

It had been too long since he'd been like this, he thought. He had been Adrissu for too long and allowed it to cloud his thinking. This was who he was: Zamnes, a dragon with the world at his fingertips and an eternity ahead of him. He could live like this, away from Ruan. It may not be pleasant, but it was possible. It all seemed so much more simple in the sky.

He flew until the first hints of sunrise began to spread across the sky, then he started to head back to his lair. He hadn't kept track of where exactly he had gone, but finding the way back to their lair was one of the most basic draconic instincts. The magic that suffused his body would guide him where he needed to go.

The sun had only begun to peek over the horizon behind him when he could see the cliffside of his home in the distance. He was entirely at peace as he coasted along toward it, thinking of the nap he would enjoy atop his hoard when he was back in his lair.

And then an arrow whistled past him from above, nicking the thinnest part of his wing. Snarling in an instant rage, he halted himself with wings outstretched, hovering for a moment to find the fool who had tried to shoot him. He could just make out a humanoid figure at the very edge of the cliff, looking down, pulling back a bow—and, realizing he'd spotted them, scrambling away.

Zamnes, Scourge of Polimnos, had not been sighted in nearly thirty years. He would find the unlucky idiot and ensure that no news of his flight spread to interrupt the peace. It took only a few thrusts of his wings to ascend the cliffside and look down on the archer that had tried to shoot him.

It was not a lone figure he spotted: on the cliffside road about a hundred feet from the edge, four densely-packed wagons pulled by mules had stopped. Humans screamed and fled from the wagons, and even the beasts brayed and wickered nervously. But between him and the caravan was a tall human, trying to nock another arrow with trembling hands—and running up behind him was Ruan.

Ruan. The caravan. Zamnes roared with anger, embers fluttering from his mouth as he barely contained his fiery rage. Damn the human, damn the caravan, and damn his own terrible luck.

He could not kill them all now. He could not kill Ruan even if he tried—he had never tried, but he felt the truth of it deep in his bones, inscribed there by the magic that had drawn them together in the first place.

"You idiot! I told you to leave it!" Ruan was shouting, glaring at the human who was now clearly too afraid to fire his bow once more. His sword was drawn, and for all the tension in his face, his hands did not tremble as he shifted to an offensive stance and stared Zamnes in the face.

Even as he glowered, a tiny thrill of pride shot up his heart at that. He knew Ruan was brave—brave to the point of foolishness, clearly—but the thought that his human would stare down a dragon without flinching made him feel... something.

But he couldn't consider that now. He had only seconds to decide on his plan of action. If burning them all to the ground was no longer an option, he would do the next best thing.

"Come on, then!" Ruan goaded him, shoving the cowering human away with one hand as he took another step toward Zamnes. "I've always wanted to kill a dragon."

Zamnes could not stop the grin from splitting his features—though he was sure that to Ruan, it was a hideous display of every one of his razor-sharp teeth.

"You will never kill a dragon," he growled, his voice a low rumble that seemed to reverberate through the earth rather than the air. The first flash of true fear crossed Ruan's face as he spoke—the knowledge that dragons *could* speak was rumored at best amongst mortals.

He knew what he would do. Zamnes lunged at him then— Ruan's sword went up to block his open maw, but it was his claws that reached for the human. Effortlessly he had the human in his grasp, ignoring Ruan's startled shout. He flapped his wings, hard enough to send the pathetic guard flying to the ground, and flew to the edge of the cliff, where he tucked his wings in and let gravity do the rest.

He was careful not to draw blood with his claws, so he knew that Ruan's screaming was not out of pain, but the primal fear any flightless creature had of falling. But he had made the exact same drop so many times before that he knew exactly when to extend his wings, halting their descent, and when to surge toward the cliff face.

Ruan must have seen how near the cliffside they had gotten, but not the narrow opening to his lair.

"Let me go!" he roared, squirming frantically in Zamnes' arms. "Let me go, you son of a bitch, let me go!"

He felt Ruan's body tense as they went right up to the cliff face; but at the last second he twisted his body to fit through the narrow gap, then pressed Ruan closer to his scaled chest and used his other three limbs to scuffle through the rest of the tunnel, until it opened to the flight chamber of his lair. Only then did he drop Ruan, moving past him to block his view into the rest of the lair and looking back at him with a snarl.

To his credit, Ruan scrambled to his feet quickly, looking around despite the meager light that streamed in from the narrow tunnel and trying to ascertain his surroundings. His sword was still in his hand, but it trembled now.

Zamnes could see himself in the reflection of his sword as Ruan lifted it in fearful determination—a hulking black serpentine shape with icy blue eyes, like bursts of lightning through the sky.

Zamnes rose up to his full height, spreading his wings in a show of dominance. He lumbered closer until Ruan trembled beneath the shadow of his wings—full of terror and fight in equal measure.

"Stop this," he growled, the thunderous bass of his voice filling the chamber. Ruan flinched as he spoke, but kept his eyes stubbornly on Zamnes's claws. He was a quick learner, at least. "Stop this now, Ruan!"

The sound of his name from the dragon's mouth made Ruan nearly jump in shock. Confusion spread across his face, his gaze finally lifting to look Zamnes in the eyes—and that was when he snapped his tail around to smack the sword out of his hands. The human shouted as the weapon flew out of his grasp, across the chamber, and clattered to the stone floor.

"How?" he panted, scowling up at the dragon. "How do you know my name?"

He knew that he would not be able to trick Ruan; he could only buy himself mere minutes, so there was no point in playing with him. He sighed, closing his eyes and lowered himself until he was standing on all fours with his head only a few feet above Ruan's eyeline.

"You know my name," he said, and this time his voice came out as a hiss, a whisper.

"Of course I do," Ruan spat. "Zamnes, Scourge of Polimnos. Every child in Polimnos grows up hearing your name. Even orphans."

"But you know me by another," he said, watching Ruan's face flicker with confusion once more.

This was it. Whatever hope he had clung to that his identity would remain secret for as long as he lived in Polimnos was dashed now. He closed his eyes and let his magic condense around him, containing him into the body of Adrissu.

"No," Ruan gaped, stumbling back the moment the glow of transmutation had faded from his body. "No, this is—this is a trick."

"It is no trick," Adrissu said softly, taking a step toward him; but Ruan backed away, shaking his head. He looked more afraid now than he had when staring down the dragon. "Ruan. It's me."

"You lie!" he shouted, still staggering back and lifting his arms in a defensive stance, as if he might strike him with his hands. "This draconic magic is—I don't know how you're doing this, but you're not real. You can't be, you can't be real!"

"I am. And I can prove it," Adrissu countered, continuing to walk toward him at a slow, even pace. "Because no one other than us knows what we did yesterday."

Ruan froze, his lips trembling. He shook his head, but evidently could no longer form the words.

"And you—" Adrissu paused, remembering with a bitter, stifled laugh the simple words of praise that had finally made Ruan melt against him. "You did so well. You were so good."

"No," Ruan rasped, and Adrissu could see his eyes glistening with tears. "No, you can't. You can't be."

"Ruan—" Adrissu started, but Ruan's eyes flickered past him for the first time and widened in shock again.

In the beat of silence Adrissu could hear the slithering sound of Vesper sliding along the stone ground. He sighed and turned to watch her coming up to them: her attention fixed on Ruan. They had always gotten along; he had been fond of the snake from the first time they met.

"Please," Ruan whispered, his voice breaking. A single tear spilled from his eyes, but many more threatened to follow. "Please don't."

But Vesper continued right up to him, her beady black eyes glinting in the meager light. She paused near his foot, then lifted herself up just enough to bump her head against his hand. When they made contact—solid and real—Ruan began to sob.

"No!" he wailed, stumbling until his back hit the stone wall, and he crumpled to his feet. "Oh gods—this isn't—how? *How?*"

Adrissu carefully clasped his hands in front of him, looking down at his feet. He could not name the feeling that simmered right near the back of his throat—not shame, not regret, but something like it.

"You weren't supposed to find out this way," he said softly. "You weren't supposed to find out at all."

"This whole time," Ruan muttered, shaking his head as if he had not heard. "All this time, and it's—you've been in the city all along."

Adrissu gave a slight nod, pursing his lips. "Yes."

"Why?" Ruan hissed, finally looking up at him. For the first time, the fear had left his eyes—replaced with anger, with hate. Adrissu stifled a scowl. At least one of them had to stay calm, he told himself, and it certainly wasn't going to be Ruan. "Why stay in the city you destroyed?"

"Because I like it here," Adrissu snapped. "I did not leave because I knew I could help Polimnos become great. The city you live in now is not the one I destroyed. The city you live in now wouldn't be possible without me!"

"You've lied to me, to everyone," Ruan said, still glaring daggers up at him. "You tricked me. For years you've tricked me."

"Ruan," he started, but his voice died in his throat. He couldn't argue with that—after all, it was the truth. Instead, he said quietly, "All that I've done since then, I've done for the benefit of Polimnos. I can promise you that. If I had wanted to bring ruin to the city, I could have done so at any time, but I haven't."

Ruan scoffed, glancing away, but had no retort. For a long, tense moment, they were both silent. Adrissu added hoarsely,

"I know there is a belief that all dragons are inherently evil, that they see their power as a reason to be above morality. But this is untrue. You've seen all I've done for this city. I may not be warm, or kind, but I'm not evil either. I'm not."

"This is madness," Ruan finally muttered, looking down at Vesper who was still peering up at him curiously. "I can't believe you, Adrissu. Gods, that's not even really your name..." A heady flush rose in his face. "I can't believe I've spent a year pining after you, after a lie."

"Ruan," Adrissu repeated. Every instinct he had cried out to gather Ruan into his arms, to force him to listen, to somehow comfort him. But how could he comfort Ruan, when he was the very source of his conflict? "Ruan, I never had any intention of tricking you. I stayed away from you for so long because of *this*: because I didn't want to have to lie to you. Because what I feel for you is genuine. What happened yesterday was... A moment of weakness. I'm sorry I let it happen."

Somehow the admission only made Ruan look more anguished.

"I can't believe this," he said, shaking his head. "I can't—I can't talk to you any more. Bring me back to the city."

Adrissu's chest constricted with grief. Ruan was going to hate him no matter what he did. It was what he had wanted this whole time, and now that it was happening, he thought it might destroy him.

"You have to promise me, Ruan, that you won't speak of this to anyone," he said, and Ruan scowled openly at him.

"I should warn everyone in town about you," he snarled, staggering to his feet. "I should gather up the rest of the mercenary's guild and storm your tower to finally drive the Scourge of Polimnos away."

Adrissu's teeth flashed in a snarl; this time he did not try to hide the savagery of his face. "You will do no such thing," he growled. "Not if you want your friends to live."

Ruan answered with a scowl of his own, but this time he visibly hesitated.

"You just said you aren't evil," he muttered.

"I'm not," Adrissu said. "But I'm not a fool, either. You think I wouldn't act in self-defense?"

"Then what was this? Today?" Ruan exclaimed, pointing upward. "Just flying around to burn a different city to the ground?"

"No," Adrissu snapped, taking a step closer to him. "I was—flying. To clear my head. About everything that just happened."

"Because that was so distressing to you? You think it was really a *mistake?*" Ruan countered.

"And you don't?" Adrissu said. Ruan at least looked cowed at that, glancing away with a mix of anger and shame rising on his face.

"Will you please," he finally whispered, not looking at him. "Will you please just let me go?"

"Promise me you will not tell anyone what I've told you," Adrissu repeated. He hesitated, then added softly, "Please. If you ever cared about me at all, please."

"I won't tell anyone," Ruan muttered. "For the sake of... Gods, I don't even know anymore. But I won't tell anyone."

Adrissu's blood had gone to ice in his veins. For one wild moment he was tempted to refuse, to keep Ruan trapped down here all for himself. He *could*—there was no way out for a human without any magical ability. The opening into the cliffs led only to a sheer drop into the ocean, certain death. The tunnel upward was entirely impossible to ascend without flight. If he refused, Ruan would be helpless to his whim. But the rational part of his mind that had always protested against the unbearable emotional pull he'd always had toward the human knew that doing so would only solidify Ruan's hatred of him.

Ruan *hated* him now. The thought was like poison sticking in his throat.

"Alright," he said softly, looking down at his feet. "When you get back into town, if anyone asks, tell them the dragon dropped you in the ocean, and you swam to shore. It couldn't have been Zamnes, because it fled from you."

Vesper had curled nervously near Ruan's feet, watching them with obvious distress. Adrissu extended a hand toward her—Ruan eyed him suspiciously, but Vesper recognized the command and uncoiled herself to slither back to him. Ruan's gaze had softened, eyes lingering on Vesper; but when he looked back up at Adrissu, his eyes were hard and cold once again. Adrissu did his best to ignore the sinking feeling collapsing through his chest.

"Let's go," he said, and turned away.

Chapter Eight

After Adrissu had flown Ruan back up to his tower, he did not watch the human leave. He remained, tense and waiting, in his home until the morning stretched into the afternoon and into the night. He did not sleep until the sun rose again the next day.

Ruan had promised that he would not tell, but part of him doubted the human's words. He waited for the sounds of an angry mob, of warriors coming to fight him, or of any telltale sign that Ruan had lied to him. But it never came.

Adrissu did not know if Ruan had made it safely back to the caravan that he was supposed to be guarding, but the human did not return the next day, nor the next week, nor the next month. Time went by at a crawl as Adrissu waited, like a spring tightly coiled and never released, for a finishing blow that never came.

But as part of the council, he had work to keep him busy: meetings and petitions and long walks around the perimeter of the city to determine where and how the borders of Polimnos could continue to expand. All the rumors and gossip that he heard about the dragon sighting died away eventually—after all, it could not have been the Scourge of Polimnos if it had fled in fear from just two fighters. It must have been frightened away, for there were no other sightings.

It was what he had always hoped for—that Ruan would finally extricate himself from whatever tangled mess they had between them, and he could go back to the way his life had been before the human had crossed his path. It was what he had always hoped for, and he hated every moment of it. He hated himself for still pining after the human, missing his presence and remembering the heat of his touch. But he could not bring himself to hate Ruan.

There was something wrong with him. There was no other explanation for how intensely he yearned for the human. Adrissu was a dragon; he should have had no need of such a lesser creature. There was no reason he could not find some other person willing to sate his base desires. He *should* have been fine on his own. He *should* have never felt the fated connection with a human. He *should* have only felt the pull toward another dragon.

These things should have been true, but they were not. He could struggle and rage against them for years on end, but that would not change reality. He *did* yearn for Ruan, and now would never have him. He would have to learn to accept it.

This was the conclusion that he came to after they had been apart for nearly three months. Every time he saw Maya, he was tempted to ask her if Ruan had returned and he was looking for work again. He did not ask, but Maya offered the information to him eventually.

"Ruan tells me he's not working for you anymore," she said, almost idly, late one afternoon while reviewing a few proposed road expansions together.

Adrissu stilled, glancing over at her from the corner of his eye. "That's correct," he replied simply, waiting to judge her reaction.

"Are you still looking for a guard? I know quite a few recruits who'd be willing to take the job, even at a lower price point if that's what's getting you," she said, still looking down at the parchment spread out before her.

Adrissu hesitated, considering his reply.

"I found that while I... enjoyed the rapport Ruan and I developed, my need for a dedicated guard was perhaps overestimated," he finally said, still watching her from beneath his eyelashes. Like himself, her head did not move, but he did notice her eyes flicker toward him for a moment.

"I see," she said, and that was the end of it.

But he knew Ruan was back in Polimnos. He knew that he could not expect Ruan to want to see him, but a small part of him ached that the human hadn't even let him know of his safe return. Adrissu silenced that part of him as much as he could and shoved it down deep into his chest until he was numb to it. He had wanted this, he reminded himself, no matter how much it hurt. He had wanted this.

He repeated it like a mantra in his head, over and over, every time he thought of Ruan. This was what he wanted. This was what was best.

It had been nearly four months since he had last seen Ruan—when Adrissu finally started to believe it—when he finally saw him again.

The knock on his door, a bit after sunset on a temperate autumn evening, was so unexpected that it did not even occur to him that it could be Ruan as he rose with a frown to answer it. Adrissu thought it might be Benil Branwood coming to bother him again—it might be any one of his fellow councilors with some new and unexpected issue—it might be any citizen seeking his aide. It did not occur to him that it could be Ruan, so when he opened the door and saw his mate standing there, he froze.

The human's countenance was serious, almost grim, and he was silent as he watched Adrissu collect himself before clearing his throat.

"Hello," he said, and luckily his voice did not waver or tremble. "Can I help you?"

Ruan looked up at him, brown eyes searching. The man's expression didn't change, so Adrissu was unsure if he saw what he was looking for, but after a beat he replied,

"Can I come in?"

Adrissu had barely processed the request before he was stepping aside on instinct, holding the door open so Ruan could step in.

When they were alone in his tower, both were silent for a long moment, Ruan's eyes flickering around the room as Adrissu watched him cautiously.

"I wanted to..." Ruan started, only to trail off. He sighed and turned to face Adrissu again. "I've... I've missed you."

Adrissu blinked. "As have I," he answered, his voice finally betraying some of the bottled-up emotion that he'd kept so carefully pushed away.

"So I'm here to... apologize, I suppose," Ruan continued resolutely, looking down at his feet. "For how I acted toward you. I was frightened, and lashed out at you."

"Ruan," Adrissu murmured, shaking his head. "I couldn't hold that against you. There is no need to apologize."

Silently Ruan nodded, but his gaze was still on the ground. There was clearly more that he wanted to say, but he remained silent. Adrissu, much as he wanted to speak, bit his tongue and waited. After a moment, Ruan swallowed hard and glanced back up at him.

"I don't want to be apart from you," he said, eyebrows furrowing together. His face was open, vulnerable. For a fleeting instant Adrissu thought that even if this was some kind of cruel trick, a ruse to lure him into a false sense of security before the town turned on him, it would be worth it for the chance to meet his gaze and drink in the warmth of his eyes again. "I don't understand it. I should hate you, but I hate being apart from you more."

A bitter laugh stuck in Adrissu's throat. It was the same feeling that he had felt toward Ruan for so long; hearing it now directed toward him, it struck him how foolish it was, and how cruel it sounded to his ear. Why had he ever wanted to hate Ruan?

"I know the feeling," he replied softly, and the first hint of a smile cracked along the edges of Ruan's lips.

"I've been able to think this all over since... since then," he continued. "I was angry at first, of course, more angry than anything. But the more time passed, the more I realized I missed you. I hated myself for missing you, but it didn't make me feel it any less. And then I thought more on what you said... That you liked Polimnos, and didn't want to see it suffer. And I thought about how you could have done whatever you wanted all this time, and you—you chose to stay, to take a weaker form and stay here. I couldn't see why you would do such a thing unless you wanted to help the city and be a part of it. And why would you do such a thing only to destroy it? The more I thought about it, the more sense you made."

A tiny flicker of hope had started to rise in Adrissu's chest, a single glowing ember amidst a pile of cold ash. He could not bring himself to speak, so instead he only nodded and continued to watch Ruan with rapt attention.

"And then I thought—I have to make a decision about all this," Ruan said. He scrubbed a hand through his hair, pushing back the tumble of his reddish-brown waves. "But to make such a choice based on just a memory... And something I don't know if I even remember accurately. I was so angry and afraid, and so hurt." He paused, and Adrissu nodded, opening his mouth to start to speak, but Ruan continued abruptly, "So I want you to show me again."

For a beat they were both silent.

"Show you again?" Adrissu repeated slowly, and Ruan nodded.

"I want you to take me back down to your... lair," he said slowly, and Adrissu could tell he was forcing himself to continue meeting his eyes. "I want to look you in the eyes, the real you. And then I'll know. I'll know what I can live with, then."

The stubborn, prideful part of Adrissu wanted to seethe against the demand, to snap at Ruan that he would not be treated as a plaything. But the rest of him—the part that had grown soft and given up trying to resist the constant tugging on his heart with anything involving the human—was ready to do anything and everything Ruan might ask of him if it meant that there was even a chance of salvaging something between them.

He swallowed hard, feeling the two parts of himself struggle, and said hoarsely, "Then come with me."

Adrissu stepped toward the back room of the first floor, where the entrance to his lair was hidden. He did not look to see if Ruan followed—he could sense his presence, could locate him only from the sound of his cautious footsteps—as he pulled open the hatch in the floor.

"You'll need to trust me," he said softly, his gaze lingering on the dark drop before them. "It's designed for me to simply fall into. You'll have to fall with me, but I will hold you."

He felt more than heard Ruan's breath stutter, but when he finally turned back, the human looked as resolute as ever.

"Okay," he said, steadily meeting Adrissu's gaze.

Adrissu turned his back to the hatch door, and slowly enough that the other man could easily pull away, he reached out and grasped Ruan's wrists. He didn't pull away, but nodded; and Adrissu stepped backward, plunging down and pulling Ruan with him.

He knew the timing of when to release his illusion by heart, pulling Ruan closer to him as his hands grew into scaled claws. He could feel Ruan's heart beating faster and his breathing stutter, as they plunged through darkness; but then Adrissu unfurled his wings, slowing their descent with a jerk. Ruan's hands pressed to the soft scales of his chest, and Adrissu held him with one arm as he twisted in the air, so his feet struck the stone floor of his lair rather than his back.

The moment they were on the ground, Ruan shifted his weight and dropped from Adrissu's arms. He stepped back and peered up into his face: into the vivid blue eyes of Zamnes, Scourge of Polimnos. Whatever he saw there, Adrissu did not know, but he met the human's gaze as evenly as he could and waited for him to speak. If he said anything now, he was sure that he would ruin whatever was to come next.

"You are him," Ruan finally said softly, taking a slow step closer to him. "I cannot call you Zamnes. You're always Adrissu to me."

He tensed as Ruan lifted a careful hand up, reaching for him. He *was* Zamnes—but he was also Adrissu, wasn't he? The conflict lasted only a moment. In the end, he thought, Ruan could call him anything, and he would only be glad to hear his mate's voice.

Adrissu's eyes flickered away from Ruan's face to his outstretched hand; despite his stern face, his fingers trembled where they reached for the dragon.

"I am Adrissu," he answered, softly as he could, but his voice still rumbled through the open chamber. Slowly, he lowered his head, and with his trembling fingers, Ruan tenderly touched his face: first trailing his fingers from the center of his snout and upward between his eyes, then tracing his broad forehead and downward to his jaw, his chin. The human's fingers were cool and silky against his scales, and a soft noise of contentment escaped him. Through half-lidded eyes, he could see Ruan stifle a smile at the sound. "I have always been yours."

"I should be terrified of you," Ruan murmured, shaking his head, even as he lifted his other hand to cup Adrissu's head. "But I... I've only missed you. I don't think I'm frightened of you at all. My feelings not changing is what scares me more."

Adrissu nodded, but remained silent. His heart was thrumming against his ribs.

"Adrissu, I..." he started, then pulled Adrissu's head closer, so his forehead was pressed between his eyes, as if he could not bear to look at him as he spoke. "I've loved you for so long, and none of this has changed that. I must be insane to feel so, but I still—I still want you, even like this. I thought maybe seeing you this way again would be enough to push me away, but it's still *you*."

Adrissu breathed in deeply, nostrils flaring with the human's scent: copper and musk and something like woodsmoke. He could smell him so much more deeply like this, could smell the lingering tang of fear and the heady beginnings of arousal. But his focus was entirely on what Ruan had said to him—*I've loved you for so long.*

"First, Ruan, I must also apologize to you," he rumbled. "Regardless of why, I did lie to you. I deceived you for years. But I hope you can believe me when I say I didn't deceive anyone out of malicious intent."

Slowly Ruan nodded, his shoulders sagging slightly as tension drained from his muscles. "I know," he said.

"And I must also tell you this," Adrissu continued. He closed his eyes, hesitating; but Ruan still held his face in his hands, waiting silently.

"I loved you from the first time I saw you," Adrissu murmured, his voice a deep growl. "I saw you in the courtyard, and I knew I was yours."

Ruan pressed his face harder into Adrissu's.

"I know," he panted, and Adrissu realized that he was holding back tears. "Gods, *why?* Why am I still so drawn to you?"

Finally Adrissu pulled away, looking down at the human. Ruan's eyes were swimming with unshed tears, but still he firmly met the dragon's gaze. He thought, distantly, that Ruan was as accomplished a warrior as he was because he didn't look away when he was afraid.

"You can accept this, then?" Adrissu asked. "That this is who I am, truly? You would still trust me?"

"Yes," Ruan said, nodding.

"You're certain?"

"Yes."

"Then take your clothes off."

Ruan blinked, the surprise obvious on his face, but the air flooded with the scent of his desire. He hesitated for only a moment, then moved to start unbuttoning his shirt. Adrissu circled him eagerly, watching until the human was naked before him, and his clothes were in a messy pile on the ground. Even in the dim light, Adrissu could see that he had a new scar on his right side just under his ribs: the mark shiny and pinkish the way human skin healed. He would be careful of the fresh wound, he thought, but Ruan was nothing if not hearty and strong.

"You trust me?" he rumbled, and though his expression had become decidedly more nervous, Ruan still nodded. His cock, half-hard already, betrayed his interest.

In one quick movement, Adrissu lifted and pushed Ruan up against the wall so his body was level with the dragon's head, then began licking him all over. Ruan gasped, his body quivering under Adrissu's grasp, the rough glide of his tongue. He started closer to Ruan's face, dragging his tongue from his chest up the side of his neck, and tousling the hair on his head. Ruan groaned as he licked over each of his nipples, and stifled a laugh as he slid his tongue in the junction under his arm, where the tuft of hair there tasted most strongly of him.

"Adrissu," Ruan panted, hands grabbing uselessly at the wall. "You act like you're going to eat me."

A grin spread across his features, all his razor sharp teeth showing a pearly white in contrast to the midnight black of his scales. It might have looked wicked, even cruel; but Ruan looked at him with such a blissed-out expression that if he had doubted Ruan's trust in him before, he had no doubt of it now. Whatever misgivings he might still have, *this,* at least, Ruan wanted very badly.

Before the human could protest, his claws had tightened their grip around him, and he lifted the human again, this time bringing his entire lower half into his mouth. Ruan yelped, muscles tensing as Adrissu's jaws closed around him, but he held him gingerly in place—and once he had settled against his teeth, Adrissu rubbed his tongue where he could feel Ruan's cock pressing against the roof of his mouth.

"Oh, *gods,*" Ruan gasped. His hands tightened around Adrissu's front teeth, holding himself up, but not struggling to escape. Adrissu growled deep and low in his chest, and another moan burst from Ruan's mouth. His hips bucked against Adrissu: he could feel his fangs piercing flesh, the first hint of blood on his tongue. If Ruan felt it, he gave no indication of being in any pain.

With the human in his mouth, he could taste the fear emanating off of him, fear that became adrenaline that became overwhelming lust. He pressed his tongue harder against Ruan, dragging it along the surface of his skin agonizingly slow to keep him moaning and thrusting against him.

"Adrissu," he whimpered. Adrissu could not get a good look at his face, but his head was thrown back in wanton pleasure. "Adrissu—Adrissu!"

The last utterance of his name was punctuated with a wordless cry, and his body tensed hard against Adrissu's mouth. He could feel his teeth pressing harder into the flesh of Ruan's back as it arched. His release was a burst of salt on his tongue that he drank down and licked clean. Ruan gasped, his voice strangled, and a few smaller spurts of come spilled into Adrissu's mouth.

When he was sure Ruan was utterly spent, his once-tense muscles relaxing limply against his jaw, Adrissu lowered his neck and deposited the human on the ground. He was panting and laid there naked, half-covered in saliva and come and small rivulets of blood, eyes rolling in his head with pleasure.

Adrissu rarely had need of his cock when in dragon form, so it was a strangely unfamiliar sensation to realize that it had emerged from its sheath and dripped with anticipation. It was easily the length and girth of Ruan's thigh, thus it would be entirely impossible to fuck Ruan in this form; but the sound and taste of his orgasm had thrown him into a frenzy. His own precome leaked steadily from the slit hidden amongst soft, pliant scales near the tip; the scales there were black as the rest of his body, but the softer, fleshier part of his member that typically remained deeper within his body was more red in tone and had no scales.

"Gods, Adrissu," Ruan muttered, his eyes locking onto it, and for the first time his voice trembled slightly in fear. "That absolutely will *not* fit."

"It won't," Adrissu agreed, his voice deeper now with need, so that it rumbled through the stone of the chamber like a distant quake. "But this is enough." He lowered his hips slightly so his cock pressed against Ruan's body and slowly rocked against him, testing the pressure. Ruan grunted, but didn't pull away, even as his softening cock dragged against the length of Adrissu's hard member.

"This will work," Ruan agreed with a slight murmur. He encircled Adrissu's cock with his hands: he could grip around the head with both, but the thickness of the rest of his length pulled his hands apart. Adrissu breathed a sigh half of pleasure and half of relief; his mate felt so good against him, even like this, that he did not think he would have been able to stop himself if Ruan had changed his mind.

He rutted against the human, his own slickness and the saliva coating the lower half of the human's body giving the perfect balance of glide and friction on the underside of his cock— Ruan's hands applying pressure to the rest. Ruan remained perfectly still at first, but after a moment he became more exploratory with his hands. As Adrissu pulled back, Ruan felt along the soft scales that were near the tip, trying to part them as Adrissu thrust against him to finger along the hidden opening that was steadily leaking precome. His hands drifted lower as Adrissu pushed forward, gliding along the soft and unprotected parts of his cock—the sensitive flesh that so rarely left the safety of his body—then his fingers found the slit where his member emerged, dipping just inside, and Adrissu bit back a cry.

"It's good there?" Ruan murmured, pushing his fingers further inside. That was far more than Adrissu could bear. This part of him had never been touched, but it sent white-hot pleasure rocketing up the length of his spine, and instantly he was coming.

He felt more than heard Ruan yelp as he came: the first burst shooting past the human's head to splatter against the stone ground, while the rest shot out with less force to coat the human's body with his come. He thought Ruan would pull away, even with only one hand to wipe the sticky fluid from his face—but he didn't pull away, rubbing encouragingly at the tender flesh just inside his sheath at the very base of his cock, and Adrissu didn't stop coming.

He felt like an animal, rutting mindlessly, tongue lolling from his mouth, and unable to focus on anything but how fucking *good* Ruan's deft fingers felt against him, as he touched where no one had before. It was all he could do to keep thrusting against the human, until the unbearable pleasure eventually became pain, and even then his cock still twitched and leaked with each motion of Ruan's hands.

"Enough," he growled, unable to pull himself away. "Ruan—Ruan—enough—!"

"But I have you entirely at my mercy," Ruan protested, the wicked grin obvious even in his voice. His hands squeezed harder around the base of Adrissu's cock. Even with both hands, he could not envelop its girth; but with how sensitive he was there, Adrissu could only gasp and shudder at the continued sensation. Ruan worked him in short, rough movements until a second orgasm was pulsing through him. He had no seed left to spill, but still his cock twitched wildly; and Adrissu *roared*, turning his head and biting down on his own claw to stop the embers that began to spark in his mouth from becoming a full stream of flame. He was going to go mad if Ruan didn't kill him first.

When the pleasure wracking his body finally ebbed away, and his wits had returned to him, Ruan had finally released his grip. Adrissu's cock began to retract back into its sheath as it softened. Somehow, even though the human was naked beneath him and absolutely coated head-to-toe in dragon come, Ruan managed to look as smug as if this had been his very intention from the moment he'd stepped into Adrissu's tower.

Adrissu grumbled, more to himself than in any discernible message to Ruan, and curled himself protectively around the human, instinctively defending his vulnerable mate, more precious than his entire hoard combined. Ruan laughed, reaching up to stroke his face.

"Can we do this every time?" he asked. Adrissu scowled.

"No," he said. He would have said more, but Ruan had leaned up to press a soft, careful kiss to the side of Adrissu's face, just above the corner of his mouth. Ruan did not speak again, only shifted slightly to get more comfortable in Adrissu's embrace, and eventually the human's eyes slid closed. Adrissu watched him silently in the darkness of his lair for a little while, but soon his eyes closed, too, and they slept.

Chapter Nine

Why had he ever wanted to be apart from Ruan?

The thought plagued him incessantly in the days following; now that he had given into his embrace, their past interactions were bathed in an entirely different light. Where before he had unconsciously waited each day for Ruan to arrive at his post, now they could wake up in each other's arms; and when Ruan invited him to dinner again, he could readily, eagerly say yes. Keeping the human at arm's length had felt so wrong. Instead he could have had *this* for a year, maybe more, but had denied himself—for what? He almost couldn't remember.

But, of course, he had avoided the human for a reason and was eventually reminded of it none too gently, when a few weeks later, Ruan told him he'd be taking a job that would take him to the next town over for several weeks.

"I guess this farmer's had a bunch of livestock taken in the middle of the night," Ruan sighed, stretching his arms casually as he explained, completely unperturbed. In stark contrast, Adrissu's heart had been suddenly seized with all the fear that he'd forgotten, remembering Ruan's meager lifespan and soft, vulnerable body. "Must've gotten pretty bad for him to put up the job with us, but I guess we're the closest city that has fighters for hire."

"I see," Adrissu said evenly, hoping his worry wasn't obvious on his face. "And he doesn't know what's been stealing his livestock?"

"No, but the letter he sent says there have been some signs of violence—blood, drag marks, all that," Ruan replied, then grinned. "Don't think it could be a dragon, could it?"

Despite himself, Adrissu scoffed. "Certainly not. If any dragon came so near to my territory just to eat a few sheep, I'd be very concerned for its mental well-being."

Ruan laughed, and Adrissu smiled. Maybe it could be worth it, if most of their moments together were like this.

"How long do you think you'll be gone?" he asked.

"Hmm, probably about two weeks. Maybe less if I don't have to go scouting after something in the woods for days on end," Ruan answered.

"And you're sure you want to take this job?"

Ruan blinked, the slight grin on his face faltering. "Well, sure. It's not exactly one of the more glamorous jobs I've taken, but I like being able to travel." He paused, tilting his head. "You're worried about me?"

Adrissu tried to scoff again, but this time it came out sounding more like he was choking. His first instinct was to deny it, but, he told himself, he was done with pushing Ruan away.

"Yes," he said. "Every time you're gone I worry about you."

Ruan grinned again. "You know, I don't think you've ever seen me fight, but I can promise you I've risen through the ranks of my own accord, not just because you overpaid me for years. I can handle some rabid animals or some sort of monster. It's only gone after livestock, so I'm not concerned."

There was much Adrissu wanted to say—that it would only take one well-aimed strike, one festering wound, to cut his tiny life even shorter than it already was. Humans were adaptable and resilient in some ways, but in others they were shockingly vulnerable, their bodies soft and easily harmed. But even now, weeks after Ruan had finally come to him again, it felt like too personal an admission to make. So instead, Adrissu forced himself to smirk over at Ruan.

"I'll believe it when I see it," he said.

Ruan laughed. "I'd invite you along, but it might raise too many eyebrows."

Adrissu agreed, but the comment set him thinking for a long while afterward. He would not presume to follow Ruan where he went—he had no desire to risk his own position, despite his worry over the human—but maybe he could help protect him in other ways.

Ruan left the next day. After he had set out, Adrissu went into town, following the main road until he was at the forge of Yue Lang. An apprentice was working the forge as he approached: a human woman probably barely out of her teenage years with familiar dark hair and soft, full features, who looked like she might be related to Yue. The girl smiled nervously at Adrissu and waved as he approached.

"Is Councilor Lang available?" Adrissu asked, hands folded behind his back.

"Yes, he's inside," the girl answered, gesturing for the door. He nodded his thanks, ignoring how her eyes stared after him, as he brushed past the heat of the forge and into the shop. The inside wasn't much cooler. Yue Lang was setting up a weapons rack in the corner, straightening up and waving when he spotted Adrissu.

"Councilor Adrissu," he said, bowing his head in greeting as he approached. "To what do I owe the honor?"

"Hello, Yue," Adrissu said, lowering his head slightly before continuing. "I am here to make an inquiry about a... custom piece, I suppose."

"Not something for yourself? I don't mean to presume, but..." the man replied, a slight grin crossing his features. His black hair was pulled back in a low ponytail, but Yue pushed a few loose pieces that were draped around his face out of the way as he spoke.

"No, not for me," Adrissu agreed with a tight smile. "A gift for a... friend."

"I see," Yue replied, still smiling. His muscled arms rippled through his shirt, but the man was entirely too friendly for his own good—despite his size and obvious strength, he was not intimidating in the slightest. "Again, I don't mean to presume, but if it's the *friend* I'm thinking of, I just made him a custom breastplate maybe a year ago, so I don't think he'd be eager to replace it any time soon."

"I understand," Adrissu said with a nod. If it had been anyone but another councilor, and particularly Yue with his affable face, he might have snapped that he certainly *was* presuming and of course Adrissu knew about the damn armor. But he bit back the quip, and instead continued, "I was considering perhaps a shield that would be suitable for a protective enchantment I could place on it."

"Interesting!" Yue said, already looking around the shop. "I have a few things that would probably work if you wanted something you could take home today. But I'd be happy to do a custom piece if you'd prefer."

"Yes," Adrissu agreed, pulling his hands from the sleeves of his robe. "I am perhaps not as familiar with the weaponry my friend uses as I should be for this purpose, but his current shield looks something like this."

He held up one hand and conjured an illusion of the shield—smaller than it truly was, but the details were about the same. Ruan's shield was rather plain, a simple but sturdy buckler without adornment.

"Easy enough," Yue said.

"I think he'd like to stick with the same sort of shield," Adrissu continued, sending the illusion dissipating with a flick of his wrist. "But if you could make it out of the best material you have available, and perhaps some sort of engraved design..."

"I could do just about any design. Did you have something particular in mind?"

"I did," Adrissu said, as he conjured a second illusion of what he imagined. Yue blinked, staring at it, then laughed.

"Fearsome!" he said with a nod. "I can definitely do something like that. Let me sketch down that design, then I'll show you the options for metals and inlays, and we can discuss the price."

Ruan returned in just under three weeks—a bit longer than he'd anticipated, but he returned whole and healthy, as he always had. He arrived at Adrissu's doorstep early one morning, not even bothering to knock. Vesper nearly bit him, rushing up to the door in surprise; but she happily crawled up his leg when she realized it was him. Her own fright had startled Adrissu from where he'd been sitting in his study, and he peered down from the second floor of the tower as Ruan laughed, petting the top of Vesper's head as he closed the heavy wooden door behind him.

"I'm home," he said fondly, glancing up to grin at Adrissu.

"You didn't knock," Adrissu said primly, but quickly descended the stairs to greet him. Ruan seemed hesitant at first, unsure whether to embrace Adrissu or kiss him; but Adrissu grabbed his face in his hands and decided for the both of them, kissing the human deeply and relishing in the curl of his lips as Ruan smiled against him.

"Missed me?" he asked breathlessly when Adrissu finally released him.

"Yes," he replied, letting his fingers trail along Ruan's face. The human must have shaved before coming; his face was smooth and clean, with no hint of stubble. "I have a gift for you."

"A gift?" Ruan asked, voice lilting in surprise. "Well, let's see it, then!"

"Come with me," Adrissu said, pulling him toward the stairs, and Ruan's grin became absolutely lecherous.

"Oh, it's that sort of gift?" he asked, eyebrows waggling, and Adrissu scoffed.

"No," he said. "Just come with me."

Ruan laughed, but did not protest as he followed Adrissu up the stairs to the second floor. Adrissu had received the completed shield only two days prior, so it worked out well that Ruan had been slightly delayed. The shield was wrapped in cloth and set carefully on one of the extra small tables in Adrissu's study. He picked it up, still wrapped, to present to Ruan.

"Adrissu," Ruan said softly, his voice dropping to a hushed whisper the moment he'd started to unveil the shield. "This is..."

Gingerly, Adrissu placed a hand on Ruan's shoulder, watching him peer down at the shield in his hands.

"I know you just had armor made, but I wanted to give you something that would help protect you," he murmured, feeling Ruan shiver at the low voice in his ear. "I spent a day enchanting it, so it deflects projectiles better. It has some force behind it, so anyone striking you in melee distance will be thrown off balance as well."

Ruan held the shield in one hand, and with the other slowly traced the symbol inlaid in the metal: the head of a dragon, horns curling upward. The visage of Zamnes, recognizable only to them. For a moment he was silent, then he glanced up at Adrissu with a watery smile.

"You don't think the dragon's too on the nose?" he asked, stifling a laugh. Despite himself, Adrissu smiled.

"So that it will strike fear in the hearts of your enemies," he said, squeezing his shoulder. "And maybe remind you of who has yours."

"Adrissu," Ruan sighed, still smiling up at him. "I think this is the most romantic thing you've ever done for me."

Adrissu rolled his eyes, but still smiled. "You'd best keep the memory close, then."

Later, when Ruan was sated and asleep in Adrissu's bed, the dragon watched him quietly, ruminating. For all that he would do to protect the human, someday he would die, and Adrissu would be left without him for what could very well be an eternity. *That* was why he had kept Ruan at arm's length for so long. But what more could he do?

There must be something. Even dragons could die, rare as it was—there were rumors of fated pairs staying together even beyond death, but how? He had not found anything in his own books and records, but perhaps there was more beyond his scope of knowledge. There were no dragons nearby, but his mother's lair was not terribly far. Would she know? He had not spoken to her in thirty years, since he had first leveled Polimnos. Maybe she would know of a fated pair that he could ask; but figuring out how to ask, without revealing his own rather embarrassing position, would prove to be tricky. If he let her suspect that he had found himself part of a fated pair, she would surely ask after his mate; and the knowledge that his mate was not a dragon, but a human, seemed like the kind of information he wanted to keep close, even from his mother. He had no draconic enemies that he knew of, but if he ever did... A human mate would be an easy target.

There must have been a piece of the puzzle that he was missing. He would not leave Ruan to find out, but the next time the human was gone, Adrissu resolved, he would seek it out.

—•⟡•⟢•—

Ruan remained in town for several weeks after that, joining Adrissu at Saltspire Tower most days. They had not exactly spoken about it, but Ruan rarely sat outside the tower and took up his post there anymore. At first, Adrissu was unsure if he should still offer him the gold piece at the end of the day. When he did, Ruan pushed his hand away.

"No need anymore," he said, laughing nervously. "I'd hardly call what I did today *work*."

The next time he took a job, as a guard to a caravan of stone down to Vlissingstadt, Adrissu was equal parts sad and relieved. Ruan would be gone a full month, two weeks there and two weeks back, so he would have plenty of time to make the trip out to his mother's island in the ocean. The day Ruan left,

Adrissu quietly set out from his lair at nightfall, flying silently over the dark waters that disguised his black scales.

He flew until the sun began to rise. It would be several more hours until he reached the island, so he found a large rock protruding from the water and settled upon it to rest. The sun warmed his scales, and he stretched his wings to bask. He could not remember the last time that he'd been in this form in the sun.

When he woke, alert and refreshed, he dunked himself under the cold ocean water to cool his overwarmed scales before setting off again. Then he flew idly, hunting fish and waterfowl as he went, until the island that was his mother's lair came into view, and he had the sense of another dragon nearby—knowing that his mother, like all dragonkind, was feeling the same awareness.

Sure enough, Ilrenth was waiting for him, standing sentinel near the peak of the rocky island for whomever her visitor might be. Alert and proud, she watched him without aggression, following his movement with her glowing blue eyes as he swooped down and perched on the rocky shores.

"Zamnes, my son," she rumbled as he approached, head low. "You are an unexpected visitor."

"Hello, mother," he said, keeping himself low to the ground. Though she *was* his mother, as a fellow adult dragon who had proven his independence from her, she no longer had any familial responsibility toward him. If at any point she thought him disrespectful, or lacking deference to her in her lair, she would be entirely justified to attack him, either to drive him away or kill him outright.

Draconic custom valued a dragon's supremacy in their own lair over anything else. It was barbaric, Adrissu often thought, but it was how dragons were.

"What do you need from me?" she said, lifting her head so she towered over him.

"I am only wondering," he said slowly, glancing between her and the ground, "If you know anything of the magic behind fated mates."

For a moment, she was silent. When he looked back up at her, the expression on her face was as inscrutable as ever; but he was sure she was considering the possibilities behind the question—some obvious, some perhaps less so.

"I know some," she finally said. "Perhaps not more than you. What are you asking?"

"I am... curious about the magic that binds them," he answered. "I am researching such bonds between souls. My curiosity lies in what might happen to one if the other were to perish."

She balked slightly at that. "Have you made an enemy of such a pair?"

"Nothing like that. I ask only to sate my own curiosity. Although, if you know of such a pair, perhaps I could seek an audience with them."

Her eyes narrowed, unsure whether or not she believed him.

"I do know of such a pair," she said. "But the ones I know of are far in the northeast, in the lands inhabited by dwarves. They will be difficult to reach from here, and may not welcome your presence."

"Are you on friendly terms with them?"

"I would not say that, no. I only know of them. They were friendly with my mother. So they would tolerate me, but their goodwill toward you would not be guaranteed."

"I see," Adrissu murmured. "Do you know anything about such magic?"

"Little," she replied, and was silent for a moment, considering. "They performed some soul-binding ritual when I was a hatchling that my mother witnessed."

Adrissu looked up quickly, his heart starting to race. A soul-binding ritual sounded like the very thing he'd been considering. "Would she remember such a ritual, then?"

"Perhaps. She had less affinity for magic than you, Zamnes," Ilrenth mused, finally turning away to pace in a wide circle. "My mother Amaranthe's recommendation might help them tolerate your presence, if you are so desperate to speak to them yourself, though."

He paused, not wanting to sound too eager. "Yes, I think that would work well. I am very... curious."

"I can see this."

"Thank you, mother," he said, scuffling toward her, while still pressed low to the ground. "I am indebted to you. If there is ever anything I can do to help you, of course, you need only ask."

"Hmm," she murmured, looking down at him with one eye. A slight grin split her features, full of fangs. "I will remember this the next time I need a favor."

Adrissu forced his expression to remain neutral and subservient. He hated the thought of being indebted to anyone, even his own mother; but already he felt as if he had learned enough to make it worth it. She, at least, was unlikely to call in a favor that would be detrimental to him in some way... Hopefully.

"You know where to find her lair?" Ilrenth continued abruptly, and he nodded.

"Yes, I will find her," he said. The last thing he wanted was to have to ask his mother for more help.

"She is closer to your home than mine," she said, turning away. "Show her the same deference as you have to me and you should be fine. Although I'd suggest perhaps not arriving in your true form... Just in case."

"I understand."

"Is there anything else?"

"No, mother."

"Then go."

Adrissu slunk away, not turning his back to her. She watched him for a moment, then slowly lowered her head and turned; only then did he also turn his back, and after a few more steps began to flap his wings, taking to the air before the rocky beach beneath him gave way to the ocean again.

Ruan was still gone when he returned to Polimnos, so Adrissu rested for a day before heading out once more. His elder mother Amaranthe was a silver-scaled dragon whose lair was not terribly far from his own; she had taken up residence in the central area of Autreth long before the dwarves lost control of it, driving dwarven workers from a deep mine and setting up residence there. He did not know exactly where it was, but no part of the world forgot a dragon. Zamnes was still spoken of in Polimnos, so he was confident that once he arrived in Gennemont, the largest city-state of Autreth, he would be able to narrow down her location without issue.

This time he flew only under the cover of night, high enough that any travelers who might be out under the stars were unlikely to spot him, touching down in a shaded copse before the sun rose. When he illusioned himself into a human-sized form, he took instead the appearance of a plain-looking human man, as generic as he could imagine. While Gennemont was sure to have more than a handful of elves, he knew that humans were still the vast majority anywhere in Autreth, and the less he stood out the better.

Adrissu walked the rest of the way into Gennemont, following a wide stone path that steadily filled with more travelers the closer he got to the city-state. Once through the city gates, it only took an hour or two of asking around the taverns to hear a handful stories about the local dragon that seemed to agree on a few key details. The abandoned mine that had been claimed by the dragon, nearly four centuries ago now, was in a stretch of foothills nearly a week to the northwest on foot. By flight, Adrissu guessed he could get there in another day. He rented a room, slept the rest of the day, and left again after the sun had set.

Finding the foothills where the mine had been was not difficult—locating the entrance to the dragon's lair from above, at night, proved tricky. He ended up landing about a mile away, and by sunrise he made his approach on foot in the same human guise. After a few false starts down collapsed mine shafts,

Adrissu eventually found a shaft with a rough-hewn sheer drop—the telltale sign of a dragon's den.

He stood at the edge, listening, but only the distant sound of wind, echoing from the way he'd come, was audible.

"Hello," he called out over the edge of the drop. "I am Zamnes, son of Ilrenth, your daughter. I seek an audience with you. Are you here, Amaranthe?"

For a long moment he listened, straining for any sign of a response. When the first hints of doubt started to creep in—making him wonder if Amaranthe truly was here, or if she had somehow been slain without his mother's knowledge—a rumbling sound echoed up from within, barely discernible as a word.

"Enter."

Adrissu hesitated, peering down into the darkness. He had never met his elder mother, and though she had allowed him entrance, there was still no telling how she might treat him. If his presence was an unwelcome enough intrusion, she might lure him down to kill him.

But he was being paranoid, he told himself. He had never met the dragon. If he truly bothered her so much, she would more than likely send him away without violence; and as long as he did not resist, he imagined things would be fine. Right?

His human disguise fell away, and he stretched into his true form, filling the mineshaft almost entirely before dropping down the wide opening. He spread his wings just enough to slow his descent and examine his dim surroundings—as he fell, he could sense the presence of another dragon rapidly drawing nearer. Beneath him, light began to glow, and with a few strong flaps of his wings, he touched down at the bottom of the drop almost silently.

Standing over him on her hind legs was Amaranthe, her silver scales gleaming in the light of many torches and braziers set up throughout the wide chamber in which he now found himself. The moment he landed, he crouched low to the ground on all fours, looking up at her with only his eyes.

"Venerated elder mother," he said, pressing himself as low as his body would go, until his whole underside was flush to the cold stone floor. Humiliating as it was, it was his best choice if he wanted to ensure that he left here alive. Even as he spoke, he seethed with how much he hated draconic custom and all its ridiculous posturing. "This humble one thanks you for welcoming him into your home. I promise I won't bother you long."

The silver dragon looked him over, still towering over him. Her eyes were not blue like his mother's, but a pale gray that was somewhere between white and the silvery sheen of her scales.

"I suppose you are Ilrenth's son after all," she finally sighed, dropping down to stand on all fours and looking away from him. "I heard she had mated with a black-scaled male. A shame you turned out like him. Her blue would have been fine, but another silver would have been better."

Adrissu bit his tongue, bristling at the rude remark. Yet another vestige of draconic custom that entirely crumbled beneath the knowledge and wisdom other dragons so loved to claim—he had no choice in the color his scales grew, yet somehow they were less valuable than her own silver hue. This, he reminded himself bitterly, was why he had eschewed the presence of other dragons for so long.

"I have come to ask you only a small favor, elder mother," he continued, ignoring the obvious goad. If she believed him to be a simpering fool, then all the better. "I do not know how much my mother Ilrenth has told you of me, but I am a practitioner and researcher of the arcane. I went to her asking for information on a particular ritual, and she mentioned you had witnessed this ritual take place."

"What ritual?" Amaranthe asked, still looking away from him.

"A ritual to bond the souls of a fated pair," he said, refusing to look away, even as she glanced back at him sharply.

"You have a fated mate?" she asked.

"No, I only ask out of curiosity," he answered quickly. "My expertise is in the nature of magic, and I have wondered why a soul bonding ritual might be necessary if two dragons are already bound by fate."

"I witnessed this ritual, yes," Amaranthe said, looking away from him again and sounding much more disinterested. "It was devised when humans finally started developing the means to slay our kind. If one of a fated pair was to die, the other suffers for the remainder of its own life. With this ritual, the souls are bound together, so the slain dragon will be reborn into the next dragon hatched in the world, and the fated pair would be reunited after a time. I thought that would be obvious, especially to one who claims expertise of the arcane."

That was *it*, Adrissu thought, exactly what he was looking for —and he was so consumed with relief that he could easily ignore her pointed jab.

"I hoped you might remember the specifics of this ritual," Adrissu said, pressing himself further into the stone, though it did not yield any more. When she hesitated for a beat, he added, "Or if you do not remember, if you might give me your recommendation to seek out the fated pair who performed it."

"*Tch*," she scoffed, rounding on him. "I remember it. Do not insult me."

"Forgive this humble one, elder mother," Adrissu rumbled, not daring to move, though internally he rolled his eyes. Predictable. "I meant no insult. Only that I am very eager to learn more about this ritual."

"Clearly," she muttered, before taking a few steps away. "Do not move. I will return shortly."

He nodded as she moved beyond his line of sight and into darkness. In the quiet he could hear her steps echoing; it seemed as though there were many adjoining tunnels in her lair, making it a labyrinthine puzzle to any unwelcome visitors. He had no doubt her hoard was scattered between these tunnels; so close to the prying eyes and greedy hands of humans, it only made sense to make her belongings as difficult for non-dragons to access as possible. So he waited patiently, even though it felt like he remained motionless on the ground for the better part of an hour, and he longed to stretch his wings. Though his own lair was also far underground, this place had a damp smell that he did not like, and he was grateful for the ocean breeze that always filled his home.

Finally he could sense her presence again, and a moment later Amaranthe returned, holding a scroll in one claw. His heart leapt at the sight of it—could he be so lucky that she had recorded the ritual? Even as he had the thought, his excitement was tempered with distrust. If she did have it, he was sure she would not give it to him out of the generosity of her heart. It was only a question of what she wanted in exchange.

"The rumor, young Zamnes, is that you brought down an entire dwarven city when you broke off from your parents and made your own lair," she said, eyeing him as she approached.

"This is true," he said slowly. "But the city was small, and most of the dwarves had already evacuated. I only got to it before the elves did."

"But I am sure their wealth left behind was not a small amount, no?"

There it was. "No, it was not a small amount," he said slowly.

"Then I will offer you this," she said, grasping the scroll in an outstretched claw. "Not only did I witness this soul binding ritual between the only two dragons I might consider my *friends*, I helped them find ingredients to perform it. This is the list of necessary components and the runes of the ritual—I trust you can read runes, at least. You may have it, in exchange for something of such value."

"You have my gratitude, elder mother," he said, eyes locked on the scroll within her claws. He would not yet take it. "I only regret that I do not know you as personally as I know my mother Ilrenth, and this humble one wonders what items you might deem of similar value."

She snorted, embers flickering from her nostrils. "Clearly I have more precious metal and gems than I could ever use. I do not want something like that. No, I understand you are the sort of drake that hoards knowledge above all else. I want some tome, some arcane text, that would give me power or protection of some sort. I am not picky, but I trust you will choose something to... *impress* your venerated elder mother."

Already he was filing through his mental list of tomes and texts. He could think of a few that might be appropriate, strong or flashy enough that she would accept it without suffering a great loss himself. He had little idea of what her magical ability was like.

"Yes, that can be arranged," he said, eyes tracking the scroll as she passed it between her claws and moved to stand over him again. "I will return with it within the week."

She eyed him for a moment, and he had the irritating thought that she was going to make him bring it first before giving him the scroll—but then with a rather disapproving sniff, she held the scroll out to him. Slowly he straightened enough to take it, shrinking back down to the ground once it was safely in his claws.

"Within the week," she said, flashing a smile that showed all her teeth. "If I don't receive it from you, Zamnes, both Ilrenth and I will be very upset, I'm sure."

"You needn't worry," Adrissu said. "I give you my word. I'll return."

"Good," she said, and turned. "I'll be expecting you."

"Goodbye for now," he growled, before turning to go. His pulse raced with anticipation as he flapped his wings, ascending until he reached the opening of the mine once again. The very thing that he'd been hoping for was within his claws.

Chapter Ten

His luck was incredible, Adrissu decided after reading the scroll that Amaranthe had given him. He had looked through it briefly before flying back to Saltspire Tower—luckily it had been a cloudy day, so he could fly during the day by staying hidden amongst clouds—but didn't fully read through it until he'd arrived back at home. But when he settled at his desk, Vesper happily curled in his lap, it seemed... *simple*. A few alchemical ungents that were uncommon, but not especially rare, some that he already owned. The runes were specific, but those would be easy enough to copy down from the scroll itself. And finally, the blood of both partners—which made sense, considering the nature of the ritual. Briefly, he thought that he must be missing something: some crucial step that made the magic work. Could it really be so simple?

But the more he read over the scroll, the more he was convinced that was *it*. The answer to all his worries was fully contained in this parchment: this spell he could cast with absolute certainty, so long as Ruan was willing.

That would be the sticking point, he realized as soon as he had the thought. It made perfect sense to him for their souls to be linked; but for all his affection for Ruan, he would not be surprised if the stubborn human was entirely resistant to the idea, at least at first. Humans always surprised him with how opinionated they were over things that seemed like simple matters. And it would require broaching the topic of fated mates first... Something about that eventual conversation made him nervous, too.

That would be a problem for the future, though. For now, he had the ritual that would eventually bind their souls together, and he was glad for it.

For Amaranthe, he decided on a tome describing the nature of enchantment, which included a spell that would manipulate a subject's opinion of someone, or something, for well over an hour. It was a relatively strong enchantment that could be used for a variety of purposes, while remaining innocuous enough that Adrissu didn't think that his elder mother could somehow use it against him to some particularly unwelcome advantage. Flying back and forth between Polimnos and Gennemont again was tiresome; by the time he'd returned home to Saltspire Tower once again, he thought that he'd had his fill of flying for the next several months at least.

He only had a few days until Ruan was set to return. He was tempted to leave and try to find the ingredients and components that he didn't already have on-hand; but to retrieve some he knew would be a journey all its own, and the last thing he wanted was to be gone when Ruan returned. For now, there was no rush, so he resolved to wait until another job took Ruan away for an extended length of time. Now that he allowed himself to *feel* what he actually felt toward Ruan, he could admit, at least to himself, that he missed the human.

When Ruan did arrive, pushing open the door of the tower without knocking, it was like he brought the sun with him.

"Hello, darling!" he shouted as he stepped inside. Adrissu could not stifle a laugh as he stepped to the landing to watch Vesper rush up to him, excitement emanating from her. "Oh, yes, you're exactly who I was talking to. Hello, girl." Only when the snake was happily wrapped around his shoulders did he look up, tired but grinning at Adrissu, who watched him from the stairs. "Hello to you, too."

"Welcome back," Adrissu said primly, though he did not try to hide the amusement on his face, nor his relief at seeing Ruan returned whole and healthy. Ruan watched him with a warm smile as he descended the stairs. "I take it the job went well?"

"Boring, so yes, it went well," Ruan laughed, reaching for him. "I missed you."

Adrissu's heart swelled as they embraced. He would deal with dragons and all their ridiculous expectations every day if it meant keeping Ruan close to him.

"As have I," he murmured, feeling Ruan's hair tickling his chin.

"You're in a good mood," Ruan said. He grinned up at Adrissu. "You're really happy to see me, aren't you?"

"Of course," he replied primly, stepping away. His smile faltered as he thought of everything he had to tell Ruan. "I had a... productive few weeks, to be sure."

"Is that so?" Ruan replied, already sounding distracted, as Vesper bumped her head against his cheek.

"Yes. I'd hoped to... to talk with you about a few things, but it can wait," Adrissu continued. Ruan glanced up at him suspiciously.

"What does that mean?" he asked.

"Just that I wanted to talk to you when I'll have your full attention. No distractions," Adrissu said. For a moment they only stared at each other, then Ruan smirked.

"No distractions, huh?" he said, heat filling his gaze as he stepped toward Adrissu.

"No distractions," he murmured, allowing Ruan to begin disrobing him.

When they were sated, they lay together quietly for a long moment, sunlight streaming through the window across their bare bodies. Adrissu watched him, eyes trailing along the beams of sunlight that illuminated stripes of his bronze skin, lingering where the locks of his auburn hair still plastered to his skin with sweat. Everything about him was drenched in sunlight.

Noticing his attention, Ruan grinned a sleepy smile and propped himself up on his elbows to look down on Adrissu.

"What did you want to talk about?" he asked. Adrissu managed only a tight smile in return.

"I think I'd like some wine first," he sighed. As he began to get dressed, he could feel Ruan's eyes linger on him with curiosity; but after a moment, the human moved to get out of bed as well.

Finally, when he had his wine in hand, and they were standing across from each other in Adrissu's modest kitchen, he swirled the glass nervously and forced himself to speak.

"I have recently made some... discoveries that I would like to share with you," Adrissu said. Ruan's eyebrows raised over his own wine glass, but he gestured for the dragon to continue.

"When we are together," Adrissu started, only to trail off, his face burning red. Why was it so difficult to say aloud? "When I... look at you, it's as if—as if the very air around you bends inward and pulls me toward you. Like I couldn't pull away from you, even if I wanted to."

Ruan blinked dumbly at him, then pressed a hand over the grin spreading across his face.

"I didn't realize you had such a flair for the dramatic," he chuckled. Adrissu stifled his own grin, trying to retain his serious expression.

"But you feel it too, right?" he pressed, leaning closer to Ruan. "How drawn we are to each other?"

"I mean—of course I do," Ruan said, still laughing.

"I felt it the first time I saw you," Adrissu sighed, leaning back. "Even then, I suspected, but... Well. Ruan, there is something I thought was just a myth amongst dragons: that some souls are inexorably linked together by forces beyond even our understanding. We call them fated mates, or a fated pair. I did not think it could happen with a non-dragon—I did not think it could happen at all. But now I think that is what we are. Fated."

For a long moment Ruan was silent, his grin slowly dropping down into a more thoughtful expression, as he processed Adrissu's words.

"Fated," he repeated—not quite a question, but testing the word out. "So... We're linked by magic? Is that what you mean?"

"Well, in a way," Adrissu stammered. Words suddenly failed him. How could he explain it when he barely understood it himself? "Yes, it's magic that links us, but—it wasn't something I cast. It just... is."

Ruan frowned, and Adrissu's heart leapt into his throat.

"Hmm," the human finally murmured, glancing away. "So I didn't even have a choice? I was always going to love you?"

He was all but helpless to answer. "I don't know. If not, then I didn't have a choice either."

He watched Ruan scratch his chin, still ruminating.

"I... have mixed feelings about that," Ruan finally confessed with a sigh. "I don't really understand, but I guess you don't either. But I trust you that it's not something you did *to* me, so... I don't know. I just want to be with you."

"If it's any consolation, Ruan, you can magically force beings to *do* things, but to manipulate their inner emotions is much more difficult. It's nearly impossible to do for an extended length of time," Adrissu said quickly, looking down at his glass of wine. Something about the conversation felt precarious. "I am an accomplished mage, but even I have my limits. I'm not capable of that level of magic."

To his surprise, Ruan laughed. "Well, now I know that must be true. I don't think I've ever heard you speak so poorly of yourself."

His laugh broke the tension that was building in Adrissu's shoulders, and he managed a resigned smile over at the human. "Unfortunately, I cannot be an expert in everything."

They were silent for a moment, and Adrissu took a deep gulp of his glass of wine. That had gone well—better than he expected, even. Maybe it would be best to save bringing up the ritual for later. Maybe it would be too much all at once—

"Was there something else?" Ruan asked, still eyeing him. Adrissu took one last drink of wine, before setting down his glass.

"It was related, yes," he sighed, folding his hands on the table in front of him. "I learned, very recently, that there is a... ritual that some fated pairs will undergo. It is to ensure that in the event one mate dies, their souls remain linked. The soul will be reborn nearby, so the two can find each other again."

"Aren't dragons immortal?"

"Immortal, yes, but not unkillable," Adrissu continued. "It was developed around the time mortals first started becoming strong enough to threaten a dragon's life. I have... come into possession of the details of this ritual."

Ruan's expression had gone stony, and Adrissu knew that Ruan already knew what he was going to ask.

"Ruan," he said softly, reaching for the other man's wrist. "You already know how much I... dread the thought of being without you. I know the idea of death seems far away to you, but for me—it's *soon*, Ruan, we will have so little time together, even if you live to the very limits of a human lifespan."

"So reincarnation is the answer, then?" Ruan retorted. He did not pull away, but his brows were furrowed together, and he stared down at the table with his fingers pressed tightly around his own glass still half-full.

"To be without one's fated mate is despair. It is *agony*, Ruan," Adrissu protested. "Even imagining it frightens me."

"I don't know, Adrissu," Ruan sighed, shaking his head. "That is... Extreme. I don't know."

Even though Adrissu was not surprised at such a reaction, it still made his heart sink to the very bottom of his stomach. But just as he'd said, forcing emotions in others was a nearly impossible task—and trying to push Ruan now would only make him more resistant. So even though he wanted to insist, to demand, to do *anything* to keep Ruan with him forever, he instead released his grip on Ruan's wrist and raised his hand in a placating gesture.

"There is no need to come to a decision now," he said. His voice was rough, a betrayal to his cool and distant expression. "I only wanted to make you aware of these things. I have no desire to... keep things from you ever again, Ruan."

There was no reply for a long moment. When he chanced a nervous look back over at Ruan, the human was watching him with an expression as carefully blank as his own. But when their eyes met, a tiny smile slowly played across Ruan's mouth, and he shook his head with a sigh.

"Maybe it is magic drawing me to you," he laughed. "Because I feel like I should be irritated with you, but all I can think about is how much I want to kiss you."

There was a strange relief that settled over Adrissu at the words. He couldn't hold it against Ruan if he felt uncertain in the moment—after all, it had taken him years to grapple with his own feelings about the whole situation. But the knowledge that Ruan did not rage or run from the magic that had brought them together soothed Adrissu in a way that he hadn't realized he'd needed.

"Why hold back, then?" he murmured, a smirk crossing his features. Ruan's laugh rang between them as he acquiesced, closing the space between them to press their lips together.

Adrissu did not broach the topic of the soul-binding ritual again for well over a year, and Ruan did not ask about it. Occasionally, he would inquire about the nature of being a fated pair—often with frustration because most of his questions Adrissu simply could not answer. But quietly, whenever Ruan was gone for longer than a week or two, Adrissu would leave town as well to find the ingredients for the ritual, those which he did not already have.

The first was a flower that grew far to the north, in the foothills of a mountain range that eventually became part of the orc wildlands. The area was remote and still disputed between the orcs and nearby elves; but the conflict meant that there were no permanent settlements there, so he flew without fear of being spotted. He came upon one orc raiding party, but there were no survivors to spread tales of having sighted him.

Adrissu knew that he would need to be careful not to be seen, as even the most remote places would occasionally have visitors. When he spotted the foothills, he dropped from the sky and took his usual elven form to search on foot. It meant not searching as quickly, but at least if he *were* seen, he'd only be some strange elf foolish enough to travel alone.

He meticulously scoured the foothills over the course of a few days, finally finding a cluster of the flowers blooming in a copse. The starburst gentian grew low to the ground and was surrounded by narrow, dark green leaves; the flowers themselves were a bright buttery yellow, which bunched together as groups of tiny blooms that burst from the same stem. The small flowers grew in the shape of a five-pointed star. Adrissu cut far more than he needed, carefully near the root, then tied the bunch of stems together with twine. Once dried, he could safely store them for a long while—hopefully long enough to convince Ruan to partake in the ritual.

Then, he needed wood from an Aefrayan willow. That would be harder—elves built their religious temples in such willow trees and regarded them as sacred. While he could certainly descend upon an unsuspecting elven village and rip up enough of their temple tree to suffice before they could mount enough of a defense to truly threaten him, such an endeavor would not go unnoticed. He would likely be tracked, or someone might recognize him as Zamnes… No, it would be better to try and get ahold of the wood undetected. That would take longer, but would be safer in the long run.

Getting into Aefraya would be easy enough—flying under the cover of night, high in the clouds, would ensure that he would not be seen—but locating a tree that he could plunder without scrutiny proved to be more difficult. He lingered in the capitol city that surrounded Castle Aefraya for a while, poring over various maps—the local cartographer was enamored with all the business, he was sure.

Nothing seemed ideal, but after a few days of study, he decided that the aptly-named village of Solitude would be his best option. It was a small logging town right along the border of its namesake, the Forest of Solitude, that had once been prosperous. But when orc forces encroached from the west, it had largely been abandoned. A nearby military post was all that remained, along with a village about a mile away, which housed the family members of the outpost's soldiers. Though the village had dwindled, it once had a flourishing temple, so the tree there still stood and was tended to by the village residents.

The temple was large enough that the elves might expect travelers to visit the holy sight, but remote enough that no one of consequence would mark his coming and going. The nearby military outpost could prove to be a problem, but if he was sneaky, he might be able to get in and out without being detected.

With that settled, he headed for Solitude the next night. Flying there was easy: he arrived in the middle of the night, landing silently amongst the trees about a mile from the sleeping village. He was sure there would be at least one guard, but the village was small enough that there were no city gates to slip through. Magically silencing his footsteps, he walked through the woods in his elven form, until it gave way to a dirt path that led to the small village—the tall willow at its center.

Just as he suspected, a single elven soldier stood guard before it, though he looked bored and sleepy. Clinging to the shadows, Adrissu crept close enough to seize the elf with his magic.

"Sleep," he whispered, letting the magic echo from his word and settle around the soldier. Still unaware of Adrissu, he blinked hard a few times, before wobbling on his feet and sinking to the ground.

Adrissu swept past him, hurrying through the open space and not slowing until he was cloaked within the low branches of the willow temple. Only then did he closely inspect his surroundings. The inside of the trunk was partly hollowed out, idols of elven deities carved inside. Simple wooden benches were arranged in a semi-circle around the tree, and grass sprouted up around its roots, although it was surrounded by hard-packed dirt, the same as the single path that cut through the town.

He would have to act quickly and quietly. He only needed enough wood to burn for the ritual; cutting from the trunk would be too noticeable. Instead, he peered up through the branches, reaching out with tendrils of magic to grasp a branch high up enough that it would hopefully not be missed.

This would be the most dangerous part—he yanked on the branch in his grasp, and it snapped off from the trunk with a resounding crack. In the silent night it may as well have been a thunderbolt.

Adrissu winced, holding the branch up where it still hung high in the tree, listening intently for any sign that his presence had been noticed, or if anyone was coming to investigate the sudden sound. But after a minute, and then two, no one came.

Finally, he relaxed his deathgrip on the branch and brought it down slowly, until the supple wood was in his hands. He wound the loosest parts of it into a wide loop, like a whip, and tucked it into his sleeve as he crept away from the willow tree, silencing his steps again as he went.

What he had just done was blasphemy under elven law, and while he could have easily dispatched any soldier that approached him, he knew it was best to simply not be noticed here. He didn't relax until he was deep within the forest of Solitude, ready to fly away once more.

Now, the only thing left was perhaps going to be the most difficult—the ingredients were to be prepared in a bowl made of dwarven beryl. The gem itself was rare; not impossibly so, but it would be a pain to track down. The bigger problem was procuring such a bowl. Dwarven beryl was mined only in the mountains of Robruolor, the kingdom of the dwarves. An artisan skilled enough to work it into a bowl would likewise only be found in Robruolor, and would certainly charge a small fortune. But since their defeat at the hands of elves some thirty years prior, dwarves had only become more secluded and insular, trading with few outsiders and keeping their borders largely closed off. Getting there would be annoying, and finding a dwarven artisan who would either sell such a bowl, or be willing to craft one, even more so.

Adrissu had no contacts in Robruolor and little knowledge of the land, aside from what he could glean from world maps and common hearsay. He had only seen a handful of dwarves in his life, but was loath to take the form of one, squat and hairy as they were.

But what else could be done? He needed the bowl, no matter how difficult it was to procure. So when Ruan was on a long assignment, another months-long caravan detail, Adrissu informed the council of Polimnos that he would be on vacation for perhaps a month; gathered up some of the more valuable dwarven relics from his hoard, along with a sizeable amount of gold; and took to the sky once more. This time it was nearly two days across the cold northern sea before the distant, rocky shores of Robruolor came into sight.

Most dwarven cities were underground, but he remained high in the sky until he finally came to the tall mountain that boasted the largest city in Robruolor, the capitol of Gylnefjell. He was unwilling to take on a dwarven guise, so instead took the form of a human: elves would still be entirely unwelcome, but humans were prone to wanderlust and thus unlikely to raise many eyebrows.

He made his way into the bustling heart of the underground city and was relieved to see a few other humans there amidst all the dwarves, so he immediately set out to find stoneworkers and jewelers that might be capable of creating such a bowl.

The first day, he had very little luck. The two most prominent jewelers in the city declined him immediately, without much reason—though he supposed their sneers, as he crouched to step through the short doorways and stood with his hair brushing the ceiling, were reason enough.

Then he broached the topic to some of the stoneworkers and mining companies, to get a sense of what the cost of an appropriately-sized raw dwarven beryl would be. One laughed him out of the shop—it took everything he had not to slap the snobby little dwarf in the face before he left—and the other entertained the idea, but quoted him nearly ten thousand gold pieces for the raw crystal alone. Adrissu knew the material would be expensive, but he was certain the proprietor had inflated the price and was taking advantage of him.

He had been asking around for several days, walking down another of the endless, dim stone streets that composed the underground city, when the hair on the back of his neck began to prickle with the sense of being watched. He would know the presence of another dragon anywhere.

The urge to flee from an unknown dragon's territory seized him, but he took only a few steps, before stumbling to a stop. They were already aware of his presence—he could feel their eyes on him—there was no running now.

Adrissu slowly turned around, eyes flickering through the street to find whoever was watching him. Across the stone avenue, standing in the entryway of what looked like a residential building, was a human—a woman, nearly as tall as him, with short-cropped blonde hair and form-fitting clothes that looked better suited to a forest hunt than whatever business a human might have in an underground dwarven city. When their eyes met, she smiled; and if he was not already certain that she was also a dragon, he would be sure of it now. The way her teeth flashed was decidedly *feral*, familiar as his own cruel grin.

"Hail, traveler," she called, raising one hand lazily. "It's rare to see another of our kind in such a far-flung place."

Adrissu hesitated, looking her over once more. She didn't look armed. Of course, she did not need to have a weapon on her illusory form to harm him. This was obviously her domain—he had not done enough research on dragons in the area, clearly—but she also didn't appear outright hostile to him, only stiff and uncertain in the way dragons often were when meeting for the first time.

"A rare occurrence indeed, but hopefully a welcome one," he answered steadily, walking slowly toward her with his hands open at his sides in an exaggerated gesture of goodwill.

"Come inside," she said, beckoning him with one hand. Without waiting to see if he would follow, she turned and stepped into the building, leaving the door slightly ajar. Now that he was looking, the door was clearly human-sized. Internally he kicked himself for having missed it—he never should have let his guard down in a new place like this. But it was too late now, and he silently followed the woman and closed the door behind him.

She was waiting for him at the opposite end of a wide foyer. A closed door was behind her, and the foyer itself was quite plain: stone walls over a stone floor with a long, narrow rug running from one door to the next with a few decorations on the walls. There was no indication if this was her actual home; considering how sparse it was, he guessed it was unlikely that she actually lived here.

In here, her presence loomed all the larger, sending goosebumps shivering down the length of his spine. Instinctively, he hunched a bit lower: a stark contrast to her, standing tall and dominant at the other end of the room.

"What's your name?" she asked, some of the friendly lilt to her voice gone now that they were alone and behind closed doors. "Your true name?"

Adrissu sighed. "I am Zamnes the Black, son of Mithantos the Black and Ilrenth the Blue." She nodded, and he hesitated. "If you are who I suspect you are... you might know of my elder mother, Amaranthe the Silver."

Her eyebrows slightly raised at that. "I do know Amaranthe. We are... on friendly terms."

"Then perhaps you know why I am here," he pressed, and she grinned again.

"I had not heard anything from her, no," she said. "But I do know why you're here. When I heard a human was asking nearly every jeweler in the central district about crafting a dwarven beryl bowl, I suspected as much."

Adrissu was silent, considering. He had not thought to ask the dragons his elder mother knew for their beryl bowl: in truth, the idea of being indebted in some way to yet another dragon was utterly distasteful. But she had approached him, and if not to drive him out of her territory, it must have been because she had something else planned for him. It was only a matter of what she wanted in exchange—and whether she would broach the topic first, or wait for him to do it out of desperation. But he did not even know this dragon's name, much less what to expect of her.

"Your suspicions were correct, then," he said slowly. "I am indeed in search of such an item."

She looked him up and down.

"Forgive my manners," she said suddenly. "I am Heriel the Red. My mate Naydruun the Blue is not home at the moment, otherwise they would be here to greet you as well."

"There is nothing to forgive, Heriel," he said quickly, lowering his head in a placating gesture. "I am an intruder in your territory, and I apologize. I was not aware you were so close to Gylnefjell. Had I known, I..." He trailed off, uncertain. He was not sure what he would have done. Not come at all? Come to her first? Neither seemed like a sufficient answer.

But she only laughed. "Well, Zamnes, if you were here for any other reason I might not be so friendly. But I know what it is to fear your mate may be lost to you forever." Her eyes flickered with pain for only an instant, just barely enough for Adrissu to catch. "Living so close to any civilization is dangerous. We only rarely make appearances in the city now." She paused, clearly thinking of what she wanted to say. After a beat, she offered,

"My mate was not first born as Naydruun the Blue, but was Grizenth the Red in their first life."

Adrissu blinked, surprise and relief flooding him all at once. "So you've proven the ritual works, then."

She barked a bitter laugh. "Yes, we've proven it works. It was a miserable five decades between Grizenth's death and Naydruun finding me, though."

"That long?"

"Not many dragons are born each year," Heriel shrugged. "Naydruun was hatched almost a full year after Grizenth died, and wandered for a time in adulthood until we found each other again."

He remained silent, thinking it over. If Ruan were eventually reborn as a human, it would not take as long—right? He could only imagine so. New humans were born every day. But even fifty years or more apart was preferable to being apart forever.

"As you can imagine," Heriel continued. "I rather have a soft spot for other fated pairs, though you're the first I've had the chance to really talk to. We still have our beryl bowl from when we completed the ritual... It was difficult to procure, so I'd be willing to sell it to you."

"Name your price," he said slowly.

"What did you bring?" she answered, and he sighed, shifting the heavy bag on his back uncomfortably.

"Some ancient dwarven pottery," he said. Her eyes brightened at that; if she had no interest in the pottery itself, here in Robruolor it was sure to fetch a far better price than it would anywhere in Autreth. "And some gold in case that was not enough."

"All the pottery you've brought," she said. "And... five thousand gold pieces."

"Done," Adrissu said quickly—probably too quickly, considering how her expression slightly faltered. But the only dwarf that took his request seriously had quoted twice that price for the materials alone, so five thousand gold seemed a trifle in comparison. He would be glad to pay it and would have some left over. "Let me see it first."

Her grin returned. "Wait here."

Heriel opened the opposite door, and he watched curiously as she stepped through. The room beyond was even larger, almost comically spacious, and seemed totally empty from what he could tell. He imagined, since the floor appeared intact, that there was no ceiling and that the room was large enough to accomodate a dragon descending from above—or taking flight to some chamber higher up, possibly within the mountain itself. But she closed the door behind her, leaving him to simply wait.

This was the last item the ritual required, aside from Ruan's consent. Anticipation boiled in his blood; he was sure that even if she came down and doubled her asking price, he would still gladly pay. Everything seemed so close now, almost within his grasp.

It felt like a long time before Heriel returned. He could feel, when she finally arrived, the overpowering sense of her presence, even without the sound of her wings and the creak of the stone at her landing. A moment later, the blonde human woman stepped back through, carrying a small bowl, far smaller than Adrissu had expected. The size of a dining bowl, it fit neatly in her hands. But it was cut like a gem, so its brilliant blood red color gleamed and sparkled even in the dim light of her decoy home.

"Here it is," she said, noticing his eyes lingering on it. "Don't let its size fool you. It will fit everything."

"All the pottery and five thousand gold?" he said, easing the bag he carried off his shoulders. She visibly hesitated, then something in her demeanor changed. She looked partly resigned, and partly... something Adrissu could not place.

"All the pottery, and five thousand gold," she agreed, stepping closer to him. When their eyes met, he knew that she knew it was a low price. He was unsure why she hadn't asked for more, but he certainly wouldn't complain.

He unloaded the five pieces of pottery that he'd brought, all carefully wrapped in cloth to avoid chipping. None of it was the finest pottery, but everyday wares meant to withstand being jostled and used: the two bowls, vase, plate, and teapot were all a glossy reddish clay with the same maker's mark on the bottom. Their value was in their age, not their beauty; but still he was glad to see that none of them looked any worse for wear, despite having been flown half a world away.

Once the pottery was set out, he pulled a coin purse from his bag and divided out five thousand gold. Much of it was in larger raw chunks, some in small pieces; but he knew that as a dragon she too would have an innate sense of its worth. When he deemed it the equivalent of five thousand gold pieces, he glanced up at her for confirmation, and she nodded. Only then did she pass the bowl to him.

It was warm in his hands. It made him think of Ruan, always warm, with the radiance of the sun.

"Thank you," he murmured unbidden, as he grasped it close to his chest. "You have no idea how much I appreciate this."

Heriel laughed, smiling over at him. For the first time her grin did not have that untamed look to it, but a genuine smile that was not at all out of place on her human features.

"Trust me, I do," she replied. "I'm happy to pass it along. Only remember our kindness, especially if you ever come across Naydruun. They're more likely to travel than I. If you ever meet Naydruun, remember our kindness to you."

"I will," Adrissu agreed, the bowl in his hands still holding his full attention. "I will remember."

Chapter Eleven

With everything in place to undergo the ritual, only Ruan needed to be convinced. Adrissu had not broached the topic in a long time, and he was unsure how to start the conversation again. So he waited until Ruan had been home for a while, and they were in his house, where his mate was comfortable, full from a good meal, and a little bit drunk on wine.

"Ruan," he murmured, nearly purring the other man's name. The human was cradled in his lap, kissing along his neck. "This is all well and good, of course, but I had something I wanted to ask you before we go any further."

Ruan pulled away, grinning up at him. The patchy facial hair he used to shave religiously had finally filled out enough that he could wear it as a short beard; Adrissu had disliked it at first, but now thoroughly enjoyed the soft tickle of it against his skin, and especially relished the satisfied sigh it would elicit out of Ruan when he threaded his fingers through it.

"What is it, then?" Ruan teased. "I would very much like to get back to this."

"Listen," Adrissu chuckled, shifting his weight so Ruan was a bit further from him. Still straddling his waist, Ruan adjusted so there was enough distance between them to meet Adrissu's gaze. "I have been... thinking about some things."

"Things?"

"Things we have previously discussed... A long time ago."

"Are you finally going to let me fuck you?"

"That is not what I was referring to," Adrissu sighed, but Ruan only laughed good-naturedly. "No, something else. Do you... Do you remember when I first told you about fated pairs?"

Ruan stilled slightly in his lap, his jovial expression faltering slightly. A slight smile remained on his face, but did not quite reach his eyes, as if he already suspected the conversation was going to take an unwelcome turn.

"Yes," he said, nodding. "I remember."

"And when we discussed this, I mentioned a... A ritual I was aware of, that would bind fated pairs' souls together."

"The reincarnation thing. Yes, I remember that, too."

"Well, I..." Adrissu started, licking his lips. For all the trouble it had taken to learn the ritual and procure its items, the thought of asking Ruan to undergo it seemed far more daunting now. "I have all the ingredients now. All the components of the ritual. I've been collecting them in my spare time, and everything is prepared. We could perform it at any time."

Ruan was perfectly still, his eyes suddenly looking faraway and unfocused. For a long moment Adrissu was silent, waiting, tension building in him. Then Ruan finally sighed, leaning back to scrub one hand through his hair, still short and scruffy as it always had been.

"I don't know, Adrissu," he finally murmured, and his tone was more fearful than Adrissu had expected. He had expected the human to be irritated, resistant—but so little seemed to frighten Ruan, warrior that he was, that to hear the slight quiver in his voice now was far more unsettling. "The thought of reincarnation... I don't know. Humans aren't meant to live forever."

"Other humans," Adrissu protested, shaking his head. "Ruan, *we* are meant to be together forever. Both of us."

Ruan winced. Every time Adrissu's lifespan came up, it seemed to pain him all over again.

"I just—I don't know, Adrissu. It doesn't seem right."

"There is no right or wrong in this, Ruan."

"Isn't there? What's so special about me that I get to know what will happen to me when I die, and other humans won't? Wouldn't they deserve the same ritual, then?"

"No. I'm the difference between you and them. *Me*. And I decide this is what you deserve," Adrissu said. It sounded wildly selfish, even as the words left his lips, but he couldn't bring himself to care. He could kill every human that he ever met for the rest of his life, if it meant keeping Ruan with him. Nothing else mattered—but he knew if he pushed too hard, came across as too frantic, he would only drive Ruan further away, when he was already clearly reticent.

"Adrissu..." Ruan started, only to trail off.

"No, it—it is a lot. I apologize," Adrissu murmured, his voice becoming gruff. He did not want to apologize, but in their time together he had become quite skilled in judging what words and tones to use with Ruan to avoid conflict. "I do not need an answer right now. I only ask that you continue to think on it. Take as long as you need."

For a long moment, Ruan was silent.

"Okay. I'll think about it," he said, nodding. They both regarded each other, Ruan's expression blank; but he had not pulled away or gotten out of Adrissu's lap, so that had to count for something. Ruan's eyes searched Adrissu's face for something, and after a long moment, he seemed to find it, as a small, familiar smile started to spread across his features again.

"*Now* can we go to bed?" he asked, leaning forward again to nip at the tender skin just below Adrissu's jaw, right above his throat. A low growl escaped him, pleasure curling along his spine.

"Yes," he agreed, and they left the conversation behind.

Polimnos had continued to expand in this time, and Benil Branwood finally got the mine expansion that he had been pursuing for years. With the increased usage of the quarry, and the opening of newer mines below, came a glut of new workers from other parts of Autreth, some alone and some with families.

The new citizens of Polimnos also brought along some troubling reports and rumors: Gennemont, the largest city-state of Autreth, was expanding its borders to push right up against other, smaller city-states. Many speculated that it was only a matter of time before their expansion exploded into violence; and at that point, who was to say whether or not Gennemont might start incorporating smaller cities into its own jurisdiction?

Knowing the constant cycles of war that mortals flung themselves into so often, this development troubled Adrissu. If Gennemont did make a bid to start conquering other cities, Polimnos was far enough away to not be in any immediate danger, but still large and prosperous enough now that there was no doubt in his mind it would eventually be a target.

But when he mentioned the rumors to Ruan, the human only laughed.

"Sounds like steady work to me," he said. He laughed, but the thought struck Adrissu like a thunderbolt, filling him with terror. If Gennemont did invade, of course Ruan would fight. He was a mercenary, a soldier. The idea that Ruan would eventually die had always been there, but it was far in the future, when he was an old man. The jobs he took now were dangerous to some extent, but they were not extended battles. They were not *war*.

Ruan noticed his sudden ashen appearance, the laugh falling away from his face. "Adrissu," he murmured, now concerned. "What's wrong?"

Adrissu shook himself out of it, before he could start spiraling. "Nothing," he replied, managing a weak smile. "I was... thinking about work. Forgive me."

They dropped the topic then, but it only bolstered Adrissu's resolve: Ruan must agree to undergo the ritual.

But Polimnos continued to grow, and Adrissu continued to guide it through his seat on the city's council. Roads were improved, old buildings were torn down and rebuilt with stronger materials, and business flourished with the increased export of stone. All in all, he was quite pleased with the direction that the city was moving, and with his place in it.

In contrast, Ruan almost never seemed satisfied in his work. He rose through the ranks steadily, taking on more prestigious jobs—dangerous hunts for rare, powerful creatures, or guarding wealthy individuals in place of caravans. Whatever pleasure he got from the jobs themselves, he always sounded disappointed when he would tell Adrissu how his ranking in the guild had risen–when he broke the top twenty, then the top ten, even the top five.

"Why do you always sound so displeased to be one of the best at what you do?" Adrissu asked him, when Ruan told him that his standing was now at number four with a deep scowl.

"I don't want to be *one of* the best. I want to be *the* best," he answered, smirking. "Even second place is only the first loser."

Adrissu had stared at him for a moment, before shaking his head and laughing. "You sound more like a dragon than me."

"Then you should understand," Ruan had retorted.

Adrissu should not have been surprised. Ruan had always been ambitious, but now that he was no longer in the throes of wild youth, that ambition had been sharpened to a ruthless point. Adrissu liked to think that maybe he'd had some influence on the human as well, fostering that sense of yearning for success and glory.

Through it all, the thought of the soul-binding ritual was always in the back of Adrissu's mind. Out of respect for Ruan he only brought it up twice a year; but like clockwork, he would ask every six months if Ruan would reconsider. The first time or two, Ruan had only echoed his previous uncertainty, asking for more time to consider.

But then he started to refuse outright. The first time, Adrissu had been so taken aback at the sudden denial that he had abruptly left, fearing he might erupt with anger, or worse, break into devastated tears. This too seemed to startle Ruan, and though he continued to refuse, he did so less flippantly and with more room for discussion.

But the conversation always ended the same: Adrissu would keep pressing, and eventually Ruan would tell him that he didn't want to talk about it any more; things would quickly settle back into their happy routine, until Adrissu asked again six months later.

Time was a strange thing for a dragon. Objectively, he knew ten years was a long time for a human to age, for a city to expand, for a relationship to grow—yet it was nothing at all. It was a season, an interlude, a welcome sabbatical from his previous studies, which he had put aside in favor of spending time with Ruan, or working with the members of the council.

A decade was so little time, yet it was nearly a third of Ruan's life so far. He had changed so much since the first time Adrissu had seen him, yet each change was familiar, as if he was becoming someone Adrissu already knew. His sharp edges were tempered, so the radiance of him shone more brightly: the parts of him that were strong and courageous and confident. Though, Adrissu often thought, he was probably biased. As far as he was concerned, Ruan could do no wrong; nevertheless, Ruan had always proven himself to be a worthy mate.

Their relationship was something of an open secret in town; they were not entirely public about it, but those who knew them could see it quite clearly. For all his intense privacy, Adrissu was glad at least that Benil Branwood had ceased all his talk of engagements and his daughter, after he saw Adrissu and Ruan together for the first time.

So it was no surprise when, at least a year after the last reported skirmish between Gennemont and its closest neighbors had ended in an uneasy truce, Maya Graylight had asked for a private sit-down, wasting no time upon her arrival and asking abruptly,

"I trust Ruan has told you the news?"

Adrissu blinked, looking at her blankly. She had already worn the signs of age when they had met. Now her hair was fully gray, and the lines of her face had deepened, partly with time and partly with stress. But her demeanor was the same, and she met his gaze with the same hawklike countenance, as he considered what she might be referring to.

"No," he finally said, gesturing for her to continue. That she expected him to know anything Ruan knew was not a surprise, but the idea that Ruan had kept something from him had taken him aback.

She sighed, pressing a hand to her forehead. "It's not good. We got word from one of our contacts in Gennemont late last night that Aqila Hill and Vizemont have fully ceded to Gennemont's governance. They're announcing that they're merging into a single nation sometime in the next few days. They're calling themselves the Federation of Autreth... which doesn't bode well for city-states like ours."

Adrissu sighed heavily, considering the implications before speaking.

"No, that does not bode well," he finally answered quietly. In light of Gennemont's aggressive expansion only a few years ago, he was sure that whatever they gained through this deal would only satiate them temporarily. And with a title like the *Federation of Autreth*, it was only a matter of time before other places in Autreth would be expected to be assimilated into the Federation that claimed its name. "Have you heard anything regarding them mounting an army? Mercenaries that have been hired, or...?"

"Not yet," Maya sighed, leaning back in her chair. "Not yet, so we'll have time to keep an eye on things and mount our own forces, if it comes down to it."

"You said Ruan already knows?" Adrissu asked, looking down at his clasped hands.

"Yes. He was with me, the instructors, and some others last night, when our runner came with the news," she said. "Ruan is already at about the highest level anyone can get in the guild without taking on a teaching position himself, so no point in trying to keep anything from him. He would have heard from Ederick if not me, I'm sure. I'm surprised he didn't tell you already."

"I see," he sighed. For a long moment, both were silent, tension palpable between them. "Well... I suppose we should start reallocating some funds, then, if we're anticipating any kind of skirmish coming to us."

"Yes," she agreed, sighing again and rubbing her temples. "Let's put together a proposal to have ready when we have our council meeting tomorrow."

When Adrissu returned to Saltspire Tower that evening, Ruan was waiting for him, lounging in one of the plush chairs with a glass of wine in one hand—Vesper curled around his arm, and her head resting in his other hand. She too had continued to grow in their time together; she was noticeably longer than she had been when Ruan first met her, and a little rounder as well.

From the nervous tension in the air and the half-empty bottle on the table—evidence that this was not Ruan's first glass of wine—he was sure that Ruan had planned to break the news to him now.

"Welcome home, love," the human called, turning to look at him in the doorway. His smile seemed forced.

"Ruan," he said, voice low and soft. He stepped closer to Ruan and could feel him shift, sensing what would come next. "I was with Maya Graylight today. She said you'd heard the news about... Gennemont."

Ruan's shoulders sagged, and he sighed, taking another drink from his glass of wine. "Yes. I... I was going to tell you about it now, actually, but I guess she beat me to it."

They were both silent, Adrissu's hand clenching at the top of Ruan's chair. After a moment, Ruan added abruptly, "It doesn't mean anything yet, of course, but I know Maya expects the worst."

"I think it's a fair assumption," Adrissu sighed, feeling the wood starting to give beneath the pressure of his fingers. He pulled away before it would break. "The cycle of war always starts up again eventually."

"It isn't war," Ruan snapped. The edge in his voice, though, betrayed his lack of conviction. "Not yet, at least, it's not war."

"It's only a matter of time," Adrissu replied. "You know Maya. We're already preparing for the worst, even if it's far off."

"How much of an army could they even put together? Aqila Hill and Vizemont are both smaller than Polimnos," Ruan said quickly, shaking his head. "She—she worries too much. And even if they do start attacking, Polimnos will hardly be their first target. Hell, Vlissingstadt has triple our population and an actual port. If there's anything in the east they'd want, it'd be Vlissingstadt."

"Ruan," Adrissu said firmly. His voice was soft, but it was enough to pull Ruan from whatever spiral he had started down, and the human fell silent. "You're correct that nothing is going to change immediately. But if their previous actions have indicated anything, it's only a matter of time before Polimnos will at least have to make a show of strength to keep the brunt of their forces away from our borders. You know that's what it will come down to."

Ruan kept his gaze down on Vesper, who was glancing curiously between the two of them. "I know," he finally said, barely above a whisper.

It was not the time of year that he would typically bring up the soul-binding again, but Adrissu could not stop the words, bubbling up out of the fear that had been simmering in his gut since his conversation with Maya. "Ruan, please, just consider the ritual—it would ensure that if anything *were* to happen—"

With a growl, Ruan threw his wine to the ground. The shattering of glass caused Adrissu to stop short.

"I knew you would say that," Ruan snarled, pressing his now-free hand to his forehead. "Gods, Adrissu, how many times do I have to tell you no? Do you ever think of anything else? Stop fucking asking me!"

Adrissu remained silent, a strange mix of anger and despair stabbing at his ribs. He wanted to snap that of *course* he did not think of anything else, how could he possibly think of anything else? He wanted to tie the human down and *force* him to submit to the ritual—but he kept his mouth closed and clamped down on the draconic, almost feral part of him that wanted to claim and take with no regard for anything else.

But the tension seemed to pass through Ruan as quickly as it came. He sighed, shoulders sagging, as he dragged his hand down his face and moved to stand.

"Sorry," he said hoarsely, still not looking at Adrissu. "I didn't... Sorry. I'll clean this up."

"No need," Adrissu replied. His voice was cool in stark contrast to his inner turmoil, so much so that it took him by surprise. Mechanically he lifted a hand, and with a swish of his wrist, the shattered glass and spilled puddle of wine were both magicked off the stone floor and into the trash chute on the wall. Ruan groaned as he sat back down.

"I don't mean to yell," he muttered, shaking his head. "I guess this is just... stressful to think about. I'm really sorry."

"You are forgiven," Adrissu replied, reaching down to touch Ruan's shoulder. The human leaned into the contact and tilted his head, so his bearded cheek was pressed against the back of Adrissu's hand. "There is nothing you could do that I could not forgive."

Ruan laughed once at that, shaking his head. "I don't know about that." But before Adrissu could answer, he added quickly, "This is all a problem for another day. I don't want to think about it any more. Come to bed with me?"

He looked up at Adrissu, reaching up to thread their fingers together. How could he tell him no?

"Yes," he agreed, pulling Ruan to his feet. "Let's go."

Adrissu did not bring up the ritual again, just as Ruan had asked. He did not bring it up when Gennemont formally announced the creation of the Federation of Autreth, declaring itself the capitol of the newly-founded nation. He did not bring it up when it was clear Gennemont was bolstering its army. He did not bring it up when, mere months after the Federation was formed, Gennemont's forces marched west to annex every village and farming town that lay on the main road to the coast.

But when the west had been absorbed, it was obvious that the Lords of the Federation were turning their sights east, where Polimnos lay in its path. Confirmation came a month or so after the west was taken, when an entourage arrived at the gates of Polimnos, carrying the flag of the Federation and requesting an audience with the Polimnos Council.

The council met the six humans who had arrived on horseback. They sat on one end of the table in the council office, and the eight councilors sat on the other. Much to Adrissu's displeasure, Benil Branwood sat next to him, visibly perspiring and wringing his hands.

"Benil, I swear to all the gods," Adrissu hissed out of the side of his mouth, leaning slightly over so it looked as if he were only whispering something. "Keep your hands still and under the table, or I'll cut them off myself. The last thing we need is these people thinking we're too fearful to speak, let alone fight them."

Benil shot him a bewildered glance, but luckily it was at that moment that Cyrus cleared his throat, and the room fell silent around them.

"Welcome," he said evenly, gesturing to the six visitors. "We are the Polimnos Council. I am Cyrus Polare, head councilor of Polimnos. I understand you're here representing Gennemont and its host of Lords?"

One of the humans, a male that looked to be no more than thirty with a sallow face and patchy facial hair, visibly bristled and retorted, "That is not who we represent. We represent the Federation of Autreth as a whole."

For a moment the group was silent. While the other five humans seemed somewhat exasperated with the young man, none spoke against him. Adrissu forced himself not to roll his eyes, and Cyrus gave a tight-lipped smile.

"Ah, my mistake," he said. "Well, please, go ahead. What business has brought you so far from home?"

One of the older humans, a female who looked like she'd be more comfortable holding a weapon than sitting here in negotiations, cleared her throat before the younger man could speak.

"We do represent the Federation of Autreth," she said evenly. "As you know, the Federation has a goal of seeing all of Autreth unified. We come offering terms to a peaceful annexation of Polimnos."

At that, Adrissu scoffed before he could stop himself—but to his surprise, it was Yue Lang who spoke first.

"Peaceful!" he spat, frowning. "And how flexible are these terms you approach us with?"

The woman's face had become stony, but she managed a cool smile that did not reach her eyes.

"Unfortunately, flexibility is not our priority," she said. She held a hand out to an older, balding man next to her, who pulled a scroll from within his sleeves and handed it to her. She spread it on the table without looking at it. "This is what the Lords of the Federation offer. Agree to these terms, and Polimnos will gladly be welcomed into the Federation. Otherwise... Well, I'm sure you've seen what has happened in the west."

"We have," Maya muttered, glancing down at the scroll with her arms folded across her chest.

"And how soon do you need a response?" Cyrus said, his tone mild compared to the others.

"We will remain in town for five days," the woman answered. Adrissu wondered why she was the one to speak for all of them—clearly she was a warrior, not a diplomat. Perhaps, he suspected, they already anticipated Polimnos would put up a fight.

"Then we shall have an answer for you within five days," Cyrus said steadily.

Adrissu did not bring up the ritual when he went home to Ruan that night, but he knew the human could feel the tension roiling off him in waves. Ruan did not need to ask to know why, and he went willingly as Adrissu dragged him to their bedroom to hold him down and fuck him hard. Here, at least, he still had control, driving himself into Ruan's body until he could forget about everything else.

Chapter Twelve

The council meeting was called the next day, and the eight councilors gathered in the meeting hall to consider Gennemont's offer.

"Has everyone reviewed the terms?" Cyrus asked when they were all seated. His eyes were sunken with an obvious lack of sleep, but his voice remained steady. A murmur of assent spread through the room. "Then let's discuss."

Everyone was silent for a moment. Ellisa offered, "I didn't think it all sounded too bad."

Yue Lang scoffed from the other side of the table. "Any terms that require us to give them taxes is too much."

An uncomfortable silence settled over them again. The terms did require tax revenue, and considering how zealously the Federation was gathering up territories, the revenue seemed to be the end goal. There was no possibility that Gennemont would agree to any terms where Polimnos did not pay them taxes, and they all knew it.

"It might be possible to bargain for a lower percentage of taxation," Cyrus said, pinching the bridge of his nose between two fingers. "But the only way we're going to get out of this without paying taxes to Gennemont is to fight."

"Then we should fight," Yue interrupted. Before anyone else could answer, Maya Graylight spoke.

"I agree," she said. "We should fight."

"Fight?!" Benil Branwood spluttered, smacking his hands on the table. "With what army? With what forces?"

"We have some of the best mercenaries this side of Autreth," Maya said.

"Some! Certainly not enough to stand up to the forces they've already gathered," Benil continued, shaking his head. "To fight against them would be a death sentence for all these mercenaries of yours, Maya. They know that, and they know *we* know it."

"Which is why they won't be expecting us to fight back!" Yue interjected. "We strike before they can and get the upper hand."

"And I take it you'll be among those doing the fighting?" Ellisa retorted, for the first time sounding frustrated. Yue visibly bristled.

"Enough," Cyrus interrupted, holding up a hand. "We came here to discuss what to do, not argue with each other."

"Yes," Adrissu sighed, speaking for the first time. "Let's try not to fight with each other."

They fell into an uncomfortable silence once again. Adrissu felt their eyes on him for a long moment, before they fell back to Cyrus, waiting for his cue.

"Let's go over what's actually in the terms for now," Cyrus sighed, flipping through several sheets of parchment in front of him.

They spent hours discussing the terms, arguing over what they should and should not accept, but almost everyone's minds already seemed made up: those in favor of a fight wouldn't budge, and those who sought peaceful negotiations with the Federation were unable to change their minds.

Adrissu thought he was the only one that truly felt torn. In his gut, he did not want to bend his knee to invading forces, whether physically or metaphorically. He was too proud to bow to anyone. But the rest of him trembled in fear at the thought of Ruan going to war, fighting, getting hurt—*dying*. It drowned out every other instinct in him, as much as it wounded his ego.

Finally, it came to a vote. Cyrus stood at the head of the table and called their names, starting on the right and moving clockwise.

"Maya. For or against Gennemont's terms?"

"Against." She nearly spat the word, without a beat of silence or hesitation.

"Benil. For or against?"

"For," he answered just as quickly. Under the table he was wringing his hands together over and over.

"Abe. For or against?"

Abe Pelagon was silent for a moment. An old human with no hair left on his head, his family partially owned the mines along with the Branwoods, which guaranteed him a seat on the council. Yet Adrissu thought that the man almost resented the responsibility; he was by far the most withdrawn of anyone on the council, and it was not uncommon for him to go an entire meeting without speaking, or else adding only a sentence here and there. Today had been no exception; Adrissu thought he had spoken no more than three times during these discussions. His sunken-in eyes flickered across the table as he considered the question and his fellow councilors, then he finally cleared his throat and and said in his raspy baritone,

"Against."

A murmur of surprise crossed the table, and Adrissu felt himself begin to sweat. He had hoped the old man would not want a fight, but...

"Ellisa," Cyrus said, moving on before Adrissu could dwell on Abe's choice for too long. "For or against?"

"For," she replied softly. In contrast to Benil, her hands were clasped firmly together and set on the table, but Adrissu could see her fingers quivering.

"Shefali. For or against?"

"For," the woman answered. Next to Yue, she was the youngest on the council, but she owned the only large-scale fishery operating in Polimnos, inheriting her seat when her father died and left his business to her. Adrissu was not surprised at her answer; though everyone around the table was successful to varying degrees, she perhaps had the most business sense among them, and the most to lose if Gennemont's reprisal led to a second destruction of Polimnos.

"Yue. For or against?"

"Against," he said, his voice tight. His arms were folded across his broad chest.

"Adrissu. For or against?"

Adrissu released a shuddering breath he had not realized he'd been holding. He wanted to roar with the frustration and rebellion boiling in his chest. He wanted to fly to Gennemont and rip the heads off the Lords of the Federation himself.

"For," he hissed through gritted teeth. From the corner of his eye, he saw Maya's head whip to look at him, the heat of her gaze prickling his skin; but he kept his eyes firmly on the table in front of him. Nothing mattered more than keeping Ruan safe, he told himself. He was the only thing that mattered.

Next to him, Cyrus let out a long sigh, looking down at the parchment where he had tallied the votes. His would be the final vote, and the council was silent as they waited for him to speak.

"My vote is against," he said softly. "Which brings us to a tie." Adrissu's heart plummeted to the very bottom of his stomach as the air in the room turned grim. "And in the event of a tie, my vote counts for two. We will not accept the terms Gennemont has offered."

He carefully folded the paper and turned to Maya.

"We should begin making plans to gather all the forces available to us. Can you have all the guild's records on available mercenaries ready for a meeting first thing tomorrow morning?"

"Absolutely," she answered.

Adrissu was on his feet before he realized what he was doing, everyone's heads swinging to look at him in surprise.

"I—" he started, only for his voice to break. He wanted to protest, to force them to listen, to smash their faces in, to go to the representatives from Gennemont and kill them all himself.

He *could* go and kill them all, he thought—right now, he could find the inn where they stayed and kill them before they could report back to the Federation. He could. He shouldn't, but for one wild instant it was so sorely tempting that he thought he might. It took a moment for his senses to return to him: if he killed them now, it would only make whatever conflict was coming even worse.

Everyone was still staring at him, silent and expectant. He cleared his throat. What could he say? He couldn't explain it, but he couldn't stand to be in the stuffy meeting hall any longer.

"Excuse me," he rasped, then turned to go. A flurry of voices erupted behind him, but he didn't turn back, and he didn't stop until he was out of the council hall and in fresh air. The sun was setting—it had been just past noon when they'd met. For a long moment he stood, looking out on the horizon, where the sun steadily sank below the jagged horizon, trying to slow his rapid breathing.

"Adrissu."

He whirled, startled, to see Maya Graylight standing in the doorway of the council hall, looking nearly as grim as he felt. He drew a shuddering breath.

"Maya," he said evenly, forcing himself to lower his head. "Forgive my abruptness. I..." He trailed off again. How could he explain how urgently he needed to get out—to be anywhere but there?

She eyed him silently for a moment before speaking. "I was surprised at your vote. You don't seem like the kind of person to let the town go down without a fight."

"Normally I would not," he said, hardly above a whisper. Heat flooded his face, partly shame, partly anger, partly something he could not describe. "But Ruan..."

"Ruan would want to fight," she interjected. "You know he would."

Adrissu looked away, scowling. "I don't care," he muttered. "I only care about keeping him safe."

"That doesn't seem fair to him. Regardless of how much you care about him, Adrissu, it's his decision to make," she said.

Adrissu bit his lip to force himself not to scowl openly at her. He suspected Maya had been one of the first to pick up on their changed dynamic all those years ago, but she had never openly acknowledged it. Once, it might have made him smile to hear someone else acknowledge that he cared for Ruan, but now it filled his chest with a sticky anger, balking at her presumption.

"You wouldn't understand," he said, turning away. "You couldn't."

"Of course I understand," she started.

"We already have so little time!" he spat, whirling on her again. He could feel his face contorting into a snarl—her eyebrows raised in surprise, but otherwise she gave no indication of being startled at his outburst. "Ruan could live to be a hundred, could die an old man, and I—I would still be in my *youth*. We already—I already have so little time with him."

His rage sputtered out as quickly as it came, and his voice broke the longer he spoke. "And now—and now *this*... We cannot win against the armies of the Federation, Maya. It's a suicide mission. We all know it."

Shame filled him as his eyes prickled with tears. He pressed his hands to his face, in part to hide them, and in part so he didn't have to see how Maya reacted to seeing the stoic mage weep.

"I cannot be impartial in this," he finally said, abruptly forcing his hands back down to his sides. Her expression had not changed, stony as ever. "I cannot. Tell Cyrus that if he doesn't want me to attend meetings regarding this, I understand. I'll step down."

"Adrissu," Maya said softly, shaking her head. "Polimnos is our home, all of us. I don't think anyone can truly be impartial."

They were silent for a long moment, until finally Adrissu turned again.

"I should go," he said softly. He did not wait to see if Maya would respond before starting down the path that would lead him through the center of town and back to his tower.

"What did the council decide?"

It was the first thing Ruan said, arriving in the doorway of Saltspire Tower. Adrissu lay on the chaise lounge in the front room with Vesper curled on his chest, her weight grounding him like a hand pressed to a bruise. When he'd come home to find Ruan gone, anxiety began to simmer in his gut; but now he sat up with a sigh, Vesper sliding down into his lap.

"To fight," he said, voice hoarse. There was no point in trying to talk around it. "They voted to fight."

Ruan sighed, nodding. He did not look surprised, only determined, as his brows furrowed and jaw tightened.

"Ruan," Adrissu said, looking up at him. He pushed Vesper off him and stood. "Let's just go."

"Go?" Ruan asked, surprise flitting on his face. "Go where?"

"Anywhere but here," he said, stepping toward him. He grasped both of Ruan's wrists. "Please. None of this needs to involve us. We can just go. I'll block up the entrance to my lair here and come back for my things when we find someplace else. But please, let's just leave."

"What are you talking about?" Ruan said, shaking his head. A nervous laugh escaped him. "You really want to leave?"

"I want to keep you *safe*," he growled. "I don't care about the Federation or Gennemont. I don't care whose rule Polimnos is under. I care about you. I care about keeping you with me as long as I can. I care about keeping you *alive*."

"You know I can't do that," Ruan said. He looked down at where Adrissu still held his wrists, but he did not try to pull away. "Adrissu. You know that."

"Then please," he rasped, forcing down the panic threatening to overtake him. "The soul-binding ritual... Please, just consider it."

"Adrissu," Ruan said sharply, but Adrissu could not stop the jumble of words escaping his mouth.

"I beg you, Ruan, please. If you must fight, if you must stay here—Ruan, if anything happened to you, I don't know how I would survive."

Vesper had slithered off the lounge and up to Ruan, curling protectively around his ankle. He looked down at her, not meeting Adrissu's eyes.

"You would survive," he said hollowly. "Of course you would."

"Ruan," Adrissu said again. It was all he could manage. The world felt like it was crumbling beneath him. What was the use of all his power, his strength, if he could not keep his mate safe?

"Stop," Ruan said abruptly, turning away. "Don't ask me again."

Adrissu's vision went red at the edges. He could feel his breathing coming hard, his heart pounding—for one wild instant he wanted to shove Ruan down the hatch to his lair and keep him imprisoned there until the fighting was over. But Ruan would hate him, and he was increasingly sure that he would hate himself too. He was more helpless than he had ever been in his life.

Silently he turned away, stepped toward the hatch, and dropped down without looking at Ruan. He could hear the human's distant shout as he fell, but all he could focus on was how badly he needed to fly, to rage.

He could not cry in his draconic form, but at least he could roar out his frustration until his voice gave up. Fire streamed from his throat like all the words he could not say, and he blasted the walls with his breath over and over until the embers were like razor blades in his mouth. When he finally went back up, Ruan was already gone.

—◆◆◆—

Ruan was going to die.

The sentence was the only full thought that his mind could produce as he sat in the council hall. Discussions were happening around him, but he couldn't focus on any of it—

could barely hear it over his own misery. Ruan was going to die, and there was little he could do to stop it.

The council would wait out the remaining four days before giving their answer to buy as much time as they could; that much he could recall, along with how terse and hopeless everyone's voices had been. He would never understand these humans' desperation to fight a losing battle.

He could feel Maya's eyes linger on him when the meeting ended, but she said nothing as he gathered his belongings and stepped out of the room. But he could not have held a conversation even if he had wanted to, so he was glad that no one tried to stop him as he quietly left.

When he arrived back at Saltspire Tower, Ruan was already there. Adrissu jerked to a stop in the doorway when he spotted him sitting at the dining table, his heart seizing all over again. It was almost worse to be around him, to see him, while knowing that the hourglass of their time together was nearly empty.

"You look like you've seen a ghost," Ruan said, leaning over in his chair to peer at Adrissu. He shook himself into action, glancing down at his feet as he set his bag on the ground. Vesper slithered up to carry it away, and he watched her drag it along for a moment, before looking back at Ruan.

"What's wrong?" Ruan asked, and Adrissu winced.

"You know what's wrong," he muttered darkly, and the veneer of concern on Ruan's face fell away to something far more grim.

"I guess I do," he sighed, turning back to the bowl of walnuts that he had been shelling. A mess of hulls was gathered on a separate plate—he would save them for Adrissu to make ink. The task seemed pointless and tedious to Adrissu now. Why waste their time?

"Ruan," he rasped. "I had a thought that... perhaps I could go with you."

Ruan's face had become pinched when he started speaking, but now the human looked back over at him in confusion.

"Go with me?" he repeated. "I don't understand."

"To defend Polimnos," Adrissu said, licking his lips nervously. "If... Zamnes went with you."

"No," Ruan said abruptly, shaking his head. "No, that's ridiculous, Adrissu. Everyone would see you, and would know you were near enough to see what was happening—it's too dangerous. You'd get found out."

"It doesn't matter. We could go somewhere else after," he pressed, shaking his head.

"No!" Ruan exclaimed. "Adrissu, that's insane. You can't. I won't let you."

"Why?" Adrissu snapped. "To keep *me* safe?"

"Yes!"

"Then you do understand!" he shouted, before biting his lip and forcing himself to continue in a strained, but quiet voice. "All I want is for you to be safe, Ruan. Please just let me protect you."

"I don't need your protection," he muttered.

"If you march with the rest of them to fight Autreth, you *will* die," Adrissu hissed. His eyes burned, and his stomach roiled with bile when he said the words aloud. "It's a suicide mission, Ruan. Everyone knows it."

"We don't know that," he protested, and Adrissu forced himself not to laugh.

"I can promise you, this rebellion will not be successful," he said, shaking his head. "The Lords of Gennemont and the Federation have been nothing if not strategic in all this. Their forces have numbers enough now that annexing all of Autreth is a feasible goal. Vlissingstadt is triple the size of Polimnos at least, and even they would be hard-pressed to fight off the full brunt of their forces. We have a mercenary's guild, Ruan, not a standing army."

Ruan's expression had darkened the longer he went on, but at least this time he seemed to be at a loss for words. They were both silent for a long moment, and Adrissu watched as Ruan's eyes flickered nervously around the room, landing anywhere but on him.

"Maybe that's true," he finally said, softly. "But I... Polimnos' freedom is worth fighting for."

"Worth dying for?" Adrissu pressed, and again Ruan had no immediate answer.

"Yes," he finally said, but his tone was tremulous.

"You truly believe that?" Adrissu said, and stubbornly Ruan nodded.

"Yes," he repeated.

All the fire drained out of Adrissu in an instant, his shoulders sagging, and a cold dread settled in its place. He could not convince Ruan not to go, could not convince him to let Zamnes go with him, could not convince the council to abandon their pointless rebellion. Ruan had told him not to bring up the soul-binding ritual again, and as much as it killed him to stay silent, he would not ask again. If ten years of asking could not convince him, he had nothing left.

That cold feeling had spread from his chest to his extremities, and he now felt distant and far away—as if it were someone else who gripped the back of the chair across from Ruan, so tightly that his knuckles were white.

"I see," he said, barely above a whisper, and he turned toward the stairs to go to his study. "Then I have nothing else to say. You've made your choice. I will respect it."

"Adrissu," Ruan said, and distantly Adrissu thought he sounded alarmed, but silently he made his way up the stairs. It did not sound like Ruan followed.

In his study, he sat down at his desk and reached for some of his old notes. Several sheets of parchment were tucked between the pages of a tome, written by a long-dead mage that argued magic was its own element in the natural world, and not a separate force that manipulated the elements, as was the leading theory at the time. It had been well over a year since he'd last touched the book, so carefully he folded away the notes and turned the page back to the beginning. His studies were familiar and safe. Those, at least, he could control.

On the fifth day, the Polimnos council met again with the representatives from the Federation of Autreth.

"I would hate to waste your time, so we'll make this short," Cyrus said, hands clasped on the table in front of him. The eight councilors sat tightly packed on one side of their long meeting table, and the six visitors sat on the other. "After much deliberation, the council and I have come to the decision that we cannot accept the terms Gennemont and your Lords of the Federation have proposed."

Across from them, the younger man's nostrils flared, and his chin turned up in obvious offense; but the warrior woman, who clearly led them, only nodded, looking entirely unsurprised.

"I trust you understand the ramifications of your decision," she said, sounding strangely stern but without malice.

"We do," Cyrus said, nodding once. "And we will be ready."

"Then we have no further business here," the woman answered, then stood. After a beat of hesitation, her companions stood as well. "Farewell."

Cyrus only nodded, and the council watched them go. Adrissu glared at the woman's back as they departed, wishing he could rip her limb from limb, then devour every one of these wretched Federation puppets who had come to steal his city away. But he was above his instincts, he told himself; and ultimately, he could only behave as any citizen of Polimnos would. To do more would risk his discovery, and that would upend whatever semblance of normalcy the city was still clinging to.

He thought of his conversation with Ruan, years ago now: he had told him that just because he was a dragon, it didn't make him evil. The thought of Ruan was too painful to hold, but he could cling to that conviction. He was not evil. He would not act like he was.

The council dispersed after that. Maya, Yue, Abe, and Cyrus walked slowly in a cluster toward the mercenary's guild—he was sure that now the mercenaries, and whatever forces they had gathered in the short time allotted to them, would begin to move with even more haste. From the corner of his eye he could see Benil Branwood nervously watch him walk away; the human looked like he wanted to say something to Adrissu, but seemingly deciding against it, he too turned away.

When Adrissu arrived back in his tower, he went straight to his study and picked up his book where he had left off. Vesper nudged her way onto his lap, coiling into a tight ball and looking up at him with her tiny black eyes. He could feel her concern and knew that she was worried about his constant tension of late. But he could not comfort her—he could not comfort himself—so he absently stroked the top of her head and said nothing.

He had been reading for a few hours when he heard the heavy wooden door downstairs swing open, and he knew it was Ruan. No one else would simply invite themselves into the tower the way that Ruan did—it was, after all, a second home to him now. Adrissu had never asked him to knock. The thought made his throat feel tight.

Ruan did not call out to him, but Adrissu could hear the dull thud of his footsteps coming up the stairs, then stop at the landing.

"You've been avoiding me," the human's voice came from behind him, tired and flat. Adrissu shook his head without turning to look. "You have," Ruan pressed, his footsteps starting up again until the weight of his warm, rough hand pressed on Adrissu's shoulder. "Please don't be like this, not now."

"I—" Adrissu started, bristling with irritation, but the feeling faded as quickly as it came. "I am not trying to avoid you."

Ruan sighed. Adrissu finally managed to muster enough strength to turn and look at him. The human had trimmed his beard, so it was tidy and short now; and although his hair was as messy as it ever was, he had at least pushed it back out of his eyes. His expression was hard to read: his eyes were tense, and his lips pursed.

"We... We march in three days," he said. Adrissu shuddered. The cold feeling had not left his limbs once, not since the council had come to its decision, but now it pulsed painfully through his chest again like a shockwave. "And I... I just want to spend as much time with you as I can."

The words should have brought him comfort, should have made him happy, should have filled his heart with affection. Now, it was only a cruel reminder that *Ruan was going to die*, and Adrissu could not stop himself from wincing. His eyes fell to Ruan's feet.

"Of course," he said simply; but from the way Ruan huffed, he knew that his response was not at all what the human wanted.

"Why are you being so cold?" he growled, stepping closer. "You haven't been this distant to me in years, Adrissu. I thought we had put this behind us."

"I—" he started, shaking his head. He had not meant to behave any differently, but he could not put into words how his chest felt like caving in every time he thought of Ruan—and of the bleak future that awaited them. Looking at him was like jabbing a tender bruise, sending fresh pain rattling through Adrissu. "I am not trying to be cold, Ruan. I am... afraid."

"You think I'm not afraid?!" Ruan exclaimed. "Look at me!" Adrissu's eyes flickered up to the human's face, where his eyes were puffy and red-rimmed. "You think I'm not frightened? Of course I am. The last thing I need is to lose you now, too. I came here because I love you. Because you comfort me. But if you're going to act as if I don't exist, as if you don't care about me, I'd rather be alone."

"I don't want that," Adrissu snapped, shaking his head. "You know I don't want that."

"I—" Ruan started, then pressed a hand to his eyes. He was crying. Adrissu's heart squeezed again, and this time he roused himself up out of his chair and gathered the human into his arms. This felt *right*, like where they belonged, and he tried not to think about how it might be one of the last times he held Ruan. "Adrissu, I—of course I'm scared. I don't want to die."

Adrissu exhaled slowly. He wanted to scream that Ruan didn't have to die: that the ritual would mean that the most important part of him would live on and come back to Adrissu, no matter what happened on the battlefield that he was so stupidly determined to fight upon—but he bit his tongue.

"Adrissu," he said softly, pressing his face harder into Adrissu's shoulder. "I—I want you to ask me."

He thought his heart might stop. He couldn't have heard Ruan right. With shaking hands he grabbed Ruan's shoulders and pulled him away, enough to look him in the face and search his eyes. Ruan's face was flushed, brows drawn, but there was an expectant look in his eyes. Years of begging, and this is what finally turned his heart? Could he have really heard him right?

"Ruan," he said slowly, slow enough that Ruan could cut him off, in case he had heard the human incorrectly. "Please. You don't have to die. You don't have to be frightened. Will you let me bind our souls? Will you come back to me?"

Ruan was perfectly still in his hands, long enough that doubt started to creep up his ribs again. But then his eyelashes fluttered—he was blinking hard against tears—and the human nodded once, so quickly that it was more a jerk of his neck than anything else. Adrissu could barely breathe.

"You're sure?" he asked breathlessly, and Ruan nodded silently again, eyes squeezing shut so hard that a stream of tears spilled from each closed lid.

"I thought—" he rasped, then shook his head. "I don't know. I thought I would be braver in the face of all this."

"You are brave," Adrissu said, squeezing his arms. "Ruan. You *are* brave. This has nothing to do with being brave or not. There is only us. Is this what you want? To know you'll come back, you'll find me again, no matter what happens?"

"Yes," Ruan sobbed, finally breaking. "Of course I fucking want that. I don't care if that means we're playing gods, or cheating death, or anything. I just want to be with you forever."

Adrissu grabbed Ruan by his face and smashed their lips together, kissing him frantically. Every inch of him was crying out in relief. Ruan was intrinsically a part of him now, soaked deep into his skin, his blood, his heart. The taste of him on his lips was as familiar as air, as water, and he would never have to leave it behind.

"I love you," he breathed, finally pulling away. Ruan gasped for breath against him, nodding his head silently. "Let's do it right now—the ritual. I can do it right now." He said nothing about the part of him that was afraid Ruan would change his mind again if he waited too long.

Ruan licked his lips, his nerves still obvious, but he nodded. "Okay. Yes. What do I need to do?"

"Wait here," Adrissu said, then flitted to the other side of his study. The components of the ritual were all stored together in a wooden crate—the herbs, the wood, the beryl bowl, a silver knife to draw blood. Atop it sat the scroll that described the ritual and its runes, and in an ivory case next to that, the red paint with which to mark them. With shaking hands, Adrissu gathered everything in a canvas bag and handed it to Ruan.

"Hold this," he said, placing the bag in one of Ruan's hands and clasping the other with his own, if only to still the trembling of his fingers. "Come with me. We'll have to do this down below. It takes up too much room."

"Okay," Ruan breathed. He slung the bag over one shoulder, waiting as Adrissu pulled the hatch open. When Adrissu stood, he wrapped his arms around Ruan's waist again. The human held him tightly, eyes full of trust.

Adrissu pressed a kiss to his forehead, then plunged them both into darkness. Ruan's breathing quickened as they fell—it always did—but his hold around Adrissu never wavered, even as his body transformed around him. With his claws he held Ruan tightly against him as he glided down through the tunnel, out of the empty landing room, and into the room he had intended to use as his nest so long ago. It was so rare that he slept down here anymore.

"Set those down," he rumbled, finally releasing Ruan from his grasp. "And we can begin."

Chapter Thirteen

Within an hour, Adrissu had the ritual set up. He had shrunk back down to his elven form for most of it—though the circle and its runes were expansive, it would be difficult to make such delicate paint strokes with claws. Ruan observed him silently, handing him components as he asked for them. Curiosity was obvious on his face, but he did not ask any questions, only watched Adrissu work.

Adrissu read the instructions as he worked, and again when he was finished, until he was certain everything was done correctly. First was the circle, then the binding runes on opposite ends of the circle. Each of the rune's intersections had to be marked and connected to its mirror with a line, and where all those lines intersected, there the fire was to be lit. He had burned the Aefrayan willow with his own fiery breath, setting it carefully in the center, then he began to grind the plants and herbs in the dwarven beryl bowl until it became a fine powdery mixture.

All that remained was to fill the rest of the bowl with their blood.

"Come here, Ruan," he said, breaking the silence that hung between them for the better part of the past hour. Ruan gave a slight start, stepping closer and eyeing the silver dagger in Adrissu's hand with some trepidation. "The ritual requires blood from each of us, enough to fill the bowl."

"Makes sense," Ruan said with a dry laugh that didn't quite reach his eyes. He held his hand out willingly to Adrissu. Grasping the human's hand, he ran his fingers along Ruan's prominent knuckles, then flipped it over to press the point of the dagger into the thickest part of his palm. Ruan hissed as the sharp blade pierced his skin, blood welling instantly along the point. Adrissu made a cut where he'd broken the skin, long enough for the blood to flow.

"Sorry," he murmured, and Ruan shook his head, watching the steady drip of blood from his hand dampen the herbs in the bowl. "I'll heal it once we have enough."

"I know," Ruan said softly. Without bothering to clean the blade, Adrissu extended his own hand and slashed through the thick part of his palm as well, letting his blood drip down into the bowl so it mingled with Ruan's. It took a moment, but between the two of them, the bowl slowly filled to the brim with dark red liquid.

"There," Adrissu said, setting the bowl down. "Let me see your hand." Ruan offered it again, and with a soft murmur Adrissu pressed his fingers to the small wound, and it began to knit together quickly. A streak of blood remained on Ruan's hand, but the cut was gone.

"Thank you," Ruan murmured, managing a small smile. Adrissu nodded, healing his own hand, before swirling the bowl to mix the components and setting it in the fire.

"Go sit in the center of the rune on that side," he said, gesturing. "I'll sit in this one, and we'll begin. It will take a bit of time, until all the liquid boils away."

Ruan frowned, but obeyed. When they were both settled, Adrissu looked down at the scroll one last time, then channeled his magic into the flame until it roared up and engulfed the bowl. As a reddish steam began to rise, he started the words of the ritual. What would have been a low, rumbling drone in the language of dragons was only a reedy chant in this smaller form, but somehow it wouldn't have felt right to finish the ritual in his true form. Ruan always thought of him as Adrissu; it was

Adrissu he was binding his soul to, not Zamnes, even if they were the same.

He repeated the words over and over, as red steam began to fill the chamber. Across from him, he could see Ruan's nose wrinkling as the strange smell filled the room—partly the metallic tang of blood, partly the pungent odor of burning herbs.

He was not sure how long he had been channeling the words when he felt a sense of... *something* in the air around them changing. The smell was headier, less unpleasant somehow, and the sensation of magic around them prickled at his skin like a sudden dry heat. This must have been it. He ignored the way his heartbeat quickened, focusing on the words of the ritual and repeating them correctly. He'd said them so many times now that they barely sounded like words anymore, but he knew it wouldn't be over until the bowl was empty, and the red smoke dissipated.

Ruan was silent through it all, watching him from across the circle, his eyes never wavering. Was he regretting his decision, wishing he hadn't given in? Was he afraid, doubting it would actually work? Adrissu couldn't linger on his thoughts, but they still crossed his mind, as he chanted and fed his magic to the flame.

It might have been hours before the tingle of magic against his skin began to fade, the red tint to the room fading with it. That was it. Adrissu fell silent, his throat raw and his mouth dry, and slowly eased back on the flame until he could see into the bowl. It was now empty, its contents burned away.

The ritual was complete.

"That's it," he said, his voice rasping with overuse.

"That's it?" Ruan repeated, looking at him with wide eyes. Adrissu nodded. He had expected to feel incandescent relief when it was over, but it seemed so anticlimactic that part of him still held onto the fear that it hadn't worked, and Ruan might soon be lost to him forever.

"That was... easy," Ruan continued, stifling a laugh. "I mean, I'm sure it was much less easy for you. But I'm... surprised, I guess."

"Gathering everything for it was the hard part," Adrissu murmured, stumbling to his feet. Ruan frowned, looking concerned, but he only shook his head. "But loving you is easy. There is no price I would not have paid."

Ruan smiled at him—the first free, open smile that he'd seen on the human's face in days, and Adrissu felt like his heart might burst out of his chest.

"Is the ritual supposed to make me feel randy?" Ruan asked, shifting slightly where he remained sitting; and Adrissu laughed, all the tension in his body starting to ease away.

"I don't know," he said, stepping toward Ruan, only to drop back down onto the stone floor with him when they were close enough to touch. "But we can do something about that, I'm sure."

"Please," Ruan agreed, and Adrissu pushed him onto his back, straddling him.

Their clothes were quickly pulled off and discarded in a pile. Ruan's mouth was open and willing against his own, and Adrissu lost himself in the heat of his mate, knowing that part of Ruan was truly with him forever now. It might not be this body, this face, but Ruan would always return to him.

There was nothing suitable to use as lubricant down in his lair, so Adrissu pushed his fingers into Ruan's mouth. The human groaned and sucked, and Adrissu could feel his mouth filling with saliva, slicking his fingers.

He pushed Ruan's legs up until his knees were at his shoulders, his hard cock falling against his stomach. Adrissu pulled his fingers from Ruan's mouth with a wet pop, reaching down to find his entrance and slowly pushing a slick finger inside. Ruan made a soft noise in the back of his throat, the muscle tensing slightly before relaxing around the familiar intrusion.

With a breathy sigh, Adrissu leaned back to watch himself open Ruan. The sight was too tempting, and after only a moment, he bent further to lick a hot stripe from where his fingers were working his hole open, up the seam of his balls, to mouth along the base of his cock.

"Adrissu," Ruan panted from above him, the human's fingers threading through Adrissu's hair. "Don't make me wait."

"Greedy boy," Adrissu murmured against his skin, licking up the length of his cock a few times just to hear him moan. "You know I won't make you wait."

"Please," Ruan grunted, shifting his hips. Adrissu pulled away, only to grab him from the back of his neck and pull him up.

"Suck," he said, pushing Ruan's head toward his cock, and with a soft groan the human eagerly complied. Adrissu hissed, Ruan's mouth hot and wet around him as he sucked hard, hollowing his cheeks. He closed his eyes, reveling in the pleasure of it until his cock was wet with Ruan's saliva, then he pulled back. Ruan followed, pouting at first, but then smiled eagerly despite himself. "Ready for me?"

"Yes," Ruan replied, nodding as he pulled his knees back up to his chest.

"I love you," Adrissu said, running his clean fingers through Ruan's hair. The human made a soft noise of pleasure, eyes closing as he leaned into the touch. "I would go and raze the armies of Autreth myself if you asked it of me. I would do anything for you."

Ruan laughed. "Right now I only want you to fuck me."

Adrissu grinned. "Get on top of me. I want to watch you."

Ruan flushed, but nodded and clambered up onto his knees as Adrissu laid back. He reached back, grasping Adrissu's slick cock, and lined it up with himself. Their eyes met, and Ruan held his gaze as he pressed the head of Adrissu's cock against his opening and sank down onto it. Adrissu's head fell back and he moaned as Ruan's tight heat enveloped him, squeezing him tight. It was as if Ruan's insides had molded perfectly to the shape of him, opening up easily now. The slight lubrication made Ruan feel tighter around him, with more friction than usual against his cock as they moved against each other. It made pleasure burn like fire up his spine, consuming him utterly.

But he had put Ruan in this position to watch him, so he propped himself up on his elbows and forced himself to keep his eyes open. The human's body was flushed, his cock swollen and steadily dripping precome as it bounced up and down with each of Ruan's movements. Every muscle in his body seemed prominent and taught, his broad thighs flexing as he rode Adrissu's cock.

"I love you," Ruan groaned, eyelids fluttering. "You feel so fucking good inside me."

"You're mine," Adrissu growled, reaching with one hand to grip hard at Ruan's cock, making him gasp. "You're mine forever now."

"Yes," Ruan agreed, panting and nodding his head. "Forever. Gods, you're going to make me come already."

"My good boy," Adrissu groaned, and Ruan whimpered above him, eyelids fluttering again. "You've given me everything I've ever wanted. You've been so good. Fuck, you feel incredible."

"Oh, fuck—tell me again," Ruan gasped. Adrissu tightened his hold around his cock, stroking him roughly.

"Good boy," Adrissu repeated. "I want to watch you come. Be good and come for me."

"Yes," he whimpered, his hips stuttering. "Nngh—I'm coming—I'm coming!" His cock pulsed in Adrissu's hand, but his hips stilled—with his free hand, Adrissu grabbed his hip and thrust up into him, hard and fast enough to make Ruan shout as he came. He tightened around Adrissu's cock, painting his stomach with thick stripes of his come—his mouth open and eyes squeezed shut in euphoria as Adrissu fucked him.

He was beautiful, and he was utterly Adrissu's, body and soul now. The thought sent his orgasm thundering through him, searing white-hot through his veins, blurring his vision. He felt himself shooting his release into Ruan, felt him twitching and quivering around him to milk out everything he had.

Everything he had was Ruan's, and Ruan was everything. For what felt like the first time in weeks, the dragon instincts inside him were calm in the assurance that his mate was his and would remain his in this life, and the next, and every life that might come after that.

When Adrissu came back to his senses, he was still propped up on his elbows. Ruan had leaned into him, their chests sticky with sweat and come where they pressed together, and his face was buried in the crook of his shoulder. The stone floor dug painfully into the skin of his arms, but he had no desire to get up. Instead, he pushed himself into a sitting position with one arm, curling the other around Ruan's waist as he pressed soft kisses to his shoulder. The human barely stirred as Adrissu shifted him.

"Come back to me," he whispered against Ruan's skin. "Ruan, come back."

Ruan stirred slightly, pressing himself closer to Adrissu, as if he could somehow merge their skin together by sheer force of will.

"I love you," he mumbled against Adrissu's neck. His voice was muffled and tremulous, almost on the verge of tears. "I... I don't know what changed. With the ritual. I'm sorry. I'm sorry it took me so long."

Adrissu shook his head. "You have nothing to apologize for. It was always your decision."

"Do you think I'll remember? When I... come back?" he asked in a small voice. Adrissu considered it, breathing deeply.

"I don't know," he said. Part of him thought that the uncertainty should worry him, but the scent of Ruan filled his nostrils: the smell of sweat and sex and musk and the particular smell that was just *Ruan*, herbal and smoky, comforting to his very core. "Maybe. But if not, I'll be sure to remind you."

Ruan chuckled at that, shaking his head. "You make it sound simple."

Adrissu grinned wickedly and pressed another kiss to Ruan's shoulder, biting down this time, then soothing the mark with his tongue.

"I have a solution," he murmured against the salt of his skin. "I'll fuck you so hard every day until you leave that it will be impossible to forget."

Ruan laughed again. "I don't know if that will work, but I won't tell you no, either."

"I love you," Adrissu said, pulling back enough to look Ruan in the face. The human's grin faltered, eyes softening. "If you remember anything, remember that. I love you."

Ruan nodded. Adrissu stared into his eyes in silence, memorizing the familiar golden brown—every part of him radiated warmth, like he carried a tiny sun within him that made him glow with its rays.

"Well, who knows?" Ruan finally broke the silence with a nervous chuckle. "I might come back from this in one piece, and then we've had all this fuss for nothing. Stranger things have happened."

In his gut, Adrissu knew it was impossible. But still he smiled and smoothed back Ruan's hair with one hand.

"Perhaps," he murmured, and pressed a kiss to his forehead. "Perhaps."

Three days later, he watched Ruan leave Polimnos on horseback with the full force of Polimnos' mercenary guild.

The shield upon Ruan's back that Adrissu had gifted him so long ago gleamed in the sun, and Adrissu watched its flickering light until his eyes watered, until the shape of Ruan was lost to the indistinct crowd of human bodies moving steadily westward. The reassurance of their soul bond was now only the barest comfort: a single ember amidst the icy cold fear that spread further through his chest with every beat of his heart.

Ruan did not return.

It took three weeks for any news to reach them.

Autreth had vanquished the forces of Polimnos, decimating almost their entire army before the last remaining warriors surrendered. Those last few were now being escorted back to the city with the invading force, who would officially proclaim Polimnos as part of the Federation of Autreth.

The courier cried the message all through town, shouting it over and over in the town square amidst the weeping of those who had remained behind. Adrissu listened from Saltspire Tower—his mind blank, his limbs cold and heavy. He did not realize Vesper had curled into his lap until she was slithering across his neck and draping herself over him, the only way she could embrace him.

She missed Ruan. She feared for his life. He could only shake his head and run his fingers along her cool skin.

The Federation forces were five days behind the courier who had come with their proclamation. When they arrived, there were a hundred of them, most on horseback, along with twenty-one survivors from Polimnos who followed on foot in a closely-guarded cluster. Adrissu craned his neck from where he stood in front of the council hall with the remaining councilors, waiting for the representatives to approach. He did not see Maya Graylight. He did not see Yue Lang.

He did not see Ruan. The cold numbness that had permeated his chest and his limbs sunk down through his veins into his bones. His mate was gone. He knew it as surely as he knew that he could breathe fire.

"People of Polimnos!" a man on horseback shouted, carrying a tall flag of the Federation with him. He was dressed as a knight, but he was not one of the original five who had come to Polimnos. It was good that Adrissu did not recognize him; if he had, he might not have been able to stop himself from killing the man then and there. "You are now all citizens of the Federation of Autreth! You will be treated with the dignity such citizenship demands. We came here not to destroy your city, but to lift it in unity, so that Autreth may never be conquered again. As long as you cooperate, no harm shall come to you."

Adrissu thought that he should be enraged, expecting the bitter sting of bile in the back of his throat as the knight's words all but denied how hundreds of citizens of Polimnos had just fought and died at the sword of Autreth. But nothing pierced through his numbness, like a sheet of ice enclosed around his body. Nothing mattered if Ruan was gone.

The knight rode up to him and the remaining councilors: Cyrus, Shefali, Abe, Benil, and Ellisa.

"You are the council of Polimnos," he said, no longer shouting.

"We are what's left of the Polimnos council, yes," Cyrus replied. His voice was hoarse as he spoke. Adrissu felt the knight's gaze linger on him as he looked them over: the only elf on the council, the only elf in Polimnos.

"Let us discuss the terms of Polimnos' annexation, then," the knight said brusquely. He plunged the long pole of his flag into the dirt and dismounted from his horse. A page came up alongside him, taking his helmet in one hand and his horse's reins in the other, and the group behind the knight began to dismount from their horses as well.

Adrissu turned to follow, as they began to file into the meeting hall, when a hiss of a voice called out to him.

"Adrissu!"

He turned back, frowning, to see one of the now released survivors hurrying toward him. It took a moment for him to recognize Ederick, the head instructor of the mercenary's guild —his armor was dirty and bloodied, as if he had not washed since they'd first set out, and both his eyes were bruised and swollen, making his face puffy.

"Ederick," he replied evenly, pausing.

"Don't let them see this, and don't tell anyone I gave it to you," Ederick said, his voice low as he loosened the bag strapped to his back. The makeshift rucksack looked as if it had once been a large bag of grain crudely affixed with rope, and was stuffed full as if all of Ederick's worldly belongings were within. With some effort, Ederick pulled out a large item: a disk shape wrapped in dirty cloth. "This belongs to you."

Adrissu took it and pulled back the cloth enough to see. The gleaming metal of Ruan's shield shone up at him, revealing one eye of the inlaid dragon. Adrissu choked, covering it back quickly and biting his lip to keep from crying out. His eyes suddenly burned, his vision blurring.

"I knew as soon as any of these bastards from Gennemont saw that, they'd try and take it for themselves," Ederick muttered, shaking his head. "But if anyone deserves it, it's you. I... I'm sorry. It was all I could find of him."

A sob escaped Adrissu, and he clapped a hand to his mouth to stifle his cry, as the other hand clutched the shield to his chest, as if he could press it through his ribs and into his heart. Distantly, he was aware of Ederick's rough hand on his shoulder, his voice low and murmuring something he couldn't understand.

His shield. The shield he had commissioned for Ruan, the one he had enchanted himself, so that it might keep him safe— it was all that was left of him. The only testament to the last decade of his life was here in his arms.

"Thank you," he managed to choke out, when he felt like he could breathe again, wiping his face with one hand. It was, he thought, the first time that he had thanked a human other than Ruan and sincerely meant it. "I can never repay you for this. Thank you."

Ederick shook his head, his own expression pained. "He was a good man. He was better for having known you. I know how much you cared for him. I'm sorry I couldn't do more."

"Thank you," Adrissu repeated. He couldn't formulate anything else. "Thank you."

"You'd better get in there before they come looking for you," Ederick said gruffly, gesturing toward the hall. Adrissu nodded, and with one last murmur of thanks, he turned and entered the meeting hall. Some of the humans looked at him curiously, their eyes flickering between his tear-streaked face and the cloth-covered shape he carried; but he ignored them, and none of them said anything.

They might have announced that Polimnos was to be set aflame, or dropped to the bottom of the ocean, and he would not have cared. Ruan's shield was in his arms, pressed to his heart. Ruan was gone, but his soul lived on. With this, at least, Adrissu thought he could bear the wait until they found each other again.

Book Two
Volkmar

Chapter Fourteen

In spite of everything, Adrissu could acknowledge that in hindsight, becoming part of the Federation of Autreth was a net positive for Polimnos.

The Autrethian officials, who facilitated the change in power, explained how each territory within Autreth had its own Lord Representative, who would be part of the Lord's Council to meet annually in Gennemont. There were federal regulations that the Lord Representative would enforce, but each territory was welcome to rule however it saw fit, so long as the Lord Representative remained the primary power. It was a strange way to rule, Adrissu thought; but all things considered, it was a relief to know that he would not be under the scrutiny of some foreign tyrant.

The title of Lord Representative was offered to him first, which took him by surprise. Each of the councilors glanced between him and the Autrethian officials, equally surprised, but Adrissu was quick to gather his wits and answer.

"I am flattered by your confidence in me, Sir Etienne," he replied evenly—the knight from Gennemont, Etienne, had taken charge of their meetings. Adrissu was not actually flattered by the irritating human's apparent faith in him, but he could not say as much. Having a Lord Representative that simply did not age or die would not be beneficial for his desire to continue his life in Polimnos in peace, so he could not accept.

"However, I must decline your offer. Much as I have enjoyed my time on the Polimnos council, I confess that I have little interest in a more dedicated civic position. I am a researcher and a mage, not a politician. Or a lord."

"Hm," Sir Etienne hummed in response, looking Adrissu over. His expression was not quite surprised—more like his understanding of Adrissu had been challenged and changed. He was silent for a moment, so Adrissu cleared his throat and offered,

"Instead, I would recommend considering Councilor Cyrus for the position." A slight murmur rose in the councilors next to him, so he continued without looking at them, "While we did not technically have a leader, and all councilors had the same standing, as the head councilor, Cyrus was the facilitator of our group. If anyone is prepared to help Polimnos into this... new era, it would be him."

"I see," Sir Etienne replied, rubbing his chin. His eyes finally left Adrissu, looking over the other councilors. Adrissu did not need to look to feel the gaze of Cyrus on him—and probably Benil Branwood as well, somehow offended that Adrissu did not recommend *him*, he was sure. "Councilor Cyrus was my second choice already, from what I was able to glean about the council in our short time together. Councilors, would you agree with this recommendation?"

For a moment, the councilors were silent. Then, Ellisa Tanner offered, "Yes, absolutely." After another beat, the others murmured their agreement. Adrissu glanced over to see Cyrus, his mouth a tight line, but his eyes soft and full of emotion. He had voted to fight against this very exchange, but somehow Adrissu did not think he would refuse.

"In that case, if you accept, Cyrus," Sir Etienne continued, gesturing toward the older human, and after a nervous huff of breath, Cyrus nodded.

Cyrus was officially declared the Lord Representative of Polimnos within the week. He was allowed two trusted advisors who might act in his stead, if he were somehow prevented from performing his duties, and who would select the next Lord Representative when he stepped down or passed away. He selected Ellisa Tanner, and after a beat of consideration, Adrissu. That, at least, he accepted.

A handful of the representatives from Autreth left Polimnos after that week. Another wave departed after a month, and the last—Sir Etienne among them—remained three months before leaving for their homes. Two remained behind to reside permanently in Polimnos: one was a human merchant, and the other an elven woman, who came to fill one of the many vacancies left in the mercenary's guild. It was the first time another elf would permanently live in Polimnos; but luckily the woman seemed just as guarded toward him as he was of her, and he never even learned her name.

He missed Ruan desperately. But time went on, and his life found a new routine. Every day he wondered if Ruan's spirit had already been reborn, if he was already in the world with him, and where he might be, *who* he might be now. At first the thought paralyzed him when it struck, filling him with a longing so desperate that he could hardly breathe. But eventually the thought became familiar, almost comforting, less of a longing and more of an eager anticipation.

Once, his thoughts took a particularly dark turn, and he wondered if the ritual could even work on a human soul, and if Ruan would ever actually return to him. The thought that it all might have truly been in vain, and he would be alone for the rest of time, kept him trapped in his bed for a day. But in the end, he knew that he'd felt the magic take hold. He could only trust that he did it right—and he pored over the scroll and his memory of the ritual over and over again, trying to pinpoint any misstep, never finding any—and wait for Ruan to find him.

It was easier to wait when he had things to do, so he kept himself busy. With the mercenary's guild clinging to life by a thread, he donated a sizable sum from his hoard, knowing Ruan would hate to see the guild that had become a fixture of Polimnos dissolved in such a way. Only the youngest recruits still in training remained, and only four instructors between them. Ederick, the most senior staff left alive, became the guildmaster by default. Adrissu could only regard him fondly, and he helped out as much as he could, often spending afternoons at the guild with Ederick to go over budgets, payouts, and contracts. It took a long time for the guild to stabilize enough that it no longer felt as if one failed job might bankrupt the entire organization, but Adrissu was thankful for the distraction.

He went back to his own studies as well: topics that he had long since put aside to remain at Ruan's side. He traveled often to neighboring cities with other mages and scholars, and even occasionally to Gennemont, taking advantage of the new alliance between the cities to visit the College of the Arcane: the foremost institute of the study of magic in the known world. Their libraries were open to him as a citizen of the Federation, so he got in the habit of visiting monthly to read as much as he could.

It was during one of these visits that a new idea first struck him: what if, instead of waiting miserably for Ruan's soul to return in a mortal body, he could make Ruan immortal like him?

The existence of undeath made him think that such a thing was possible. If a body could be animated without the presence of a soul to continue living, then the opposite could also be true, at least theoretically. Necromancy was a topic of which he knew little, and while not outright forbidden, it was certainly taboo. The College of the Arcane's library held almost nothing on the topic that did not simply condemn it and move on. One of the professors there had a passing interest in necromancy and would discuss Adrissu's idea with him—a hypothetical, of course—but nothing concrete ever came of it. Adrissu filed the thought away: there was *something* there, he was sure, but Gennemont was not the place to discover it.

Several years passed this way. His advisor position to Cyrus as the Lord Representative was more a formality than anything, so his presence on the new council was rarely missed. Between his studies throughout Autreth and his increased involvement with the mercenary's guild, he kept busy enough not to dwell on Ruan, and with time the pain of it became the dull ache of an old wound.

Nearly five years after Polimnos became part of Autreth—as it was generally known, since the entirety of the continent of Autreth was now part of the Federation—Cyrus passed away in his sleep, and a new Lord Representative was chosen. Had it happened even a year prior, Adrissu would have expected Benil Branwood to vye for the position, ambitious as he was. But his daughter had finally married, he now had a grandchild, and the Branwood mines were prosperous and productive. Whatever goals he seemed to once have for civic life or political power had been put aside, at least so it appeared. Adrissu hadn't had a one-on-one conversation with him in several years.

He and Ellisa discussed the matter—she too was now advanced in age and was unlikely to survive Cyrus by far—and decided to appoint Kira Lang as the next Lord Representative, which she accepted. Kira was the younger cousin of the late Yue Lang, whom Adrissu had met a handful of times when she'd been apprenticed to the forge. She had taken over when Yue died, and under her care, it was more prosperous than ever. Polimnos was a place of trade and commerce, so it only made sense for their Lord Representative to be one of the most successful merchants in the city.

Kira was brusque, but intelligent, and Adrissu got along well with her. Like Cyrus, she obeyed the law of the Federation only as required, and otherwise tried to keep Polimnos as independent as possible, promoting trade and encouraging a diversity of business beyond the primary export of stone.

"I have an idea for you," she told him once, nearly ten years on, when he had returned from one of his regular trips to the College of the Arcane.

"I'm listening," he replied, brows raised in curiosity.

"You should set up your own school of magic," she said, blunt as ever. "It would be good for the town."

Adrissu laughed, shaking his head, but Kira frowned at him.

"I'm serious," she continued, folding her arms across her chest. "We already have the mercenary's guild to train up fighters. Why not a school for mages and scholars as well? Polimnos could become a place of learning for everyone."

"You *are* serious," Adrissu repeated, still smirking. "Well... I'll give it some thought, I suppose. I don't think I'm cut out for teaching, frankly."

"Then don't teach," she said. "Be the headmaster. Design a curriculum. You're good at dealing with people, Adrissu. I think running a school of magic would play right to your strengths."

"A headmaster," he mused, leaning back. "I think I do like the sound of it."

He considered it for a few days, then returned to Kira and agreed to at least give it a test run. With her endorsement, it was relatively simple to gather the funds for a new building, where the school would be housed. Adrissu shifted much of his time from working on his own studies to creating lessons and designing a curriculum that started with the very basics of arcane knowledge, which eventually grew to a three-branched path that focused on mastery of the elements, alchemy, and enchantment.

To his surprise, his contacts at the College in Gennemont were happy to help him design and refine his curriculum; and two students, who were set to graduate the following year, took a contract to be the first instructors in Polimnos. Everything fell into place far more easily than he'd expected.

But when signups began, interest was meager, and the only students to enroll were the children of merchants in Polimnos who were well-off enough to afford the risk that the school might not survive long enough to confer a degree. While a small student body was not necessarily a bad thing, Adrissu hated the idea of such a weak start.

After some discussions with Ederick, still the head of the mercenary's guild, a collaboration was formed. Three guild recruits who showed some aptitude and interest in the arcane would receive a scholarship to attend the academy, entirely at Adrissu's expense. At first he thought of naming the scholarship in memory of Ruan, but it left a bitter taste in his mouth. After all, Ruan was not dead. Adrissu was only waiting for him to return. He called it the Headmaster's Scholarship, instead, and selected the three recruits.

It took nearly a year for all the moving parts to come together; but in the end, the Polimnos Academy of Magic opened its doors to ten students with two instructors to guide them. Spending his mornings in the brand-new, four-room building was far more pleasant than Adrissu first anticipated; and many of his afternoons he ended up either studying in his office, or occasionally stepping in to teach a lesson or two in the classroom.

"Aren't you glad you listened to me?" Kira laughed, a week after the school's grand opening, as they shared a bottle of wine in his new office.

"Very," he admitted. He *was* glad Kira had convinced him. It was not something that he would have thought to do on his own; but now that the Academy was open and running, he wondered why he had not considered such a venture sooner. If nothing else, it would make the procurement of magical texts and tomes much easier. Their library was tiny now, but he already had plans on how to expand.

The first year required his near-constant attention, so his studies largely went to the wayside, and anything that he could not accomplish from Polimnos was abandoned entirely. The second year, they lost three students, but gained a new one, for a total of eight. With the curriculum already in place, and the teachers less wet behind the ears, Adrissu allowed himself to step back a small amount. He took one trip to the college in Gennemont in the autumn, partly to gather texts for the academy, and partly to resume his own studies. He had not forgotten his idea about mortal souls becoming immortal.

During his two-week stay at the college, the most he could find was a study that proposed the idea of soul containment as a means of stasis; but the tome made no mention of putting a contained soul into anything other than its original body. He made a note of the author—an elf called Caemar Illuren, studying in service of the royal library of Aefraya—and considered perhaps taking a trip to Aefraya sometime in the future.

Adrissu wrote a letter to Caemar, introducing himself as a fellow scholar, expressing his interest in the study and Caemar's findings, and requesting permission to visit him at a later date. He passed it to a courier, paid the exorbitant fee to have such a letter delivered halfway across the known world, and tried not to think of it thereafter. Long-lived as they were, elves were notoriously slow to act on anything, and he doubted that he would hear back from the scholar within a year, if not a decade. Luckily, the one thing that he had in abundance was time.

He put his head down and focused on the Academy. If he dwelled too long on Ruan, the thought of waiting for him to return became unbearable, so he tried to keep busy as much as he could.

Polimnos grew significantly around him. What had once made up the whole of the town was now only a central inner city, which was surrounded by new buildings: homes and businesses alike. His tower was still far enough out of town that he was largely isolated; but for the first time, he could see his nearest neighbors from his door. Luckily, Kira knew how much he valued his privacy, and when any building proposals that edged too close to Saltspire Tower came before the council, she kindly suggested an alternate location closer to the city center. So far, no construction had intruded too close, and he intended to keep it that way.

He used to know every resident of Polimnos by name. Now he recognized most on sight, but knew the names of fewer and fewer as the city's population grew every year.

It had been twenty years since Ruan's death, and the population had grown so much that he began to wonder exactly how close "nearby" was for the purposes of the ritual. So once a week, Adrissu started going for long walks around the city. Sometimes he would be accompanied by instructors, or other city officials, or occasionally students who wanted to discuss some topic or another, but most often he would walk the streets alone. His eyes would flicker across the face of every man that he saw who looked to be about twenty years old, whether they were workers performing manual labor, artisans crafting their wares, or merchants calling out for his attention.

While some seemed to recognize him, more and more as his walks continued, none gave him that sense of the world stopping around them—he could still remember it so clearly, the first time that he'd seen Ruan over thirty years ago.

Whenever he would return to his tower, Vesper would eagerly come to peek down at him from where she typically lay on the upper floor, radiating a bit of disappointment when she saw he was alone. She had continued to grow and was now too heavy to go out with him—plus, loose, flowy robes with large sleeves had fallen out of fashion, and the tighter robes that he wore now had no room for her to nestle in the sleeve.

"Maybe next time," he would sigh, patting her head and trying not to think about it until his next walk.

This too became a part of his life's routine. He oversaw lessons at the Academy, met with Kira and other officials, and went for long walks around the city. Time passed quickly and easily when every week had the same structure as the last.

Adrissu had started to fear that maybe the man he was looking for was not in Polimnos after all, when one day his feet carried him through the back streets of the town center, and the world came to a halt around him.

Chapter Fifteen

As much as he had tried to keep an open mind about who Ruan would be when they found each other again, Adrissu still could not stop the hot prickle of shock in his chest when he found him standing just outside the doorway of a brothel.

He had been walking as usual, eyes scanning the crowd, when that feeling of *knowing* caught him by surprise, so much so that he didn't notice the brothel until he was already standing at the front. The human man was unlike Ruan in appearance in almost every way—petite where Ruan had been tall, slender where Ruan had been bulky with muscle, and fair where Ruan had been tan.

He was standing idly in front of the brothel's entryway, watching people walk by. It was clear that he worked there and was enticing customers with sultry looks and winks; his tight pants and lack of shirt only reinforced the message. A delicate golden chain looped around his neck, draping down to wrap around his waist and encircle his narrow wrists. It seemed to be ornamentation, but Adrissu had the unsettling thought that it was perhaps some mark of ownership.

He did not have long to dwell on it, though; the man turned his head, as his gaze followed the path of a passerby walking in the opposite direction, until Adrissu entered his line of sight. His eyes were a vivid blue in the sunlight. He blinked, noticing Adrissu's attention for the first time, and a slow smile spread across his lips. There was some slight recognition in his expression, but in a way that was familiar. Adrissu was known, being one of now only a handful of elves in Polimnos, so it was a look that he had seen a hundred times over. The man knew who he was, but not in the way Adrissu had hoped.

The man leaned forward, eyeing Adrissu. His hair was slightly wavy, cascading just past his shoulders, and was somewhere between a light brown and a dirty blonde. Adrissu hesitated for only an instant longer, then continued walking toward him.

"Hello, sir," the man said, his eyes flickering up and down the length of his body. "I can't say I've seen you grace our establishment before. Adrissu, isn't it?"

He did not try to stifle the smile that spread across his lips. The sound of his name in his mate's voice would never cease to be a source of pleasure, even if that voice was new.

"Yes," he said, stepping right up to the man. Any other human would have stepped away in discomfort, but this one only smiled wider up at him. "And what is your name?"

"I'm Volkmar," he said, almost a purr. Seeming to take Adrissu's boldness as an invitation, he pressed his hands to the thick sash of a belt on Adrissu's waist—another style that had been in fashion of late—and slid them higher up his chest. "Welcome to the Garden of Delight."

Adrissu almost laughed. "Is that what this place is called?"

"It certainly is," the man—Volkmar—said, pulling one hand away to gesture behind him. Now that he looked, Adrissu could see that the entire entryway was covered in ivy. This time he did laugh, shaking his head.

"So it is," he agreed, pulling his gaze back to the man that had nearly thrown himself into his arms.

He considered where to go from here. He could agree to Volkmar's obvious invitation for a romp, probably in a room upstairs, but then what? Leave him behind to visit again some other day? He knew that as soon as he had Volkmar, he would be entirely unwilling to leave his side. But it would be the same if he brought Volkmar home with him—and how could he explain that he couldn't stand for the human to leave when they had only just met? It was clear that Volkmar had no memory of him, perhaps no memory of his time as Ruan at all, so it truly was as if they were strangers. *That* would be an entirely separate conversation, too.

It took only a moment for him to decide what he had to do.

"Volkmar," he said, testing the sound of his new name on his lips. It did not flow from his mouth as easily as Ruan had, but there was a certain cadence to it that he liked. He was sure he would learn to love it just as much. "Since you know of me, you might know that I... value my privacy. Would you consider, perhaps, making a house call?"

He let the question settle in the air between them, heavy with promise, hoping his anticipation didn't come across as desperate. Slowly, Volkmar grinned up at him.

"Such a thing could be arranged," he said. "But... it will cost extra."

"Of course," Adrissu said, bowing his head. "That will be no problem."

"Your place, then?" he asked, stepping back.

"Yes," Adrissu said. "Only it might be prudent to... change into something a little more... discreet." Volkmar's smile faltered, and he added softly, "I would very much like to unwrap you like a gift."

Volkmar laughed at that, the easy grin returning to his face. "Well, when you put it that way..." he said, as he moved past Adrissu to enter the building. Judging from the bulge in his pants that had not been there a moment ago, either he was very good at his job, or Adrissu's words affected him more than he let on. "Why don't you come in? There's a little sitting room right here. I won't be long."

Adrissu nodded and followed Volkmar inside. The entrance was dimly lit, and the hazy smoke of incense wafted through the room. More flowers and plants were along the walls and in pots on the floor, and distantly, Adrissu could hear the sound of flowing water like a fountain—clearly they were leaning into the garden imagery.

A woman, just as scantily dressed, was sitting near the door. She started to rise as they entered, but seeing Volkmar, smiled knowingly and settled back into her seat.

"Wait right here," Volkmar said, turning to face him again. "Don't go anywhere." He winked, then moved toward a staircase on the opposite end of the hallway.

Adrissu watched him go, admiring the supple movement of his backside as he climbed the stairs, then turned to the woman.

"Could you direct me to the person who owns this establishment?" he asked.

She led him past the stairway that Volkmar had ascended and through a large, dark atrium, where a topless woman played a harp and hummed as couples sat in dim corners. Adrissu kept his head down as they passed, but the visitors all seemed preoccupied. On the other side of the sitting room was another hallway, this one more brightly lit, and the woman knocked on the door at the very end.

"Come in," a woman's voice called, and she opened the door.

"A visitor to see you, ma'am," the woman said, and gestured for Adrissu to enter.

The office was perfectly mundane and would not have been out of place alongside his own office at the Academy. The woman sitting at the desk was an older human, thin as a whip and with long fingernails painted with red lacquer. Her dark hair was set in short curls around her face, which was painted with makeup, but the robes she wore were much more leisurely and casual than the rest of her appearance would suggest. She peered at Adrissu curiously for a moment, before gesturing to one of three chairs set around the room.

"Please, sit," she said, and Adrissu sat across from her. "How can I help you, headmaster?"

"I see my reputation precedes me," he said with a dry smile.

"I can assure you everyone in my establishment will treat you with the utmost discretion, including myself," she said. "Ah—

you can call me Madam Crowe, by the by. Pleased to meet you."

"I don't know how to ask this, Madam Crowe, so I will get to the point to avoid wasting anyone's time," Adrissu said, before he could think better of it. "I would like to buy out one of your... workers."

The woman regarded him for a long moment before leaning back in her chair, her lacquered nails tapping on its arms.

"Buy out," she repeated. "You seem to be under the impression that I have some measure of ownership over my workers. I can assure you, everyone under my employ is free to leave whenever they see fit."

Adrissu hesitated. "But surely they are under contractual obligations to you. A portion of their earnings goes to you, correct?"

"There are contracts in place, yes," she said, then sighed. "Which one of my workers are you interested in, headmaster?"

"Volkmar," he said brusquely. Clearly, his attempts at subtlety were in vain here. "Whatever he earns you in a year, I will pay triple that amount to you now."

Her eyebrows raised. "Volkmar," she repeated again, then laughed. "You're in luck, then. He's one of my only workers who *is* contractually obligated to stay. He's paying off his late mother's debt."

"I will pay it," Adrissu said. *That* was sure to be its own conversation—who his mother was, and how they ended up in debt to a brothel—but he would much rather hear it all from Volkmar, and later.

"You don't even know how much he owes."

"It doesn't matter. I will pay it," he insisted.

"His debt is in the amount of..." she started, then reached for a box of small scrolls on her desk. Filing through them, she selected one and unrolled it, looking it over quickly. "As of today, he still owes two thousand, one hundred and seven gold to the Garden." Her eyes flickered back up to him. "I'd estimate he brings in about a thousand gold per year. We can call it five thousand gold to buy him out and end his contract."

It clearly did not add up—if Volkmar owed two thousand gold, Adrissu highly doubted that he brought in one thousand gold to the brothel a year, unless the establishment took out such an exorbitant amount that its workers lived in poverty. She was almost certainly taking advantage of him; but for all that he bristled in indignation, five thousand gold was not so steep a price to pay to ensure Volkmar never had to return here.

"Done," he said, ignoring the way her eyes widened as he reached for his coin purse. With tight robes and slim silhouettes being the trend, he had only a small purse tied to his belt, but he emptied its contents on her table. "This is fifty gold pieces. Consider it a deposit, and I will bring the remainder to you tomorrow."

He could practically hear her mind working as her eyes flickered between him, the gold on the table, and the parchment in her hand. She had expected him to balk at the price—or at least to call her bluff, to try and bring the price down, so that she would have grounds to refuse. He did not care. There was no price he would not have paid to bring his mate home.

"Well, headmaster," she finally said, clearing her throat. "You... drive a hard bargain. Let me amend the contract."

She scribbled over a fresh sheet of parchment in silence for several minutes before presenting it for him to sign. When he did, she took it along with the gold, eyes downcast.

"I must warn you," she said, looking back up at him as he stood to leave. "I've been in this line of work for a long time. This happens every once in a while, some lovesick patron comes to beg me to release the object of his affections. Usually they're grateful for a little while, but this life is all they've known, and eventually the gloss starts to wear off. They usually come back." Her mouth pressed into a hard line. "Volkmar grew up here. This is truly the only life he knows. You may be wasting your money."

Adrissu stifled a smirk. "I will take it into consideration, Madam Crowe," he said, bowing his head stiffly, then he left without waiting for her to reply. He passed through the atrium again—the same woman was singing, but two of the couples that had been lounging before were now gone.

When Adrissu arrived in the entry hall, Volkmar was waiting for him, dressed in a tight, thin white robe that was nearly see-through with how sheer it was. It was barely a step up from walking around topless, the way he had been, but the sight of it made Adrissu instantly hard. Getting him to Saltspire Tower without devouring him first was going to be difficult.

A relieved smile crossed Volkmar's face as Adrissu strode in.

"Everything alright? Elle said you went to go talk to Madam Crowe," he said, a slight hint of nervousness in his voice.

"Yes. I... paid ahead a bit, so we'll have some extra time," Adrissu said. It wasn't a complete lie, after all. "So we have plenty of time to get to know each other."

Volkmar's grin became wicked, the lust in his eyes nearly palpable. "Oh, I intend to," he breathed, and took Adrissu's hand. "Let's go."

It was their first direct contact, and Adrissu's fingers buzzed with the sensation of Volkmar's skin against his own.

Adrissu was sure that they garnered stares as they walked, but he could only focus on the sensation of Volkmar alongside him, their fingers entwined. It was strange, he thought, to feel this way about someone that was not Ruan, while knowing that somehow it *was* Ruan. Even if it was not the shape of Ruan next to him, it felt familiar and right. Lightly, he rubbed his thumb up and down the back of Volkmar's hand, and the human grinned up at him almost shyly.

"You live in the big tower on the cliffs, don't you?" he asked, and Adrissu nodded. "And you walk all the way to town? That seems so far."

"I enjoy the exercise," Adrissu replied, shrugging. "It doesn't feel like such a long walk when you make the trip every day."

"I don't think you're in our part of town every day, though," he said, a teasing lilt in his voice. "I think I would have noticed you before if you were."

When he thought back to it, he had walked down that side street perhaps once or twice before, but evidently not when Volkmar had been out. Part of him stirred with jealousy that he might have been *occupied* the last time he'd been down that way, but he did his best to push it aside. He would not let some phantom of the past mar the incandescence of their reunion.

"Well," he said slowly, returning Volkmar's wicked smile. "I think I found what I was looking for."

The human laughed, his head tossing back the way Ruan's would when he was particularly tickled by some joke or remark, and Adrissu's chest constricted with familiarity. He had ached for this for so long.

"And now you always know where to find me," the human purred, and Adrissu's grin faltered for only an instant. Telling Volkmar what he'd done now was the right thing to do, but he selfishly did not want such an interruption, not yet. After, he told himself. Even if they did not have sex—although it seemed readily apparent that they would—now that they'd finally found each other again, he wanted to be in the company of his mate in peace. Everything else could wait.

When they arrived at Saltspire Tower, Adrissu ushered Volkmar in and closed the heavy door behind him.

"Oh!" Volkmar exclaimed, just as a burst of excitement welled in Adrissu's chest—Vesper had seen him and knew.

"Oh, my apologies," he said quickly, moving to intercept her for fear that her rapid approach would frighten him away. "My pet snake. She's harmless." He could hear the familiar *thud-thud-thud* of her body sliding down the stairs, and as she slithered up, she only had eyes for Volkmar.

"Aww," he cooed, kneeling down and holding a finger out for her to sniff. Her tongue flicked rapidly, tasting him; but she hardly seemed to care, as she went straight for his hand and bumped her head against his palm, the way she used to with Ruan. "She's sweet. What's her name?"

"Vesper," he said softly, remembering how Vesper and Ruan had gotten along right away, too. Somehow she had an affinity for him, as if she too felt the pull of fate that drew Adrissu toward him. "She likes you."

"Vesper," Volkmar repeated, lightly stroking the top of her head. "I like her, too."

Adrissu watched them for a moment, his heart aching in his chest. The world had righted itself again.

Finally, Volkmar straightened, glancing back at Adrissu. "There's another snake I'm much more interested in, though."

Adrissu stifled a laugh. "You have a sense of humor."

"Of course," Volkmar replied, as he stepped closer to Adrissu. "Don't you?"

"I have been told I come across as stern," Adrissu said, keeping his gaze on Volkmar's eyes as the human sauntered up to him, until their bodies were barely an inch apart. "Or perhaps that I am too serious. Humans tend to be wary of me."

Volkmar grinned. "I'm not wary of you," he said. He ran his hands up Adrissu's chest again, and he hummed softly in satisfaction, his eyes slipping closed. The human's hands were smaller than Ruan's, and softer by far, but somehow the sensation still felt familiar.

As Volkmar's hands snaked along his sternum toward his collarbones, Adrissu reached up and clasped his wrists, stilling the movement. Volkmar glanced up at him curiously, and Adrissu hesitated for only a moment before dipping his head down to kiss him.

He felt Volkmar smile against his lips, before returning the kiss eagerly. Adrissu was chaste, kissing him softly; but when Volkmar's tongue swiped against his lips, he groaned and pressed his own into the human's pliant mouth. He tasted like mint and summer melon, sweet and fresh.

Volkmar was the first to pull away, looking up at Adrissu through his lashes. His blue eyes had gone dark, pupils blown wide with lust.

"Is your bedroom upstairs?" he asked. Adrissu nodded.

"Come," he said, his voice rasping, maintaining his hold on Volkmar's wrists to lead him up the stairs and into his bedchamber.

They tumbled into bed, Volkmar laughing as they went. He easily fell into place underneath Adrissu, his hair splayed out around his head. It was more wavy than curly, soft beneath Adrissu's fingers as he ran a hand through and leaned down to kiss him again.

"I thought you said you were going to unwrap me," Volkmar teased when he finally pulled away, both of them breathless.

"I did say that," Adrissu agreed, leaning back on his knees over Volkmar, straddling him at the waist. He could feel the human's erection pressing against him, but remained focused on the task ahead of him, as he slowly moved his hands down the length of Volkmar's body. The human sighed, eyelids drooping closed. Adrissu untied the loose knot of the sash holding the robe shut, then slid his hands beneath the opening. Volkmar's skin was warm and smooth against his palms as they ran up the length of his torso—the golden chain that had adorned his bare chest before was gone, which gave him a strange sense of relief. He pushed the robe open when his hands reached Volkmar's shoulders, and Volkmar slid his arms out of the sleeves so the full expanse of his torso was bare.

Now that Adrissu could look at him more closely, he noticed that both of Volkmar's nipples were pierced, along with his navel. Tiny gold beads adorned each side of the small pink peaks, and a similar gold bar affixed a flat disk just above his belly button to what looked like an opal that protruded from just inside his navel.

"You like them?" Volkmar asked, seeing his interest.

"Yes," Adrissu said softly, lightly touching one of his nipple piercings.

"I have more," he said, grinning; and from the heated way he met Adrissu's gaze, he was quite sure that Volkmar was not referring to the studs in his ears. If Adrissu had not already been achingly hard, he would be now at the thought of Volkmar's pierced cock. "Don't you want to see it?"

Adrissu smirked. "I think I'm going to take my time with you."

Without waiting for a response, he leaned down and took one nipple into his mouth, relishing in the slight gasp that escaped Volkmar and the shiver that coursed through his body. The metal was warm against his tongue, the same temperature as the rest of the human. Adrissu licked and sucked it for a moment, before moving to the next, and this time Volkmar made a low, throaty moan in response and writhed underneath him.

His hands traveled lower, even as his mouth remained occupied, unlacing Volkmar's trousers with little effort. Volkmar gasped and bucked his hips as Adrissu palmed him roughly, stopping to lean back and watch himself peel the human's trousers down. His hard cock sprang free, slender and warmly pink. The piercing was on the underside of his cock, through the skin that connected the head to the rest of his shaft: a gold bar like the others with a golden bead on either end. It suited him somehow, Adrissu thought—delicate and pretty.

"What do you think?" Volkmar murmured from underneath him, wiggling his hips so his cock swung back and forth along his belly. "People always ask if it hurt."

"Seems like a foolish question," Adrissu said, and Volkmar laughed.

"Right?" he agreed. "Of course it hurt. But only for a minute."

"Does it bring you pleasure the rest of the time?" Adrissu asked, finally tearing his eyes away from the human's cock to look him in the face. A slight flush had risen in Volkmar's cheeks.

"I like knowing that it's there," he said, then his voice dropped to a more husky tone. "But I'm guessing that's not what you meant."

Adrissu shifted back, so he was now between Volkmar's spread legs, and bent his head to take his cock into his mouth. Volkmar yelped, partly in surprise, and Adrissu felt his cock jump and flex in his mouth, the human's hand fisting in his hair.

He felt around the warm metal beads with his tongue, lightly moving them back and forth; it did not seem to bring him to any great height of pleasure, but it did not appear to hurt him either.

Volkmar's cock was smaller than he remembered Ruan's being, but that only meant he could get all of it into his mouth with little effort. Volkmar groaned as Adrissu's nose pressed to where his pubic hair would be, but the skin was mostly smooth and hairless. Clearly, Volkmar was meticulous with grooming—Adrissu could not recall seeing any body hair on him, and even this close, he only felt a tiny prickle against his skin, where it might just be starting to grow back.

The taste of him was overwhelming. Adrissu moaned low in the back of his throat at the strange familiarity of it—entirely new on his tongue, yet as familiar as if he'd always known it. His smell, his musk, made the most feral parts of him growl with the need to claim, to protect. Adrissu sucked him greedily, until Volkmar was gasping and trembling above him.

"Wait, wait," he panted, his grip tightening in Adrissu's hair in a weak attempt to pull him away. "I don't—I don't want to come yet."

Adrissu growled, but slowly pulled away, letting his tongue drag against the underside of Volkmar's cock as he did. As he straightened, Volkmar laughed weakly and covered his eyes with one hand.

"You," he said, peeking up at Adrissu through his fingers, "are probably the most attentive lover I've ever had."

Something hot sparked deep in the pit of his stomach—jealousy at the thought of how many lovers Volkmar must have had before him. But it was pointless to be jealous of something in the past, he told himself, forcing himself to focus. Nothing would ruin this.

"I've barely begun," he murmured in reply, his voice gravelly. Volkmar's cock twitched under him.

"At least get out of some of those," Volkmar said, tugging on the belt of his robe. Adrissu blinked—he'd forgotten he was still clothed—and smiled softly. He allowed Volkmar to loosen his belt before slipping out of the robe, peeling off the undershirt beneath it, and pushing down the breeches that hugged his waist. Volkmar watched him hungrily, his eyes lingering on Adrissu's chest as he disrobed, before flickering down to watch his hands loosen his breeches, and lighting up in delight as he pulled them down.

"Gods, you look delicious," Volkmar groaned. He started to push himself up, lips parted eagerly—Adrissu was tempted to push him back down, but the human was quick, capturing the head of his cock in his mouth before he could pull away. Adrissu bit back a moan as heat enveloped him. It had been years—decades—since someone else had touched his cock, and Volkmar had jumped right into it effortlessly.

But he especially did not want to come already, so he allowed Volkmar to bob up and down the length of his cock for only a few moments, before running his fingers through the human's long hair and gripping it near the base of his neck to pull him away. Volkmar's gaze was entirely smug as he looked up at Adrissu, evidently already certain of why he'd been pulled away.

"Lay back," Adrissu said, and Volkmar obeyed without hesitation. "There should be a bottle of lubricant in the drawer to your right."

Volkmar blinked, then reached for the bedside drawer. When he retrieved the glass vial, he looked at it and laughed.

"Gods, this is *vintage,*" he chuckled, shaking his head. "The label looks older than I am."

It was, Adrissu thought with a slight pang of... *something*. Not quite sadness, not anymore, but maybe a pining for the way things had once been. But he only smirked and said softly, "It probably is. My kind live rather long lives, after all."

Volkmar's gaze became serious. "Don't tell me you haven't *used* this in that long."

Adrissu laughed. "Guilty as charged. But again, long lives and all... It doesn't feel like it's been too terribly long."

Volkmar's face went through a few different expressions very rapidly. He seemed at first startled, then confused, then an almost shy smile spread across his lips. "Well," he murmured, pressing the bottle into Adrissu's hands. "I'm glad to be the one to finally be ending your dry spell, then."

"As am I," Adrissu said. "Pull your legs up." Volkmar immediately obeyed, pulling his knees up to his chest. Adrissu gripped his thighs, spreading him further apart till his asshole was on display, just as carefully groomed as the rest of him. He had not planned to, but something in him snapped at the sight of Volkmar splayed out and vulnerable beneath him, barely an hour after they'd first met—so he dove down to lick a hot stripe from the soft bud of his opening up to the seam of his balls.

"Oh, *fuck*," Volkmar gasped. Even from where he was, Adrissu could practically hear the way his eyes rolled with pleasure. "That feels so good."

Adrissu kept his attention on Volkmar's opening, trailing his tongue around the ring of muscle until it twitched against him, opening up enough for the tip of his tongue to dip inside. Volkmar moaned, his hips bucking slightly with weakly restrained movements.

"Please," the human whimpered, fingers moving restlessly along Adrissu's scalp. "Please just fuck me."

The words were a thunderbolt straight to his cock. Adrissu pushed himself up, relishing the blissed-out, dazed expression on Volkmar's face, his eyes dark with desire. Precome glistened on his stomach where the head of his cock was pressed.

"Since you asked so nicely," Adrissu murmured, shifting so he could watch as he pushed a finger inside of Volkmar. He was already slick and glistening with saliva, combined with oil from the glass bottle, so his first finger slid in with little resistance. Volkmar made a low, soft sound of satisfaction, and Adrissu stifled a groan that threatened to break free from the back of his throat. The human was hot and tight around him, perfectly pliant, and he knew he would feel incredible around his cock.

Volkmar opened up for him easily, and for all that Adrissu wanted to savor the moment, the human seemed more than eager to get to the main event. He begged first for a second finger, then a third, then his cock—a plea that was impossible to ignore.

"So impatient," Adrissu murmured, kissing along the warm expanse of the human's thighs. "Is that what you want?"

"Yes, please," Volkmar panted, squirming beneath him. "Please, I want your cock."

He laughed breathlessly and answered, "How could I tell you no?"

He pulled his fingers away to spread lubricant along the length of his cock, hard and heavy with anticipation. Then he braced himself over Volkmar with one arm, and with the other he took the human's chin between his fingers and murmured, "Look at me."

Again Volkmar obeyed, blue eyes meeting his own. Adrissu released him to line himself up, and pushed into Volkmar's entrance slowly, feeling the friction of their skin as Volkmar's eyelids fluttered.

"Oh, fuck," the human groaned as Adrissu pushed all the way in, watching his face all the while. "Yeah, just like that." Adrissu rocked his hips, finally breaking eye contact with Volkmar to close his eyes with a gasp. He drew back just as slowly, until only the head of his cock remained inside, before pushing back in. "Fuck, you feel good."

Adrissu nodded, panting. He had almost forgotten how good it was, how long it had been. His instincts were roaring to move faster—to fuck him hard and make him his own—but he loved how the human writhed and moaned in response to the slow slide of their bodies. He kept the same languid pace for as long as he could manage, until Volkmar was trembling beneath him.

"Adrissu," he groaned, and the sound of his name on his lips made his cock twitch. "You're going to drive me mad."

"You don't like this?" Adrissu teased, rocking his hips a little bit faster.

"I'm a big fan," Volkmar said, shaking his head. A few strands of his long hair were sticking to his sweat-dampened forehead, and his cheeks were flushed pink with arousal. "But I would love to watch you come all over me."

It was as if he somehow could hear the voice in the back of Adrissu's head, urging him to mark and claim his mate. Adrissu growled, hips stuttering, and could not stop himself from speeding up. Long, languid strokes soon gave way to short, rapid thrusts; Volkmar cried out in pleasure, his head tipping back. Ruan would so often cover his mouth or bite back his cries, but Volkmar clearly had no qualms about being vocal.

"Gods, yes," he moaned, one hand fisting in Adrissu's sheets, and the other moving down to stroke his cock. "Nngh, right there—don't stop—you're going to make me come."

Adrissu groaned, curling his body around Volkmar's so he could press his mouth to the side of the human's throat, feeling the thrum of his rapid pulse against his lips and the salt of his sweat on his tongue. His cock was the only thing that mattered in the world, Volkmar's tight hole around him the only place he'd ever belonged.

"There, there, there," Volkmar panted, words seeming to escape his mouth without thought. "Fuck, you feel good—gods, I'm so close—"

His head fell back with a wordless cry as his hand around his cock stuttered and squeezed. Adrissu leaned back just enough to watch him come, cock pulsing in his hand and shooting come up the length of his torso. Adrissu's hips continued to piston, mostly of their own accord; but Volkmar clenched and pulsed around him as he came, and he knew he wouldn't last much longer.

He nearly said Ruan's name as he came, stopping himself just as he felt his cock pulsing hard. He pulled his hips back, making Volkmar gasp, and bit back a moan as he shot his release onto Volkmar's chest. Heat coiled around his cock, making him gasp and shudder as his orgasm pulsed through him. Volkmar hissed as Adrissu painted him with come, their seed mingling on his chest.

"Do all elves run so hot?" Volkmar panted, grinning in amusement with eyes half-lidded. Adrissu barely heard him. "Gods, you feel like fire."

"Just me, I think," Adrissu grunted, leaning back. Volkmar's legs were still around him; they had loosened, but he didn't seem eager to try and push him away. They were both panting and eyeing the other, Volkmar with a soft mix of affection and a hint of apprehension—Adrissu suspected that perhaps he had not expected to enjoy himself, but it was only conjecture. Idly the human's fingers were trailing through the come on his chest, swirling the sticky mess together.

"Here," Adrissu said, pulling up a sheet to wipe him down. When he had been mostly cleaned up, and the sheet was tossed aside, Adrissu tentatively crawled into bed with him, though the sun had not yet begun to set. Volkmar leaned into him, so he wrapped his arms around the human's waist, breathing his scent in deeply.

"Stay the night?" he murmured. "...I'll make you dinner."

He could hear the smile in Volkmar's voice as he answered. "I'd love to."

Chapter Sixteen

Adrissu woke the next morning to sunlight streaming in through his window and his mate sleeping in his arms. It was not Ruan, but it was his mate. It felt strange and right, all at once, for Volkmar to be in his bed: his eyes closed, his breathing slow and even. Adrissu watched him as he ran his fingers through his hair, until the human stirred and his eyes slid open. Blue irises flickered back and forth, taking in his surroundings, then met Adrissu's gaze. A slow, sleepy smile spread across his face.

"Good morning," he murmured, his voice low and raspy with sleep. Adrissu smiled back at him, affection bubbling low in his chest.

"Good morning," he replied softly. "Are you hungry?"

Soon he had set up a platter of bread, cheeses, and dried meats for Volkmar to pick through. Since Adrissu did not have to eat as often as humans did, most of the food he kept were things that would last longer than a few days, or things he could keep in his small icebox. He hated the hassle of continuously getting blocks of ice, so when one of the enchantment students at the academy developed an icebox that did not require ice to keep food cold, he made sure to review the student's notes and diagrams carefully when the project was submitted.

Volkmar had been very interested in the little magical icebox, but was now happily munching on bread and cheese as Adrissu made tea. Vesper had wandered over to them and was now coiled on the table, watching Volkmar eat with a low simmer of contentment radiating from her.

"So," Volkmar said over his last bite of bread. "How long do you have me for?"

For the first time that morning, Adrissu's happiness at having his mate with him faltered. He still had not told Volkmar what he'd done, but he couldn't exactly hide it much longer. For better or worse, he couldn't avoid telling Volkmar how he'd bought his freedom.

"Well," Adrissu said slowly, setting down the tea kettle and slowly turning to face the human. "Yesterday, I went to speak with the proprietor of the Garden, Madam Crowe, and..."

It felt impossible to say.

"And?" Volkmar prompted, lifting one eyebrow quizzically. It was an expression that he had never seen on Ruan's face, and a soft swell of affection broke through his nerves for just an instant at the sight of it. Adrissu thrummed his fingers on the table for a moment before answering.

"I paid off the remainder of your contract," he said quickly, before he could stop himself. Across from him, Volkmar went very still. "So you can stay as long as you'd like."

"I... I don't understand," Volkmar stammered, brows furrowing. "What do you mean? Paid it off?"

"I paid everything you owed to Madam Crowe," Adrissu said, glancing away nervously. "So you are no longer under a contract with her. You don't have to work there anymore."

Volkmar stared at him silently for a long moment, eyes wide. First he was perfectly still, then slowly his hands came up to cover his mouth, though his eyes were still locked on Adrissu.

"Why? Why would you do that?" he finally managed to ask, pulling his hands away only to press his fingers to his temples, an obvious sign of stress.

How could he explain? Somehow he thought that telling Volkmar that he was the reincarnation of his former lover, and that they were fated to be together, would not go over well at the moment.

"I don't know," he said, then shook his head. "I... I wanted you. I didn't want anyone else to have you."

"What am I going to do?" Volkmar said, an edge of panic starting to overtake his voice. He stood abruptly, pacing anxiously along the length of the table—Vesper watched him curiously, but seemed much less perturbed than either of them. "Where will I go? I don't—I don't have anywhere else to go."

"You can stay here," Adrissu said quickly, taking a step toward him, to—to what? Comfort him? As far as Volkmar knew, they were essentially strangers. "You will need for nothing. I'll make sure you're taken care of."

Volkmar blinked, going still, but Adrissu could practically hear the gears whirring in his mind.

"You bought me," he finally said—Adrissu expected him to sound angry or upset, but somehow he sounded almost relieved. "You're... You're keeping me. Is that it?"

Adrissu frowned. The implication of it was unsettling, but he supposed that, in a way, he *had* bought Volkmar.

"Well, yes," he said slowly. "I bought your freedom. I would certainly like for you to stay here with me, but I will not force you. If you want to go elsewhere, you may. I would be happy to help you either way."

"I—I don't know how I could possibly repay you," Volkmar stammered.

"Not necessary."

"Are you sure? What will I do?"

"I would love for you to stay with me. And you can do whatever you wish."

"You bought me," Volkmar repeated, and to Adrissu's surprise, he laughed. "You *bought* me. Gods, I wish you would have just told me from the start that's what you wanted."

"I... apologize," Adrissu said slowly, trying not to sound as confused as he felt. "I feared perhaps the prospect would be... unwelcomed."

"Well, if anyone is going to keep me, you're certainly at the top of my list," Volkmar laughed again, and he sat back down at the table to pick at the last piece of cheese that was on his plate. He still seemed nervous, pulling the cheese apart into small pieces rather than actually eating it, but not panicked in the way that he had been a moment ago. "This is... This is fine. This is good. Can I at least go back to get my things?"

"Of course," Adrissu said quickly, taking another cautious step closer to him. "We'll go together. I have to bring the rest of the payment anyway."

Volkmar nodded absently, his smile still lingering. Whatever he was feeling seemed a complete mystery to Adrissu—for all that he *was* Ruan, he was also a different person entirely. He had felt that fated pull, certainly, but part of him wondered if the differences between them now were too great, if there was any remnant of the man that he had loved there. But he pushed the thought down before it could blossom into worry.

"Whenever you're ready," he said softly, looking down at Volkmar's hands still fidgeting over his food.

Volkmar smiled slyly at him, eyes going dark. "I suppose I'd better earn my keep, then."

They didn't leave until later that afternoon, walking quietly back down the path that they had come up the afternoon before. Adrissu had offered him one of his own robes to wear out, but it was far too long for the smaller man, so he kept on his same sheer white robe from the day before.

"Not like I wore it for very long," Volkmar laughed, looking up at him, and Adrissu relished the faint blush that rose in his cheeks as he said it.

They walked in silence most of the way, but when they turned onto the street where the Garden of Delight stood, Adrissu could feel Volkmar tense, his pace slowing. The human's hand touched his forearm lightly.

"We don't have to do this if you don't want to," Adrissu blurted, though he was entirely sure that he could not turn back now, even if he tried. "You can just... go back, if you want."

Volkmar laughed, though it had a nervous undertone to it now. "That's not what I was thinking. Truly, what you're offering me has its appeal. I liked my job, but I did want to eventually leave when I'd paid everything off. I guess I just don't know what to expect. My friends might be... Well, I don't know. They could be mad or sad or... anything, really."

Adrissu wanted to snap that none of that mattered—that they could not be good friends if they were angry or upset with him for such a thing—but he held his tongue. He had to remind himself that Volkmar didn't know him like Ruan did, even though he slipped too easily into the old rapport that they once had. He was still nearly a stranger to Volkmar, no matter how much burgeoning fondness they shared.

"Will you stay with me?" Volkmar asked, before Adrissu could decide on what to say, looking up at him with a sudden earnestness. "I... I don't want to pack up alone."

"Of course," Adrissu murmured, starting to reach for Volkmar's hand on his forearm, before becoming suddenly very aware of the heavy coin purse in his opposite hand. "I'll drop this off with Madame Crowe first, and then we can go gather your things."

When they entered the building, going from the bright street to the dim interior, a different girl was sitting in the foyer reading a small book. She glanced up as they entered, smiling, but the smile faltered slightly upon seeing them.

"Oh, Volkmar," she said, lifting one hand to wave at him uncertainly. "Hello."

"Hi," he said breathlessly. "Is Madame Crowe in?"

"Is it true you're leaving?" she asked without answering his question, glancing between him and Adrissu.

"Well, yes," Volkmar replied, grinning nervously. "Headmaster Adrissu paid off the rest of my contract, so..."

"Wow," the girl said, grinning over at Adrissu. "How lucky. We'll miss you, Volkmar."

Something in her tone seemed strained, but Adrissu couldn't place it; and Volkmar seemed to ignore it. The human murmured a thank you, and together they walked through the hall, into the atrium, and toward Madam Crowe's office.

"There you are," the woman sighed as they entered. "I've been expecting you."

"I've brought the rest of the payment," Adrissu said. Her eyes flickered toward him briefly, but when she spoke again, she addressed Volkmar.

"I assume headmaster Adrissu has explained to you what's happening," she said sharply. Adrissu frowned—it was rare that he was ignored, and he did not like the way she spoke to him.

"Yes," Volkmar said, nodding. He, at least, did not seem surprised. Perhaps this was just the way she always was. The thought was not comforting to Adrissu.

"And you're alright with this?" she pressed, clasping her hands on her desk in front of her. "You can always stay here, Volkmar, even if he does pay off your contract. Don't feel beholden to him."

Adrissu bristled, but remained silent. Ultimately she *was* right—while his instinct was to keep Volkmar with him regardless of what he wanted, the more rational part of him balked at the idea of doing anything against Volkmar's will. If he truly did not want to leave the Garden, Adrissu would let him stay, or at least try to.

"I understand," Volkmar said, nodding. "But I... I appreciate what Adrissu wants to do for me, and..." He glanced over at Adrissu, who maintained his stony, silent face as much as he could manage. A slight smile wavered on the human's face. "I like him. He's... nice."

It was hardly a compliment, but it still made Adrissu's body tingle with pleasure to hear, and he stifled a smile.

"So, yes, I'm going with him," Volkmar continued. Across from her desk, Madame Crowe sighed.

"I thought you'd say that," she said. "Well, Volkmar, you know we've all loved you, and you're welcome back any time. I mean it."

Adrissu stopped himself from rolling his eyes as he stepped forward, setting the coin purse on the table.

"That's the rest of it," he said, and without waiting for her to answer—after all, she had ignored him—he turned to go, leading Volkmar by his elbow.

"Bye!" the human called brightly over his shoulder. He led Adrissu to a different staircase, so they did not have to pass through the atrium again. When they were on the stairs, he looked up at Adrissu and grinned.

"She hates you," he laughed, and Adrissu smiled.

"I noticed," he said dryly. "I take it you were one of the... better performers? I can imagine she'll miss the business you bring."

"Well," he said, suddenly seeming almost shy, his smile faltering. "It's really just that there's only one other man who's here regularly. And she liked my mother, so I think it's more nostalgic for her. My numbers were pretty average."

Adrissu still wondered about his mother, but it could wait. They would have plenty of time. Instead, he followed Volkmar silently as the man led him to his room, and they packed up his personal belongings. It wasn't much—several skimpy outfits with a handful of plainer robes and pants, some books and trinkets and toiletries. Among his belongings was a small box of what seemed to be old children's toys that Volkmar held and sighed over, before setting it in the pile of things to carry out. Again Adrissu wondered, but remained silent. Volkmar was so much more different from Ruan than he had expected.

"That's everything, I think," Volkmar sighed, looking over the small room once more. They each had a full rucksack on their backs, and Adrissu held a crate with the other items. The linens and furniture all belonged to the Gardens and would remain behind. "Shall we go?"

Adrissu nodded. Part of him wanted to ask if Volkmar truly wanted to do this, if it was too much, too fast—but the rest of him knew that he wouldn't be able to handle being told no, not now, and Volkmar had already agreed, so again he held his tongue.

As they descended back down the stairs, a few women called out to him to say goodbye. He was polite and answered each of them in turn, but didn't seem particularly emotionally invested in any of them. His gaze was distant, as if he were thinking of a hundred other things.

Their trip back to the tower passed mostly in silence, as well. Adrissu watched Volkmar walk a few steps ahead of him, his gaze fluttering around and looking at the city as if he might never see it again. The thought made him frown. He thought he had made it quite clear that Volkmar was free to do as he pleased, but...

"So will I get my own room?" Volkmar asked as the tower came into sight.

Adrissu blinked. It had not occurred to him.

"Of course," he answered, mentally rearranging some of the rooms in the upper floors of the tower. One of the larger ones, certainly, but he'd have to find a new place for the equipment that he stored there—it was mostly glass items, vials and jars that stored bulk alchemical ingredients, like salt and stone. Most of it would probably fit in one of the smaller rooms that held some of his older, out-of-fashion clothes, which he probably should get rid of anyway. Even with his magic, it would probably take the better part of the afternoon to move everything around. "It will take some rearranging, but that's no issue."

He could feel Vesper's attention in his chest as they drew nearer; she must have heard them coming. Sure enough, when Volkmar opened the door to the tower, she was right at the entrance, peering up at them—if her physiology would have allowed it, Adrissu was sure she would be grinning.

"Oh!" Volkmar exclaimed, carefully stepping around her. "I forgot about you, little one, I almost stepped on you! What did you call her? Viper?"

"Vesper," he said.

"Vesper," Volkmar repeated, still looking down at her. She lifted her head up off the ground, her tongue flicking against his forearm. "Sweet girl. I'll just be a minute. Okay?" Her head bobbed, and he burst out laughing. "Did you see that? I swear she just nodded at me."

Adrissu stifled a smile. She certainly had. "I did see."

He showed Volkmar to the room that would be his. He had decided on the largest room on the third floor, just above his own. The room was dark and cool to better preserve the materials within, but as they entered, Adrissu strode to the large window on the far side and opened the thick curtains to bathe the room in sunlight.

"As you can see, I was using this room for storage," Adrissu sighed, gesturing around to the various crates and shelves. "But I can get all of this out before sunset." And to emphasize his point, he flicked his wrist, magically lifting the first crate into the air. It floated through the doorway out into the hall; Volkmar watched him with wide eyes, his lips parting as his mouth hung open.

"That's amazing," he said, tearing his gaze away from the crate to look back at Adrissu. The wonder in his gaze was almost childlike, and Adrissu found himself entirely flustered.

"Telekinesis is quite simple, really," he said, forcing his tone to remain even, as he set another crate floating out of the room.

"Could you show me how?" Volkmar asked.

Adrissu hesitated, and the crate faltered slightly as it floated through the doorway. Ruan never had any interest in learning magic, and even less aptitude for it, so he suspected the same would be true of Volkmar. But as he glanced over at the human, his eyes were so eager in a way Ruan's had never been. They were so different, but his heart ached all the same.

"Of course," he said, forcing himself to smile back at Volkmar.

But he seemed to sense Adrissu's hesitance, adding quickly, "You don't have to. I understand you must get tired of teaching all day."

"On the contrary," Adrissu said. "As the headmaster, I do very little teaching. I would be happy to give you private lessons, but it's important to know that arcane ability can vary wildly in humans. It's possible you may simply not have the ability to do more than the most rudimentary tasks."

"I still want to try," Volkmar said, softer this time, but with the same bright expression. He flushed slightly, and added in an even smaller voice, "I want to try everything. I feel like there's so much I've missed out on."

Adrissu's heart could have burst. He wanted to promise Volkmar that he *would* do everything, that together they would do everything, and that he would want for nothing ever again—but for all that it was true, their relationship still felt so new that he could not say any of it.

"I will do my best to teach you to the fullest of your potential," he said, and a tiny smile spread across Volkmar's lips.

"So do all elves have as much magic as you do, then?" he asked, eyes following the box of empty glass vials that Adrissu was carefully sending into the hall and through the opposite doorway.

"No," he replied, smirking. "There is less variation in magical ability with elves, but it is still possible to have more or less aptitude. I am... particularly gifted. There are some who would match my ability and few that would exceed it." That, at least, was not a lie.

"You're powerful," Volkmar said, still smiling, but his gaze became more heated. This time Adrissu laughed, bowing his head in mock humility.

"You don't know the half of it," he murmured.

Chapter Seventeen

Ruan had never lived with him full time, so it was a strange adjustment for Adrissu to acclimate himself to Volkmar's constant presence in his home. Once they had moved all his belongings into the room on the third floor, though, Volkmar seemed to mostly keep to himself, as if he too were unsure of his standing in Adrissu's life.

Adrissu had taken a week off from his duties at the school to spend that time with Volkmar and help them both adjust, although much of their free time together ended with them in his bedroom. That, at least, Volkmar had no qualms about. But otherwise he was nervous and asked permission for everything—to use the kitchen, to go on a walk, to hold Vesper.

"You don't have to ask me these things," Adrissu finally sighed. He put down a book as Volkmar hovered in the doorway of his study, having asked if he could bring some of the extra blankets that were in storage into his room. "You live here now too."

"Well, it's your house," Volkmar protested, smiling slightly.

"I give you permission to do whatever you want," Adrissu replied, and Volkmar laughed.

"Whatever I want?" he asked, before clambering into Adrissu's lap. The conversation ended there.

So far the only similarities Adrissu could find between Volkmar and Ruan were that Volkmar was also an orphan, and that he was just as stubborn. It still seemed too soon to ask about his mother, but it was clear that Volkmar had no living relatives. And his stubbornness became obvious in the way that Volkmar continued to constantly ask permission to do things—regardless of how often Adrissu told him he need not ask—and the way he continued to attempt the test of magic that Adrissu had given him, even when it was apparent that he had no aptitude for it.

"This is the most common means of detecting magical ability in the untrained," Adrissu explained, lighting a candle on the table between them. They were in his study, Volkmar sitting across from him and watching him with his eyes big and attentive. "Snuff out the flame without using your breath or touching the candle. I will show you."

He gestured to the candle, before clasping his hands in his lap. Looking at the flame, he concentrated, smothering it out with his magic. The light winked out instantly.

"You didn't do anything," Volkmar protested, eyebrows furrowing.

"I focused on filling the space around it with only arcane power," Adrissu said, as he snapped his fingers and the flame sparked back to life. "So the flame was starved and went out. Others might manipulate wind or water to blow the flame out or quench it. Some arcanists find particular hand motions help them cast. The only limit is that you do not touch the candle, and don't blow it out yourself."

Volkmar sighed, leaning back in his seat with a displeased expression. But after a moment of looking at the candle, he straightened, folding his hands on the table in front of him. His eyelids quivered as he stared intently at the candle. For a long moment he was motionless, only staring at the candle's tiny flame; Adrissu did not sense any magic coming from him, nor anything touching the candle.

"Try a hand motion," he encouraged, lifting his own hand and showing a waving motion. "This can help focus the power."

Volkmar nodded. He lifted one of his hands and tried a few different motions: first waving how Adrissu did, then circling his wrist, then clenching his fist. As his fingers snapped into a fist, the flame flickered slightly—it shrunk and sputtered, but did not go out. Still, Volkmar grinned up at him, eyes bright.

"I think I felt something," he said. Adrissu smiled in return—he had felt it too, but the thread of magic coming off of him was so small that he knew instantly it would never manifest as anything more powerful than snuffing a candle.

"Try again," he said, and Volkmar did.

Each time the fire flickered and shrunk, but he could not get it fully extinguished. Adrissu watched him try, over and over, for the better part of an hour before murmuring,

"I don't think you have much more than that, Volkmar. I'm sorry. It's nothing to be ashamed of. It's not uncommon for humans to have no significant magical ability."

"I can do it," Volkmar insisted, his eyes never leaving the candle. He kept trying. The sound of his fingers snapping into a fist echoed over and over in the quiet room, as Adrissu leaned back and observed, eventually moving to his own desk to read, then later down into the kitchen to make him something to eat.

When he returned with a warm bowl of soup, the candle was no longer lit, and Volkmar's head was on the table in his folded arms. He looked up quickly at the sound of Adrissu's footsteps, a bright smile fixed on his face, but his lower eyelids shone with moisture, as if he had been crying.

"I did it," he said, his gaze flicking between the candle and Adrissu's face. Adrissu forced himself to smile in response.

"Good job," he said, even as he felt his heart constrict at the human's hastily-hidden tears. He would give Volkmar anything and everything he wanted, he decided at that moment. There was nothing the human would ever want for again that he would not get.

When Volkmar had been with him for a little over a month, things seemed to settle into a more comfortable routine between them, and carefully Adrissu asked about Volkmar's family.

"I am only curious," he said quickly, before Volkmar could answer. "Madame Crowe had mentioned your mother, so I wondered. But you don't need to tell me anything you don't want to."

"No, it's okay," Volkmar said, shaking his head. He was sitting cross-legged on the floor of the living room, Vesper coiled over his legs. His back was against the chaise lounge where Adrissu sat, so that he could idly run his fingers through the human's hair as he read; but now he turned to face Adrissu. "It was always just my mother and I growing up. My father died just before I was born. He was one of the soldiers that went to fight Gennemont for Polimnos' independence, before the Federation took over." Volkmar paused. "You must have been there for that. I bet you even remember when that happened."

A pained smile crossed Adrissu's face. "Yes, I remember." He wondered if he might have known Volkmar's father, if Ruan might have known him. It was strange to consider. He glanced over at Ruan's shield, displayed prominently on the wall of his study, wondering whether to mention him. But he hesitated too long, and Volkmar spoke again before he could decide.

"Anyway, when he died, my mom got a little bit of money from the mercenary's guild, but not much," Volkmar continued, looking down at Vesper as he spoke. Her dark, beady eyes were fixed on him. "I think we had a house, but she couldn't keep paying for it. And when you're a young widow with a child, sex work starts looking like the best way to make decent money. So she joined the Garden, and we lived there. She got sick and died when I was about sixteen, so I started working there too, to keep our room and pay off the last of the debt she had."

"What was the debt for?" Adrissu asked, frowning. Volkmar shrugged.

"I'm not sure. Living expenses, I guess," he said, sounding far more nonchalant about it than Adrissu felt. "Especially from when I was a little kid. Probably still cost more to take care of me than she made, so she borrowed money from the Garden."

"I see," Adrissu said. It still sounded suspicious to him. If he did not know what the debt was for, how did he know he hadn't been taken advantage of? He could have been paying more than he needed for years. But it was paid off now, he supposed, so there was nothing to do.

"What about you?" Volkmar asked, grinning up at him. "What are your parents like?"

Adrissu chuckled dryly, shaking his head. "I have not seen either of them in a long time. Although, I did see my mother about thirty years ago now. My parents and I have never been particularly close."

"Oh," Volkmar said, and for a brief moment he looked almost disappointed. But then he laughed, looking back up at Adrissu. "I can't even imagine you as a baby."

"Elven babies are basically the same as human babies," Adrissu said, shrugging.

"How old are you, anyway?"

At that, he hesitated. "Much older than you."

"But how old exactly?" Volkmar pressed. "And don't try to tell me you don't know. I won't believe you."

Adrissu sighed, leaning back as he considered it. He did not pay much attention to his birthday, and had to think in earnest about how old he was.

"I am getting close to two hundred," he finally said. "One hundred and sixty.... four, I think."

Volkmar blinked, eyes wide. "How long do elves usually live for?"

"Over two hundred and fifty is average," he replied. "Some make it over three hundred."

"I see," Volkmar said, as he looked away with a thoughtful expression, eyebrows furrowing. Whatever he was thinking of, he did not speak aloud, so Adrissu didn't press. He didn't need to ask.

Volkmar did not have his memories as Ruan, at least not consciously that Adrissu could tell. It had become more and more obvious as they spent time together, and Adrissu was unsure how to address it. How could he casually just ask if he had memories of another life? How could he bring up Ruan, the ritual, his reincarnated soul? It seemed easier not to. What Volkmar didn't know wouldn't hurt him, after all. It was easier to just enjoy their time together.

He found that Volkmar dearly wanted to travel and see new things; he had lived in Polimnos his entire life, but had heard stories of many other places. When he mentioned it to Adrissu, he planned immediately to bring Volkmar with him on his next trip to Gennemont. It was usually a business trip, but he would take some extra time for leisure. Normally he would fly, but this time they took a carriage along a scenic route, so Volkmar could watch the countryside go by. It was tedious and boring by his own standards, but the joyful expression on Volkmar's face as they traveled made up for it. He was entirely enamored with the city as well, following Adrissu down the bustling stone-paved streets with wide eyes.

"This is amazing," he murmured, looking out from the window. They had rented a room for one month, near the college so Adrissu might still attend to his research. "I can't believe how big the city is. I knew it was bigger than Polimnos, but..." He turned to face Adrissu, smiling. In the months they had been together now, his smiles came easier, his affection feeling more true. Whatever he had felt toward Adrissu at the beginning, and whatever he thought about being "bought" by him, had started to melt into genuine regard.

"Thank you," he said softly. He stepped toward Adrissu and pushed himself into his arms, his slim hands snaking around Adrissu's waist. "Thank you for bringing me here."

"I'm glad to have you with me," Adrissu murmured, pressing his lips to the soft skin along the crook of his neck.

"I love you," Volkmar said, barely above a whisper, and Adrissu stilled, heat flooding his veins. He felt Volkmar tense.

"I love you too," he said quickly, before Volkmar could pull away, before his silence became damning. He squeezed his arms harder around the human's slight frame. "I loved you the first time I saw you. I knew right then I had to have you all to myself."

He felt more than heard Volkmar laugh slightly against his shoulder, as he squeezed around Adrissu's waist in response. "I know."

"You didn't know," Adrissu muttered, only to be cut off with a stifled groan, as one of Volkmar's hands released his waist to palm at his cock through his clothes.

"Let me thank you properly," Volkmar murmured, tilting his head up. Adrissu leaned down to devour his mouth, kissing him roughly, as Volkmar eased his hardening cock out of his pants. They broke apart, and Volkmar dropped to his knees, lips parting to take him into his mouth, as Adrissu's hands fisted in his hair. A moan escaped each of them in turn, Adrissu gasping as Volkmar sucked him eagerly and whimpered around his length. He rocked his hips and watched his cock slide in and out of Volkmar's pink lips stretched around his girth, pleasure shivering up his spine at the sight.

"Look at me," he panted, pulling Volkmar's hair so his head tilted up. The human looked up at him, eyes dark with lust, and groaned around him as Adrissu pushed himself as far into Volkmar's mouth as he would go, until the head of his cock pressed to the back of Volkmar's throat. "So good for me," he muttered, smoothing back his mate's hair to watch him. "Thanking me properly like this. You're being so good, aren't you?"

Volkmar only whimpered, his pace quickening. One hand fisted around his shaft, so he could focus his mouth on the head of his cock, and the other reached down to slip beneath the waistband of his own pants. Adrissu groaned, imagining Volkmar's slender fingers wrapping around the pink length of his cock slicked with his own precome. His own cock twitched, eager to bury itself in a different warmth.

He pulled back, withdrawing his cock from Volkmar's mouth with a wet pop.

"Get on the bed," he growled, hauling Volkmar to his feet. The human shook his head stubbornly.

"I want you to fuck me right up against this window," he panted, pulling Adrissu with him as he took a step backward.

"Filthy boy," Adrissu murmured, though his cock jumped at the prospect. Their balcony was high up enough that it was unlikely anyone would be able to fully see them, but evidently Volkmar did not care either way. "Wanting everyone to see you. Wanting everyone to know you're mine."

"Yes," he gasped, quickly pulling his robe off and letting it fall to the floor in a heap. "I'm yours."

Adrissu pushed him forward until his back was against the glass-paneled door to the balcony. He hauled Volkmar up, and obediently the human lifted his legs to wrap them around Adrissu's waist. Adrissu held him up almost effortlessly with one arm, back braced against the door, and reaching up with the other, he shoved his fingers into the human's mouth. Volkmar groaned around his fingers and sucked eagerly, his mouth flooding with saliva. Once his fingers were wet, he pulled them back out and reached down to find Volkmar's asshole, pushing two of his slick fingers into the pliant ring of muscle. Volkmar panted, voice ragged with half-pleasure and half-pain; but soon the tight channel relaxed around him, and he slipped a third finger in, fucking him until the human was moaning and trembling against him.

"I'm ready," Volkmar urged, pressing feather-light kisses to his neck, up his jawline. "Come on. I want to feel you."

Adrissu growled, pulling his fingers out to grasp his cock and line himself up. Volkmar yelped as he pushed himself in roughly—hardly giving him any time to adapt to the intrusion before rutting against him with his hips. The glass rattled in its frame in time with each of his thrusts, but was nearly drowned out by Volkmar's cries.

"I love you," he whimpered, one hand fisting in the cloth of Adrissu's robes, the other curling around the base of his neck. Adrissu groaned, eyelids fluttering in bliss. He was buried to the hilt, his mate whispering in his ear, his mate who *loved* him. He would never let Volkmar out of his sight. Why had he ever let Ruan leave him for weeks, months at a time? All he wanted was to bask in Volkmar's presence forever. His mate belonged nowhere else but here, in his arms, tight and hot around his cock.

Adrissu dipped his head down to bite at the tender flesh between Volkmar's neck and shoulder, relishing in the gasp it drew from Volkmar's lips.

"I'm going to come inside you," he grunted, lips still pressed to Volkmar's skin. The human's legs tightened around him encouragingly, shifting his hips so he thrust even impossibly deeper. With his free hand, he found Volkmar's cock bouncing between them, making him moan as he stroked, squeezing hard. "Want to feel you first."

"Yes," Volkmar panted, voice rough, words flooding from his mouth apparently without thought. "Nngh, you feel so good—fuck, right there, right there—yes—yes—!" His head tipped back, his channel tightened and pulsed around Adrissu's cock. His cock jumped and strained against Adrissu's hand stroking him rapidly, and he came with a cry, seed spurting onto his belly.

Adrissu groaned, giving only another few thrusts before his orgasm erupted through his body. For a long moment the only thing he could feel was Volkmar's warmth around him, the scent of his mate and their sex flooding his senses. Nothing else existed but their bodies entwined with each other.

"I love you," he panted against Volkmar's skin. "I love you. You're mine. I love you."

He could feel Volkmar's heart hammering against his chest, his ribs expanding and contracting with rapid, hard breaths.

After a moment his hands trailed idly through Adrissu's hair, fingernails scraping against his scalp and sending soft tingles shooting along the length of his spine.

"I love you too," he whispered. Adrissu tightened his hold around Volkmar's waist, uncaring of the mess he was making, as he pressed their bodies closer together. "I'm yours."

Their life continued idly and comfortably this way. When they returned to Polimnos after their leisure trip to Gennemont, Volkmar slept in Adrissu's room each night. His room still held most of his things—and Volkmar loved trinkets, so he had many things—and he still spent large portions of his day there. But each night he came to Adrissu's bed, and that was all that mattered.

The human clearly enjoyed being "kept", as he would often tease Adrissu, since it meant a constant supply of new clothes and baubles and things to occupy his time. He wanted to try everything there was to do, and Adrissu was only too eager to give him anything he wanted. He was interested in painting, so Adrissu bought him all manner of canvases and brushes and oil paints. Then he wanted to learn to play music, so Adrissu paid for lessons for him to sing and play the lute. He wanted to learn to swim, so they went down to the beach every day for nearly three months. He had never received a formal education, so he read through the vast majority of Adrissu's books, before working through new ones he bought from traveling merchants and the local bookshop: everything from history to philosophy to pulp romance booklets.

He lived a life of utter leisure, wanting for nothing. Compared to their last life together, the time they spent together was utterly decadent.

The only thing that ever bothered Adrissu was that the topic of Volkmar's past life and his own true nature never came up. Not that either subject would come up in normal conversation, but every time Adrissu considered broaching the topic, something stopped him. The words would die far before they left his throat, his chest constricting with fear, or something like it. And the longer they went without it coming up, the harder it was to even consider talking about.

In the end, it was easier to let things continue as they were. After everything with Ruan, Adrissu thought, maybe they deserved something easy and comfortable this time around. And everything with Volkmar felt comfortable now, so why change anything? He deserved this, didn't he?

And so nothing changed. Polimnos continued to grow, the position of Lord Representative changed hands to Benil Branwood's grandson, and Adrissu's duties as the headmaster shifted and grew along with the academy; but his relationship with Volkmar was even and smooth for years on end. Sometimes he wondered how much Volkmar and Ruan had in common, considering how often Adrissu and Ruan had butted heads in their briefer time together; but any time he doubted that they were the same, he would see glimmers of his past life in Volkmar —the things he found amusing, the cadence of his voice when it trembled with emotion, his stubborn pride that sometimes bordered on vanity. He never doubted for long.

Volkmar was thirty-eight before doubt crept in and stayed.

Chapter Eighteen

Volkmar was thirty-eight, softer around the middle with laugh lines and crow's feet eking out their domain along his face, and Adrissu was no different than from the day they met. The evidence of the passage of time only made itself known in the human's form, which Volkmar often complained about—sometimes teasingly, sometimes less so. It only amused Adrissu; after all, it was no surprise to him.

It had been a long time since Adrissu had taken his true form—at least a year, probably more. He rarely did so anymore, since now even his mate did not know. But he was not meant to be condensed down into his tiny elven form for so long, and the yearning to spread his wings and fly steadily increased over time, until eventually he could no longer deny himself.

It was midsummer and the night was warm as he slipped out of bed well past midnight. Volkmar lay asleep beside him, and he could feel Vesper's eyes on him as he walked out of their bedroom.

"*Back soon,*" he thought toward her, and in the center of his chest he felt her acknowledgement. A slight rustle broke the silence, as she coiled up more firmly in the little nest she often made for herself in the corner—Volkmar would regularly leave clothes on the floor for her to hide beneath before laundry day, and tonight she was tucked under a light cotton robe.

He made his way down to the ground floor, carefully skipping the step that always creaked under his weight. The trap door hadn't been opened in a long while, so he magically silenced the groan of long-unused hinges, before taking a step and relishing the cold whistle of air against him as he plummeted.

He burst forth from his elven form as he fell, the wind snapping against his open wings, equal parts painful and satisfying. Groaning in pleasure, he stretched his long-dormant muscles first in the comfort of his lair, stale and dusty as it was. But he had not come down here to tidy up his lair—he came down here to *fly*. So once the braziers were lit with his burning breath, he soared out through the cliffs of Polimnos and out onto the ocean.

Even the spray of the waves almost felt warm against his scales as he flew, nearly silent as he glided mere inches above the surface of the water. His black scales disguised him against the black water, but he was sure that all his teeth showing in a wide grin would give him away if there were anyone so far out on the water. It had been so long, *too* long. He'd have to make a point to get out more often.

Adrissu flew aimlessly for a long while, just enjoying the chance to spread his wings: the simple, instinctual pleasure of doing what his body was made to do. It had been hours by the time the cliffs of Polimnos came back into view. When he clambered back through the narrow passageway that led to his lair beneath the cliffs, his whole body was buzzing with a relaxed sort of joy that he had only ever felt after long flights like this. It took a moment for him to become aware of a different sensation in the center of his chest—Vesper, sleepy but worried. He nudged at her awareness—*what's wrong?*

Woke up. Looked for you, the answer came, wordless but unmistakable. *Sleep now.*

Adrissu huffed in slight irritation, embers fluttering in the air around his mouth. He paced the length of his lair, considering what it might mean. But if Volkmar was asleep again now, he could pass it off as simply going for a nighttime walk, a passing restlessness. It was not entirely a lie.

With several heavy beats of his wings, he flew up through the tunnel that led to the tower; just as the passageway grew too narrow for him to flap his wings again, he shunted himself back into his elven form, letting the momentum and one last surge of magic carry him the rest of the way. His fingers found the rungs of the short ladder that he kept attached to the trap door for this very purpose, and he climbed back up as quietly as he could manage.

The room was dark, and as he remained motionless, listening, the tower seemed silent. Slowly, he closed the door at his feet and made his way back up the stairs, skipping the creaky step and listening intently for any sign that Volkmar was awake.

The door to his bedroom was closed, where he had left it slightly ajar, but standing there he did not hear any noise coming from within. Hopefully Volkmar was still asleep.

The handle clicked as he opened the door, but otherwise he padded in silently. He could see the shape of Volkmar under a light sheet, curled away from him. The human's breathing was slow and steady, even as Adrissu slipped back into bed. But his senses were sharper than either humans or elves—Volkmar was pretending to sleep, he thought, carefully controlling his breath as he listened for Adrissu.

He did not know what it meant. He rolled over and wrapped one arm around the human, pressing his face into Volkmar's long hair and breathing in deeply. Volkmar tensed under his arm, but slowly relaxed. Adrissu held him, awake, until his measured breaths slowed into the true pattern of sleep.

"I heard you leave last night."

The words were more an accusation than anything. When he had woken the next morning and Volkmar hadn't said anything, Adrissu had hoped that would be the end of it, but evidently that was not the case. Adrissu stifled a sigh, glancing up at

Volkmar standing on the stairs, who was looking down at him with his mouth pressed into a tight line and the beginnings of tension between his brows. Adrissu wiped his hands, setting aside the herbs he had been preparing.

"I couldn't sleep," he said, a chagrined smile crossing his face, the image of innocence. "Sorry I woke you."

"You were gone for hours," Volkmar said, looking unmoved as he took a few more steps down.

"I went for a walk."

"For hours?" Volkmar pressed, openly scowling now. "Where did you go for hours in the middle of the night?"

"Volkmar," Adrissu said, pressing his lips together. "What are you trying to say?"

"You—" he started, then looked away. Even from the distance that separated them, Adrissu could see his eyes glimmering with tears. "You know what I'm trying to say."

Silently, Adrissu approached where he stood on the last step.

"Do you truly think I would do something like that?" he said softly, brows furrowing. He reached out to the human, slow enough that he could pull away if he did not want to be touched, but Volkmar did not pull away. He remained stiff and kept his gaze averted, but allowed Adrissu to wrap his arms around his waist. "I love you. I was feeling restless and went for a long walk. I'm sorry I made you worry, but truly, I promise that's all it was."

Volkmar nodded stiffly, but his expression didn't change. Adrissu's heart started to quicken now, unsure of what else he could say that might convince him. He had not expected resistance.

"Volkmar," he repeated, voice still low, as he tilted his head slightly to try and peer into the human's eyes. "Why would I ever do such a thing?"

"Because," the human replied, his voice sounding strained. "Because I'm old and fat now, and you're—you're always going to be beautiful."

Adrissu stilled, taken aback, then despite himself he laughed once. It made sense now that Volkmar said it, but the idea that the human might be feeling insecure, of all things, had truly not occurred to him.

"Old and fat?" he repeated, shaking his head. "I have never, ever thought either of those things in regard to you, love. And even if you were old and fat, I would still want no one else. You know who's truly old and fat? Flint the fishmonger, and I can promise you, you look nothing like that man."

"I—I—" Volkmar stammered, then let out a noise of frustration as he pressed his hands to his eyes. "You're right, of course. I'm... I'm sorry. I just heard you leave and couldn't find you and I suppose I just felt... paranoid. That you decided you wanted something better."

"There is nothing better than you," Adrissu said, shaking his head, and this time as he leaned in, he kissed Volkmar softly on his cheek. "I have always known that my time with you would be limited, that you would... get older faster than I will. I came to terms with it a long time ago, I promise you. But I'm sorry that I didn't realize you were still struggling with it."

Slowly, he felt Volkmar smile against his lips.

"I'm sorry," he answered, a watery smile on his face, as he finally met Adrissu's gaze. "I trust you. Really. I'm sorry I even said it."

"I'm sorry I worried you," Adrissu said, shaking his head. "Now. Have you had lunch yet? We can have whatever you like."

The matter passed and nothing else came of it, at least not at first.

Several weeks later, Adrissu and Volkmar were returning from the market, coming up the worn path to Saltspire Tower and talking amicably about a new wineseller who had just opened a stall in the town square, when every hair on the back of

Adrissu's neck stood on end. He fell abruptly silent, stopping in his tracks—the presence of another dragon was unmistakable.

Why would another dragon come so close? Polimnos was his territory—any dragon would be able to sense his presence as acutely as he felt theirs now, but the feeling persisted. Whoever it was, they weren't turning away.

"Adrissu?" Volkmar asked, turning back to look at him where he'd stopped walking. "What's wrong?"

He first looked up, eyes scanning the horizon in half-dread and half-anger. But the sky was empty, clear and cloudless in the heat of the summer afternoon.

"I..." he started uncertainly, looking back to Volkmar. The human was looking at him, then his eyes flicked to a point behind Adrissu.

He could feel it behind him. Slowly he turned, keeping his face as blank as possible. Walking up the path marked with worn stepping-stones was a lithe human figure, androgynous and nearly as tall as him, with dark hair that was pulled back in a low ponytail, but barely extended past their shoulders. They were dressed in fine traveling clothes, a light and loose cotton tunic over darker pants, leather boots, and topped with a hooded cloak that looked too thick to be comfortable in the heat.

Their eyes met Adrissu's gaze, and he knew immediately that this was the dragon he was sensing.

"Hail, traveler," he called out, his tone short and clipped. The figure raised their hand in a lazy wave, still walking toward them. "You must be lost. There is nothing up this path except for my home." He stressed the last word, smiling, but letting the feral cruelness of his teeth show as he did.

"Luckily, it's you I'm seeking," the traveler replied. Even their voice was hard to place, low in tenor for a woman, but high and nasal for a man.

Something in their demeanor was familiar—he thought of the lazy wave given to him by the last dragon he'd seen in person: Heriel, who had given him the dwarven beryl bowl, over forty years prior in Robruolor. *They're more likely to wander than I*, she had said of her mate. He would have bet the five thousand gold he'd given her that this was the very dragon whom she had mentioned, her mate, Naydruun the Blue.

"Volkmar," he said, finally tearing his gaze away from the intruder to look back up at the human, curiosity plain on his face as he watched their stilted interaction. "Go inside, please."

"What?" he asked, eyebrows lifting in surprise. "But I..."

"Go. Inside," he repeated, giving him a look that he hoped would communicate that it was an order, not a request. Volkmar frowned, eyes flickering between him and the stranger for an instant longer, then with a polite nod at the other figure, he turned and headed for the door. Adrissu watched him until the tower door had closed behind him, and with his one free hand he flicked his wrist, hearing the lock click. Only then did he turn back to face the traveler, whose gaze lingered on the door with a perturbed expression.

"Are you Naydruun the Blue?" Adrissu asked sharply, his voice just above a hiss as he took a step closer. A distance of only about five feet separated them now—he hated being so close, but did not want their voices to carry, and to cast a silencing spell around them could very well be seen as an act of aggression, even though this was his territory.

The figure did not look surprised at the question. "I am," they replied, nodding once. "You are Zamnes the Black?"

Adrissu nearly winced at the name—it had been a long time since he had heard it. It had been decades since Zamnes had been sighted anywhere near Polimnos, and when the town's citizens discussed the beast, it was always Zamnes the Scourge of Polimnos. Only another dragon would know him as Zamnes the Black, and he had luckily avoided the presence of other dragons for many years.

"Yes," he said, openly scowling at Naydruun now. "You are bold to come into my lair, right up to my home."

Naydruun lifted their hands in an appeasing gesture. "I mean no harm. Heriel told me about you when I visited home, how you bought the beryl bowl. I wanted to meet you and perhaps offer my congratulations to you and your mate, but..." Their eyes flickered up to the tower door again. "I wondered why I only sensed one draconic presence as I approached. Was that human really your mate?"

"He *is* my mate, and you would do well to remember where you are," Adrissu growled. Indignation flared in his chest. Every time he had been in another dragon's territory, he had practically humiliated himself with how he'd crawled and begged; yet this strange dragon had the audacity to walk right up to him, as if they were equals in his own home? They were acquaintances at best, and even that was generous; but Naydruun clearly had no intention of lowering themselves before Adrissu. He barely knew the dragon and already he hated them. "What do you want?"

"As I said, I intended to come here to introduce myself to you and your mate, but I see now that won't be necessary," Naydruun sighed. Their lips pressed together in an expression that was not quite a frown, but was decidedly unfriendly. "I have half a mind to take our bowl back, frankly. To do such a thing with a mortal... I don't know how it was even possible. The possibility of it disgusts me."

Adrissu's vision went red with rage, as he took a step closer to Naydruun, feeling his face contort in an expression of anger. Every instinct in him was screaming to kill this intruder, to defend his mate from this threat, and it was only the knowledge that Volkmar was likely watching from the upstairs window that kept him from pulling down a thunderbolt onto their head.

"You know just as well as I that I could kill you right here and be completely justified under our laws," he hissed, lifting one hand to point threateningly. "I do not care what you think of me or my mate. We are fated, and we are soul bound, and your opinion doesn't change that. You are in *my* home, so it doesn't matter that you're older. Your mate treated me with kindness when I met her, and asked me to treat you the same should I ever come across you. For that, for Heriel, I'll let you leave. If I *ever* sense you in Polimnos again, I won't be so forgiving, so I would advise you to never return."

Naydruun's posture had stiffened throughout Adrissu's tirade, and now they took a careful step back to restore the distance that had once been between them. Adrissu realized he still held a cloth bag filled with vegetables in one hand; the sight of him couldn't have been remotely threatening, but at least his words seemed to unsettle Naydruun enough that they remembered their manners.

"If any other dragons find out your mate isn't a dragon, it's going to go poorly for you both," they said stiffly.

"Then it would be best if no other dragons find out, wouldn't it?" he said. For a long moment they were both silent, staring each other down.

"I... *apologize* for the intrusion," Naydruun finally said, their face twisting with distaste as they said it. Adrissu wanted to punch them—he hated lowering himself as much as any other dragon, but at least he had the decency to keep a straight face when he had to. "You won't have to worry about seeing me again. And I won't tell others about your human. I don't keep secrets from Heriel, but no one else will hear it from me."

"Good," Adrissu spat. "Farewell."

He stared down Naydruun for several long, silent seconds, until finally the traveler lowered their head in a curt bow.

"Goodbye," they said, just as unceremoniously, and took a few steps back before turning and walking away. Adrissu watched them until they disappeared down the next hill, and only then did he turn back to his home. With a sigh he scrubbed a hand over his face, willing his hammering heart to slow, and stepped up to the door of Saltspire Tower.

Inside, Volkmar was standing at the top of the stairs and looking down at him with red-rimmed eyes. The bags of fruit and grain that he had brought had been tossed haphazardly onto the table in their sitting room, evidence of how quickly the human must have hurried upstairs to peek out the study window overlooking the path.

"Who the fuck was that?" he asked, voice trembling.

"An unwelcome visitor," Adrissu growled, regretting his angry tone almost immediately. He sucked in a deep breath as he set down his sack of groceries, clenching and unclenching his fists on the tabletop, before looking back up at Volkmar. "We should... talk."

Volkmar's expression didn't change as he took a step down the stairs, but his voice rasped with barely-constrained emotion when he spoke. "Yes. We should."

Chapter Nineteen

"First, whatever you think this is, it isn't," Adrissu said, looking at Volkmar from across the low table in their sitting room. Volkmar had come down to sit in the chaise lounge where Adrissu often read; Adrissu had pulled over one of the cushioned chairs that was normally pushed up against the wall to sit across from him. He watched Volkmar wince at the abrupt words, rubbing his forearms nervously and looking down at his feet. The human's distress and anxiety were sharp against Adrissu's nose, the scent roiling off him like steam. It would have gutted him, if he were not already feeling distressed and uncertain himself.

"Whatever I think it is?" Volkmar muttered, shaking his head. "So you leave in the middle of the night, and a few days later a stranger approaches you in the street and you send me away? And they're not related? That sounds awfully *convenient* for you, doesn't it?"

"It does," Adrissu sighed, biting down on the angry retort in the back of his throat. "I know what it looks like, Volkmar, but I promise you it is nothing of the sort. I have never met that person before today."

"They certainly seemed to know *you*."

"Yes, and that happens quite a lot," he protested, frustration starting to rise in his voice. "I'm the headmaster of the only school of magic in this part of Autreth, not to mention that I can count the number of elves that live here on one hand. Most people in Polimnos know me on sight, Volkmar. You know that, and it isn't fair to act like that isn't the case."

Cowed, Volkmar kept his eyes on the ground and was silent, but Adrissu could see his expression twist.

"I asked you to go inside because I could tell they were dangerous," he continued, forcing his tone to become more even. "I didn't know why they were here, and I wanted to keep you safe."

"Dangerous? How?" Volkmar laughed, finally looking up at him incredulously. "I didn't even see a weapon on them anywhere."

"I could sense their magic," he said, the lie coming easily. It was only halfway a lie, after all—the ability to sense another dragon's presence was certainly linked to magic, even if it was more territorial instinct than anything else. "That's how powerful they were. They knew me, and I didn't know them, so they had me at a disadvantage. I wasn't going to risk anything happening to you in a situation like that."

"A human," Volkmar scoffed. He leaned back in the chaise lounge as he said it, folding his arms across his chest. "I don't believe you. You'd never be so scared of a human."

Adrissu rubbed his eyes in frustration. The veneer of their simple, easy life was about to be ripped away, and he wished he could enjoy its last few moments, rather than dread what was to come. But he did not know what else to say that might have any chance of assuaging him, so all he was left with was the truth.

"They were not a human," he said softly, pulling his hand away from his eyes as he said it. "They were a dragon."

Volkmar stilled, looking at him with wide eyes. For a moment they were both silent, tension palpable in the air between them, but Adrissu forced himself to hold his gaze.

Finally, Volkmar barked out a bitter laugh. "What the fuck are you talking about?"

"They were a dragon in disguise," he sighed.

"Now I know you're hiding something," Volkmar spat, folding his arms across his chest. "Don't lie to me."

"I'm not lying."

"Even if they were a dragon, how could you possibly know that?"

This was it. He wanted to look away, but he kept looking at Volkmar, hoping things would somehow work out.

"Because I'm one, too," he said. "That's how I knew."

Again Volkmar went utterly still, but this time his face twisted in anger.

"Do you really think so little of me?" he hissed, standing up quickly. "That I would believe such an obvious lie?"

"I'm not lying," Adrissu continued, keeping his voice low. He reached for Volkmar, grasping his wrists—he felt the human flinch, but he did not pull away. "You don't remember it now, but you knew this about me. You knew, a long time ago."

He could tell Volkmar was right on the edge of panic, feeling his pulse thrumming rapidly from where he held his wrist, his breathing fast and shallow. All he could do was keep his voice low and even as he spoke.

"I know you don't remember anymore," he continued softly. "But we've known each other longer than you've been alive. Please, you have to trust me on this."

"I don't believe you," Volkmar said sharply, tugging his hands futilely. Adrissu did not let go. "I don't care what you say anymore. I don't believe you."

"I can help you remember," Adrissu said, though he was unsure if he actually could. "Would that prove it to you then? If you remember?"

Volkmar stared down at him, eyes wide and bloodshot. That, at least, seemed to take him aback. Adrissu's heart spiked with fear that Volkmar would still refuse, would still *leave*—so without waiting for an answer, he reached out with his magic to touch the human's mind.

He had long ago studied the basics of altering memory and other such magic. However, these were typically frowned upon amongst both dragons and mortals, if not outright condemned, so he had never had the chance to try anything like this before. He felt his magic touch Volkmar's consciousness, and he thought of Ruan, the time they had shared, and the ritual they had done to bind their souls together. *Remember*, he thought, as if that might somehow unlock whatever was buried deep in Volkmar's subconscious. *Remember me.*

He could feel his consciousness catch on something, a tugging sensation—then Volkmar was wrenching his hands out of Adrissu's grasp with a cry.

"What did you—what did you—" he gasped, clutching his hands to his chest as he collapsed back onto the chaise lounge. His face was glossy with sweat now, his eyes frantically moving back and forth around the room, as if he were seeing things that were not there.

"It's okay," Adrissu said softly, ignoring the fear and worry that had started to trickle down his spine. He had expected that the process would be distressing, but the human looked as if his heart were about to burst. "Do you remember now? Do you remember being Ruan?"

Volkmar sobbed. He reached for a spot low on the left side of his ribs, looking down at himself with obvious worry. "They stabbed me," he whimpered, looking at his hands as if expecting them to come away bloody. "I—You—" His eyes flicked up, lingering on Ruan's shield where it was displayed on the wall, and his face went even more pallid than it already was.

And then he looked back at Adrissu, and terror filled his eyes.

"Volkmar," Adrissu said softly, reaching for him.

"Stay away from me!" Volkmar cried, stumbling off the chaise lounge and onto the floor with how forcefully he recoiled away from Adrissu. His blood turned to ice in his veins, every part of him becoming numb all at once. His mate feared him—his mate *hated* him. He watched, frozen, as Volkmar scrambled back on the stone floor, putting more distance between them, before stumbling to his feet. "Don't—Don't touch me!"

Volkmar was weeping now, his whole body trembling. Adrissu stayed where he was, motionless. Everything was going as poorly as it possibly could, and he had no idea how to make anything better. How could he ever fix this?

"You lied to me," Volkmar hissed, shaking his head as tears streamed down his face. "All these years and you—you thought you could trick me forever?"

"That's not what happened," Adrissu protested, moving to stand up. Volkmar flinched, taking a fearful step back. Adrissu instead dropped to his knees, crawling along the floor toward the human to wrap his arms around his legs. It was humiliating, entirely unbecoming to prostrate himself in such a way before a human, but draconic custom was far from his mind. "I promise you, that wasn't my intention at all. I love you. I just wanted—I just wanted this time to be *simple*. I couldn't bear losing you again. Please, Volkmar, I never wanted to lie to you. I just wanted..." He trailed off, unsure of how to even express it. He had only wanted to keep Volkmar with him for as long as he possibly could, but saying that aloud now seemed foolish.

"You're *Zamnes*," Volkmar muttered, still trembling. "I can't —I can't believe this. I can't believe you. I have to go."

"Go where?" Adrissu asked abruptly, his head snapping up to look into his face

"I can't deal with this," Volkmar muttered, shaking his head and trying to extricate himself from Adrissu's arms. "Let go of me."

"Where will you go?" Adrissu asked again, sounding anguished even to his own ears. He clung to Volkmar for only an instant longer; the human pushed against him frantically, and he released his grasp around his legs.

"I don't know," Volkmar snapped, heading for the stairs. "I just—I can't be anywhere near you. I need to be alone."

Tears burned at Adrissu's eyes. How had he fucked this up so spectacularly? He leaned against the table, not bothering to stand back up, and pressed his hands to his face. What could he do? What *should* he do?

He was unsure how long he remained there, head in his hands, listening to Volkmar's rapid footsteps that moved back and forth on the upper floor. Muffled as it was, he could tell Volkmar was packing a bag. Maybe he could take the memories away, if he could just touch Volkmar again—maybe that would be enough. The thought made him feel sick.

"How much gold is in your desk?" Volkmar's voice came sharply from the top of the stairs.

"A thousand," Adrissu croaked, voice still muffled against his hands.

"I'm taking it all."

At that, he looked up abruptly.

"You shouldn't have so much on you—" he started.

"What? Now that's too much money to spend on me? I know you spent so much more to fucking *buy* me," Volkmar shouted, looking down at him from the landing, his face twisted savagely.

Adrissu balked, mouth working soundlessly for a moment. "I didn't—I only meant, it's not safe to carry so much with you," he protested, forcing himself to get to his feet. His hands were trembling now, thinking of all the terrible things that could befall a human, weak and defenseless, with so much gold jangling on their person. And if he was taking that much with him, maybe he planned on never coming back. "Please, Volkmar, I won't stop you, but please, be reasonable about this—"

"Reasonable? *Reasonable?*" Volkmar repeated, his voice rising shrilly. Adrissu could smell the panic and shock wafting off him even from the bottom of the stairs. "You don't get to fucking tell me what's reasonable, Adrissu, not when you've been a fucking dragon this entire time! *That's* what's unreasonable."

He had no answer to that. He stood frozen in place for a moment longer—the distant sounds of Volkmar opening and slamming drawers and cabinets barely registering—before walking stiffly to the kitchen, bracing himself on the counter as his legs trembled, and taking a long drink directly from an open bottle of wine on the table.

It had never once occurred to him that his mate might eventually *want* to leave him. He had fought so hard to keep them together beyond death that he had never even considered not being together in life. Was that truly what was happening? Would he ever see Volkmar again?

He had the thought, as he sometimes had with Ruan, that he could quite easily prevent Volkmar from leaving. But the thought of Volkmar truly growing to hate him hurt worse than the thought of Volkmar leaving him, and he knew he could not bring himself to actually, physically stop him. If he let Volkmar leave, there was always the chance that he would come back. If he trapped Volkmar here with him…

"I'm leaving," Volkmar said sharply, coming down the stairs without looking at Adrissu. "Don't come looking for me."

His chest felt heavy as he watched Volkmar cross the sitting room, a full rucksack on his back. He could barely focus over the painful thudding of his heart. "Okay."

"I…" Volkmar stammered, and finally glanced back at Adrissu. His eyebrows were furrowed, and for an instant he looked more sad than he did angry. "I'll—I'll check back in with you in a few days. Or something."

Slowly, Adrissu nodded. "Please just let me know you're safe."

"Goodbye," Volkmar muttered, and without waiting for his response, he hauled the heavy wooden door open and left the tower.

The first day Volkmar was gone, Adrissu couldn't even bother to pull himself out of bed. What was the point? What was the purpose of his magic, his power, even his life, if his own mate rejected him? The summer day was hot, which normally did not bother him, but now it only compounded his misery as he laid atop his sheets and sweated the day away. Vesper curled on the bed near him, echoing his despair with a soft sadness of her own in his chest. He could not tell if he appreciated her commiseration or hated it.

On the second day, he spent most of his waking hours pacing anxiously around the tower. He had not heard from Volkmar. They had never been apart so long; it was as if he had forgotten how to exist without his mate at his side. He was sorely tempted to go looking for Volkmar, but he had promised that he would not, and it seemed all he had left was his word. But if he were to simply walk about town and happened to see him, though, surely that would not count as *looking* for him.

As he prepared to leave, he could feel that Vesper desperately did not want him to go alone.

Come with, she thought to him. *Come with.*

He sighed, then got a canvas bag for her to coil in. She was too big now to hide in his sleeve the way she used to, but he slung the bag around one shoulder, and her head peeked out from the top.

Adrissu set out, walking at a rapid pace down to the town square, where he made a careful circuit of all the main streets and the side street that housed the Garden of Delight. He did not truly think Volkmar would have returned there after so long, but he lingered on the street anyway, watching people go in and out. But it seemed quiet and slow, only a handful of visitors entering in the hour Adrissu loitered around the building, and he left without any leads. He saw no sign of Volkmar as he continued around town, and eventually came back to the footpath that led to his tower. He doubted Volkmar had left the city, but wherever he was, he wasn't walking about town.

When he came home, he methodically went through all the things Volkmar had left behind, as if he could make some sense of it all from what he had taken and what remained. Only about a week's worth of clothes were gone from his closet, and most of his valuables had been left behind—though, Adrissu noted, Volkmar had taken a necklace with him that he particularly loved. Adrissu had bought it for him during one of their many trips, when they had spent the summer in the west of Autreth, visiting several small beachside towns that attracted tourists for their warm shores and lovely views. The necklace was a silver chain with a single, large blue pearl on it: one that could only be harvested in Naymere, along the western coast.

Maybe that was a good sign, he thought. Maybe he had brought it with him because deep down he knew Adrissu cared. Or maybe he had only been wearing it when he left and hadn't thought to take it off. Adrissu couldn't remember if he had been wearing it or not.

On the third day, Adrissu woke from a restless sleep, already feeling sick and hating himself. Never before had he felt so completely useless. He couldn't even track his mate down in their own city, much less convince him to return. He thought of going out to look again, but Vesper curled heavy and tight around his shoulders.

Stay, he heard clearly from her. *Sleep.*

"How can I sleep when I don't even know where he is?" he muttered, scowling at her. But she did not budge, and he didn't have the will to fight. The cool weight of her on his bare shoulders was almost comforting in the summer heat, and he managed to sleep a little longer.

Adrissu woke with a start, uncertain of how long it had been, to the sound of someone pounding on his door. Vesper was slithering off him the moment he woke—they must have only just arrived, otherwise she would already be at the door.

Stranger, she thought. He scowled, getting up slowly; but the pounding on his door continued, so he descended the stairs, pulling a clean summer robe over him as he went.

The pounding stopped as he unlocked the door, and it swung open to reveal a spindly, fair-haired human that Adrissu did not recognize at first. He was red-faced and breathing hard, leaning forward with his hands on his knees as he squinted up at Adrissu.

"Headmaster Adrissu," the man panted, and recognition dawned on him as he spoke. "I'm Dr. Allar with the surgeon's office—"

"What are you doing here?" Adrissu interrupted, a chill overtaking him despite the afternoon heat. The human hesitated, looking at him with something like sympathy, and instantly his heart plummeted to the very bottom of his stomach. "What happened?"

"It's your, ah, your husband—your partner, sir," the doctor stammered, still breathing hard. "Well, he's with us."

"What *happened*?" Adrissu asked again, hissing through his teeth. The wood of the door cracked as he said it—he had clenched the door handle so forcefully, it splintered in his hand. Angrily, he yanked his hand away, looking back into the tower where Vesper was watching from the stairs. He waved his now-empty hand, sending his shoes sliding along the floor to him.

"I can tell you on the way, sir, you should really come with me," the doctor continued. Adrissu stifled a growl of frustration, pulling his shoes on with one hand and reaching out with the other, until he felt his coin purse come sailing into his palm. Adrissu had never had to make use of the handful of physicians in town, and he guessed that they were not operating out of the goodness of their hearts.

"You said the surgeon's office?" he said, stepping out of the tower and closing the door behind him. "Near the town square?"

"Yes, this way," the man said, starting to turn. Adrissu seized his shoulder before he could get more than a step away. The doctor looked back at him, confused; but Adrissu snapped his fingers, thinking of the building where he knew the surgeon's office to be. There was a lurching sensation, then they were standing in the town square.

"Gods above!" the doctor exclaimed, eyes wide as he looked about. A woman walking near them yelped at their sudden appearance, stumbling backward.

Despite the heavy exhaustion that immediately settled over him—teleportation was by far the most taxing magic he was capable of, even a short distance like this—Adrissu ignored them, pushing past the doctor to enter the building. The human seemed to shake himself and hurried after Adrissu.

"You should know before you see him," he said quickly, jogging to catch up and pushing his hair out of his perspiring face. "He's been here about an hour—he was hurt when someone found him and called us over, but we don't know for how long. It's—" He hesitated, and Adrissu stopped to look back at him, frowning. "It's bad, to be honest, sir. I wanted to tell you before you saw him."

"How bad?" Adrissu said. He already felt cold, but now he was shaking. "How bad?"

The doctor didn't answer him right away, glancing away anxiously, and Adrissu had the cold realization that he had not brought him to help or comfort Volkmar. He had been in a rush to bring him to say goodbye.

Chapter Twenty

"Where was he when you found him?" Adrissu asked tersely, following more slowly, as Dr. Allar led him through the hallways of the physician's office. His whole body felt numb with shock, but he had already been useless enough. He had to see this through, whatever was going to happen.

"A citizen found him collapsed in town, behind the inn near the harbor. He must have been robbed, but we don't really know exactly what happened. He had a, well, a stab wound in the abdomen... He managed to walk out into the street before collapsing, where someone spotted him and brought him here. He woke up a bit and asked for you, but... I'm sorry." He opened his mouth to say more, glancing back at him anxiously, then shook his head and only repeated, "I'm sorry."

He stopped in front of a closed door, his hand hovering nervously over the handle.

"Let me in," Adrissu said, his voice choked. "I need to see him."

The man nodded and opened the door.

The first thing that struck him was the smell—blood and something like ammonia. The room was cramped, just large enough for one narrow bed and space on the sides for someone to walk by. In the center of it all was Volkmar, pallid and unmoving. Adrissu's stomach lurched—already he looked like a corpse—but then he stirred slightly, eyelids fluttering, but not quite opening. A thick layer of bandages was wrapped around his abdomen just below his ribs, bloodied on his right side. His hair was a mess, dampened with sweat and sticking to his face. A nurse was on the other side of the bed, gathering a bundle of bloodied sheets in her arms. She glanced at them with a start, then pushed past them to hurry out the door, leaving them alone.

He couldn't move, frozen in the doorway. His mate was dying, and he couldn't move. Before, he had anguished over not being with Ruan when he died—now the thought of being with his mate as his life so obviously faded away made him want to flee in terror.

"The dagger cut him through the liver," the doctor murmured next to him, shaking him from his stupor. "We've tried to stop the bleeding, but... By the time he got to us, it was already too far gone. We've done our best to make him comfortable. I'm... I'm sorry."

"How long?" Adrissu rasped, holding his hands tightly in front of him to keep them from shaking.

The doctor shook his head. "An hour, maybe. At most."

The air left Adrissu's lungs. An hour. Probably less. And then he would be alone, maybe another two decades, maybe more.

"I know you are practiced in the arcane, of course," the doctor continued, his voice still low. "If you know any healing magic..."

Adrissu's stomach lurched again, his heart squeezing painfully in his chest. His knowledge of healing magic extended only to superficial wounds. A deep, mortal wound like this was far beyond his capabilities. Could such a thing be healed by even the most accomplished magicians? He did not know. He had never cared before.

The man was still looking at him expectantly, a tiny, irritating sliver of hope on his face. But Adrissu shook his head once, shame flooding him as he did, and that hope dimmed from the doctor's eyes as he looked back at Volkmar.

"I'll leave you alone," the doctor sighed, stepping back. His tone was more brisk now, a cool veneer over the sympathy he had just shown. In a profession like this, Adrissu supposed, that was necessary; but part of him burned with rage that his mate was dying and this man no longer cared. "A nurse will be just outside. You should say goodbye while you can."

Adrissu only nodded, stepping past him into the room without looking back. When he heard the door click behind him, he took another slow, fearful step toward Volkmar, sitting down on the edge of the bed at his side.

A tiny sliver of his eyes was visible, eyelids flickering with movement as if he were sleeping. Adrissu reached up to brush his sweat-soaked hair out of his face, and Volkmar's eyes flew open, bloodshot and frightened.

"I'm here," Adrissu murmured, ignoring the way his lungs constricted at the way the human's eyes fluttered frantically around the room. "Volkmar. It's alright. I'm here."

Volkmar's eyes found his, focusing now, and immediately his breathing quickened. Weakly, he lifted one hand and grasped Adrissu's wrist where he was touching Volkmar's face. It trembled violently against his own. Instantly he stank of fear: whether Volkmar was afraid of him, or afraid because he knew he was dying, Adrissu did not know. He did not want to know.

Volkmar made a soft noise in the back of his throat, lips parted, but when he managed to speak it was barely a whisper. "S-Sorry."

Adrissu squeezed his eyes shut, shaking his head. The last thing he needed was to cry now, but tears burned his eyes all the same.

"No, I'm sorry," he murmured, reaching with his other hand and continuing to push hair out of Volkmar's face. "I'm sorry I couldn't protect you. I'm sorry I let this happen. I'm—I'm sorry I hurt you."

Volkmar nodded, eyes sliding away, as he allowed Adrissu to pull back his hair and tuck it behind his head against the pillow. He almost looked worse with his face more visible–his skin was waxy and pale underneath the sheen of cold sweat. The skin under his eyes was blotched and dark like a bruise, yet the color seemed to have drained entirely from his lips.

"Hurts," he groaned, his voice rasping. His free hand came up to press against the bandages packed tightly to his side; a red patch had started seeping up through the center, even in the few moments Adrissu had been beside him.

"Let me help," Adrissu murmured, pressing his fingertips to Volkmar's forehead. This, at least, he could do. Reaching out with his magic, he could feel a sharp burst of agony in his own side, a mirror of where Volkmar had been wounded. He winced, nearly wrenching his hand away, but kept the contact long enough to draw all the pain to him. Volkmar let out a long breath and sagged weakly against the pillows that propped him up, the relief obvious in his face.

"Took the—the gold," he rasped, eyes a little wider now. With his free hand he weakly patted at his collarbone, before letting the limb slide back down onto the bed. "My necklace. Should have—listened to you—sorry."

"You have nothing to apologize for," Adrissu said, shaking his head, even as the mention of the necklace sent another spike of despair through his chest. If Volkmar had continued to wear the necklace, maybe he had brought it intentionally after all. Maybe there would have been hope after all. "You know I don't care about the gold."

Volkmar nodded silently, closing his eyes. He was still for a moment, Adrissu watching him, then he whispered without opening his eyes, "I'm—I'm scared."

"You have nothing to be afraid of," Adrissu said, though his voice cracked as he spoke. "You came back to me. You'll always come back to me."

A tear slid out from beneath Volkmar's lashes, but he nodded. The smell of fear still permeated the room, but his hand was no longer trembling where it rested on Adrissu's wrist.

It took less than an hour, as the doctor had said. Adrissu managed to pull Volkmar closer to him, so he could wrap both arms around his small frame—could feel the slight expansion of his lungs with each shallow, labored breath. He spoke softly with Volkmar's head leaning against the crook of his shoulder, telling him all the places they would still go, and the things they would still do together. Volkmar had nodded or murmured every so often at first, but before long his responses became less and less distinct, with longer and longer delays.

When it had been several minutes since Volkmar responded, Adrissu fell silent, listening closely for the sound of his breathing and the beat of his heart. He remained sitting perfectly still, silently counting the seconds between each breath.

Finally, after one last shallow gasp, his breathing seemed to stop. Adrissu squeezed his shoulder.

"Volkmar," he whispered, voice breaking. The human did not stir, did not breathe. He could no longer feel the faint flutter of his heartbeat. "Volkmar."

He was gone.

Adrissu was still holding Volkmar's body when a nurse came back in to check on them, and everything after that was a blur. He could not remember the exact details of how Volkmar's body was taken away, nor describe the face of the mortician who had come to make burial arrangements. He did not know how he ended up back in his tower, curled on the chaise lounge with Vesper coiled tightly in a ball that he held to his chest.

His body was leaden with grief. He regretted ever letting Volkmar leave his sight, regretted ever trying to bring back his memory, regretted ever keeping the truth from him in the first place. The thought that someday his mate would return to him did not soothe him at all, the way it had when Ruan died. That too was now tinged with its own pain, knowing he would be alone until then, when he had grown so used to having his mate at his side. That hope had been tainted with the fear that he might somehow drive his mate away from him again in the future.

The idea of going to the funeral was entirely distasteful. In all his years he had been to only a few; when Cyrus had died, Adrissu had attended his funeral as one of his advisors, but that was a notable exception. He did not like them. Dragons did not have anything comparable to them. Most dragon deaths involved more violence, and vengeance on whatever killed it, than any sort of mourning for the dragon itself. Their bodies were burned, not buried, with little ceremony. No, most dragons believed that eventually a dragon's soul would be reborn, so deaths were not mourned the way humans mourned.

But his mate *was* human, and he had already paid for the rites with the mortician, so he dragged himself out of his tower, dressed in black robes despite the summer heat, and walked down into the city.

Polimnos had a few graveyards now, but the largest overlooked the sea on a cliff that was down along the southern edge of town. The grass and leaves of the trees were all a vibrant yellow-green as Adrissu approached, making the dark clothing of the priest that would perform the rites stand out. The man bowed his head in greeting to Adrissu.

"My sincerest condolences, headmaster Adrissu," the priest said, with all the rehearsed cadence of a man who had said the same thing a thousand times before. Immediately, Adrissu hated him. "This way, please."

Adrissu followed him down the meandering path through the graveyard, until he could see the wooden box that housed Volkmar's body, set up on a small wooden platform over a hole in the ground that would be its final resting place. A few flowers were set up alongside it, as if that could mask the macabre nature of their task.

"If there are any words you'd like to say, there will be a moment for that before the rites begin," the priest started, but Adrissu shook his head sharply.

"No," he said, his voice coming out raspy. He cleared his throat before continuing. "No. I want this over with quickly."

"Of course," the priest replied, though he sounded uncertain. "I'll return in fifteen minutes for the rites."

The priest stepped away, walking a little ways back down toward the path. He would wait there to direct any other guests to the correct spot; Adrissu doubted more than a few would come. Volkmar had friends and acquaintances, of course, and he knew the teachers of the academy planned on coming out of respect for him; but in Volkmar's lifetime, Adrissu had sequestered himself in his tower far more than he had during Ruan's life. He was not as involved with the current governance outside of how it concerned the academy; he was well-known throughout town, as he had always been, but he had fewer friends now than when he'd first met Volkmar. Part of him wanted to flee, balking at the idea of these humans who knew so little about him, yet came to grieve with him. But he was already here, and maybe this was what Volkmar would have wanted. He did not know; he had not thought that he would need to discuss it with Volkmar for a long time yet.

The first few guests were coming up the path now, their figures indistinct in the similar black robes they wore, save for one in white. There were four of them, which he knew were the four instructors of the academy: three humans in black, and another elf in white.

Ayeval had been with the academy for a few years now, the first who had approached him about potentially teaching. Adrissu had been surprised that an elf was interested in teaching magic so far from Aefraya, but she was young and eager to see the world. She seemed like the type that would only put down roots for a decade or two, before wanting to see somewhere new; and she was very good with illusions, the subject she taught, so he had been convinced. The other three were human, two of his original instructors and the third who had only been brought on the year after Ayeval. As they drew nearer, they all bore expressions of sympathy, but Ayeval's was particularly sad, which irritated him.

"Headmaster," one of the humans murmured as they stepped up alongside him. "We were all so sorry to hear what happened. What a terrible tragedy."

"Truly heinous," another sighed, shaking his head. "I hope they find whoever did this."

"Thank you," Adrissu said, his voice clipped. He looked away, eyes lingering on the wooden box. They seemed not to know what else to say, so they stood in silence.

After a moment, Ayeval leaned closer to him.

"I'm surprised to see you in black," she murmured, just loud enough for him to hear.

In truth, he had not been aware that the elven mourning dress was, apparently, white instead of black. But he shrugged, and answered simply,

"He was human."

She paused, then nodded, leaning back.

They waited a bit longer. The next figure to approach was the current Lord Representative, which took Adrissu by surprise at first, then left a sour taste in his mouth. Benit Pallestride was the grandson of Benil Branwood, who had died perhaps five years ago. The man had achieved what Benil had never been able to accomplish, having a much shrewder mind and a better disposition for civic responsibility. Adrissu was not one of his advisors, as he had been to Cyrus and Kira Lang. He liked Benit well enough, but the human was a year younger than Volkmar, and the sight of him now made Adrissu's blood boil with something like envy. It was irrational, Adrissu told himself, as Benit bowed his head deeply in front of him, and he forced himself to nod slowly in reply.

"So sorry to hear of all this," the human sighed, folding his arms across his chest and looking past Adrissu toward the coffin. "Absolutely terrible. I never thought something like this could happen in our city. The harbor is usually so safe."

Adrissu stopped himself from rolling his eyes. "Thank you for coming."

"We will find who did this, and they will pay," he continued.

"Yes," Adrissu nodded. This, at least, seemed little enough for Benit to work with, and the lord fell silent.

Two more figures were coming up the path, one walking slowly and leaning on the other, both wearing black. Adrissu frowned; he did not recognize the one bearing the other's weight.

It took him a moment to recognize the other: Ederick, head of the mercenary's guild, who must have been eighty years old, if not past that now. Most of his hair was gone, and his face was lined with age, but he glanced up and caught Adrissu's gaze, lifting his free hand slowly in a somber greeting.

"Adrissu," Ederick panted as he got within earshot. "I hope you don't mind me coming. I heard what happened—just awful."

"I do not mind," Adrissu said softly, bowing his head at the human. "Thank you for coming."

"Gods, I can't even imagine," he sighed, looking up at Adrissu as he straightened. His dark eyes were slightly yellowed, his lower lids sagging with age, making his expression all the more downtrodden. "When I heard you found someone, after— after Ruan—I was so glad for you. And for this to happen—I can't imagine." He reached out with one spotted hand and gently squeezed his forearm.

Adrissu patted his hand once, before clasping his own over it. Ederick had always been on friendly terms with him, but he had not expected the old man to come, especially since Adrissu had stepped back from the mercenary's guild significantly in the past several years; but now that he was here, he felt more grateful for Ederick's presence than all the rest put together.

"Ah, forgive me. This is my nephew, Elvard," Ederick said, gesturing to the man who was standing next to him. The human nodded stiffly at Adrissu, looking slightly uncomfortable. "Elvard, this is headmaster Adrissu, an old friend and headmaster of the Polimnos Academy of Magic."

Adrissu pressed his lips together as Elvard bowed his head. He supposed Ederick was his friend.

"I'm honored to meet you, though I'm sorry it's under these circumstances," Elvard murmured, his eyes flickering around the graveyard, looking everywhere but at Adrissu, or at the coffin behind him.

"Likewise," he muttered, looking away as well. He spotted the priest at the end of the walkway, but did not think anyone else would arrive.

"I'll, ah, leave you to it," Elvard continued, clearly trying to be polite, though his tone was awkward and stilted. He gave Ederick a look, and the old human nodded, before stepping away to stand at a polite distance across the footpath.

A few more people trickled in: friends of Volkmar that he'd known from selling his paintings and taking music lessons. Adrissu acknowledged each of them tersely, realizing he couldn't put a name to any of their faces. If they felt snubbed by his reaction, they didn't show it.

It was late in the morning and already seemed to be another hot, humid day; he was starting to sweat in his dark robes. Luckily, the priest seemed cognizant of the time, and he started heading back up the path a moment later. Relief spread like a cool balm in Adrissu's chest; the sooner they got this over with, the sooner he could go home.

The priest started his monologue, speaking of the souls of the dead that would never truly die, that went to be in the presence of the gods, and that would continue to live on there and in the memories of those they left behind. It was all very nebulous and sentimental. Like Adrissu, Volkmar had never seemed particularly interested in the trappings of religion and the gods. The whole ceremony felt pointless.

Then the coffin was lowered into the ground; Adrissu could feel the flow of magic coming from the priest, not particularly strong, but enough to pull the coffin from its stand and lower it into the hole. It was sprinkled with salt, ash, and water, then the priest gestured toward Adrissu.

"Please, if you'll be the first," he said, gesturing to the mound of fresh earth alongside the grave. Adrissu sighed, steadying his breathing as much as he could. He took the shovel, scooped up some dirt, and dropped it down into the grave. He passed it to Ederick next to him; with some effort, the human repeated the action, and passed the shovel to the next. Each of them took a scoop of dirt and poured it into the grave in turn, until the shovel made it back into the hands of the priest.

"And thus we say goodbye to Volkmar and send our best wishes to his spirit, as he basks in the presence of the gods," the priest said, and with a swish of his arm, the rest of the dirt followed to mark the fresh gravesite.

A few more words were said, but at that point it was basically over. Adrissu had no plans of hosting some sort of party or dinner, which humans often would host after a funeral—he could not imagine wanting anything less.

"Thank you for coming," he said stiffly to the small group around him, when the priest finally finished the rites and politely stepped away, his job done. "I am sure Volkmar would appreciate it, as—as have I." He cleared his throat, clasping his hands tightly in front of them to keep them from shaking.

"We're here for you, headmaster," Ayeval said softly. The others murmured their assent. "You have our support."

"Thank you," Adrissu repeated. More than anything he just wanted to go home. "I... Pardon me."

He turned, ignoring the voices of the people around him, and started walking away. He did not stop until he was alone.

We will find who did this, and they will pay.

Benit's words were echoing in his head each time he woke over the next few days. Vengeance, he thought, would not truly make him feel any better about what happened, but the most primal part of him burned to find the one who had done this to him, to his mate.

The human's words were meaningless—after the funeral, Adrissu did not hear anything from the Lord Representative about tracking down whoever had killed Volkmar—so when he could no longer bear the ache of not knowing, he set out to seek his own justice.

He started at the harbor, sitting outside the inn where Volkmar had stayed, and began to watch. He asked the innkeeper if she had seen what happened; she had not, she said, and had told the city guard as such. He had no leads and no idea what he was looking for; but sitting outside the inn watching people walk to and from the harbor, or else walking along the harbor himself, felt better than sitting alone in his damned tower.

For several days, he did not see anything that seemed related to what had happened—not that he had any idea of what he was looking for, of course.

It was late in the afternoon on the third day, when he saw the faint flicker of a bluish-tinged pearl that reflected the light of the setting sun, as it bounced on a silver chain in the hand of what looked to be a dock worker. The worker was presenting the necklace to another man who looked down at it with obvious disinterest.

It had to be Volkmar's necklace. Adrissu turned abruptly to watch the exchange; the dock worker's back was to him, but he could see the other man's face as he reached for the necklace, holding the pearl up closer to his face to inspect it. The man sighed and handed it back, and over the noise of the harbor Adrissu could just barely hear him speak.

"How much?" he asked. The dock worker's answer was too faint to hear, but the other man visibly balked. "No, that's too much."

The man gesticulated with both hands, but seemed to purposely be keeping his voice low. The pearl flashed again in the sunlight, swinging in his grasp. The man Adrissu could see shook his head, frowning.

"That's not my problem, now is it?" he said, folding his arms across his chest and taking a step away from the man. "Look, ask me again tomorrow if you still haven't sold it, and maybe consider a discount if you're trying to get rid of it quickly."

"Yeah, fuck you," Adrissu heard the man say, waving a dismissive hand as he turned. Adrissu pretended to look out toward the sea as the man turned, but he continued to watch him from the corner of his eye. The human was tall with a sinewy build, and he wore a set of sailor's clothes that looked brand new, though his hands were rough and dirty. His hair was dark and cropped close to his scalp, his hairline receding, but patchy facial hair covered his face, as if he were growing it out—as if he were trying to disguise himself. Adrissu's eyes narrowed, and he turned to watch the man start walking away, having not seemed to notice his attention.

The man was heading away from the docks, toward the path that led further into town. Adrissu followed, keeping a safe distance at first, then closed the gap between them quickly as they left the crowded harbor, and the man turned toward a more quiet street.

"Excuse me," Adrissu said, and the man turned around quickly, looking startled. "I couldn't help but notice you on the dock. Is that a Naymerese pearl necklace you're selling?"

From the way the man's eyes shifted quickly from Adrissu to the docks behind him to the buildings surrounding them, Adrissu could tell he was nervous and did not know what Adrissu was talking about exactly, but was eager to hand off his stolen goods. Best of all, he did not seem to recognize Adrissu; he guessed the man was a sailor, here for a week or two, until the boat that he worked on set out again.

"Why, yes it is," he said after a beat, his tone sounding far more chipper than Adrissu would have expected. "If you're interested, I can part with it for a hundred gold."

Adrissu forced himself not to flinch; while the pearl was rare and the necklace pricey, a hundred gold was easily double what it was worth. The man seemed to be an idiot as well as a thief and a murderer; somehow, he thought, that was worse than the idea of Volkmar being killed by someone calculating and intelligent. It made his death seem all the more pointless, set in motion by a mere opportunist.

But he came here for a reason. Adrissu forced himself to smile, despite the way his blood burned in his veins. "Done," he said quickly. "I don't have that much on me, but I live just up the road. Would you mind?"

A nervous look flitted over the man's face for a moment, and he shifted slightly to the left—just enough that Adrissu could spot the dagger on his hip, though he purposely did not look at it.

"Sure," the man said, gesturing up the road. "Please, lead the way."

Adrissu grinned wider, and the man glanced away. "Of course," he said, overtaking the man with a few long strides. "In fact, I know a shortcut."

The road ahead was empty; Adrissu did not care if anyone could see them from behind him. He reached one hand out to clasp the man's shoulder; the sailor flinched away instinctively, but Adrissu's reach was longer. He clamped his fingers around the man's shoulder the moment he made contact, thought of his lair, and snapped his fingers.

The world lurched around them, and the street went dark.

"What the fuck!" the sailor exclaimed, leaping away from Adrissu only to stumble in the sudden darkness. "What the fuck did you do?!"

Adrissu ignored him, his true form surging forth from his body. His draconic sight clicked into place, piercing through the darkness of his lair, just in time to see a look of horror dawning on the sailor's face, eyes turning up as Adrissu grew to tower over the human. He smiled again, feeling the heat gush from his throat as he exhaled, embers fluttering around his bared teeth.

Before the sailor could react, Adrissu lunged forward, grabbing the man with his claws and flapping his wings to glide through his lair. The man was screaming, the sound echoing through the chamber; luckily, he didn't start pissing himself until Adrissu had cleared the entrance, and light surrounded them again as they rocketed over the ocean.

The man was begging for mercy as Adrissu flew, eyes scanning the horizon for somewhere to land. It would not be enough just to drop him into the ocean. He was going to completely eviscerate the bastard that had taken his mate from him.

He had flown maybe two miles, and the man's desperate cries had faded into hyperventilating breaths, when Adrissu spotted a narrow rock formation rising up out of the waves. It would barely support the weight of his body, but it would work. He turned sharply toward it, holding the man out in front of him to slam him into the rock as he landed. There was a satisfying crack and a howl of pain that became a wail of fear as Adrissu towered over him, wings spread out to block the light of the sunset.

"*Give me the necklace,*" he growled, lowering his jaw close enough to the man's face that the skin of his face reddened with heat as he spoke. The man froze, eyes wide with shock and confusion. Adrissu snarled, and the man cried out again. "*Give me the fucking necklace!*"

"Here!" he sobbed, scrambling with one hand to reach into his pocket. He pulled out the necklace, holding it up by the chain.

The pearl had been cracked with the impact, and as he held it up, the cracked half fell off completely and splashed down into the ocean below.

Adrissu screamed in rage and ripped the man's hand off with his teeth, the coppery taste of blood filling his mouth. The sailor was shrieking now, kicking against him uselessly, as Adrissu flung his severed hand out into the ocean and the remains of the necklace with it. He had wanted to make the man suffer, but now a blind fury filled him. The only coherent thought he could put together was that this was the man who killed Volkmar, and he had deserved to die days ago.

He drove his head down again, powerful jaws closing over the man's chest. His ribs crunched and parted against Adrissu's teeth, and his screams became a burst of bloody air on his tongue as his tiny human lungs were crushed. When Adrissu reared back, entrails dripping from his teeth, the man was looking down at his obliterated body with an expression of absolute agony, even as his face drained of color and the light left his eyes.

Adrissu inhaled hard, then sent a stream of flame shooting into the man's face, the fire consuming the human's body and skittering across the rocks. When he finally stopped to inhale again, the human was dead, his skin blistering and sloughing off.

It was not enough. He breathed fire again, and again, and again, until every last bit of flesh was burned away, and only blackened bones remained. Even then, he smashed the burnt bones with his claws, splintering and crushing them until they were like gravel. It still was not enough, but there was nothing left.

With one last slash of his claws to send the mess of ash and bone spilling into the waters below, Adrissu took to the sky again, screaming flame down into the ocean as he went, where it boiled and steamed away uselessly. He almost hoped someone spotted him, even miles out into the ocean, so he had an excuse to keep killing and destroying everything. But he was alone, and when the flames no longer came and the blood dripping from his mouth was now his own, he turned and flew home.

He had his revenge. He didn't feel any better.

Book Three
Braern

Chapter Twenty-One

After taking his revenge, Adrissu did not leave his tower for well over a month. An instructor from the academy would drop by once a week, mostly a formality to ensure he was kept in the loop of the goings-on at the school, but largely he did not care what was happening. To care about anything felt pointless. He had done all that he could do to avenge Volkmar, but he was still alone, without his mate, so what was the purpose of it all?

Volkmar's death wrecked him in a way that Ruan's had not. He could not place it, not at first, but in the end it felt as though he were at fault with Volkmar in a way he had not been with Ruan. Ruan had understood the risks of the conflict he joined and accepted them, forcing Adrissu to make his own peace with it. Volkmar had no such acceptance. If anything, Adrissu had driven him into the very situation that killed him.

Guilt was not an emotion that he had often felt prior to this, but for weeks he was paralyzed with it. Their last argument played in his head, over and over, as he considered every word he might have said differently that could have prevented this. Part of him wished that he had killed Naydruun on sight, or when they had turned to go—part of him wanted to go find the dragon and kill them right then, as if that would somehow make him feel any better, or bring Volkmar back to him. But as much as Adrissu hated the other dragon, he would not have had the energy or drive to truly seek them out. And he did owe Heriel,

Naydruun's mate, a debt of gratitude. He would not seek the dragon out, but if he ever saw them again, he *would* kill them. The decision was something like a balm to his other troubled thoughts.

He was miserable, but eventually the sight of the same walls around the same room was driving him to the brink of madness. So when he could bear it no longer, Adrissu forced himself to go to the academy in the mornings, hating every moment. He did almost no actual work, but it made him feel a little better to be moping somewhere other than Saltspire Tower.

As it had a knack of doing, time eventually took the sting out of it all. Adrissu's grief settled into the old, familiar longing— waiting for his mate to return—and he could think of other things for long enough that the guilt began to ebb away. There was nothing left to do, except to wait, so he might as well pass the time doing something other than being miserable.

Much like he had before, he threw himself back into his work, devoting most of his time and attention to the academy. In the nearly forty years since its founding, its growth had stalled after the first decade. With their attendance at around fifty students each year, the four instructors were enough; but if he could bring in more instructors, he could bring in more students. He spent the following year revising and expanding the current school curriculum; he added extra lessons to the existing concentrations and designed new areas of study that included protective and offensive magic, expanding the slight overlap they already had with the mercenary's guild.

The new curriculum was time-consuming, but not especially difficult to put together. Finding instructors would prove more difficult.

Adrissu went to the College of the Arcane in Gennemont again, alone for the first time in many years. He met with the instructors that he already knew, showing them his improved curriculum and offering them a place at his own academy. So far, he had seemed to be little enough of a threat to the college of Gennemont that he was free to peruse their libraries and consult with their teachers; if all went as he hoped, he might not have such freedom with their resources in the future. But only one of the current Gennemont instructors seemed interested enough in relocating to Polimnos; his three most promising leads were students on the cusp of graduating.

Normally, he would do some research at their expansive library while in Gennemont; but this time he was too busy consulting with students and professors to spare more than an hour or so in the evening, before the library closed for the day. Besides, it felt too soon to restart his research on making mortal souls immortal.

But when he returned from his trip, a letter was waiting for him from an elf, Caemar Illuren, to whom he had written several decades ago. Of course, he thought bitterly as he opened the letter, *now* was the time that the elf would finally respond. The letter was long and meandering, explaining the research the elf had done in the years between receiving Adrissu's letter and his leisurely response: how he had largely moved on from his theories regarding soul containment, but that he would be happy to discuss the topic with Adrissu should he ever find himself in Aefraya.

If Adrissu remembered correctly—and he was quite sure he was—Caemar Illuren was certainly more than two hundred years old now, approaching advanced age even amongst elves. It would behoove him to take advantage of the elf's standing invitation, sooner rather than later, in the unfortunate event that he would not live long enough to receive Adrissu. So he wrote back that he would love to discuss the topic with Caemar as such an authority on the subject, and would plan to come to Aefraya the next summer, when he was not so busy with the academy. The timing would not be ideal, but it would have to do.

The following year, Adrissu was preoccupied with attracting more students to Polimnos. The city's population had continued to swell with the expansion of the harbor and the continued success of the mines. The mercenary's guild did not flourish the way it once had, but remained a stalwart, if niche, presence in the city's economy. Poaching students from the mercenary guild's roster seemed pointless when their own attendance was smaller than ever; and besides, he did not want to do anything to threaten the rapport he had with Ederick, who somehow was still alive and still the guildmaster, though it seemed to be largely a courtesy title with little actual duty anymore.

He would have to explore other avenues. He and the instructors provided incentives for current students to recruit new ones, posted listings on each message board in every inn and tavern in Polimnos, and even set up a booth each weekend on the docks, which they hoped would spread the word of the academy to the many sailors and laborers that traveled from port to port.

Though it did not work as well as Adrissu would have liked, it did work. By the time the school term ended, they were on track to have sixty-two students after the summer recess with room for up to twenty more, if there happened to be any last-minute enrollments. It was more than they had ever had before, so Adrissu counted himself lucky and solidified his plans to continue scaling up.

As soon as he was free for the summer, though, he flew to Aefraya. Traveling alone did not feel quite so wretched now: being alone in the air, away from the constant noise and movement of the city, was its own reward.

Caemar Illuren resided in Castle Aefraya itself, as an arcanist in service of the royal library. Neither the library nor the castle would be accessible to Adrissu. The current rulers, Queen Taviriel and her King-Consort Aeroven, had recently announced that they were expecting their first child, so security around the castle was excessive. Even with Caemar's invitation, Adrissu was not an Aefrayan citizen and would thereby not be allowed into the castle. Instead, they met at the most luxurious inn within the walls of the capitol city: the Magenta Marigold, which was quite refined, despite its silly name.

"Headmaster Adrissu, I presume?"

The elf was visibly old and wizened, meaning he was almost certainly within the final decade or two of his life. His hair looked like it may have once been dark, but was now mostly gray, pulled back in a low ponytail that fell past his shoulders. Adrissu managed a smile as the man approached him where he sat in one of the tavern's private meeting rooms.

"Is it that obvious I'm not from around here?" he replied, standing to greet the elf. Though Caemar was old, he moved easily, bowing his head in greeting smoothly, and smiled politely when he rose.

"It is obvious you are not from Aefraya," he replied, and gestured to Adrissu's clothes. "Those tight sleeves and the belt are all human fashion. Here in the capitol especially, you'd be hard-pressed to find any robes without the ruffled sleeves or billowing length that Queen Taviriel prefers. All the fashions are modeled after hers."

"I see," Adrissu said, maintaining the smile that was plastered on his face. He had not been aware of the current elf fashions, but he did not particularly care. Still, he wanted to stay in the elf's good graces, so he would suffer through the small talk. "I am afraid I've been living amongst humans so long, it did not occur to me how drastically my dress might differ now."

Caemar waved his hand, laughing. "No, no, it is more practical if nothing else. I can't tell you how many times I've accidentally dipped these damned ruffle sleeves into my tea. I've had to stop wearing white shirts for all the stains."

Despite himself, Adrissu chuckled. "Thank you for taking the time to come see me."

Caemar sat down across from him and poured himself a glass of wine from the bottle on the table. "It's no trouble at all. I'm glad to meet you. The research I did was very interesting, but never really went anywhere, so I'm glad for the opportunity to discuss it with you. I'm only sorry it took so long for me to get back to you. I meant to do it sooner, but your letter got lost with some of my other belongings, so..." He shrugged, taking a sip of his wine before continuing. "You must be dedicated to still come all this way after so long, though, so I won't bore you with any more small talk."

This time, Adrissu's smile felt a little more genuine. "I only found one paper about it. Is that all you wrote?"

"It is, though I did a bit of research after, which was never published."

"Please, tell me. I've been curious about your work all these years."

"Yes, well, as I'm sure you know, I was involved in some theoretical work of housing souls separately from their bodies as a means of stasis. When I wrote that dissertation, it was purely theoretical." He leaned closer to Adrissu, lowering his voice in a conspiratorial tone. "However, we were able to get in a few decent experiments before moving on."

Adrissu's heart leapt. This could very well be exactly what he was looking for. He reached for his bag, fishing out parchment and a quill to take notes. "What sorts of experiments?"

"Now, of course, we did not use any elves for this purpose," Caemar said quickly, raising a placating hand—not that Adrissu cared. "What we were studying already bordered on what the priests would declare immoral, and none of us wanted to have to deal with that. So we did experiments on animals. We purchased some livestock from local farmers, pigs and goats mostly. We first experimented to see if our soul retrieval process was even possible, and it did work. The creatures' souls were stored in gems that were suitable for use as magical conduits, and the bodies did not die, though they no longer had consciousness. We waited a week, put them back, and it was as if they woke up from a deep sleep. They were a little confused and tired at first, but in less than an hour they were all going about their business, the same as they always had. Their personalities and memories seemed to remain intact."

"I'm curious how you retrieved their souls in the first place," Adrissu said, filing away as much of the information as he could in his mind, even as he noted down the major points.

"I thought you might," Caemar said, pulling a scroll from an inner pocket of his robe. He set it on the table in front of them without unrolling it, then pushed it toward Adrissu. "I still have the notation we used. It's runes, mostly; a circle around the subject, the gem over their heart, a bit of force and some herbal components. Frankly, as long as the gem is suitable, it's not an exceedingly difficult task, especially for those with particular aptitude for the arcane such as you and I."

Adrissu's hands itched to look at the scroll, but acting overeager now could raise Caemar's suspicions. "But what makes the gem suitable, then?"

"The size, and the clarity," Caemar explained. "Since our test subjects were limited, this strays back into the theoretical, but the larger and clearer the gem, the more complex of a consciousness it can house. I think this because the pigs required larger, clearer gems than the goats, and pigs are regarded as more intelligent creatures. We also had a horse, just one. We used a diamond for it, smaller than some of the other gems, but much finer quality."

"Size and clarity," Adrissu murmured, frowning slightly as he wrote it down. If something as simple as a horse needed a diamond, the soul of a human or elf might need something unfathomably pristine. "And how did you put them back in?"

"Once the gem made physical contact with the empty body, it went right back," Caemar said, shrugging. "It didn't even require any magic on our part. I think the soul is naturally drawn to its own body, so physical contact is enough."

"May I?" Adrissu said, gesturing toward the scroll. Caemar nodded, and Adrissu rolled it open, scanning the runes quickly. It was a circle, as he had described, with a series of symbols all along the inner and outer edges, markings for essence and containment and the spark of life. Intricate and complicated, but not unexpected. He glanced up quickly, noting that Caemar was watching his hands closely. He probably would not be able to copy this in his notes, and certainly would not be allowed to keep it. He dropped his eyes back to the chart, memorizing as much as he could. His memory, while not eidetic, would be enough to copy the instructions down later in the evening when Caemar was gone.

"It's all very interesting, isn't it?" Caemar said as Adrissu looked it over. "We speculated perhaps medical uses, taking a person's consciousness so as not to suffer, while they were injured or gravely ill. The body does not seem to age or decay while the soul is outside of it, but imagine being able to do a surgery without the danger of the patient waking up, or a negative interaction with the sleeping draught... It could completely revolutionize medicine as we know it."

"Could the body still die, though?" Adrissu said, frowning. "If it were injured, as you said—what if the body succumbed to its injuries while the soul was outside it?"

Caemar hesitated. "Well. In the case of death, the soul should be released to join the body."

"You don't think the soul could be put in a different body?"

There was a long moment of silence, as Caemar seemed to process the question. When Adrissu briefly flicked his gaze upward to peer at the elf's face, he had an almost absent expression, his unfocused eyes remaining on the scroll in Adrissu's hand.

He finally spoke, his voice quiet and conspiratorial. "Theoretically this would be possible. But I do not see how it could be done without extremely questionable moral practices, at best."

It was a dangerous topic of discussion, but Adrissu pressed on while he still could. "Not necessarily—perhaps a man wished for a female body, and found a woman who wanted a male body. In this case both would be willing subjects. Would such an exchange work, do you think?"

Again Caemar was silent for a long moment, before answering, "I suppose so, yes."

"So do you think the soul might survive being placed in the body of a different race entirely?" Adrissu asked, keeping his eyes carefully on the paper in his hand, his tone light and speculative. "Like a human soul being placed into an elf body?"

Caemar laughed at that, shaking his head. "These are dangerous ideas you are suggesting, Adrissu."

Adrissu plastered a pleasant smile on his face, setting down the scroll to lift his hands in a placating gesture. "This is all purely theoretical, of course. I am only curious as to the limits of such magic. Much of my research has pertained to what the nature of magic truly is, and so far it seems to me that it is inexorably linked to the living soul of the magic-user. There may be implications that the souls of more accomplished arcanists, such as ourselves, are made of more resilient stuff than the souls of those less talented in the arcane arts, which would cast an interesting light on my own studies."

"Regardless, you should be cautious of the things you're saying, and who you're saying them to," Caemar said. His expression had become less jovial the longer Adrissu spoke; there was no open hostility, but the elf seemed concerned more than anything else. "I understand that what you're discussing is entirely in the realm of hypotheticals. But others might be less open-minded. The very notion of taking an elf's soul and putting it in some other body is…" He made a face, shaking his head. "I am not especially pious, and the thought even makes me uncomfortable."

"I understand," Adrissu said smoothly, rolling the scroll back up and sliding it back across the table to the old elf. Better to end the discussion now, before he became suspicious; and after all, Adrissu had gotten the building blocks of what he truly needed. The rest of the theory he could work out himself. "So what have you been working on more recently?"

Caemar smiled, clearly eager to move on as well. He chattered for a long while about the research that he was currently conducting for the royal library, obviously content just to hear himself talk. Adrissu barely listened, going over the list of runes that he had observed over and over in his mind. He had all the pieces of the puzzle: all that was left was to put them together.

This was, of course, easier said than done.

The population growth of the academy meant that Adrissu's attention was constantly needed, organizing classes, assisting instructors, and adjusting the curriculum as the school term went on. The original three-room schoolhouse had expanded with three more rooms already, but the promise of more students in the future would require further expansion, which meant Adrissu had to secure all the necessary funding and permits. While he was still liked by the Lord Representative, Benit Pallestride, he was not as closely involved with civic duty as he had been in the past, so it would be a more tedious process than simply bringing up the idea to whoever on the council wanted to be in his good graces and letting them do the footwork.

He put together a proposal for a new school building entirely, this one larger than the previous, and dormitories to house their larger student body. They would be built adjacent to the hill where his tower overlooked the rest of the city, which would have the added benefit of ensuring that no unknown neighbors would encroach any closer to his home. The council might still deny this location, so he chose as an alternative a larger plot of land on the outer reaches of the city, which would still be a short walk from Saltspire Tower.

Benit considered his proposal for several weeks before giving him a straight answer.

"As it is now, you just don't have the attendance to justify this much expansion," he explained to Adrissu, gesturing at the papers that had been presented to him. "If you had a hundred students I could consider it. But sixty? I couldn't justify building something the size of the mercenary guild's hall for less than half their students."

"Of course," Adrissu said stonily, taking back his papers.

Garnering more students was necessary, so he doubled his efforts, spreading word of the academy and providing incentives to current students in hopes of attracting more. He cut the price of tuition as much as he possibly could for the following year, funding almost half of his instructors' salaries out of his own pocket.

He was not sure why he was so hellbent on seeing the academy grow and succeed. Continuing his research on soul transference could very well be a better use of his time and money, but when faced between prioritizing the two, his instinct always drew him toward his work expanding the academy. There would be time for both, he supposed, so for now he focused on the school.

His efforts paid off, but not as quickly as he'd hoped. The following year, they grew from sixty students to just over eighty. It was not until the next year that they finally broke one hundred. But it was also that year that Ederick finally died, an old man asleep in his home. Adrissu was sorry to see him go and worried that whoever took his place at the mercenary's guild would not be as staunch a supporter of the Academy as he had been. Without the funnel of warriors who had some aptitude for magic filling the ranks of their offensive and defensive magic tracks, their student population was likely to stall, or even drop back below one hundred.

But they did have over one hundred for now, so Adrissu approached Benit again with his proposal. This time the human took even longer to consider it, and some modifications were made—the worst was that the dormitories Adrissu proposed were slashed to house only twenty students, instead of fifty—but he gave his approval in the end. With the funding secured and construction begun on the plot of land that Adrissu could see from his tower, some of the stress eased away.

Partway through construction, the Federation of Autreth decreed a standard of living for all city-states within its jurisdiction—namely, that all Autrethian cities with more than one thousand residents were to pave their roads with stone, and every building needed meet the new standards set by a group of architects in Gennemont.

Because of this decree, construction was paused until the roads were re-paved, and the building plans reassessed. The decree benefitted Polimnos at large, driving an unprecedented level of business to the mines; but it meant that every available laborer in the city was now preoccupied with harvesting the stone, readying it to be laid, and paving the new roads. The skeleton of the new academy, now left unfinished indefinitely, was an eyesore from his tower: a constant reminder of everything that was just out of his reach. Adrissu seethed, but it could not be helped. All he could do was wait.

Each existing structure in Polimnos was inspected according to the new standards, but Adrissu could not let anyone into the tower who might discover the entrance to his secret lair. So when the inspector came to his door—a young human man wearing thick spectacles and tight, fashionable robes—Adrissu did something that he had never done before; as he allowed the inspector through the door, he grasped him by the shoulder, reached out with a tendril of magic, and planted a false memory in the human's mind that he had inspected the tower thoroughly and found nothing that needed altering.

"Please, no need to leave so soon," Adrissu said quickly, the moment the spell had taken effect. "Why don't you stay for tea?"

The human smiled widely at him, though the way his eyes darted around the room betrayed his disorientation. "Well, I'm running a bit ahead of schedule, so I don't see why not."

Adrissu expected to feel some measure of guilt for having forced the fake memory onto the unsuspecting human; but if he did, it was drowned out by the relief that a stranger would not enter his home to scrutinize every inch—dealing with the delays on the new academy building was frustrating enough.

Slowly, the world changed around him, but he had nothing but time. It took a year for all the roads in Polimnos to be paved with stone; by the time construction resumed on the academy, they were poised to have a hundred and fifty students the following term. When it finally opened, they were closer to two hundred.

Ten years after Volkmar's death, the Polimnos Academy of Magic was thriving: the foremost location of arcane study in Autreth, second only to the esteemed College in Gennemont. The city had continued to expand, and in many ways bore no resemblance to the quaint town where he had met Ruan, nor the growing city where he and Volkmar had lived in leisure. Sometimes it felt like he was the only constant thing in Polimnos.

When the growth of the academy seemed to have stabilized, and he had enough trusted instructors in place that he did not feel the need to constantly monitor everything that happened during the school year, Adrissu stepped back a bit to resume his own studies. With the knowledge he had gleaned from Caemar Illuren, and the hastily-noted copy of the runes that the elf had used, he started his own experiments.

He started with animals, the way Caemar had described. Vesper hated having other animals around and strangled the first two chickens he brought home, much to his chagrin; after that he took them directly down into his lair, instead of trying to work in his study. In his hoard he had more than enough small gems to start with simple creatures like this, not to mention the utter privacy that provided few distractions, so it turned out for the best.

The first time he tried it, he accidentally killed the chicken when he pulled its tiny soul from its body. Fuming, he went over the runes that he had notated, checking and double checking his work, but all seemed correctly placed and executed. He could not find where he went wrong, so he erased the entire array and started over, drawing the circle out again from scratch. The components of the ritual were uncommon, but not nearly as difficult to procure as the soul-binding components had been.

The second time he tested the ritual, he did everything more slowly, closing his eyes in concentration: one hand on the bird to feel the exact spark of life that was the creature's soul, before guiding it, still painstakingly slow, out of its body and into a small ruby that he held in the other hand. This time, the chicken survived, the ruby flickering with an almost imperceptible glow, as its body lay limp on the ground, warm and breathing.

Adrissu grinned down at the ruby in his fingers. As small a step as it was, it proved that his theory was possible. He only had to continue down this path until he reached his goal.

Chapter Twenty-Two

Twenty-one years after Volkmar's death, two city advisors quietly approached Adrissu about removing Benit Pallestride as the Lord Representative.

The two humans were in their middle years, one male and the other female, not significantly younger than Benit himself—at least, not as far as Adrissu was concerned. They had been the Lord Representative's two chosen advisors for the past decade or so—the two that Benit appointed, when he took the position almost thirty years ago, had long since died.

Much as Adrissu liked to think he was difficult to surprise, the proposition did take him aback. He looked silently between the two humans for a moment, gathering his thoughts, before speaking.

"And who do you propose to take his place?" he asked, noting the tension that grew in the man's—Varold's—eyebrows at the question. "I do not care about Benit one way or the other, but unless the laws of the Federation have significantly changed very recently, someone would need to take his place quickly. One of you?"

"No," the woman, Maeve, interjected quickly, before Varold could answer. "Actually, headmaster, we wanted you to take his place."

Adrissu laughed bitterly, covering his mouth with one hand. "No, thank you. If you knew anything about me, you'd know I have no interest in the position. I was offered it myself when Autreth first conquered Polimnos, and I have less civic ambition now than I did then."

"As I told you," Varold grumbled, shooting Maeve a dirty look, but the woman seemed undeterred.

"Then at least help us remove Benit from the picture," she said. "If not you, perhaps someone with your endorsement."

"What has Benit done that is so egregious you want to remove him *now*?" Adrissu asked. It would have made more sense if one of them had wanted the position for themselves; perhaps they had only offered it to him out of some misguided flattery. Otherwise, he could not surmise their intentions.

The two humans glanced at each other, then Maeve spoke again.

"He's been pocketing city funds for his own purposes," she said in a low voice, as if some invisible assailant might be eavesdropping on them. "That's why taxes went up two years ago. It was no decree of Autreth, but his own."

That took him by surprise, though he supposed that he should not be shocked. With their short little lives, humans were too ambitious for their own good and seemed to have no qualms about harming other humans to make their own existence even a fraction more comfortable. Adrissu bit his lower lip, considering.

"Why not simply expose his wrongdoing to the Lord's Council?" Adrissu finally asked. "Let the Federation handle it."

Again the humans shared a look, then Maeve nodded, and Varold turned to him.

"We do not want to get anyone in Gennemont, or the rest of Autreth, involved," he said slowly. "We'd... like to form a city council separate from the office of Lord Representative, but having the scrutiny of Autreth on us for an investigation into Benit would set back all our plans."

Adrissu blanched. "So you propose rebellion? A bid of independence for Polimnos?"

"Not rebellion," he said quickly, shaking his head. "We would still be part of the Federation. It would only be... an addition, so that one person does not hold so much power within the city."

"What makes you think Autreth will accept such a thing? They certainly were against it when they came to conquer Polimnos," Adrissu countered.

"Because Polimnos has power now that it didn't have then," Maeve said, before Varold could speak. "And that's largely because of you, and your school."

"Gennemont's power has grown just as much," Adrissu replied coolly, shaking his head. "Listen. I do not care what you do about Benit, or this new city council. But I don't want to be involved. I'm not going to risk everything I've built up with the academy on something so... bull-headed."

"Fine," Maeve said abruptly. Varold shot her a dark look, but she ignored him. "We'll figure something else out. And worst comes to worst, we can call for his... resignation. Or force his hand."

"You should be more careful of who you're saying these things around," Adrissu sighed, though he looked idly down at his fingernails as he said it. "As long as it does not affect me, I don't care what you do. But others are... unlikely to be as impartial."

"We're not stupid," Varold muttered, and Adrissu had to consciously stop himself from rolling his eyes.

"Thank you for your time," Maeve said, sounding only slightly less frustrated, and she grabbed Varold by the elbow and turned to leave. At the doorway of his office, she hesitated, turning back slightly as if there was more she wanted to say. But whatever it was, she seemed to think better of it, and they both turned away and stepped out of his office.

Nothing came of Maeve and Varold's plot. About a year and a half later, Benit Pallestride was kicked in the head by a horse and died. Part of him wondered if Maeve and Varold had something to do with it, but for two humans to somehow get a horse to kick a man in the exact spot to kill him seemed unlikely to say the least. No, it was more likely a random occurrence that had worked out very much in their favor. It was something of a relief to Adrissu; while he had no particular ill will toward Benit, neither did he want to see a large-scale conflict split the city.

The woman who was next appointed as Lord Representative, Rowena Allistair, was unknown to Adrissu. The Allistair family was one that came to Polimnos when the stone mines were first booming, which was the extent of his knowledge. But coming from working stock, she seemed capable and practical, and she was particularly interested in improving the city's education system, which bode well for him. That was all he really cared about. If the two advisors had tried to enact their plan of establishing a city council alongside this Lord Representative, the attempt was quashed before Adrissu ever heard of it.

He started walking around town again, looking for wherever Volkmar's soul had gone. It took much longer to make a full circuit around town now, so instead he broke the city up into small sections and walked a few streets at a time, once or twice a week. He only tried to avoid the small corner of town that was home to most of the city's elven families, few as they were. He had always taken care to keep his distance from long-lived species, like elves, as much as possible. It was easy to lie to humans about how long he'd been alive, but much harder to come up with a story that would convince an elf, who would see that even a hundred years had not aged him. It was best to avoid them, which was easy enough—there were only three elven families in Polimnos still, and they seemed aware of his distaste for them, even if they did not know why. Skipping those few streets, Adrissu was able to make a full pass through the rest of Polimnos every two months, depending on how often he walked.

But he did not seem to be so lucky this lifetime. While he was acutely aware of how long it had been since Volkmar had died, he one day realized with an unpleasant start that fifty years had passed, and he had been waiting now for much longer than Volkmar had been alive.

But he knew the ritual had worked. Volkmar *was* out there, somewhere. Adrissu started taking walks more often, but still never felt that recognizable pull toward any of the people that he encountered.

He kept his focus on the school and his own studies, and he tried not to think about his mate unless he was out looking for him.

Time was a strange thing. The longer he lived the more quickly it seemed to go, yet it still made him unsettled each time he realized that another year had passed, and still he had not found his mate. When it had been eighty years since Volkmar had died, Adrissu quietly accepted that he had somehow missed his mate in this lifetime, and he would have to wait until the next to find him. The realization was bitter and stuck in his throat, but he had nothing but time. All he could do was wait.

One hundred and three years after Volkmar's death, Polimnos may have very well been a different world entirely.

What had once been a small seaside village now rivaled Gennemont as one of the largest cities in Autreth, sprawling out along the southeastern coast of the continent, and joining the southern rocky beaches to the tall cliffs that rose along the eastern edge and swept northward. Stone paths and stone buildings were all a testament to the productivity of the quarry along the southern edge of the city, depleted now, but with a smaller ore mine deep beneath it. Aqueducts and sewers now ran through the streets, allowing plumbing and clean water to nearly every building—thanks in no small part to the magic-users who kept the water purified and running, even through the summer.

The Polimnos Academy of Magic now boasted twenty instructors and nearly five hundred students, with room for one hundred to live on the school grounds, which had also grown and expanded. The campus wrapped around Saltspire Tower in the shape of a crescent moon with a generous distance between the tower and any of the nearest buildings. The practical applications of magic, fostered by the academy, had helped the city flourish and grow—not only by maintaining the waterways, but providing security and cleanliness in the streets, as well as a myriad of small applications that simply made life more convenient for the citizens of Polimnos. Adrissu was surrounded by his life's work; it satisfied him in the same primal way as his hoard of treasures deep within his lair.

Eventually, Varold and Maeve got their city council, although it came a good fifty years after their deaths. Autreth still had a Lord Representative in each city-state, but now the title's primary focus was the enforcement of federal regulations within the city, and as a representative of their people's interests at the annual Council of Lords in Gennemont. The city council handled more of the day-to-day goings-on of a city that was now far too large for one person to handle themself. Adrissu was again offered a spot on the council. This time, he was more tempted, but ultimately declined. He had lived in Polimnos for a long time, too long in fact, and was now known as Adrissu the younger—claiming that it was his elven father who had first taken up residence in Saltspire Tower, and that he had only inherited it a hundred or so years ago now. No one was old enough to remember, so the lie was uncontested, and after some time, it came so easily that Adrissu nearly believed it himself. Nearly.

With the population as large as it was now, though, it was much harder for Adrissu to take his usual walks and be confident that he had canvassed the entire city. He still had not found his mate, but his long walks along the major streets became less and less frequent.

The midpoint of winter had just passed, and the air was cold and damp with fog. Adrissu was not often cold, but this morning had been particularly chilly, so he sat in his study bundled in a thick robe with a steaming mug of tea on his desk, when Vesper uncoiled just enough to peek her head out, looking toward the stairs.

Stranger, she thought. Adrissu idly looked down toward the stairs, and sure enough, a knock sounded at his door a moment later.

Adrissu sighed and got up. With his home in such easy reach of the school, it was not uncommon for instructors, or occasionally even students, to come see him for one reason or another. If Vesper did not recognize the visitor, it was probably a student coming to get his help on something. He generally did not mind, though he did wonder who would be out and about on such a cold morning.

The heavy door creaked as he opened it—he kept meaning to replace the hinges, but hadn't yet—to reveal a figure that had started to walk away, but turned back to look as the door opened.

The world stopped, a spark jolting through Adrissu's limbs—he blinked, slack-jawed, as his mate turned around to face him. Big brown eyes peered up at him from a slim, delicate face. A few pieces of long, wavy blonde hair framed the visitor's features, while the rest was pulled into a low ponytail. His ears, tapered to slim points, peeked out from beneath the long tresses.

"You *are* real," the man said, sounding nearly as surprised as Adrissu felt.

"You're an elf," Adrissu replied, looking him over quickly. Everything started to click into place—his elven-style clothing, the worn traveler's cloak about his shoulders, and all else told him that the man was not at all local to Polimnos. He had not missed his mate's last lifetime: his mate had ended up further away and longer-lived than he had expected.

The elf smiled nervously in response, one side of his mouth lifting slightly higher than the other. "Do you know who I am?" he asked.

Adrissu tilted his head, considering. His mate now seemed far more aware of the situation than Volkmar had, but Adrissu doubted the elf entirely understood what was happening, or had any idea of what had already happened so long ago.

"In a way, yes," he said slowly, stepping to the side and holding the door open. "Come inside."

"Thank you," the elf said, quickly coming up the three stone steps and brushing past him. Adrissu closed the door and turned to face the elf again. Behind them, Vesper had already come down the stairs and was making a beeline for the elf who watched her with wide eyes, but no obvious fear.

"Vesper," Adrissu warned. The snake slowed, veering closer to Adrissu, though her gaze remained on the newcomer. He could tell that she wanted to greet him; but already the elf seemed nervous and unsure, and somehow he thought a giant snake wrapping herself around him would not make him feel more comfortable. He was looking at her with wide eyes; while he didn't seem entirely shocked, neither did he seem eager to be the subject of her affection.

"Please, sit," Adrissu continued, gesturing toward the comfortable chairs in the front sitting room arranged around a low table. "Are you hungry? Thirsty?"

"No, I'm alright," the elf replied stiffly, pulling his cloak off before sitting down. Beneath the cloak he was dressed in an elven-style open robe and long tunic, over thick winter pants and boots. He must have come from Aefraya, Adrissu thought, and he wondered how his mate managed to end up so far from him this time. The worry was distant, though—in the moment, all he could focus on was the sheer relief and happiness of finally being reunited.

"You seemed to know me," Adrissu started, sitting down across from him and fighting to keep a neutral expression on his face, when all he wanted to do was grin like an idiot. "But I am Adrissu, headmaster of the Polimnos Academy of Magic."

"I know," the elf said, watching him with an inscrutable expression. He somehow looked all at once surprised and relieved and uncertain. There was a beat of silence, then the elf seemed to shake himself, blinking rapidly before speaking again. "Ah, I'm—I'm Braern Rolastra."

"Braern," Adrissu said, testing the name on his tongue. It felt right, as if he'd always known it. "I'm glad to meet you."

"Me too," Braern said, flashing that same nervous smile. "I was—well, I'm hoping you'll have some answers for me."

Adrissu smiled in return. "Of course. How can I help?"

"I..." the elf started, finally looking away. His smile faltered and faded, as he seemed to gather his thoughts. "I've had dreams. For most of my life. About... this place, and you. And me, I think." His brown eyes flicked up to watch Adrissu's reaction. "I didn't think anything of it for a long time. But you're really... You're really here."

He could not stifle the laugh that escaped him. "I assure you, I am certainly real. And I am... not surprised you've dreamt of me. How much do you remember of these dreams?"

"I've dreamt of going places with you," Braern said, a faraway look crossing his face. "Of being in a tower, and seeing the ocean, and..." One hand unconsciously lifted to hold his side, just under his ribs. "Being stabbed and dying. I dreamt of being a soldier."

"These are all things that have happened," Adrissu said softly. "Memories of your past lives."

"Lives?" Braern said, blinking up at him owlishly. "Multiple lives?"

"Just two," Adrissu said quickly. "Do you remember why? Do you remember us?"

A flush rose in Braern's cheeks—evidently, he remembered enough. "I think so. But I don't know why I've dreamt of you. Why I know you. And I've dreamt of..." The elf licked his lips nervously, eyebrows furrowing. His gaze fell away from Adrissu as he said it. "I've dreamt of a dragon."

Adrissu went still. He had sworn that he would not keep his true form a secret from his mate any more, not after the disastrous end of Volkmar; but he had not anticipated Braern already knowing the truth. It unsettled him to suddenly be so vulnerable with a man that was nearly a stranger.

"That's you, isn't it?" Braern pressed, evidently unnerved by Adrissu's silence. "Isn't it?"

Adrissu sighed, leaning back. "I vowed I wouldn't hide it from you. Yes, that's me."

He watched Braern as he said it. There was no hint of surprise on the elf's expression, but a host of other emotions crossed his face as he processed the answer. Uncertainty and concern and maybe fear were all recognizable in the furrow of his brows and the tension of his mouth. But it was a far cry from the absolute terror that had seized Volkmar when Adrissu had restored his memories, which had to be a good sign.

"Why?" Braern finally asked. Adrissu blinked in surprise—whatever host of reactions he had expected from Braern, such a simple question had not been among them. "Why do you do this? Living amongst humans, disguising yourself?"

It was a reasonable question, and not unwelcome, but Adrissu still hesitated before answering. "Long ago, the original Polimnos, a dwarven city, was destroyed by a dragon. I am that dragon. But... I like it here. I liked it when they first started rebuilding it, and I liked it more as it grew. My home is here, but I'm happy to share it."

Something like recognition stirred in Braern's eyes, but the elf remained silent. He still seemed tense, almost troubled. Adrissu wanted to reach out to touch him, just to place a comforting hand on his wrist, but such a gesture felt too intimate. Though he was Adrissu's mate, they were still strangers.

"You have known all of this in the past, as well," Adrissu continued softly. "If you'd like, I can help those memories resurface. If you want more than just dreams. But only if you want."

Braern looked at him, then back down at his hands clasped in his lap. He opened his mouth, then closed it again, before shaking his head.

"No—not yet," he said. "There's something I should tell you first."

To Adrissu's surprise, the elf's eyes were suddenly swimming with tears, his voice constricting with emotion. Unsure of how to respond, he murmured, "What is it?"

Braern took in a deep breath, rubbing at his eyes almost angrily. His lips trembled, then the words all left him in a rush. "I'm—I'm already married. My husband doesn't know I'm here, but I'm sure he'll come looking for me eventually."

Chapter Twenty-Three

Fury exploded through Adrissu's veins, his vision going red. He didn't realize that he'd stood until his vision cleared, and he could see Braern looking up at him, eyes wide and fearful.

"I—" he started, feeling heat building in his throat—he clamped down on it immediately, before his true form threatened to burst forth out of rage. Such a transformation had never happened to him before, but neither had he experienced the sudden fit of mindless jealousy and hatred that the elf's words had so easily elicited in him.

He cleared his throat, clenching his fists tightly at his sides to contain his anger, and forced himself to sit back down. How could his mate have bound himself to another? Why, then, was he even here?

"I apologize," he said, his tone clipped. "You... This comes as a surprise to me, as you can see."

"I understand. I'm sorry," Braern said, looking away with an expression that was utterly miserable. Despite his best efforts, his eyes were glossy with tears again—then his face twisted in anger, tears spilling over his lids and down each cheek, and he hissed with absolute contempt, "I *hate* him."

Again, everything seemed to click into place—his fear, his unannounced arrival, the wretchedness with which he'd spoken of this husband. Possessive rage flooded Adrissu anew, but this time he forced himself to remain sitting, though he could not stop the snarl that crossed his face.

"He has hurt you," he growled, the words coming out as a statement, rather than a question. Braern flinched, then slowly nodded, still unable to meet Adrissu's eyes. "And that's why you came here." Braern nodded again.

Adrissu leaned back, sighing heavily. So much of the joy of meeting his mate again had dissipated in an instant. Evidently, it would not be as simple as starting up where they'd left off. Elves were so different, in both their custom and their physiology—Adrissu had no idea how an elf might remove themselves from a marriage, especially if—

The thought made him shudder with dread. "As you know, I am not truly an elf, so forgive me if this is... rude or blunt," Adrissu said, rubbing his forehead. "But do you have children with this man?"

Braern let out a bitter laugh and shook his head, much to Adrissu's relief.

"No, luckily," the elf said, managing a smile that faded as quickly as it came. "I... Well, I did conceive, once, early on, but I —I lost it in such a way that I was... injured, and couldn't anymore."

"I... see," Adrissu said slowly, frowning. "I apologize for bringing it up, then."

"Don't," Braern replied quickly, shaking his head again. "It's a relief, honestly. I never liked him, even from the start. And things have only... gotten worse."

"Tell me everything," Adrissu prompted. This time he did reach forward, gently placing one hand atop Braern's fists, clenched in his lap. The elf's gaze softened, and his grip relaxed. Adrissu could only hope that his affection was more obvious than the anger, still simmering low in his stomach. "Start from the beginning."

"Well," Braern said, a slight smile starting to spread across his face again. "I was born in Polimnos, actually. My family owns a business selling Aefrayan silks. My mother's side of the family makes them, and my father sells them. My parents were here on business and I was born early, so they had me here, instead of back home in Aefraya like they'd planned."

"I see," Adrissu said. Another surge of relief rushed through him, knowing that the ritual still kept his soul nearby. He had only gotten lucky that Volkmar had been born in Polimnos and never left. He filed it away as something to consider for next time, then gestured for Braern to continue.

"I grew up in Menserine, which is a larger city in the south of Aefraya, the closest to the Autrethian border," Braern said. "I'm the youngest of four, but all my siblings already had families of their own, when another silk business approached my father about combining their efforts. They accepted, and married me to the owner's younger brother to... solidify things." His gaze darkened, and he unclenched his fists to grasp Adrissu's hand. "But then they ended up taking everything. My mother's side of the family still provides the raw silks, so there's money coming in that way, but my father's business was entirely squandered. It all belongs to his family now."

"How long have you been married?" Adrissu asked.

"Thirty years now," Braern sighed. "Once my father's business was out of the picture, Lorsan—my husband— became... worse. I tried to convince him to give some of it back, or at least pay my family a fair amount for the business they'd taken, so I stayed longer than I wanted to, but... I don't know. I don't know why I thought I could convince him. He's always been cold. His whole family is that way."

"So you decided to leave?"

"I... yes." Braern's gaze shifted away as he said it—there was obviously more there. "I had been reading about Polimnos, since I knew I was born there, when I saw the Academy—and your name—and I couldn't believe it. I'd always thought they were just dreams. So when I decided to go, I thought... I thought I'd come here to see if you were actually real. I figured even if not, Polimnos seems like a nice place. And if worst came to worst, I could probably find a boat to somewhere else, somewhere far away." He smiled, though the grin didn't reach his eyes. "I'm sorry if this is presumptuous of me—I paid for a room at an inn when I got here yesterday, but I only paid for a few days—but I feel... drawn to you. I don't want to leave."

"You don't have to leave," Adrissu said forcefully, shaking his head. He squeezed Braern's hand, and after a moment, Braern squeezed back. "It is not presumptuous. I want you here, with me. And we will figure out how to deal with this... Lorsan."

Braern peered up at him through his eyelashes and smiled. "I hoped you would say that."

"You can stay as long as you want," Adrissu continued. "Forever, if you want. You are... well." He bit his lip, unsure of how much to say, considering how vulnerable Braern had just been with him. "As I said, I can restore the memories of your previous lives, if you'd like. But if you'd prefer, I could just... explain the necessary basics."

The elf hesitated, eyes downcast again as he considered. "I think... just explain the basics of this all to me, first."

"Okay," Adrissu said. He gave Braern's hand one last squeeze, before releasing it and leaning back in his chair to consider his words carefully. "Amongst dragons, there is a... phenomena, I suppose, in which two souls are drawn together. The means or reason behind this is unknown, but the pull of it is undeniable. We call them fated mates, or fated pairs." He paused, glancing at Braern who was nodding, his brown eyes wide with rapt attention. Adrissu's heart squeezed: he was beautiful, as elves so often were, but in a way that was familiar, that somehow still felt like he was looking at Ruan and Volkmar all at once. "You are my fated mate. I hadn't thought it was possible for a human to be fated to a dragon—because you were a human, the first time we met—but I felt that pull toward you the first time I saw you. But because I knew you would die, and I would live, we..."

He trailed off, biting his lip. What was the most succinct way to explain the ritual, and in a way that wouldn't upset him, the way Volkmar had been? He looked at Braern, who remained silent, but nodded encouragingly.

"While dragons are immortal, we *can* be killed," Adrissu continued, rubbing his chin with one hand. "And so a ritual was devised, so that if one of a fated pair were to die, their soul was bound to their mate's and they would be reborn, so that the pair could find each other again."

"And we did that," Braern said, before Adrissu could finish. He smiled, a fond pride already welling in his chest; Braern did not seem upset at all, only curious.

"We did," Adrissu agreed, nodding. "And so, when you died the first time—you were a soldier—I waited and met you again in your second life, when you were about twenty—a human again. It didn't occur to me that you could be reborn as an elf, so I admit I was surprised when I saw you standing there."

Braern laughed—a soft, delicate laugh that suited his delicate elven features perfectly. "Understandable."

Adrissu eyed him, affection swelling in his chest that drowned out everything else. "You're taking all this rather well."

Braern laughed again. "I think I already knew everything you've told me. I've dreamt about it for... well, since I can remember. I've had a long time to adjust to it, I think."

"You're not afraid?"

"I'm *terrified*," Braern said, a nervous flash crossing his face. "But not of you. I feel like I've always known you."

"You have," Adrissu said softly. This time, Braern reached for him, almost imperceptibly; and Adrissu reached out to meet his hand, squeezing his fingers between his own. "What inn are you staying at? We can go get your things and bring them here."

Braern seemed entirely normal as they went and gathered his belongings from the inn where he'd been staying—Adrissu insisted on paying the rest of the balance, unsure of how much money Braern had on him—but Adrissu could tell that he was barely holding it together as they walked back to the tower. The elf kept his eyes downturned, and his hands trembled as he carried a bag of clothes.

"There's a spare room you can stay in," Adrissu said, keeping his tone casual despite his worry. "It might be a little dusty, but it gets a lot of light."

Braern nodded silently, but when Adrissu glanced back over at him, his gaze was faraway.

When they arrived back in the tower, Braern preoccupied himself with unpacking his things; Adrissu cleaned out the room a bit first, but the elf seemed to want to be alone, so he kept his distance.

He had not expected to have a visitor, so he didn't have much in the way of food; leaving Vesper to keep an eye on Braern, he headed back out and walked down to the market for fresh vegetables and other grocery items. He had no idea how to make any kind of traditional elvish meal, but he figured that he would prepare one of Volkmar's favorite dishes and hope for the best.

He could feel a slight hum of concern coming from Vesper when he arrived back in the tower. *Crying*, she thought toward him, as he peered up the stairs.

He wondered if he should go and talk to Braern, comfort him somehow—but Vesper felt protective, like she didn't want him to come up, so he resigned himself to making a meal. Eventually Braern came down of his own accord, Vesper following him eagerly.

"Are you hungry?" Adrissu asked, looking over at him. The elf's eyes were rimmed with pink, but otherwise, he looked better than he had when Adrissu had left him.

"No, I—" Braern started, biting his lip. "I... want to see you. Your true form."

Adrissu stilled, brows furrowing as he looked him over. "Why?"

"I feel like... I need to know," he replied, sounding uncertain. "I just... I remember it, a little bit. But I feel like I need to see for myself to know if I can... if I can do this."

Slowly, Adrissu nodded. It sounded very much like what Ruan had told him once, that he had needed to see him—see *Zamnes*—to know if he could live with the knowledge that his lover was a dragon. Then, all those years ago, the prospect had made Adrissu afraid, but now he had no such qualms. If Ruan had accepted him then, he had no doubts that Braern would do the same.

"Are you sure?" he said, but Braern already had a look of determination in his eye.

"Yes," he said with a nod, so Adrissu led him over to the trap door in the front room.

"I don't know if you remember this part," he said slowly, pulling the door open. "It's a long drop. But I'll hold you."

Braern frowned, looking down at the drop with some consternation—the ladder obviously only went down a few rungs, and beyond it was only darkness.

"I..." he started, sounding afraid, then visibly shook himself. "Alright. I... trust you."

"Come here," Adrissu said, extending a hand. Braern took a deep breath, stepped closer, and wrapped his arms around Adrissu's waist. Desire shot through him as their bodies pressed together, the scent of his mate wafting to his nose, clean and herbal despite his arduous journey. His long-dormant cock instantly stood to attention in response—but he ignored it, holding Braern tightly against his chest, while trying not to think of his mate finally, *finally* in his arms. "Hold on tight. Ready?"

"Ready," the elf breathed, and Adrissu stepped forward, sending them both sailing over the edge. A cry of fear died in Braern's throat; he could feel the elf press his face into his shoulder, eyes squeezing shut and breaths coming rapidly. Adrissu counted off the seconds, then let himself transform.

By the time they landed, Braern was trembling against him—pressed to his warm, scaled chest by one claw.

"Can you stand?" he rumbled, causing Braern to yelp in surprise, as he gingerly set the shaking elf on his feet.

"Y-Yes," Braern stammered. He glanced around nervously. "It's dark—I can't see."

Adrissu laughed despite himself. The deep tenor of it echoed through the cave until it was a low, droning reverberation. "I haven't been down here in a while. Just a moment."

He turned, slinking away to light the various braziers and torches set up throughout his lair with streams of fiery breath. When the cavern was finally lit, he turned back around to face Braern, who was looking up at him with wide eyes and a pale face.

"I..." the elf started, only to trail off. Despite the obvious trepidation on his face, his eyes were locked on Adrissu. He did not look away, even when the dragon crouched low to return his gaze at eye level. "You... You look exactly how I dreamt."

Adrissu stifled a grin, knowing the toothy display was unlikely to bring any comfort to Braern, as obviously nervous as he was. "I would hope so."

Slowly, Braern stepped forward, until he was close enough to reach out and touch Adrissu's snout. His fingers felt cool against his scales.

"Do you want me to call you Adrissu, still?" he asked, barely above a whisper. "I know you are Zamnes, but..."

Adrissu shook his head. "I have always been Adrissu with you."

Braern nodded, and to Adrissu's surprise, he stepped even closer, holding Adrissu's chin in both his hands to press their faces together.

"I'm not afraid," he panted, though Adrissu could feel his pulse hammering from where his wrists touched his neck. "I feel like I should be, but I'm not afraid of you."

"I know," Adrissu rumbled, deep in his chest.

"You'll keep me safe?" Braern asked, his voice rasping. Adrissu growled, his insides burning at the thought of anyone hurting his mate.

"Yes," he answered, his voice filling the cavern.

"You'll protect me?"

"Yes."

"And I can—I can stay with you? As long as I want to?"

Adrissu rumbled again, wanting to press his face further into Braern, but knowing he would knock the elf over if he did.

"I am your home," he said. "I will always be your home."

Braern was silent, but he could feel him nodding against his skull, could feel tears dripping from his eyes onto his scales. More than anything, Adrissu wanted to kill whoever had put such fear into his mate. It made him think of when he had ripped apart the sailor that had taken Volkmar from him; and it was a small comfort to know that he would do the same to this cruel elf, who had kept Braern from him for so long.

"Okay," Braern finally said, clearing his throat. "I've seen what I needed to see. We can go back."

When they both emerged back in the tower, and Adrissu straightened from closing the trap door behind them, Braern grabbed him by the forearms, pulled him close, and kissed him.

Adrissu groaned against his mouth, every nerve in his body lighting up with fire. It was sudden and chaste, but consumed him entirely. Braern started to pull away, but Adrissu followed. The elf yielded to him, mouth opening against his tongue. The feel of him was new and strange—at the same time as familiar and easy as breathing. With one hand Adrissu held the back of Braern's neck, and with the other he pressed against the small of his back, grinding their hips together as they kissed. He tasted floral, like pine and lavender, and the hard evidence of his desire pressed flush against Adrissu's groin, making the elf gasp—

"W-Wait," Braern stammered against his lips, and immediately Adrissu stilled. Braern leaned back, still in Adrissu's arms, but with some space between their bodies now. He looked at him with dark eyes and flushed, swollen lips. "I... I don't think I can do this yet."

Adrissu blinked, forcing his racing heart to calm. "I... Alright. Of course. Whatever you want."

"This is going to sound so stupid," Braern groaned, squeezing his eyes shut. "I feel... guilty, doing this. With you."

Adrissu had no idea how to respond. It *did* sound stupid, but he could not say as much. "I want you to be comfortable."

"I am. I will be," Braern said. "I... do want this. Just not yet. Not so soon."

Adrissu nodded, and in one smooth motion, he loosened his hold around Braern and took a measured step back, separating them fully.

"In that case," he said, clearing his throat and trying his best to ignore his cock that still ached for attention. "Lunch is ready for you."

Braern blinked, then laughed, a genuine smile crossing his face. Any lingering frustration Adrissu might have had melted away entirely. He had waited a hundred years—what was a little more time? His mate was *here*, at his side, and that was all that mattered.

Chapter Twenty-Four

The longer Braern was able to decompress, the more he seemed like the person Adrissu remembered. He was not exactly Ruan, nor was he entirely Volkmar, just as they had been different from each other; but more and more clearly, he could see the thread of personality that connected them: the streak of stubborn resilience that must have driven Braern to travel halfway across the world in the hope that his dreams had some root in reality. He was curious as Volkmar had been, with an elven sense of pride that somehow reminded him of Ruan, too.

For having spent the last hundred years alone, Adrissu thought he adapted rather well to the sudden presence of another in his home. Vesper was over the moon and most often stayed with Braern in his room, or slithering along behind him as he explored the tower. To his credit, Braern had no fear of the huge snake, and after adjusting to her presence, he seemed to enjoy her company nearly as much as she enjoyed his.

It all felt homey and cozy again, like things had finally gone back to how they were supposed to be. Of course, in those first weeks together, the quiet urge for vengeance was a tight ball in the pit of Adrissu's stomach. He could ignore it most of the time, but never entirely. They had not discussed the issue of Lorsan: what they would do about him, or how they would respond if he did come looking for Braern. It seemed like the kind of topic that he shouldn't bring up on his own, so Adrissu waited for Braern to discuss it with him.

Eventually, Braern did broach the topic, in a way. Adrissu had been at the school for most of the day, and he was tired when he arrived back at the tower; but Braern seemed eager to see him, grinning up from the book he was reading on the couch. Vesper was coiled over his legs—he shifted them gently to coax her down, and she uncoiled herself to drop down to the stone floor with a thud.

"Welcome home," Braern said, standing up. Adrissu smiled back, surprised.

"You're in a good mood," he said, pulling off his winter cloak and hanging it by the door. Braern nodded, biting his lip, though the smile on his face lingered.

"I've been thinking," he said, stepping closer and letting his hands settle around Adrissu's waist. "I... don't want to wait anymore."

"No?" Adrissu said, raising an eyebrow and hoping his slight smirk did not betray how quickly his heart had started to hammer in his chest.

"No," Braern said, shaking his head. "I came here for a reason. I came here to get away from... from him. You're my home. Like you said. I have no doubts about his own faithlessness, so..."

The spark of rage, which he'd kept so firmly contained, roared at the mention of the other man, but he clamped down on it. He wanted to ask about what they would do about Lorsan, to fully make a clean break from the other man, but even that seemed too presumptuous—and would certainly detract from what Braern would obviously rather do right now. Instead, he raised his hand and gently pushed a strand of Braern's hair behind his ear, searching his wide, eager eyes.

"You're sure?" he asked.

"Yes," Braern replied, nodding quickly. Adrissu smiled, then pulled his face closer to press a quick, chaste kiss to his lips.

"You have no idea how glad I am to hear that," he murmured, and Braern laughed, eyes crinkling with mirth. "But I think you will like it better if I bathe first, and maybe we can have a meal together."

"I'd like that," Braern replied softly, pulling away to head for the kitchen. "I can make something."

Adrissu bathed quickly, observing himself in the mirror as he preened. He could make himself look however he wanted; this form was handsome, though, and he did not think anything needed to be changed. If he altered his appearance too much, anyway, it would probably have the opposite effect on Braern now. It had been a hundred years since he'd done this, but that was not so long when he had already lived for three hundred.

When he came back down, Braern was still cooking, so Adrissu watched him with hunger in his eyes as he finished the meal, obvious enough that he was certain Braern felt his desire as intensely as he did. The elf enjoyed cooking and often prepared elvish dishes for them, making modifications with local ingredients that were easier to procure here, far in the southeast of Autreth. Today was no different: he had prepared a light broth that was a common elven dish, alongside a plate of grilled fish with vegetables, which was more like the standard human cuisine found in a seaside city like Polimnos.

They chatted while they ate, as casually as they had over every meal that the two had shared together during the last few weeks; but when he caught Braern's eyes on him from across the table, they were full of heat, flickering up and down his body with the same hunger that ached in Adrissu's groin. *This* was going to be worth it.

"Delicious," Adrissu murmured when he was done, smirking over at Braern. The elf flushed, a prideful smile twitching at the corners of his mouth. "Are you done?"

"Yes," Braern said quickly, pushing his plate away. "Your room?"

Adrissu nodded, standing. He took Braern by the hand and led him upstairs, the points of contact between their skin tingling with anticipation. Vesper started up the stairs after him, but he shooed her away with a pointed look and a nonverbal order to stay. She remained on the ground floor, but he could practically feel her rolling her eyes, if she had been physically able to do so.

Braern's hands snaked around his waist, bringing him back to the moment. "Lay down," the elf murmured in his ear, as he nudged Adrissu toward the bed, sending a shiver down his spine.

"Like this?" Adrissu teased, falling back onto his pillows and pulling his shirt open seductively. Tight, high-waisted breeches with looser, flowy shirts tucked into them were in fashion now, so between his open shirt and his obvious erection straining beneath his pants, he must have been a sight. Braern laughed, but straddled him still fully clothed.

"I want to... go slow," he murmured, running his hands up the length of Adrissu's exposed chest.

"Be my guest," Adrissu groaned, back arching to follow the path of Braern's touch. It had been so long, *so long*, since his mate had touched him—this alone had him so painfully hard that he couldn't imagine lasting at all, but if Braern wanted to go slow, they would go slow.

"I sort of remember..." Braern started, then frowned, flushing. "I think I dreamt once of doing this but in your, ah... true form."

The memory made Adrissu's body flood with heat all over again. It had been a rare occurrence; it had never happened with Volkmar, of course, but Ruan was sometimes particularly adventurous. He remembered Ruan's hands on his slick cock, teasing the slit where it emerged from his body, until he came so hard his vision would blur and embers would spark from his mouth.

"Yes, sometimes," Adrissu panted, bucking his hips against Braern. "Not often, but sometimes. If you want to again, we can, but maybe not now. Not yet."

Braern nodded, eyes wide as he seemed to consider what exactly such activities would entail. He stilled on top of Adrissu, distracted, until Adrissu frowned and grabbed him by the waist, rocking their hips together so he could feel the elf's erection pressing against him.

"Don't keep me waiting," he teased, and Braern laughed breathlessly.

"Can I undress you?" he asked softly, hands hovering at Adrissu's waist where his shirt was tucked in.

"Please undress me," Adrissu urged, and without any further encouragement, Braern was pulling his shirt off. Adrissu leaned forward so he could pull it over his head, tossing it to the side as Braern unbuttoned Adrissu's pants. He panted when the first layer was pulled away and only his underwear separated them, then he gasped when Braern palmed him through the thin fabric. The elf stifled a groan of his own, squeezing his hard length.

"You're big," he murmured, looking down at the outline of cock with his eyes dark with lust. "You're going to feel so good inside me."

Adrissu stifled a whimper; he wanted to be inside Braern more than anything he had ever wanted. But Braern made no move to pull down his underwear, instead leaning back to start pulling off his own clothes.

Adrissu had bought him a few new articles of clothing in a more human style to help him blend in, but he still mostly wore his elven robes. Beneath the multiple layers of open robes and long tunics, his body was lithe, but soft in a way that spoke to his upbringing in a wealthy family. A faint dusting of light hair made a small patch in the center of his chest, almost imperceptible; and around his navel there was a bit more that trailed down and disappeared into the waistband of his pants, just a shade darker, but still quite light. With the layers of robes gone, Adrissu could see the evidence of his arousal as well, tenting the front of his breeches. Every instinct in him wanted to reach out to touch, but he stretched his arms up and kept his hands firmly away, both to ensure that Braern stayed in control and to encourage his mate to touch him again.

.

Braern descended on him then, kissing and licking his way down Adrissu's body–starting along his neck, slowly meandering to his collarbones and the divot of his sternum, getting tantalizingly close to his nipples before moving away. Adrissu groaned, half in pleasure and half in frustration. Braern smiled against his skin.

"You're teasing me," Adrissu protested, and Braern laughed.

"Of course I am," he said, tilting his head to smirk up at Adrissu. "Not a fan?"

He couldn't exactly say that he *didn't* enjoy it, so he only made a frustrated noise in the back of his throat and let his head fall back onto the pillows.

Braern resumed kissing along the length of his torso, pausing near the waistband of his underwear to take in a deep breath, as if steeling his resolve. But rather than pull them down, he mouthed along the head of Adrissu's cock through the fabric, a teasing grin still on his face.

"*Fuck,*" Adrissu choked, stifling himself with one hand. He was going to lose his mind. "Braern, *please.*"

"What?" Braern asked, smiling innocently up at Adrissu, with the bulge of his cock still pressed against his cheek. He was enjoying this entirely too much.

With an easy show of strength, Adrissu lunged upwards, taking Braern with him and flipping the elf onto his back with a surprised cry.

"Not so fun now, is it?" he growled, pressing his face into Braern's neck and biting.

"I'm not complaining," Braern gasped, eyelids fluttering as he tilted his head and exposed more of his neck for Adrissu to kiss and bite.

Adrissu growled. With how nervous Braern had been for so long, he had not at all expected him to be so... whatever this was. Teasing and irreverent—it almost irritated him, but then the thought of taming him into submission went straight to his cock.

"I'm done being teased," Adrissu murmured against his skin, before propping himself up to look down at his mate, face flushed and lips swollen as he grinned blissfully up at Adrissu. For a long moment Adrissu admired him, eyes traveling the length of his torso and settling on the swell of his arousal beneath his underwear. It was far past time for them to be naked.

He leaned back to pull his own off first, catching Braern watch him hungrily from the corner of his eye, as he nonchalantly kicked them away.

"You know," he murmured, as he settled over Braern again, letting his lips ghost against the tender skin where his neck met his collarbone. "In all my years, I've never fucked an elf before. The rumor is that fucking elf men is just like fucking elf women. Any truth to that?"

"Well, I've never fucked a dragon pretending to be an elf," Braern quipped. "And I've never fucked a woman, elf or not, so I couldn't tell you."

Adrissu stifled a laugh. "Neither have I, on either account. I'll have to decide on a final verdict once I'm done with you, I suppose."

A soft moan of anticipation escaped Braern from the back of his throat, and whatever pretense Adrissu had of teasing Braern, or drawing this out, was gone. He trailed his hands down the length of the elf's torso and hooked his thumbs in the waistband of his underwear, hesitating for only a second to see if Braern tried to pull away. He didn't, so Adrissu pulled them down, and Braern shifted his weight so he could kick them off. His cock, now freed, sprang up eagerly, the dark pinkish tip already glistening with precome. Braern bucked his hips, rutting himself against Adrissu, and pressed their cocks together in one hand. Adrissu gasped, panting at the sensation of Braern's skin sliding against his own. One touch, and he was nearly undone. It had been far, *far* too long. He squeezed his eyes shut, trying to think of anything else to help him last a little longer.

"Braern," he groaned, pulling away enough that his cock slipped free of the elf's hand. "*Fuck*. Give me a moment."

"Let me on top again," Braern said, pushing slightly against him. Adrissu hesitated, but acquiesced, swinging one leg around so he no longer straddled him, before laying down on his back. This time it was Braern who devoured him with his eyes, his gaze trailing obviously from his face down his torso to his aching cock.

"We do have one advantage over humans, I think," Braern murmured, settling on his knees over Adrissu and reaching back with one hand to grip his cock. "I can do this." He leaned back, pressing Adrissu's cock to his asshole—already warm and unbelievably slick—and sank down onto it in one easy motion with a breathy sigh. In contrast, Adrissu swore loudly, squeezing his eyes shut and tossing his head back, as pleasure burst through every nerve in his body. Already he could feel pressure building in his groin. Braern rocked his hips, sliding up and down on his cock, and Adrissu slapped a hand to his mouth to stifle the very undignified cry that escaped him.

"That good, huh?" Braern laughed breathlessly, hips stuttering.

"In my defense," Adrissu forced out through gritted teeth. "It *has* been more than a hundred years."

"Worth it?" Braern pressed, gasping softly with each deliberate bounce.

"Yes," Adrissu panted. "Gods, yes, you feel incredible."

"Tell me," Braern prompted him. His breathing was more ragged now, his cheeks flushed and lips parted.

Adrissu hesitated, remembering how quickly both Ruan and Volkmar had come undone with the slightest word of praise. If that indicated anything, he guessed Braern would be the same. He reached out to seize Braern by his hips, stilling him when he was buried to the hilt.

"It's different. Better. Because it's you," he said, grinning with all his teeth. "You've been so good, let me take care of you."

Braern whimpered, pulsing impossibly tighter around Adrissu, who held the elf in place as he started to pump his hips and fuck him in earnest.

"There," Braern groaned, his eyes slipping closed and his mouth hanging open. "Fuck, yes, right there—"

Adrissu's body was buzzing with stimulation, pressure building in his cock. He absolutely did not want to come already, but his hips were thrusting of their own accord now, driving up again and again into Braern's slick channel enveloping him.

"So good," he panted, squeezing hard where he gripped Braern's hips. "Fuck, you feel so good—I'm going to come inside you."

"Please," Braern gasped, and the hitch in his voice was more than enough to send Adrissu over the edge. He moaned and shuddered, as he gave one last hard thrust and his cock pulsed deep inside Braern, filling him. His mate squeezed around him as he cried aloud, pulling a few more spurts of come out of him.

"S-Sorry," he panted, when it had finally run its course, his tensed muscles relaxing back into the bed. "I usually—I swear I'm not usually like this."

"It's been a hundred years, after all," Braern teased, grinning. Adrissu smiled blissfully back at him, though even in his post-orgasmic high, he could see the need still dark in Braern's eyes.

"So understanding," he murmured, releasing his hold on Braern's hips to grip his cock instead, where it jutted out above his abdomen. "You deserve to be rewarded, don't you?"

Braern whimpered again, nodding and biting his lip, as his gaze dropped down to watch Adrissu's hand working his cock—squeezing it and stroking in long, slow motions.

"Does this feel good? My cock still inside you while I'm touching you," Adrissu panted. Braern moaned, pulsing around him. That was answer enough. "I want to make you come. Will you let me watch you come?"

"Fuck," Braern gasped, thrusting against Adrissu's hand. He could feel his own over-sensitive length sliding in and out of

Braern, as he pushed his cock in and out of Adrissu's hand.

"Will you let me watch you come?" Adrissu repeated, stroking him fast without warning. The elf cried aloud, the rhythm of his hips stuttering—Adrissu could feel him clench and pulse around him, harder now—he lifted his gaze to watch Braern's face as his cock pulsed wildly in his hand, painting his abdomen with come. His eyes were squeezed shut, eyebrows drawn together, and flushed lips open as he came, moaning and gasping in pleasure. Adrissu's cock twitched from where it was still buried in Braern's ass; one of the only drawbacks to this form, Adrissu thought, was that he could not come again so quickly. Still he rocked his hips to keep fucking Braern through his orgasm, ignoring the almost-painful edge of sensation shooting up his spine, so he could watch him come utterly undone.

"Good boy," Adrissu murmured encouragingly, relishing the shiver it sent up the elf's spine, then released his cock to drag his fingernails along the length of Braern's thighs, feeling the muscles tremble then relax.

Afterward, Braern laughed under his breath as he rolled over, pressing himself close to Adrissu.

"Sorry," he said, covering his grin with one hand at Adrissu's quizzical eyebrow. "I... I guess I feel free now. It's strange. Like it's real that he's not... part of my life anymore."

Slowly Adrissu nodded, considering. He had wanted to ask Braern what they would do about this apparent husband, waiting for the elf to bring it up himself; yet still it seemed too serious of a conversation to have now, naked and messy in the immediate aftermath of their coupling.

"You are free," he finally decided on, flashing Braern a small smile. "I'll make sure you're entirely free from now on. You don't have to worry about anything anymore. I'll always take care of you."

Color had crept into Braern's face as Adrissu spoke, and now the tips of his ears were a flushed red.

"I know," the elf murmured, pressing his face into Adrissu's shoulder. "Thank you."

"I love you," Adrissu said, pressing his lips to Braern's hair. While they had known each other in this form for only a short while, and he knew Braern might consider it too soon to have such strong feelings, it didn't feel too presumptuous for Adrissu to say. For him, it was only a continuance of where they had left off a hundred years ago. Braern as a person was new, but Adrissu had never stopped loving his mate. It would never be too soon to say it.

"I know," Braern repeated softly, sounding shy. "I..."

"You don't have to say it," Adrissu said quickly. "I know it's different for you. I know you remember a little bit, but I remember it all. I've loved you longer than you've been alive."

"You know, that only makes me feel *more* pressured," Braern laughed, but his eyes were full of affection as he looked up at Adrissu. "I get it. At least I think I get it. So I... I'll say it when I'm ready."

"I wouldn't want anything else," he replied, and kissed his forehead again. The rest of their evening was spent in bed, Braern laying curled against Adrissu's side, exactly where he belonged.

Chapter Twenty-Five

The topic of Braern's husband did not come up again for a long time. Not for lack of trying—Adrissu thought of the mysterious, cruel elf from whom his mate had fled almost every day, turning the situation over and over in his mind. Something would have to be done, but he knew Braern was the one who needed to take the reins going forward. He had learned that lesson with Volkmar and had no intention of making the same mistake in this lifetime.

A thought came to him, when he was reorganizing his notes on his soul-transference studies, which he had largely paused in the past decade or so to focus on the academy. He had all of the theoreticals worked out, and his experiments on animals had all been successful. All that was left was to try it on a humanoid creature, but doing so was far more difficult to justify to himself, thus the experiments had ceased. But would he have the same qualms if the creature was evil: someone who had harmed others and would likely continue to do so if left to their own accord? No, he thought—and he already had someone in mind.

Bringing that up to Braern seemed nearly impossible, though, so he would continue to wait for him to broach the topic of *what they would do about the husband*, then perhaps they could discuss his experiments and Lorsan's potential role in them. It was aggravating to wait, but he hoped that they had many years left together. It had not occurred to him that his mate might come back as an elf, but now he was grateful for the extra time that it allowed them to spend with each other. Maybe, he hoped, Braern would agree that even that extended time was not enough.

Several months passed, and Braern had fallen into place in Adrissu's life quickly, taking on some clerical work at the academy to keep busy. As an elf, he had notably more magical prowess than either Ruan or Volkmar, though it was still nothing remarkable. Adrissu told him that he could take any classes that he wanted at no cost, but so far he hadn't taken him up on the offer. For the most part, he seemed happy with the busy work and spent the rest of his time quite leisurely. He had a fondness for elven poetry, so Adrissu bought him as many books of it as he could find.

It was late in the evening when Braern finally spoke on the matter. They were both in Adrissu's study: Adrissu at his desk, and Braern sitting in a lounge chair on the other end of the room. Adrissu was reviewing lesson plans that his instructors had submitted for the following year when he felt Braern's gaze on him. When it lasted longer than a few seconds, Adrissu glanced up with a questioning look.

"Sorry," Braern said quickly, flashing an apologetic smile. "I was just thinking about something."

Adrissu set down his notes. "About?"

Braern's eyes flickered down to the book that he'd been reading. "I was... considering what we should do about... well, about Lorsan."

Adrissu's pulse quickened—now was the moment he'd been waiting for. But he kept his breathing calm, clasping his hands in front of him, as he turned his full attention to Braern.

"What do *you* want to do about Lorsan?" he asked. Across from him, Braern bit his lip, worrying it between his teeth for a moment, before speaking.

"I'm... not really sure," he finally admitted, sighing. "Part of me doesn't want to do anything. As long as he's not nearby, it's like he doesn't exist, you know?"

Adrissu blinked slowly, unsure. "I... see."

Braern gave him an odd look, then his eyes widened, and he slapped a hand to his mouth. "Oh, gods, I forgot you aren't really an elf—you don't know about the bond, do you?"

Adrissu frowned. It was a point of pride that there was little in the world of which he had no knowledge. But this, at least, was one such thing.

"No," he said simply, and he stood up from his desk to settle in a reading chair next to Braern. "Enlighten me."

"It's part of the elven marriage... rites, I guess," Braern said, gesticulating in the air with an almost derisive expression. "It's meant to bring people closer, foster a connection between them. The bond is a sort of mental link, so when you're within a certain radius of each other, you have a... a *sense* of them, I guess, and a feel of their thoughts and emotions."

"That sounds extremely unpleasant," Adrissu muttered, frowning. "And invasive."

Braern laughed bitterly. "It can be, on both accounts," he said. "We almost always kept our bond mostly closed. But even with it closed, if we're ever within about a mile of each other, we'd know the other was near. So if he *really* wanted to find me, he could."

"Do you think he wants to find you?"

"I don't know," Braern sighed, sinking down in his chair slightly. "I don't really think so. But even after all our time together I feel like we never knew each other very well. So maybe. He never seemed fond of me, but I can see him being angry that I left because it makes him look bad."

"Let me see something," Adrissu said quickly, leaning closer to him. He held one hand up—Braern eyed him for a moment, then nodded—and Adrissu reached forward to touch the side of the elf's face, his fingertips brushing against Braern's temple just below his hairline. Adrissu closed his eyes and reached out with his magic, letting it course through him into Braern. He could feel the elf's aura, the beating of his heart, the slight tingling sensation of his life force—and there, like a tiny bead in the back of his head, was *something else*, the presence of another. He had never sensed anything like it before. Did all married elves really live with such an invasion of their privacy? Although, he thought, he could see the romanticism of it, if it were with someone he loved. Even then, a *constant* presence in his head? It sounded nightmarish. Maybe that was why it was, apparently, a secret amongst elves.

"I can sense it," he said, opening his eyes to see Braern watching him with a slight smile. "What?"

"You're handsome," Braern said simply, his grin widening. Adrissu felt himself flush, but smiled in return.

"Stay focused," he chided, though there was no reprimand in his tone, and Braern only smiled wider at him. "As I was saying, I can sense the magic that connects you to him. If you want to, I think I could remove it."

"Remove it?" Braern asked, his eyes going wide and the teasing expression falling away from his face. "You could? Really?"

"I think so," Adrissu repeated, nodding as he let his hand slide down Braern's face to cup his cheek. "It seems like a simple enough enchantment—strong, but not entirely complicated. It really just feels like... a little point of someone else they stuck in your brain, so I don't see why I can't just take it back out or cut it off entirely."

Where Adrissu's fingers just barely brushed Braern's neck, right below his jaw, he felt the other man's pulse quicken, felt him swallow nervously, though his expression remained mostly the same. His big brown eyes flickered away from Adrissu, eyebrows drawn together in thought.

"Only if you want," Adrissu added quickly, his own brows furrowing in concern. Braern gave a start as if being pulled from deep reflection, eyes flicking back up to meet Adrissu's gaze.

"I'm... not sure," he said softly, grimacing. "Isn't that ridiculous? I don't ever want to see him again, but the thought of ending the bond feels... frightening, somehow."

"Well," Adrissu said slowly, leaning back. "If the thought of that doesn't appeal to you, we could approach this a different way."

"How?" Braern asked. Adrissu sighed, worrying his lip between his teeth for a moment, before looking up at Braern with a pointed expression.

"We could get rid of him," he said simply. Braern blinked. Adrissu raised his eyebrows, giving him a knowing look. Braern's eyes widened.

"Adrissu!" he exclaimed, stuttering. "Suggesting such a thing!"

"It would be the simplest solution," Adrissu replied, shrugging. Braern laughed, but the edge of hysteria to his laugh made Adrissu certain that outright killing the man was probably out of the question. "But let me suggest something slightly different. We could get rid of him as a problem without necessarily killing him."

Braern frowned at that, but at least he didn't look as affronted as he had before. "What do you mean?"

Adrissu was silent for a long moment, considering what exactly to say, how much to give away. To bring up the possibility of doing something with Braern's soul now was unlikely to be successful; but if he only brought up the concept of soul transference now and asked about Braern's soul later on, then it might work out. Maybe.

For now, he would only discuss what was necessary. "I've done some research on the... nature of souls," he started slowly, choosing his words with care. "It was an elven scholar, actually, who introduced me to the concept of taking a soul and removing it from the body without killing it. Inducing a stasis sort of state."

From the way Braern leaned back slightly, he could tell that he had already guessed what he would suggest, but he continued anyway.

"If he ever came here, I could do that to him," Adrissu said. "I've experimented with animals and such. I know I could do it.

It would completely incapacitate him without actually harming him."

"But then what?" Braern asked, frowning. "We would just leave him like that forever?"

Adrissu shrugged. "Why not? It seems like a fitting punishment to me. Let him remain alive, but deny him the ability to truly *live*. Whatever happens to an elf's soul when they die, prevent his from participating."

"It would be kinder to kill him," Braern scoffed. Again Adrissu shrugged.

"Perhaps. Then we should just kill him," he said.

"I don't know about all this," Braern sighed, shaking his head.

"There's no need to make a decision now."

"Would it hurt him? Taking his soul out?" he pressed. Adrissu hesitated—he did not think so, but he wasn't certain.

"No, it wouldn't," he said, more decisively than he felt. "I don't think he would even be aware of it."

"What would happen to it? Can you just... stick a soul in a jar?"

Adrissu laughed in dark amusement at the suggestion. "No, it's unfortunately not so simple. I've only been able to do it with precious gems as a conduit for the magic. So his soul would be in such a gem."

"And his body?"

"It would stay alive, as if he were sleeping. I'm not sure if it would age. I haven't done anything long-term yet."

Braern's eyes narrowed. "You just want to do it as an experiment, don't you?"

Adrissu smiled wryly. "I can't get anything past you."

"I... This is all a lot to think about," Braern sighed, running a hand through his hair anxiously.

"Like I said, we don't need to decide to do anything now," Adrissu murmured, reaching over to clasp his other hand. "Just something to consider. And if you think of what, exactly, you *do* want to do, we'll do that. I promise. I won't do anything that you don't want me to do."

A small smile played at the edges of Braern's mouth. "I know," he said softly. "That's not what I'm worried about. Truly."

"Are you worried?"

Braern laughed, tossing his head back. "We're discussing possibly killing my husband. So yes, I'm a little worried." The grin on his face faltered slightly, and he added in a more serious tone, "In truth, I'm worried he might show up before I've made a decision, and then I'll be forced to choose."

"I understand," Adrissu murmured, squeezing his hand. "I won't let him find you. I'll keep you safe."

Braern nodded silently, his eyes unfocused. "Maybe don't get rid of the bond just yet," he said softly, barely above a whisper. "That way, if he does turn up... We'll have at least a bit of a warning. I'll know if he's close. It lasts up to about a mile or so."

That could be helpful if it came down to it. Adrissu nodded, still holding the elf's hand in his own. "I'll keep you safe," he repeated.

Braern was quiet for a long moment, then he moved to sit in Adrissu's lap, pressing his face into the crook between his neck and shoulder. Adrissu wrapped his arms around him, squeezing his waist and rubbing his back with one hand in a slow, soothing motion.

"I love you," Braern said, barely above a whisper against his skin, and Adrissu froze. Braern had not said it before. Slowly, Adrissu smiled and pulled back a bit to look Braern in the face; the elf's cheeks were flushed, but he met Adrissu's gaze earnestly.

"I love you too," Adrissu replied, leaning in to kiss him. There had never been any doubt in his mind that Braern *did* love him, but to hear it in his mate's own voice was a soothing balm, easing a tension that he had been unconscious of until now. "And I'm proud of you. For doing this, all of this. It took a lot of bravery to reach this point."

"I don't feel brave," Braern replied, shaking his head with a bitter laugh. "But thank you. If anything, you're the one who makes me brave. If it weren't for you, I don't know what I would have done."

Adrissu shrugged. "You still would have come to Polimnos. You still would have gotten away. You didn't even think I was real when you decided to come here. Everything up to now has been because of your own strength."

Braern's face had flushed warmer and warmer as he spoke, the tips of his ears red, but an expression of pride on his face.

"Maybe," he relented, laughing. A darker look gleamed in his eyes, and he removed himself from Adrissu's lap only to drop to his knees in front of him. "Let me show you how much I love you."

Adrissu grinned, all his teeth showing. He spread his legs, and Braern shifted to kneel between them. "Please, show me."

After that conversation, Adrissu didn't want to push the matter too hard and did not mention it again for a long while, so Braern could consider the information. Similar to his approach with Ruan and the ritual, he set a schedule for himself, asking every few months if Braern had decided how he wanted to handle the problem of Lorsan. But the elf remained uncertain, so he always let the subject drop without pressing him for an answer.

They had lived together in Polimnos for nearly a year when a sudden sense of foreboding prickled up Adrissu's spine, making all the hairs on the back of his neck stand on end. An instant later, Vesper uncurled from Braern's lap and looked up abruptly, her beady eyes wide as she craned her head toward a nearby window. *Danger!*

"Braern," Adrissu said quickly, trying to sound calm, even as he leapt to his feet to look out the window. "There's a dragon approaching. Go to your room and lock the door."

"I—What?" Braern stammered, eyes wide. He had been with Adrissu in the study, reading aloud from a book of poetry, but had taken a short break to brew a fresh pot of tea, still steaming on the table next to them. "My room?"

"Yes," Adrissu said, scanning the sky. He did not see the dragon, but felt them approaching as surely as if he were tracking the movement with his eyes. "Until I can find out who they are and why they're here. They can sense me too, surely. And if they know what's good for them they will turn around and pass by Polimnos, instead of cutting over it, but..." He could not finish the sentence. If some dragon had truly come for nefarious purposes, being behind a locked door in a tower was unlikely to protect Braern more than Adrissu's presence—but the thought of Volkmar and the cruel way Naydruun had looked at him entered his mind's eye, as freshly as if it had only happened a day ago instead of a century.

The sense of the approaching dragon did not grow any smaller or go away. Behind him, he heard Braern get to his feet, but then sensed how he hovered nervously in the doorframe, as if trying to think of what to say.

"Adrissu," he finally said, a worried edge to his voice. Adrissu could practically see the way his brows knit together in concern, even with his back turned. "Why would a dragon come here?"

Countless possibilities were already going through his head. The most likely, Adrissu thought, was that either Naydruun or Heriel had come for some reason: to take back the bowl they had given him, or to express some dissatisfaction with his choice of mate, the way Naydruun had when they first met. But it just as easily could have been one of his ancestors, come for some reason still unknown to him. It was less likely, but not impossible.

"I don't know," he finally said, still peering through the window. "I'll get you as soon as I know it's safe."

Again Braern was silent for a long, lingering moment. "Okay," he finally said, and Adrissu could hear his padding footsteps head through the hallway and up the stairs. He listened intently until he heard the door close and the lock click into place above him, before hurrying out of the study and heading down the stairs. Vesper started following him; he pointed at her with an unspoken command to protect the tower, and Braern above all else, and did not need to look back at her to sense her understanding.

The dragon was not leaving, it seemed, so he left the tower, locking the heavy wooden door behind him. Like Braern's room, if some wayward dragon truly wanted to try and attack him, or claim his hoard, a locked door would do little to stop it; but the thought of leaving it unlocked felt somehow more vulnerable.

Whatever this dragon was, they evidently were not flying, so Adrissu stopped looking toward the sky and peered down the hill into the campus grounds that he could see from his home. At this distance, he couldn't make out any specific figures, though he did see a few people walking around; his eyes flickered between each of them in turn, until they alighted on one he recognized, heading for the path that would lead up to his tower.

It looked like a tall human woman with short-cropped blonde hair. Heriel. Adrissu sighed, irritation and unease making his heart leap up into his throat. His last encounter with a dragon, Naydruun, had been a disaster; though over a century ago, for this meeting to be with their mate, turning up unannounced on his doorstep, did not bode well.

She seemed to catch sight of him as she started up the stone path up to his tower, but did not slow down. He folded his arms across his chest, silently watching her approach. Now that she was in *his* territory, he hoped she felt all the discomfort and nervousness that he himself had felt when he had presented himself at her home, nearly two hundred years ago now.

"Heriel," he said curtly, as she got within earshot. She took a few more steps, but stopped a sizable distance from him.

"Zamnes," she replied evenly, and he had to stop himself from flinching at the name. "Forgive me for the... unannounced visit."

"Can I help you?" he asked brusquely. From the way she hesitated, he knew that Naydruun had told her about their stilted interaction so long ago. Though whether her visit was due to this, or some other reason, he had not quite determined.

He had no idea why else she might be here, but he would entertain the thought until she proved otherwise.

"May I come in?" she asked, gesturing toward his tower, and his eyes narrowed.

"No," he replied. "Whatever you have to say to me can be said out here."

Heriel sighed, looking irritated. "I allowed you into my home."

Adrissu scoffed. "You allowed me into the facade of a home. It was an empty room, hardly a home."

She frowned, but clearly had no rebuttal. So after a beat, she leaned back with her arms folded across her own chest, mirroring his body language.

"I had hoped to come speak with you," she said slowly. "My mate Naydruun told me some... disturbing things when they returned to me from their travels."

This time Adrissu did not stop himself from rolling his eyes. It was his home, after all, and she was the one who had to be respectful; he was under no such obligation. "Is that so?"

"I wanted to see for myself what the truth was," she said. Adrissu raised an eyebrow and gestured for her to continue. Her eyes were dark and searching, as she seemed to consider what she would say, then she pressed, "Naydruun told me your mate was a human."

Adrissu sighed, leaning back on his heels, considering what to say. To lie would be pointless, but to tell her that his mate was, in fact, now an elf: that felt like giving too much information to someone who likely did not have his or Braern's best interests in mind.

"My mate was human at the time, yes," he finally settled on. "Although Naydruun's presence caused a... sequence of events that eventually killed him."

A series of expressions crossed Heriel's face all at once, but she caught herself quickly, reining in her expression, until only lingering hints of surprise remained. "Did the ritual work, then? On a human?"

Adrissu scowled. "It did."

"A human," Heriel repeated, and this time the revulsion was obvious in her voice. "To think a dragon would debase themself in such a way."

Anger flared in Adrissu's chest, hot and bright. "I did not lie when I told you we were a fated pair. I didn't expect it to happen with a human, either, but it did. And as long as you're here, in *my* territory, you will not use that tone for my mate."

Her mouth clamped down into a tight line, her eyes becoming hard and cold. He wanted to kill her then. She was disrespectful, and she *was* in his territory, so he would be entirely justified under draconic custom to attack her now. Two thoughts stilled the rage pulsing through him: she *had* given him the dwarven beryl bowl that allowed him to perform the ritual in the first place; and the more pressing thought, if they started to fight now, all of Polimnos would see two dragons scuffling at his doorstep. That was the last thing he needed on top of everything else. So he stifled his anger, but maintained his cold glare down at her.

"Give me my bowl back," she finally said, a forced coolness to her voice. "You don't deserve to keep it."

Again Adrissu rolled his eyes. The request, though reasonable, reeked of juvenile pettiness. But if giving it to her would get her to leave, it would be a small price to pay.

"Stay here," he said, watching her with narrowed eyes as he took a few steps back, not turning to face the tower until he felt his foot make contact with the first stone step.

He unlocked the door and ducked inside quickly, taking the stairs two at a time as he headed up to his study. Vesper watched him suspiciously from the top of the stairs.

"Just me," he sighed, stepping over her. "She'll be gone soon."

"Adrissu?" Braern's voice called from above. "Is everything alright?"

"It's alright, love," he answered, though he could hear the sharp edge in his own voice, in spite of his attempts at reassurance. "I'm just getting something. Stay up there a little longer. I'll be right back." The elf did not answer, but Adrissu could hear the dull sound of his footsteps pacing the floor above.

Though his study was not as neat and tidy as it had been when he lived alone, all his most valuable components were carefully documented and organized, the dwarven beryl bowl among them. He found the crate where it was stored, wrapped in parchment paper that was tied neatly with twine, and did not bother to put the crate back in its place as he carried the little bowl back down and out the door.

Closer, Vesper warned, just in time for him to open the door and see that Heriel had walked nearer, now only six feet from the doorway.

"Here," he said, holding it out to her unceremoniously. She snatched it from his hand and made a big show of unwrapping it, until the deep red of the beryl peeked out from beneath the plain paper, sparkling in the sunlight. Her hands stilled, as she looked at it for a moment—then, just as quickly, she re-wrapped it and placed it in the traveling bag slung around her shoulder.

"You will be hated for this," she finally said, looking back up into his face. Something in her expression seemed less hard, less cruel, but he did not know what that meant. "Any dragon who finds out about this will shun you at best, or try to kill you and your mate, at worst. To allow a human to know our ways..."

"I have no desire to be part of draconic society," he replied curtly, but she shook her head.

"It's not only about that," she said, her voice dropping low and urgent. "If it gets out how few dragon souls there really are in the world—what you've done, bringing a human into our cycle, it could unbalance everything. It could spur mortals into a real effort to eradicate us once and for all."

Adrissu scoffed. The belief that there were only a handful of dragon souls in existence at any one time—no more than a hundred, which simply cycled through different bodies to be reborn when one dragon was slain—had gained some traction in the past centuries amongst draconic society. But as far as

Adrissu was concerned, there was no evidence that pointed toward such a belief being rooted in reality. He put no stock in such a superstition.

"I cannot say I share your belief that the souls of our kind have a limited number," he replied, and she scoffed. "And obviously my mate has no desire to see me harmed or found out. If mortals do decide to someday mount a true defense against the presence of dragons in the world, it will not be because of me. I have lived here in peace as an elf for nearly two hundred years, and I have no intention of doing anything else for several more generations."

Heriel shook her head, eyes growing cold again. "On your own head be it, then," she sighed, taking a step back while still facing him. "Naydruun is more honorable than I, and promised not to spread word of your... unusual situation. I make no such promise. If any other dragons grow suspicious of you, Zamnes, I will not deny what I've learned here. I would advise you to make your position as an elven scholar a permanent one."

The unspoken threat hung heavy in the air between them.

"Luckily, I have no desire or intention of being part of draconic society, as I said before," Adrissu growled, anger flaring up again. He had treated her with such respect when he was in her territory, and this was how she repaid him? Threatening him on his own doorstep? "Let me make you a promise as well, one I made to Naydruun. I have not harmed either them, nor you, out of respect and gratitude for the kindness you showed me. In light of that I'll let you leave, despite how rudely you've behaved here today."

She opened her mouth to protest, but he lifted a silencing hand and continued before she could speak. "But just as I told Naydruun, if I ever see you again, I *will* kill you. I do not care what you did for me before, not any longer. You've made your true colors known, and I have no more qualms about whatever misplaced loyalty I might have thought you deserved. Our business is done, and you will no longer be welcome in my territory. Either of you."

Heriel's face had flushed red—probably with anger, but a small, petty part of him hoped she felt ashamed of how far she'd overstepped the boundaries that draconic custom had placed on her in their interaction.

"Go," he said curtly, turning away. "Before I change my mind."

Chapter Twenty-Six

Adrissu was on edge for several days after his unpleasant interaction with Heriel, but luckily neither she, nor any other dragons came again. For now, at least, it seemed he could continue to live his life in peace.

The next week, Braern slept in later than usual, and he was irritable and tired when he woke. When he did get up, he sat on the edge of the bed for a long moment, squinting and blinking in the morning light; then he scowled, groaned, and pressed his hands to his face.

"What's the matter?" Adrissu asked, frowning. "Are you sick?" Braern did not reply at first, so Adrissu took a step toward him, reaching out to feel his forehead—but Braern swatted his hand away quickly.

"It's not that," he muttered, though his face looked warm. "I just... I'm going into heat. It's been over a year so it took me by surprise, I guess."

Adrissu froze, his hand still hovering in the air between them, as he processed Braern's words. He had known male elves went through heats, of course, but had not entirely known what to expect. With how long they'd been together, he had quietly thought that perhaps Braern did not go into heat any longer, since he had mentioned not being able to conceive, and Adrissu did not want to make him uncomfortable by asking about it. But evidently, he had been wrong.

"I see," Adrissu finally said, shaking himself and sitting down next to Braern. "Well... I don't entirely know what to expect. What will you need from me?"

"I'm just going to be a horny mess," Braern sighed, folding his arms across his chest. "Probably by the end of the day, or maybe tomorrow morning, is when it will be the worst. But mine usually only last a day or so."

"I'll clear my schedule tomorrow and the day after, then," Adrissu said. Braern shook his head.

"No, no, it's okay," he stammered, his face burning red. "If you don't want to—I can just deal with it on my own. I'll be alright. It's uncomfortable, but I can just hide out in my room—"

"Why?" Adrissu asked, unable to mask the surprise in his voice. "I do want to. Do you not want my help?"

"I don't want you to have to rearrange your schedule for me," Braern murmured, looking down at his feet. "It's... embarrassing, I guess."

"Braern," Adrissu said, and the elf glanced up at him nervously. "Do you really think I would rather go to work than spend an entire day fucking you senseless?"

He had not thought it possible for Braern to blush any darker, but somehow the elf managed it. "I—I suppose not."

"If you don't want my help, then I'll let you do whatever it is you need to do for yourself," Adrissu said, raising his hands in a placating gesture. "But it is no inconvenience to me, so if you *do* want me there, I'm more than—"

"Please," Braern blurted out before he could finish, grabbing his hands. "It's so much worse alone."

Adrissu could not stop himself from chuckling, despite Braern's scowl. "I'd be happy to. I promise." He wrapped one arm around Braern, and the elf leaned closer to him. He felt warmer than usual, but not quite feverish. "Is there anything you need now?"

Braern shook his head. "I'll still be alright for the rest of the day, I think. It's usually best to rest up the day before it really hits, though, for... both of us."

Adrissu chuckled again. "Well, I'll still drop by the academy in the afternoon so they know not to expect me for the next few days. And I'll be sure to rest, and to hydrate." He grinned salaciously at Braern, whose flushed face went a shade pinker.

They went about the rest of their day in much the same way; when Adrissu left after lunch to spend a few hours at the academy, Braern was curled on the couch and wrapped in a blanket with Vesper as he flipped listlessly through a book. When he returned just before sunset, Braern was still on the couch, but had tossed the blanket to the floor and lay sleeping, Vesper coiled on the ground beneath him.

Sick, she thought, starting to slither toward him, as he hung up his cloak and took off his boots.

"He's not sick," Adrissu whispered, patting her head lightly. "He'll be okay." She felt doubtful, but when he gestured for her to go upstairs to his study, she obeyed.

Braern was still asleep on the couch, laying on his back with his head tossed to one side, hair splayed messily around him. Adrissu approached, and even from a few steps away he could clearly see the outline of the elf's hard cock pressing against his breeches. Maybe his heat had already begun.

Adrissu knelt next to him and situated himself comfortably, pulling off his outer robe and folding it neatly before pushing it under the couch, then untying the laces of his trousers so they would be easy to remove. He turned toward Braern's sleeping form and clasped the waistband of his pants.

Braern woke with a start. "A-Adrissu," he stammered, starting to push himself up into a sitting position.

"Shh," Adrissu replied, pushing him back down with one hand. Braern started to sit up again, confusion on his face—then Adrissu palmed his erection through his clothes, and Braern moaned, shuddering, and fell back down against the couch. "It's started?"

Limply, Braern shook his head, allowing Adrissu to undress him now. "No—not quite. Probably tomorrow morning."

Adrissu wasn't sure if he believed him. Braern's cock was rock-hard and sprang up eagerly when Adrissu pulled his pants down. There was a damp spot in the seat of his underwear, and his inner thighs glistened with his own slick. He even smelled different now—less herbal and more musky.

"What's all this, then?" he murmured teasingly, running one hand up Braern's thigh. A soft sigh of pleasure escaped from the elf's lips before he answered.

"It's not *just* that," he said. "It makes me feel different, too. It's hard to explain, I guess, but—oh, *fuck*."

Adrissu had taken the head of his cock into his mouth, sucking it gently. Already he tasted salty with precome, and he could feel Braern's length twitching frantically, as if he'd been teasing him for hours already.

"Adrissu," Braern whined, one hand grasping mindlessly at the pillow behind his head, and the other coming up to the back of Adrissu's neck. He slowly lowered his mouth around Braern's cock, until he felt the tip of it press to the back of his throat. "Gods, this feels so good."

Adrissu only made a soft noise of agreement, making Braern moan and rock his hips. He had come undone so quickly, already panting and flushed with desire. If this was before his heat even started, Adrissu couldn't imagine what it would be like when it truly began.

His own body had responded in kind, his cock hard and eager beneath his loosened trousers; but if it would only get more intense, he would wait before he allowed himself to come. Instead, he slid his fingers in the cleft of Braern's ass; the elf whimpered and spread his legs wider. Adrissu found his entrance easily, and there was no resistance as he slipped one finger inside.

"Fuck!" Braern hissed, bucking against him as if it had been his cock that pressed inside him, instead of a single digit. He groaned as Adrissu added a second, then slapped a hand to his mouth to stifle a cry as a third slipped in just as effortlessly. His entire body trembled with each drag of Adrissu's tongue against the underside of his cock, and his insides felt hotter and wetter against his fingers than usual. "Fuck, Adrissu, I'm close."

Adrissu made an encouraging noise in the back of his throat, sucking harder and thrusting in and out of him with long, slow strokes of his fingers. Braern moaned, his cock pulsing hard before flooding Adrissu's mouth with come. That was much more than usual, too; though Adrissu tried to swallow each spurt, some still overflowed and spilled from his lips, dripping down his chin. Braern whimpered when his cock finally stopped shooting, and Adrissu pulled away to wipe his mouth.

"Your—your hand," Braern moaned, rocking his hips to push Adrissu's fingers deeper inside him.

"Still want more?" Adrissu murmured, easing his fingers in and out. Braern nodded desperately, biting his lip and squeezing his eyes shut.

"Please," he whimpered. "Adrissu, please."

"Good boy," he said, and stifled a smug grin as Braern clenched and pulsed around his fingers. "Asking so nicely. So politely. Even though you want it so badly, don't you?"

"Yes," Braern panted. "Yes, p-please."

Adrissu crooked his fingers, feeling for the most sensitive spot inside him. Braern gasped as his fingers brushed against it; what was normally a soft, tender spot that was difficult to feel, now was prominent and swollen against his fingertip. Adrissu hesitated, not expecting it to feel different. He did not want to hurt Braern, but the elf groaned and rocked against him, desperate for stimulation.

"Don't stop," he whined. Adrissu nodded, and experimentally rubbed his fingers against the hard nub in slow circles. Braern shuddered around him, gasping and moaning with the movement. "Gods, yes, please, r-right there—harder, Adrissu, harder, please!"

A desperate edge was in his voice now, so Adrissu obeyed, pressing harder and stroking relentlessly against the tender spot until his slick channel tightened and clenched around his fingers. Braern wailed, bucking his hips against him as his cock twitched against his stomach; rather than shooting his load this time, though, it was steadily dripping thick, pearly drops into a puddle on his stomach.

"Gods, you're incredible," Adrissu murmured, watching him come again and trying to ignore his own aching cock.

"A-Again," Braern stammered hoarsely, eyelids fluttering. "Again."

"Again?" Adrissu repeated, half in disbelief. Braern nodded, so Adrissu started to finger-fuck him in earnest. The lewd, wet sounds of his fingers thrusting in and out of him were barely audible over Braern's fevered cries of pleasure. Adrissu brushed against the hard nub inside him again, shifting the angle of his hand so he hit it each time that he pushed further inside. His wrist ached, but it only took a moment longer for Braern to seize around him—his entire body shuddered, and his cries became strangled. This time, as he came, his cock only twitched wildly against his abdomen, nothing left in him to spend.

When the tight ring of Braern's asshole finally stopped twitching against his fingers, Adrissu asked softly, "More?" If Braern did still want more, he did not think that he would be able to stop himself from pulling his cock out and sinking it into the elf's needy, pliant hole. Luckily, this time he finally shook his head, a weak smile crossing his features.

"N-No," he panted. "I'm—I'm okay now."

Adrissu nodded, then eased his fingers out. His entire hand glistened with Braern's natural lubrication, and he met Braern's eyes as he pushed his fingers into his mouth and licked them clean, the heady taste of his mate filling his senses.

"If I was deep in it, I'd definitely want you to keep going," Braern groaned, letting his head fall back. "You'll have to know when to tell me no more, though, to—to sleep, and eat. Okay?"

"I can do that," Adrissu promised.

Adrissu woke in the middle of the night to a heavy, warm weight on him. Disoriented at first, he struggled against it, only to realize it was Braern, climbing on top of him.

"Adrissu," he said, his voice a breathy whine. There was an urgency in his tone that was strange and unfamiliar. "Please—I need—"

"I have you," Adrissu murmured, running his hands up the length of his bare thighs and letting his fingernails drag against Braern's soft skin to feel him shiver. "I'm here. Whatever you need."

"Please," Braern said softly, rocking his hips. His body was warm to the touch, and his cock was already slick with precome where it rubbed against Adrissu's stomach. With one hand Adrissu held him at the base of his cock, as his other hand ran soothing circles along his thigh. He stroked slowly but firmly, squeezing harder around the head. Braern groaned, his hips grinding down harder into Adrissu's groin.

"Come on," he panted.

"Let me make you come first," Adrissu urged. His own body, still recovering from waking in such surprise, had not quite responded the way Braern wanted. But already his cock felt heavier between his legs, and Braern was clearly in no state to wait even a moment for him to be ready.

Braern made a faint noise of frustration in the back of his throat, but nodded, leaning back slightly to push his cock harder against Adrissu's hand.

There was no point in being tender or romantic now, he thought. Braern would only want to come, over and over again, until his heat had passed. So Adrissu wasted no time, immediately stroking him hard and fast. Braern yelped, shuddering, his fingers digging into Adrissu's thighs where he had braced himself. It took only a moment to finish him off. He came loudly, his head falling forward as he moaned, as his cock seized in Adrissu's hand and shot a few stripes of come up his chest. It twitched against his palm for nearly a minute longer, as Adrissu continued to squeeze and stroke him slowly.

"Ready for me?" Adrissu murmured. His cock was rock-hard and eager now, seeing Braern come undone so easily. The elf nodded eagerly. In the moonlight his dark eyes shone with lust, and he made no move to resist as Adrissu pushed him off and positioned him onto his hands and knees, moaning faintly as Adrissu manhandled him.

"Please come inside me," Braern begged, lifting his ass high in the air as Adrissu settled on his knees behind him. "Please."

Adrissu groaned, spreading his ass cheeks apart; the elf's slick had thoroughly coated his ass and inner thighs, glistening in the moonlight. Braern was more than ready for him. "Gods, I'm going to enjoy you."

"Please," Braern repeated. That was all the invitation he needed; in one smooth movement, he pressed the head of his cock to Braern's entrance and slid inside. Adrissu gasped at the wet heat that surrounded him, nearly sucking him in as he buried himself to the hilt. Braern made a noise of such visceral relief that Adrissu thought he might have come already.

"You feel so fucking good," Adrissu groaned, grabbing Braern by the hips and rutting into him with short, sharp strokes. "This is what you wanted, wasn't it? My cock so deep inside you."

"Nnngh," was all that Braern could manage, though he nodded weakly. "H-Harder."

"No," Adrissu sighed, closing his eyes. "No, I'm going to take my time with you." Beneath him Braern whimpered, but made no other protest. He had never been so... *agreeable.* He was fiery, stubborn, as he had been in all his lives. Adrissu did not expect or even want Braern's constant submission, but there was certainly an appeal to how compliant and needy he now was.

He released Braern's hip with one hand and took a fistful of his hair right near the nape of his neck, pulling his head back. Again, the elf submitted to him utterly, giving no resistance as Adrissu moved his body to his own liking.

"Fuck," Braern panted, as Adrissu felt him tighten around his cock. "Fuck, you're going to make me come."

"Good boy," Adrissu purred, and that was more than enough. Braern clenched and shuddered around him, moaning as he came; barely a dribble escaped his cock, but he felt all at once tighter and wetter around Adrissu.

"D-Don't stop," the elf managed to gasp, even as his thighs trembled against Adrissu's. "Please—don't stop—I need you—come inside me."

"I will, sweet boy," Adrissu groaned, closing his eyes. His pace so far had been rhythmic and even, but now it started to stutter, growing frantic as he drew nearer to the edge. "I want to feel you come again first, though, can you do that for me?"

Braern groaned, and Adrissu could feel his hesitance. He had come a third time so easily, even before his heat had fully begun, but now he seemed uncertain. Adrissu pulled his hair harder, leaning down as he did, so his mouth was right against Braern's ear.

"Don't you want me to come inside you?" he murmured. Braern whimpered, shuddering against him. "Don't you want to come again for me?"

"Touch me," Braern gasped. Wordlessly, Adrissu obeyed, releasing his hold on the elf's hair and skimming his fingertips along the length of his spine before reaching down to grasp his cock. Braern grunted and shifted his hips to rut into Adrissu's hand, gasping as the angle that Adrissu entered him shifted along with them. "T-There, right there."

"I feel you," Adrissu panted, stroking him roughly in time with his short, hard thrusts. The front of his thighs felt slippery against Braern's—coated with the slick that was still leaking steadily from him. "Gods, you feel so good."

"I can't—I can't," Braern said. There was an anguished edge to his voice, as if he could not bear the thought that Adrissu would not come if he didn't first.

"You don't want me to come inside you?" Adrissu teased.

"Please," Braern begged him. As much as he enjoyed teasing him, having Braern beg was going straight to his cock.

"Then hold still," Adrissu said, gripping Braern's hips tighter and fucking him harder; the lewd sound of his thighs slapping against Braern's ass nearly drowning out the elf's cries. "Fuck—I'm close."

"Please," Braern begged again, pushing his hips back to meet each of Adrissu's thrusts. "Please, Adrissu, please."

It was more than he could bear. His orgasm came rushing over him too quick to stop, and his hips stuttered and stilled as he buried himself as deeply as he could.

"*Yes,*" he felt more than heard Braern gasping, his cock twitching in his hand. "Gods, yes, *yes—*"

Braern came as Adrissu filled him, which sent another bolt of pleasure shooting up his spine and through his cock. Panting, he leaned heavily against Braern, whose limbs trembled as he struggled to stay on his hands and knees.

"You've been bad," he sighed, though he ran his fingernails up and down Braern's back as he said it. "Told you you had to come first."

"Sorry," he panted, his words slurring. Slowly, Adrissu leaned back, easing out of him—Braern followed rapidly. "N-No!" he whined, trying to keep Adrissu inside him. He grabbed Braern's hips to still him as he pulled all the way out, a thick rivulet of his come mixed with Braern's lubrication dripping down his cock as he did.

"You have to rest," he said, even as Braern whimpered and tried to back himself up against Adrissu again. "Let's clean you up, alright?"

Adrissu thought he might still resist, stubborn as he was. However, after only a moment of sulky silence, Braern obeyed: he waited as Adrissu went to clean himself, then allowed Adrissu to wipe him clean with a damp cloth.

"Drink," Adrissu said, pushing a cup of water into his hands. Braern's face was flushed, but his eyes seemed brighter and more alert now.

"You don't have to boss me around," Braern muttered, but he took the water and drank it anyway. Adrissu grinned down at him.

"I think I like this," he murmured, running his hand through the elf's hair, damp with sweat along his hairline. Braern grumbled, but leaned into the touch. Neither had bothered with clothes; the elf's cock was still hard and ready between his legs, though his half-lidded eyes and sweat-dampened face made him look exhausted.

"I hate it," Braern muttered, setting down the now-empty cup.

"Try to rest," Adrissu said, pushing him back to lay on the bed. "You'll feel better when you sleep."

Braern grumbled, but closed his eyes. His mutterings trailed off quickly; he must have been just as exhausted as he looked.

Adrissu looked down at him until he was sure that the elf was truly asleep, then leaned back with a sigh and drank deeply of his own cup of water. Enjoyable as that had been, an entire day of the same thing was... daunting. He would need his rest just as much as Braern, so he laid back down next to him, arms wrapped protectively around the elf's waist, and listened to the deep, slow cadence of his breath until sleep took him again.

The day passed with a similar rhythm: they would sleep for a few hours, Braern would usually wake first, they'd fuck until Adrissu could no longer keep up, then they'd wash and eat and drink and fall back asleep. They had cycled through this a few times when early in the afternoon, Braern shook him awake with a different request.

"I want your true form," the elf was saying breathlessly, the absurdity of it snapping Adrissu to wakefulness.

"Absolutely not," he answered out of instinct, frowning. He had never expressed any interest in Adrissu's draconic form outside of the one time that he had asked to see; it must be his heat, Adrissu thought, clouding his judgment.

"You've done it before," Braern pouted. "When I was... well, before. I want it."

"Even in heat, I'd rip you apart," Adrissu sighed, shaking his head again. "No, Braern."

"*Please*," Braern repeated, grip tightening on his arm. "Just to try. I know you liked it."

"Not enough to risk hurting you, love," Adrissu sighed, gathering the elf into his arms. Despite his frown, Braern relaxed in his grip, his body warm and pliant against Adrissu's. "What else can I do for you, hm?"

By that point they were both tired and sore, so Adrissu used his fingers instead to make Braern come. After, he doubled over on himself with a groan of distinct pain, rather than pleasure.

"Are you all right?" Adrissu asked, frowning; still doubled over, Braern nodded.

"Sore," he said, after a moment of catching his breath. "T-That's all."

"My poor boy," Adrissu murmured, rubbing the tense muscles of his abdomen with one hand, while carefully easing the other out of his asshole. Braern sucked in a sharp breath through his teeth, before meeting Adrissu's eyes, a chagrined smile wavering on his face.

"This is always the worst part," he groaned, slowly pushing himself back up into a normal sitting position. "When it starts hurting like this, but I still want it."

"Let's get you something to eat and drink, then maybe a warm bath will help," Adrissu said, and Braern nodded.

Braern was quiet as Adrissu fed him and gave him a glass of water, watching him with dark eyes as he did the same for himself.

"You know," Braern said, the smirk obvious in his voice, as he watched Adrissu gulp down some water. "I bet this would be less tiring for you if you were a dragon." Despite himself, Adrissu laughed, wiping his face as he set down his cup.

"You're not wrong," he laughed, shaking his head.

"Then just do that," Braern pushed, leaning closer to him. "You're not an elf. You're not built for this. But if you were a dragon—"

"I don't think you understand just how *much* bigger I would be," Adrissu said quickly. "You're already in pain. The novelty of it would be exciting, of course, but afterward you'd be in even more pain." Braern's face shadowed with disappointment, but he didn't reply. Adrissu eyed him for a long moment before speaking again. "Not this time, Braern. I will maybe consider it for the future. With some extra planning, maybe. I don't think you'd ever be able to truly take my cock in that form, no matter how much you wanted it, but maybe we could figure something out. But not now, not in the state we're both in at this point."

Braern looked at him blankly for a long moment, then a slow smile spread across his face.

"Next time," he said, sounding all too satisfied at the prospect of it. Adrissu shook his head, but didn't bother to correct him. "Okay. I can live with that."

"Now, how about that bath?" Adrissu said, standing up; and with the same self-satisfied grin, Braern followed.

The warm water was obviously soothing to the worn elf, who made soft noises of pleasure and appreciation as Adrissu bathed him—paying special attention to the tense, aching muscles of his abdomen and lower back. When Adrissu joined him in the bath, though, Braern's interest immediately shifted. An apologetic grin crossed his face even as his eyes darkened with lust.

"Sorry," he murmured, as he leaned closer to Adrissu, the water splashing around them. "I know you're tired."

"Don't apologize," Adrissu said, pulling Braern into his lap. "Come here."

Over and over Braern whined that his fingers were not enough—even when four were buried to the last knuckle in Braern's slick hole, and the elf was moaning and writhing on top of him–but Adrissu's cock was utterly spent. He teased two weak, shuddering orgasms out of the elf this way, before Braern was too sore and tired to continue.

For all that the experience was utterly exhausting for each of them, when the sun set and they once again got into bed,

Adrissu watched Braern fall into a deep sleep and thought that he could live with this and be happy. An excuse once a year or so to be completely alone with his mate, doing nothing but following his most primal urges? To eat and sleep and fuck, and nothing else? Not that he really needed an excuse for such a thing, but it was appealing all the same.

Yes, he could gladly do this for a long time. Maybe forever. Hopefully forever.

Chapter Twenty-Seven

By the next day, Braern was mostly back to normal. His heat usually lasted a day, he explained, and he counted himself lucky for it; some elves had it closer to two, or even three days, which sounded miserable. Enjoyable as some parts of it had been, Adrissu was mostly glad to resume their daily life. Braern was quieter than usual the day after, mostly tired, but also seemingly embarrassed or uncertain whether Adrissu's opinion of him might have changed. The day after that, he had largely returned to his normal self, even going with Adrissu to the academy to help him catch up on the work that he'd missed.

Life settled back into their normal routines; but more than ever, Adrissu wanted to ask Braern to let him find a dragon to put his soul into, so that they would not have to be apart again. While a century was not an impossible length of time to spend alone, if Adrissu could avoid it, then that was certainly preferable. And as tolerable as Braern's heat had been for him, the elf clearly found it a hassle at best. What was the point in dealing with it every year if he could not bear children? Adrissu could make Braern like him, allowing him to take the form of an elf without any of their body's unusual inconveniences. He was thinking of it more and more after that first heat, and he finally managed the courage to broach the subject a few weeks after.

"Do you remember the trick I mentioned we could do to Lorsan, if he were to ever show up?" Adrissu asked, keeping his tone light as he watched Braern from across their dinner table at the end of their meal. Braern raised his head, mid-bite, with an inquisitive look on his face.

"Of course I remember," he said, covering his mouth. "I still haven't really come to a decision about it, I suppose."

"I wanted to ask you something different this time," Adrissu replied, taking a steadying breath. He was suddenly nervous. It felt altogether too much like the time he and Ruan had fought about the first ritual: how Ruan had so stubbornly dug in his heels whenever it came up. He mentally prepared himself to be refused, the way Ruan had always refused him, but quietly hoped that maybe this would be different—maybe now that he'd done it twice, Braern might be more amenable to the idea of not having to die again.

"What is it?" Braern asked after a few seconds of silence, sounding unsure.

"How would you feel about something similar on—well, on yourself?" Adrissu asked. Braern's eyes went wide, startled, and he added quickly, "Not in the way we discussed for Lorsan, no. But taking your soul and putting it in something more... more permanent."

"I don't understand," Braern replied, shaking his head. Adrissu bit his lip—for all the time he had spent turning the idea over and over in his head, that was the best he could come up with?

"Let me start over," he said, sighing. "We have only discussed using this soul transference technique in a... weaponized way. But we could also use it to swap souls between bodies. I... I missed you very much in the hundred years we were apart, and if we could avoid having to wait through such a thing again, wouldn't you prefer not to be apart?"

From the way Braern's expression had changed from bewilderment to concern, Adrissu knew Braern understood what he was suggesting. The elf was silent for a long moment, looking down at his nearly empty plate, and considered the information. Nervously Adrissu added, "If I were to... make you a dragon, like me, you would not have to change your appearance at all. Any dragon can take a humanoid form and make it appear however they wish. And you wouldn't have to deal with heats again, or your bond—any of that. It would truly be a clean break from everything."

"That's an awful lot to drop on me over dinner," Braern sighed, leaning back in his chair. Despite himself, Adrissu chuckled nervously, and Braern echoed it with a sharp, breathless laugh. "So we would—what, take my soul out and stick it in a dragon's body?"

"Exactly," Adrissu said, perking up; he didn't refuse outright, so that must have been a good sign. "That's exactly what I was considering."

"Where would we get a dragon body to do this, though?" Braern asked, frowning. "I mean, even if I wanted to—and I'm not saying anything either way yet—but even if I wanted to, how would we go about something like that?"

Adrissu hesitated. That *would* be the most difficult part, of course, but not prohibitively so. It would take some careful planning, but Adrissu had a solid idea of where all the nearest dragons were—their best bet would probably be one of the younger ones, who were about his age and unmated. There were three he could think of within a few days of travel: a green, a gold, and a red. The red was the youngest, only about a hundred: just old enough to have set out on his own, but not old enough to have gained any significant strength or power. The green was a female, so probably not ideal for Braern. The gold was a bit older than Adrissu and had a similar interest in magic, which meant he might be strong enough to seriously threaten Adrissu's life; they would need a meticulous plan to incapacitate him.

"It would be tricky," he admitted, considering his words. "But I have a few different dragons in mind that we could probably, ah, procure without too much difficulty."

Braern nodded slowly in acknowledgment, but the same frown lingered on his face. Adrissu waited, watching him anxiously as he mulled it over.

"I don't think so, Adrissu," he finally said in a soft voice, and Adrissu sighed, deflating into his seat. "That's just... a really big deal. Becoming a dragon. I don't think I would *want* to be immortal."

"Even if it meant we would be together? That you wouldn't have to keep dying and coming back?" Adrissu pressed. Braern winced. He was unsure how much Braern recalled about his past deaths, but he did have at least some memory of them, and Adrissu doubted they were pleasant.

"It's not so bad," Braern said, despite his expression. "At least, I don't think it is. Not yet. Who knows, Adrissu? Ask me again when I'm older. For now, I don't think I want to."

It was unsurprising, almost exactly what Ruan had told him. But he had in time changed Ruan's mind—maybe he would eventually change Braern's, too.

"Of course," Adrissu said after a beat of silence, standing to take his dishes to the wash basin. "I understand. Just something to consider."

He could feel Braern watching him as he stepped away, but he did not look back, fearing his face might betray the mix of emotions swirling in his chest. He knew he would have to be patient; still, the rejection stung.

But by the time Braern had come to stand next to him, placing his own dishes in the wash basin, Adrissu managed a fond smile at him; and after a moment of hesitation, the elf smiled back.

"You're not upset?" he said softly, leaning against Adrissu, who sighed and wrapped one arm around the elf's shoulders.

"It's not what I wanted to hear," he said, considering his words. "But how could I be upset with you? I learned a long time ago that you're going to do what you want to do. I can tell you what I want all day long, but in the end, you've always been stubborn. If you don't want to, you won't. If eventually you come to the conclusion you *do* want to, you will. There's little I could do or say to really change your mind."

"I'm not *that* stubborn," Braern said, stifling a smile. He pressed closer to Adrissu, wrapping his arms around the dragon's slim waist and burying his face in his shoulder. "I love you."

"I'll always love you," Adrissu murmured, squeezing him. "Even when we're apart, I'll love you."

Life went on, as it always did. The academy took up most of Adrissu's time, but Braern was often there with him, so they never had to spend too much time apart. Adrissu would occasionally ask if his feelings had changed at all about the soul transference ritual; they never did, but Braern never seemed uncomfortable with the conversation.

In his own time, Braern was working on a book of elven poetry. As was the elvish custom, he hand-made the paper and bound the booklet himself, carefully sewing the reams together with a thick needle and red thread. Then he carefully transferred the poems that he'd written in a careful, even script, using some of the finest inks Adrissu owned.

He worked on the project for several months, but when he was done, he presented it to Adrissu with a wide grin.

"It's done," he said softly, beaming with joy, as Adrissu carefully flipped through the pages. The swirls of fanciful elvish script made Adrissu's heart swell with pride; he thought of Ruan, who could not read at all for so much of his life, and marveled at how far his mate had come since then.

"You should be very proud," he said, smiling softly back at Braern. "Why don't you hold a reading? I'm sure plenty of people would come to listen."

Braern shook his head. "It's for you," he said, folding his hands over Adrissu's, as if to signify his ownership over the book. "You're the only one I care about reading any of it."

Adrissu's heart skipped a beat again. He knew they were mostly love poems, of course, but he had not thought the book itself was for him alone. He nodded silently and looked down at the book in his hands, his vision swimming, unsure of how to respond.

"Thank you, love," he finally managed, his voice rough. Next to him Braern laughed, pressing closer to him and hugging him tightly.

"It's all for you," he repeated softly against Adrissu's ear. "It's always for you."

When Adrissu had read all the poems, he carefully displayed the book in his study, atop a shelf that was just beneath Ruan's shield still mounted on the wall. He had something to remember Ruan, and now Braern. He still had most of Volkmar's belongings, but even after all these years, those somehow felt too painful to look at. Maybe someday he would go through it all, find one of his favorite paintings, and set that up somewhere. It would be nice, he thought, to have something on display from each of his mate's lives. It would be better for Braern to stay with him forever; but if he could not convince the elf, then he could look at the things that had been left behind, and remember, and wait.

A month or so after Braern's second heat, a little over two years since they had been together, a crash from the kitchen startled Adrissu out of his studies. His head snapped up, immediately alert, and an instant later, a wail rose up from the lower floor.

"A-Adrissu!"

Braern's voice was not startled or upset, but absolutely *terrified*. Adrissu was at the stairway in an instant, looking down into the lower floor; he could not quite see into the kitchen, but could hear Braern's frantic breath and a scuffling sound, as if he were struggling to walk.

"What happened?" Adrissu called, hurrying down the steps as Braern emerged from the kitchen. His face was pale and his hands trembled as he reached for Adrissu.

"He's here," Braern sobbed. His hands were cold as he clutched at Adrissu's robes. "He's here—he's here, I felt him—

he found me."

Adrissu froze, processing. His shock lasted only a moment, though; without even having to think, he knew what he was going to do. The man who had hurt his mate was near, somewhere in Polimnos, and Adrissu was going to end things. A cold calm settled over him as he grasped Braern's trembling hand with his own, swishing the other to gather up the pieces of the broken plate that Braern must have dropped and sending the mess into the trash chute.

"Can you tell where he is?" he asked softly, holding Braern but leaning back enough to look into the elf's eyes. For all his panic, Braern managed to stay focused on him—his gaze wide and fearful, but completely locked on Adrissu.

"No," he croaked, shaking his head. "Just—he's close. Somewhere in the city. A mile or so."

"A mile," Adrissu repeated, mapping out Polimnos in his mind. Nothing of note was to the north of the tower, and to the east was the ocean. The school surrounded his tower to the south and west, but not so far out. The town square, with all the inns and the main road, was to the southwest, further than a mile. If the elf had found out about Adrissu, it would have been easy to find the tower, and he could already be making his way up the main road toward them.

"Braern, listen to me," he said, his voice low and even. His calm tone surprised even himself; Braern blinked up at him, as if Adrissu's relaxed tone shocked him as well. "I know we discussed this before. But you don't have time to be unsure anymore. I'm making this decision for us. I'm cutting off your bond, now, so that you won't feel anything that happens to him in the future."

Braern's eyebrows knit together, his hands trembling anew in Adrissu's grip—but after a beat, he gave an almost imperceptible nod. Adrissu released him to place one hand on the elf's temple, just beneath his hairline.

Adrissu closed his eyes and carefully reached out with his magic. The tingling warmth of Braern's life force was familiar now, and he could easily hone in on the bond in the back of his skull: the singular point that resonated differently to the touch of his magic. He had the faintest sense of whatever it was being *aware* of him—then he surrounded it, found the tether that linked it to the elf he had never met, and smothered it until the strange resonance that resisted him was crushed.

Braern hissed in pain; Adrissu felt him flinch, but not enough to pull away. That was all it took for Braern to now be unmarried by elven law: it was so simple that for a moment Adrissu hated himself for not simply doing it of his own accord sooner, and he wondered why Braern had been so reticent for so long. But when he opened his eyes again and let his magic fall away, Braern's eyes were still squeezed shut, and a small stream of blood was trickling from his nose down his lips.

"Are you in pain?" Adrissu asked, frowning as he swiped at the trickle of blood with one finger. There was not a lot of blood, but still he had not expected it. Braern slowly opened his eyes, breathing hard and shaking his head as he reached up with one hand to touch his nose. He blinked down at his fingertips when they came away with blood, before absently wiping his hand on his robes.

"It stung at first," he said, his voice stronger, but still tremulous. "But I'm alright now."

"I think it's safe to say he felt that as well," Adrissu said, releasing Braern to stride toward the front door, locking it. "My guess is that he somehow knows you're here, with me, and is already on his way here. Vesper!"

He could feel the snake watching him with uncertainty from the top of the landing, but when he called, she started thudding down the stairs.

"Guard the door, Vesper, and stay close to me when our *guest* arrives," he said, and obediently Vesper headed toward it.

"What are we doing?" Braern asked softly, still standing where Adrissu had left him. When he glanced back over at the elf, for a moment he looked like a lost child, afraid and unsure. Adrissu's chest boiled with hate—somehow, someone had hurt

Braern so badly that his mere proximity was enough to fill his mate with terror. But he was going to make him pay.

"I am making a decision for us," Adrissu continued briskly, heading for the stairs. The necessary alchemical ingredients were all in his study, but the gem that he needed was down in his lair. "And I am doing exactly what we discussed doing. When he arrives, I'm going to take his soul from his body, so he can't harm you ever again."

Braern's expression twisted in a way that Adrissu could not quite place; but then he nodded, once, holding Adrissu's gaze. His agreement sent a wave of relief through Adrissu, even through the cold calm that had otherwise overtaken his body. He managed a tight smile, before turning away to head up the stairs and into his study, gathering the materials that he would need. He was sure Lorsan would turn up at their doorstep before long, so he moved quickly.

When he arrived back down on the first floor, Braern sat rigidly on the chaise lounge in the front room, still looking shaken. Adrissu set down the crate of his supplies on the table before him, then knelt at Braern's side, meeting his eyes.

"I'm going to let him in here when he arrives," he said, voice still low. "Do you want to wait in our room? You don't have to see him at all if you don't want to. But I need to let him in here to get him down into the lair."

Braern shuddered, glancing away nervously. "No, I—I want to be here," he finally said, after taking in a shuddering breath. "I want him to know this was my decision."

Adrissu looked up at him silently for a long moment, considering. Despite the obvious fear in his voice, Braern now met his gaze steadily, and a slow smile crept across Adrissu's face.

"Brave boy," he murmured, leaning up to kiss him softly. "I'm going to go stand outside. I'd expect him to come up the main road, so I'll keep an eye out."

"Alright," Braern murmured, nodding once. "I... I'll be here, I suppose."

"You can change your mind, if you want," Adrissu said as he stood. "There's no shame in it."

"I won't," Braern said firmly, and he managed a weak smile at Adrissu.

When Adrissu stepped outside, he could feel Vesper's fierce protectiveness well within his own chest—wanting to keep Braern safe just as much as he did. It was a small comfort to know that she was just behind the door, only feet from Braern, watching over him.

He pushed all distractions from his mind as he took a few steps away from the tower, surveying the town below. From the hill, he had a wide view of the city, though the academy grounds on all sides blocked most of the view to the west. He stood, hands clasped behind his back, and waited.

Just as he had suspected, it did not take long for a figure to become visible coming up the path. At first, it was simply a shape with no distinguishing features, formless amidst all the other humans that he could barely make out milling about town. There was no indication it was an elf, or the man Adrissu was waiting for, but as the figure continued up the path to Adrissu's tower, his eyes followed their path with cold interest. The figure did not turn down a side street or veer away down a different path; and by the time they had passed the last fork in the road, continuing their course toward Saltspire Tower, Adrissu knew it was him.

Lorsan was tall for an elf, probably of a height with Adrissu. He looked like a merchant, wearing traveling clothes that were finely made, though slightly faded and worn. When he got close enough for his features to be visible, he caught sight of Adrissu at the top of the hill and stopped in his tracks.

A streak of blood was smeared between his nostril and upper lip—he must have begun bleeding from his nose, the way Braern had, and hastily wiped it away. His eyes were dark, as was his hair, which was quite long and tied back in a low ponytail. Hesitation was obvious on his face even from a distance: the thought that he'd hoped to have some element of surprise was darkly amusing to Adrissu, but he kept his expression as one of cool indifference. The bastard had no idea what was coming for him.

Lorsan remained where he was for a few seconds, eyes narrowing as he seemed to consider his options—then he continued to walk up the path, scowling and keeping his eyes on Adrissu the whole time. His features became clearer as he approached, and Adrissu was struck that he did not look particularly cruel. He had imagined the man as some caricature of an abuser, bigger and stronger than Braern, with a perpetual snarl and beady, brutish eyes. But he looked like every other elf that Adrissu had met: a pretty face with an air of arrogance, but nothing more unforgivable than that.

Then Lorsan, now within earshot, opened his mouth. "You know who I am, don't you?" he shouted in elvish, sneering up at Adrissu; and in that moment Adrissu could see him exactly for what he was.

A cold smirk spread across his lips. "I do," he called back, his voice even and calm as ever.

"Fucking bastard," he heard Lorsan say, quieter, but not so low that he could not catch it. Then, raising his voice, "Where's my fucking husband?"

This time Adrissu waited until he was close, then gestured to the tower behind him with a grin that showed all his teeth. "Why don't you come inside?"

Chapter Twenty-Eight

Braern still sat in the front room when Adrissu swung the door open, a resolute expression on his face that faltered as his eyes moved from Adrissu to the elf behind him.

Adrissu felt Lorsan starting to push past him at the same moment that Braern rose to his feet; he reached out, one hand slamming into Lorsan's chest to keep him in place. The elf swore under his breath, but Adrissu took a step to put himself between his mate and Lorsan, who seemed to take the message and did not try to get past him again.

"Now," he said primly, and the door slammed shut behind them. He felt more than saw Lorsan give a start, and he stifled a grin as the elf hissed in surprise. Vesper had closed the door behind them, and her unexpected presence was—he hoped—terrifying to Lorsan. "Why don't we discuss this like adults?"

"Oh, fuck you," Lorsan muttered, surprising Adrissu with how bold he was despite the giant snake that watched his every move. "You think you can make a cuckold of me and then try to talk this out like *adults*?"

"Lorsan," Braern said quickly; his voice did not waver, making Adrissu's heart bubble with pride. "You shouldn't have come here."

"That's rich, coming from you," Lorsan snorted, stepping closer to Braern. This time, Adrissu let him. "Thought I couldn't find you? Thought I'd just let you do whatever the hell you wanted?"

"I thought you'd take the hint," he muttered, shrinking back as Lorsan stepped closer.

"I considered it," the elf hissed. "Then I felt every fucking second of your heat, both of them, and *that* was the last straw."

Braern's face went pale. "You—You could feel it?"

"Surprise, huh?" he said. "Fucking triggered my own, too, which only pissed me off more. But it let me figure out which direction you'd gone. I suspected, but that only confirmed it." A cruel grin split his features. "And now here I am."

"And you suffered through those heats alone, then?" Adrissu said, reveling in the way Lorsan's expression faltered with obvious irritation. When he did not reply, Adrissu sighed. "I see. And, of course, it was only wrong for Braern to have a partner through his, but not for you."

"It's *different*," Lorsan spat, whirling on him. "I don't need to hear anything from you, you bastard."

"Leave him alone," Braern protested, straightening as his eyes flashed in anger.

"Are you the one that did this?" Lorsan said, ignoring Braern to glare at Adrissu, gesturing at his nosebleed. This time Adrissu did not try to stifle the smug smile that crept along his face.

"I did," he replied, relishing in the rage that twisted the elf's face. He could have ended this the moment Lorsan stepped inside his tower, but there was a playfulness to their exchange that he was still enjoying. "As you might have heard, I am something of a prodigy. I am the headmaster of the Polimnos Academy of Magic, and this is a title I earned through prowess. Removing the... unfortunate bond that you and Braern shared was a simple task, once he agreed to it."

Lorsan's expression had become darker and angrier the longer Adrissu had spoken, but his own smile had only become wider.

"Bastard," the elf muttered again, looking back toward Braern.

"What do you want, Lorsan?" Braern interjected, frowning. "What did you even hope to do by coming here? I'm not going back with you. There's nothing you could say that would convince me of that."

"Not even if your mother is ill, on her deathbed?" Lorsan retorted, and Braern's determined expression faltered once again. "Would you turn away what is perhaps your last chance to say goodbye? Don't you think it would hearten her, to see her baby boy happy with his husband one last time?"

"I—" Braern stammered, eyes sliding away nervously. "I—"

"This has gone on long enough," Adrissu sighed, stepping closer to Lorsan. Whether or not there was any truth to what Lorsan said, he would not let him try to manipulate Braern any further. Lorsan started to round on him, fury plain in his face, but Adrissu grasped him firmly by the back of his neck—this close, he could tell Lorsan was a tiny bit taller than him—and hissed, "*Be still.*"

His magic seized Lorsan's frame, freezing his muscles where he stood. Lorsan made a choked sound, as if trying to speak or make a noise of surprise, but he remained helpless to Adrissu's command.

"Braern," Adrissu said evenly. The elf's eyes flickered between Adrissu and Lorsan's still form. "I'm ending this now. If you'd like to help me, bring me the crate on the table, and we'll go down into my lair. Otherwise, I will take him down myself, and I'll return when I'm done."

Braern hesitated. Adrissu's heart squeezed: if Braern still had some lingering affection for this man that made it too difficult to help Adrissu with his task, he could not exactly begrudge him of his feelings, but it still felt like a blow. Then Braern took in a deep breath, visibly steeling himself, and stood.

"I'm going with you," he said softly, meeting his eyes. Adrissu smiled. How could he have doubted his mate?

Braern gathered the crate into his arms as Adrissu pushed Lorsan's rigid form toward the trap door. When Adrissu pulled it open, a choked sound came from Lorsan's throat—when

Braern stepped over to him with the supplies in his arms, and Adrissu kissed him, he made another faint noise of protest. Adrissu could feel him straining against the spell, but his magic held fast. His lips curled into a smile against Braern's.

"Let's go," he murmured against Braern's ear, gathering the elf into one arm. With the other he reached out and grabbed the lapel of Lorsan's robe. Once they were both secure in his grasp, he pulled them down with him into the drop.

There was a particular gratification to releasing both elves from his claws when they reached the bottom. Braern easily found his footing, looking up at his true form with an expression of adoration; and beside him, Lorsan lay rigidly on the floor—eyes wide, breathing rapid and shallow, stifled cries barely audible from the back of his throat.

"You have *no* idea what you walked into," Adrissu growled, his features split with a toothy grin, as tears started to stream down Lorsan's unmoving face.

They set to work; Adrissu did not bother to change back, and Braern handed him things out of the crate as needed. None were so small and fiddly that it would be easier to do in his elven form, and the abject terror radiating from Lorsan was reason enough to remain as he was.

When it was mostly done, Adrissu turned to Braern. "Wait here," he rumbled, and Braern nodded. He turned and crawled to the innermost chamber of his lair, where the bulk of his wealth was stored. It had all been carefully organized at first, but over the decades this chamber had become more and more of a mess. All the gold was generally in the same place, but much of the other riches—gems and stonework and pottery—had been strewn about over time, and little of it remained in its original holding place.

It took only a moment of digging through his gems to find one that would work for the ritual. Adrissu was loath to use something valuable on the wretched elf, but the soul of a sapient creature would require a much larger gem to house it than the ones that he'd used in his experiments. At least the amethyst that he selected was common enough, and this one was large and clear with an odd shape that made it rather ugly.

When he arrived back in the main chamber, Braern was staring down at Lorsan's still-unmoving body with an expression that Adrissu couldn't place. But he looked up as Adrissu approached, a relieved smile crossing his face.

"Is everything ready?" he asked, looking up at Adrissu.

It struck him, then, how full of trust Braern's eyes were. He looked up at a dragon—an immortal creature so much larger than him that Adrissu could have killed him in an instant—and he did not so much as flinch. They were here not to kill his former partner, but perhaps do something worse, trapping his soul in a gem for eternity. Yet Braern looked up at him with eyes full of love and trust, with no fear of him, nor the power he wielded.

Slowly he leaned down, lowering his head until it was level with Braern. The elf smiled at him, half-laughing before reaching out toward him, pressing both hands beneath Adrissu's chin to hold his head in place.

"What is it?" he said softly, his voice a faint breeze against Adrissu's scales. Adrissu made a low, rumbling noise of contentment that resonated through the cavern.

"You are so strong," he murmured, and felt more than saw Braern smile. "And I love you."

"I love you too," Braern replied, stepping away. "Let's finish this, then."

Adrissu nodded, then turned back to the body on the ground. Lorsan's eyes quivered in their sockets, struggling to move, yet desperate to see. With a smirk, Adrissu leaned down close to him and hissed, "I'm going to be the last thing you ever see, you piece of shit."

The elf, of course, did not react, though his eyeballs seemed to quiver more frantically. Adrissu straightened up, the gem in one claw, and looked back toward Braern.

"We need to knock him out," he said, his voice a deep growl. "I won't be able to keep him paralyzed while casting the ritual."

Braern hesitated, looking down at the motionless elf.

"Do you want me to do it?" Adrissu asked. He was slightly unsure if he could knock out the elf without killing him, but he would try it if Braern could not.

But then Braern shook his head, and he silently turned to the cavern wall, searching. After a moment he leaned down, then straightened, carrying a rock large enough that he had to hold it with both hands.

"I can do it," he said firmly. Adrissu's trepidation must have been obvious on his face.

"Here," he said, holding down Lorsan's torso with his other claw to keep the elf's arms pinned to his sides. "Be ready to drop that once I say."

Braern nodded, then took a position behind Lorsan and lifted the rock above his head.

"Now," Adrissu growled, releasing his magical hold on the elf. He felt Lorsan's body shudder beneath his claw.

"Braern," the elf cried, immediately starting to struggle. "I'm sorry, please—I'll go, I'm so sorry, please just let me go—"

But Braern's face had twisted, and he threw the rock down onto Lorsan's skull with a resounding crack that echoed ominously through the cavern; and the elf's pleas died away. Adrissu kept his claw over his limp body for a moment, making sure—he could barely feel the rise and fall of his chest, still breathing, but there seemed to be no consciousness as his muscles went slack.

"Good job," he said, glancing up at Braern, who was backing away. The elf's expression was pinched, and his eyes remained on Lorsan's unconscious, bleeding face; but he nodded sharply in acknowledgement of Adrissu's praise. If he was having mixed feelings about what he'd done, or what they were doing, Adrissu supposed he couldn't fault him for it. So without saying anything else, he lifted his claw away to mark the ground around the unconscious elf with the necessary runes. It would be a quick process now.

"Back up a little more," he warned Braern. The elf nodded, stepping away until his back was against the wall of the lair. Adrissu nodded, then turned his attention down to the unconscious elf.

Looming over him, he pressed the amethyst to Lorsan's chest, making sure that the broadest side of the crystal was in direct contact with his skin. Then he closed his eyes, concentrating, and reached through the crystal and into his consciousness.

Rooting around his mind did not feel especially different from the few, brief instances that he'd touched Braern's mind in the same way. Somehow, the thought unsettled him, wishing the sensations were as distinctly different as the elves themselves. With the tendril of magic he could feel where the elf's memories would be, the center of his emotions—and a little deeper down, the strange tingling sensation of what was a creature's very essence, the spark of magic within that fueled every other process.

With his own magic he grasped that deepest core, loosening it from where it sat and tugging it forward. There was some resistance, which was different from his previous attempts with animals; but it was barely enough to register, and certainly not enough to stop him. With some careful pulling and guiding, he eased the soul out of its body; when it was halfway between them and fully ensconced in the amethyst, Adrissu lifted the gem away to break contact with the skin, and at the same moment he released his grasp on the elf's soul.

The runes around them flared and burned away, echoed by a light that burst within the crystal for a moment, then ebbed and flickered out. Adrissu pulled it up closer to his eyes—looking carefully, he could see faint glimmers of light from within, barely enough to illuminate the surface. It would never draw the eye of someone who was not already looking for it.

A slow smile spread across his face. It worked. His soul-transference ritual had *worked* on a mortal, an elf; and for an instant, he felt like the most accomplished sorcerer who had ever lived. After all, no one had ever done what he had just performed.

"Is it finished?" Braern asked softly, centering his attention. Adrissu set the gem down on the ground and gestured for him to look.

"It's done," he affirmed, as Braern took a cautious step closer. "See? The body still breathes, but there's nothing there anymore. If you look closely at the gem, you can see the evidence of the soul within."

Braern stopped just short of the body, looking down at it with a dark expression.

"What will you do with it?" he asked, eyes still not leaving the elf. "The soul? The body?"

Adrissu shrugged. "I had no plans for the body. As for the soul, I'll probably hold onto it to see if I can put it back into something, but it will never perish, as long as the gem endures. I can leave it as it is for years, centuries, before trying anything new with it."

"What will happen if the body dies?" Braern asked, his voice rough. Adrissu opened his mouth to answer that the absence of a soul put it in a state of stasis: it would not age nor hunger, and thus would not die—but then he realized what Braern was *truly* asking, and he paused.

"To my understanding, nothing will happen to the soul if the body were to perish," Adrissu replied, and he took a step back, as if giving him permission.

Slowly Braern nodded, still looking down at Lorsan. His face had been carefully neutral during their brief conversation, but now something twisted in his expression—the pull of his mouth, the angle of his eyebrows.

"Do what you need to do, Braern," Adrissu urged him, pressing his body low to the ground, so they were at eye level. "Whatever you want to do, he deserves it."

Braern nodded, a short, sharp movement. He was still for a moment longer, considering; then he quickly reared back one foot and kicked Lorsan in the head, so hard his limp neck twisted to the side, and blood splattered across the stone floor.

After that first kick, something seemed to snap in the elf, and the floodgates were opened. He kicked and stomped, his breaths coming more rapidly at first—then he was grunting in exertion with each kick—then he was screaming, shouting expletives down at the unmoving body.

"That's what you get!" he finally sobbed, stumbling back with his feet covered in blood. Lorsan's face had been thoroughly smashed in; his features now only a mess of meat, and there was no rise and fall to his chest. "That's what you fucking get, you sick bastard, that's what you get for laying your fucking hands on me!"

Adrissu watched silently, his gut twisting at the anguish in Braern's voice and the tears streaking his face. But then Braern looked up at him, eyes bright and glassy, and his scent of grief and anger almost instantly became something softer. Blood and viscera squelched beneath his feet as he stumbled toward Adrissu, wrapping his arms around the dragon's neck and burying his face in the cool, supple scales there.

Adrissu lowered his head to return the embrace, drawing his wings up and around Braern's body, as if he could cocoon him within—as if he could hold him there forever away from the world, from anyone or anything that could harm his mate.

"Adrissu," Braern gasped, his breathing ragged. He pulled away enough to meet Adrissu's eyes. "I need you—now, right now—like this—please."

Adrissu's body responded to Braern's plea so quickly that he had not even processed what he was asking until his cock had already started to emerge, parting the soft slit between his legs.

"Now?" Adrissu rumbled, uncertain. "Are you sure?"

"Please," Braern said again, kissing the spot on his face between the hinge of his jaw and his lower eyelid. "Please."

Adrissu sighed out a long breath. How could he say no? He gathered Braern into his arms and pulled him into the chamber with his hoard. Adrissu set him on his feet and saw that an almost-smug grin had crossed the elf's face, though it became a look of surprise as Braern's eyes flickered around the room, taking in the piles of gold and jewels.

"Lay down," Adrissu murmured, pacing around him to clear the floor. A deep, primal part of him was suddenly nervous to have another living creature in his hoard—but it was his mate, who already owned all that he had. Even as he was pushing the thought away, Braern started undressing, which consumed his attention.

"I bet I could take it, if I was in heat," Braern murmured, as he laid his clothes on the ground and settled onto them, eyeing Adrissu's cock with an all-too-confident grin. "I bet I could."

Adrissu bit back a laugh, shaking his head. He absolutely could *not*, Adrissu was certain; but the thought of Braern stretched impossibly wide around him did have a particular appeal, and his cock twitched with interest. "I don't think so, love."

Adrissu curled around him protectively, as if his naked body were also part of his hoard. Braern settled closer to him, his back against Adrissu's side, as he sighed heavily.

"I love you," Braern murmured, stroking the softer scales on the underside of his belly. Adrissu rumbled deep in his chest in response, curving his long neck around to start licking Braern clean. The elf laughed, startled at first, but made no move to resist. Adrissu started between his neck and shoulders, tasting the sweat and salt of his skin. He could feel the rapid thrum of his heartbeat, still quickened by adrenaline, and kept licking him in slow, long movements until his pulse began to ease back into a more normal rate.

Adrissu moved lower, across his chest and sternum; when his rough tongue passed over Braern's nipples, the elf groaned and squirmed against him, fingernails scraping against his scales. His soft moans coaxed Adrissu's member fully from its sheath. Braern leaned toward it, shifting so that Adrissu's tongue now dragged along his ribs and his back; he began to carefully touch the soft scales on the head, then felt along its length. His hands were small, and his tongue even smaller, but a shiver of pleasure still shot up Adrissu's spine as Braern licked away the bead of precome that had welled up on the tip of his cock.

"Gods, you're boiling hot," Braern groaned, leaning back against Adrissu.

"Spread your legs," Adrissu murmured, and without missing a beat Braern obeyed, spreading his legs wide as Adrissu lowered his head. He first licked one long stripe up the length of Braern's cock, making him gasp; then teased him with smaller licks along the junction of each of his thighs; then tongued his balls and the sensitive skin beneath them.

"Adrissu," Braern panted as Adrissu's tongue dipped lower, tasting his slick that now steadily leaked from his asshole. The fluid had a different taste from the rest of him, salty like his come, but muskier too. "Nngh—there, yes, right there—"

Adrissu groaned as his tongue slid easily into Braern's entrance; he had only intended to lick over it, but his body was so open and ready beneath him that he slipped in effortlessly. Braern moaned; Adrissu gave him a few more exploratory licks, pushing a little deeper each time, until finally he pulled away to growl,

"Touch yourself. I'm going to make you come just like this."

He lowered his head once more as Braern nodded, panting. The elf's fingers brushed against his tongue as he gathered some of his own slick onto his hand, then stifled a cry as Adrissu's tongue plunged into him again at the same moment he began to stroke himself.

Adrissu's tail had curled protectively around Braern's body; with his free hand, the elf absently grasped and squeezed at it, the other working his cock in time with the shallow, quick motions of Adrissu's tongue inside him. The taste of him was addicting: dark and salty and herbal, the way he smelled, only far more concentrated here.

"Adrissu," Braern panted, hips bucking against him. "Fuck, you feel so good."

Adrissu growled, a deep sound from the pit of his chest that reverberated through the room. Braern yelped, tightening around Adrissu's tongue—he liked the danger, Adrissu thought, so he growled again just to hear Braern moan.

"I'm close," Braern said breathlessly, trembling. "D-Don't stop."

Adrissu growled again, wishing he could speak only so he could tell Braern that he absolutely would not stop. But that seemed to be enough—Braern gasped, contracting around him. A flood of slick coated his tongue as Braern came, his hand stuttering to a stop around his cock as he shot his release up his chest.

"I love you," Braern panted, when his body finally shuddered and relaxed around him. "I love you, I love you."

Carefully, Adrissu withdrew, slick and saliva dripping from his maw. "You're mine," he rumbled, nuzzling just under Braern's jaw as he repositioned himself. "I'll never let anyone hurt you again."

"Yours," Braern agreed breathlessly, eyelids flickering. "Yours."

"Don't get too comfortable, I'm not done with you yet," Adrissu teased. He grasped Braern's legs just below the knee to push them up and press his thighs together, careful not to break skin with his claws. "Still want me like this?"

"Gods, yes," Braern laughed, eyes full of adoration as he looked up at Adrissu with a blissed-out smile. "Just like this. Just as you are."

Warmth seeped through every inch of Adrissu's body, as he smiled back down at Braern. His true form should have terrified him—even his smile, with his rows of razor teeth, should have been unsettling—but Braern looked up at him with no less love and affection than he had when they were both elves in his tower bed.

"Mine," Adrissu sighed, lowering himself over Braern's body to push his cock between his thighs. He would never truly fit inside Braern in this form, but his thighs were slick with his own lubrication, and his torso was painted with come, creating enough pressure and friction that Adrissu could rut against him. He could not really be dignified or tender—his body was far too long to look at Braern from this position, and if he was too rough, he could easily crush Braern beneath him. But he could glide his cock through the silky pressure of his legs, and if Braern wanted him this way, then this way he would remain.

"Here," Braern panted, reaching past his bent legs with one hand. "You liked this before, didn't you?" Adrissu groaned as Braern's hands found the base of his cock: the tender fold of skin and scales where his cock emerged from his body and the sensitive flesh within. The elf's fingers skimmed the soft surface, but even that feather-light touch set his body aflame.

"Braern," he moaned, forcing himself not to rut harder against him.

"You do like this," Braern murmured, sounding far too pleased with himself, as he leaned forward to dip his fingers further into the slit. Adrissu grit his teeth, embers fluttering at the back of his throat as pleasure overtook him. Of all the things he could have remembered from his past lives, of course it would be *this*. "I want to watch you come like this, make you come all over me."

"B-Braern," Adrissu grunted again, this time as a warning. He turned his head to the side to try and stifle the threat of his fiery breath that rose in the back of his throat, tongue lolling and claws scrabbling on the stone floor. He was mindless, utterly overcome with the need to mate, to mark. Braern's fingers rubbed insistently at the base of his cock and the sensitive walls around it, and he was undone. Adrissu growled and roared as his orgasm shuddered through him, barely registering Braern's gasp when he pumped his load across the length of his body. This was *his* mate, the most primal part of Adrissu's mind purred—completely and utterly his, marked with his seed and bound to him by fate. He would never let anyone touch him again.

When he could focus, Adrissu pushed himself off Braern with trembling limbs. The same adoring smile was on his face, entirely unbothered with the mess all over his torso and legs—and, Adrissu noticed with a scowl, some even past his head and onto the nearest pile of gems. *That* would be a frustrating clean-up, a problem for the future.

"Dirty boy," he grumbled deep in his chest, then he set to work licking Braern clean again. "You'd die trying to take my cock."

"That doesn't make me want it any less," Braern laughed, catching Adrissu's head between his hands to hold him still as their eyes met. "I love you. I love *this*. I feel like I should... I don't know, be afraid or upset or... Or regret what we did. But I don't, not at all. I want this forever. I want to be bonded to *you*, Adrissu."

Adrissu paused, meeting the elf's earnest gaze for a long moment. The idea of the elven bond was strange to him, but the admission seemed tender and honest. It filled him with affection, knowing Braern had essentially asked for them to be married. The idea of marriage meant nothing in draconic society, which was why in his past lives they had never formally been married, but he knew mortals held the concept in high regard.

Of course, Braern was asking him this *now*, when he had just coated his mate in come—after they had just, essentially, killed his former husband. It was an understandable question, but not something Adrissu thought he should answer anytime soon.

"I have no regrets about this, either," Adrissu replied evenly. "I do not know if such a bond would work between species in this way, but I will consider it. But at the moment, I'm trying to get you cleaned up."

Braern blinked owlishly at him, then a grin split his face as he laughed.

"Well, considering half-elves exist, I'd guess the bond would still work between us," he sighed, settling back and allowing Adrissu to clean him. "Even if not, I'd at least go through the ritual with you. You'd be my husband then."

When he was done, Adrissu let out a long, contented breath as he curled himself protectively around Braern. "Perhaps... that would be nice. Perhaps."

Chapter Twenty-Nine

"Do you think he was telling the truth about my mother?"

The question was barely more than a whisper, much later that night when they were laying in bed. Exhausted from the day's exertion, Adrissu was right on the edge of sleep, but Braern's soft voice pulled him back into consciousness.

After they'd cleaned up, Adrissu had tossed the body out into the ocean far beneath them, carefully set the amethyst inside a metal chest that was placed amongst the rest of his hoard, then carried Braern back up to the tower. By then it was past sundown, and they were both dirty and tired, so they bathed and went right to bed. Evidently, rest was more elusive to Braern than it was to Adrissu.

"That she's sick?" Adrissu asked, his voice rough with sleep. He cleared his throat as he pushed himself into a sitting position, finding Braern curled on his side facing him, eyes gleaming in the moonlight coming in through the window.

"That she's sick," Braern agreed, nodding. His eyebrows were knit together with worry. Adrissu sighed, then reached out to rub his shoulder.

"I don't know," he said. "It's possible, but it's just as likely he was lying to try and lure you back home, away from me."

"Could we... go there? To check?" Braern asked, voice even softer now, as if he were ashamed to ask.

Adrissu was silent for a long moment, gathering his thoughts in the dark.

"Dragons do not have these kinds of relationships with their parents," he finally said, rubbing his eyes wearily. "So I do not understand why your mother being ill would have any bearing on what you do. But if it is important to you—and I can see that it is—then of course we can go. Braern, you do not need to ask me permission for something like that."

A small smile had spread across Braern's face as he spoke.

"I think my parents will like you," he said, and Adrissu scoffed, shaking his head.

"I think they might be concerned if we give them any reason to suspect Lorsan is... gone by our hand," he replied.

"Knowing them, they won't ask questions," Braern said, shaking his head.

"I can fly us there," Adrissu said, settling back down into bed. "If you want to leave soon. I can tell the Academy I'll be gone for a week or two while we check up on them."

"How soon could we go?"

"The day after tomorrow, I think," Adrissu yawned. He felt Braern nod next to him.

"The day after tomorrow, then," he echoed quietly. Neither said anything after that, and by the time Adrissu drifted back off, Braern's breathing had taken on the slow rhythm of sleep.

Two days later, they set out for Aefraya.

Although Braern was nervous about flying for so long, both agreed that the need to get there quickly outweighed his apprehension. So at sunset they went down to Adrissu's lair, and under the cover of night they slipped out over the sea—Braern secured to Adrissu's back as he flew.

"It is *not* a saddle," Adrissu had grumbled, as they affixed the leather straps that would lash them together. "If I hear you call it that, I'm tossing you into the ocean." Braern laughed, and did not call it a saddle.

For all that he trembled and made noises of fear for the first hour or so, Braern soon fell asleep on Adrissu's back, so the night went by quietly. They touched down before dawn in a forested area about a day's walk from Menserine, the city where Braern was from, and where his family still lived. Adrissu did not relish the thought of walking for most of the day, not when he'd already flown through the night, but it was far safer than continuing to fly in broad daylight. They rested for an hour or so in the forest, before heading for the road, which they would follow all the way to the elven city. When they'd been walking along the stone-paved road for about thirty minutes, Braern laced their fingers together, smiling up at Adrissu. Adrissu returned the smile, and they walked hand-in-hand for a long while.

They passed a handful of others, some merchants and some lone travelers: mostly human, but a few elves among them as well. Now late autumn, the majority of travel was winding down before the first snows arrived, so the limited presence of other travelers was expected. Some gave them polite nods or waves, but for the most part they were left alone.

At sunset, they approached the border between Autreth and Aefraya, marked by a large stone tower that served as a checkpoint, with two elven soldiers standing guard. No other travelers were at the checkpoint when they arrived, so one soldier held up a hand as they came into view, partly in greeting and partly to signal that they'd been spotted, Adrissu was sure.

"Greetings," the soldier said as they drew nearer. "State your business, please."

"I am Braern Rolastra," Braern said quickly, before Adrissu could speak. "My... my husband, Adrissu Rolastra, is a citizen of Autreth. We are coming to visit my family, who live in Menserine just up the road."

Adrissu stifled the smile that threatened to split his features. *Adrissu Rolastra*, Braern had called him. It had a nice ring to it. He had never chosen a surname for himself—dragons did not have them, and he had never needed one—but maybe he would take Braern's.

The soldier nodded, first looking Braern up and down, then doing the same to Adrissu—his eyes lingered on Adrissu's face for a beat longer than they had Braern's—perhaps memorizing his features, or searching for some resemblance to wanted criminals, or whoever else such guards might keep watch against. But he did not seem to find whatever he was looking for, and the soldier simply nodded.

"I wouldn't recommend going further into Aefraya without a guard," the soldier told them. "Not sure how long you've been away from home, sir, or how quickly news has traveled, but Prince Ruven is now King Ruven as of last week. And there have been reports of orc scouts pushing further and further in toward the capitol."

"What?" Braern said quickly, visibly shocked. "Is the Queen dead?"

The soldier nodded grimly. "You must've been coming from far into Autreth if that news hadn't reached you yet. Yes, about a week and a half ago, now."

"By the gods, what happened?" Braern asked. The soldier shook his head.

"Nothing official has been released, which doesn't bode well," he sighed, then leaned a bit closer, his voice lowering conspiratorially. "The rumors are that she was poisoned, maybe by someone in her own court. King-Consort Aeroven was suspected, but evidently was cleared of any involvement, and just abdicated to be reinstated as a general. So their son is king now. No one's sure if the orcs were involved, but they've certainly been mounting more and more attacks in just the past week. The roads should be safe enough this close to Autreth, but... Things are tumultuous, to say the least. Be careful out there."

Slowly, Braern nodded, brows still furrowed in uncertainty. "We won't be leaving Menserine, I think. Thank you for the news. I had no idea. Gods, what a week it must have been!"

They walked on, and after a moment Adrissu wrapped an arm around Braern's shoulder, pulling him close.

"What a week it's been," he echoed in a low murmur, and with a bitter laugh, Braern nodded. "That might work out to our advantage, though. Let's say Lorsan confronted us a week or two ago, left before we did, and hasn't been seen since... If everyone knows the roads are dangerous, no one will wonder too much."

Braern was silent as he seemed to consider the alibi. "That does sound feasible."

Adrissu nodded. "Then that's what happened."

"I can't believe the queen is dead," Braern muttered, shaking his head. Adrissu did not have a response, so they walked quietly as the sun set ahead of them.

By the time it had dipped below the horizon, the city gates of Menserine were in view. The gate was open, and although two guards were stationed there, they waved them through silently.

"This way," Braern said, taking Adrissu's hand and leading him along the main road. It seemed similar in size to Polimnos, but was evidently more carefully planned out; rather than a formerly small city that had built outwards as needed, Menserine was intentionally divided into districts that were clearly delineated by the size and appearance of the buildings they passed. The first district that they walked through seemed to be industrial, which gave way to smaller buildings that looked like workshops for artisans and skilled laborers. Next was a market district full of colorful storefronts and market stalls, with more and more elves milling about, shopping or hawking their wares.

Finally, the bright colors faded to a more austere residential district, and it was here that Braern finally veered off the main road. He led Adrissu past wide streets with large homes, to more narrow roads where homes were smaller and closer together. It was here that he finally stopped in front of a house with a pale wooden door, turning to face Adrissu with a nervous expression.

"This is it," he said, squeezing Adrissu's hand hard, before releasing it. "I... Let me do most of the talking, I suppose."

"Of course," Adrissu murmured, nodding. "I'll follow your lead. Whatever you want."

Braern managed a tight smile up at him. "I love you."

Before Adrissu could respond, Braern had turned and was heading up the walkway to the home, a mostly-wooden domicile that appeared tall enough to have a second floor—nothing extravagant by any means, but comfortable and pleasant-looking with a few fruit trees in the fenced-in yard. It was a relief to see that his family at least appeared to be making ends meet.

Braern hesitated at the door, evidently unsure if he should just go in or knock. After a beat, he knocked. Adrissu waited a step behind him, Braern wringing his hands nervously, his attention focused on the closed door in front of them.

It took a few moments, but the metallic sound of the handle soon broke the nervous silence, and the door swung open to reveal an elven man. He did not look any older than Braern, with similar features but lighter eyes and lighter, longer hair. Considering how ageless most elves appeared until they were quite elderly, the man could have been Braern's father, or one of his brothers.

The elf stared at Braern for a long moment, eyes wide, then seemed to visibly shake himself, blinking rapidly. "Braern?"

"Father," Braern said, the word leaving him in a rush. "I—I'm sorry for the unexpected visit."

"No, no, don't apologize," the man said quickly, as he reached out to hug Braern. The elf froze, surprised, then tentatively hugged him back. "Gods, I'm just glad to see you. Your mother will be so happy. Come in, come in."

The man's eyes flickered to Adrissu, as if seeing him for the first time. "Oh—and your, um, friend, too, of course."

Adrissu lowered his head respectfully, an unexpected nervousness in his belly. He had never needed to meet his mate's parents before, and suddenly felt entirely out of place. "Thank you for your hospitality."

"It's a long story," Braern said, before his father could speak. "I'll explain when I see Mother. Is she well?"

"She's well," the man said quickly, looking back at Braern. "Although, she had a long bout of pneumonia a little while back that had us a bit worried. But she's been on the mend for a week or two now."

Braern let out a long, sharp exhale. "I... I see."

Adrissu followed at a polite distance as they were ushered inside. It seemed that while Lorsan had certainly been manipulating Braern to try and get him to return, he had not lied entirely, only exaggerated. Braern looked visibly relieved that his mother was well; Adrissu was glad, but could only focus on how much he still hated the dead elf, who had caused all this stress and worry in the first place.

"Who was it, Aram?" a woman's voice called from further into the house, as the elf—Aram—closed the door behind them.

"It's me, Mother," Braern called before his father could reply. There was a sudden scraping sound, as if she had been sitting in a chair and quickly stood.

"Braern?" her voice repeated as footsteps came from the hallway. A female elf emerged from an archway further down the hall, her hair darker and curlier than Braern's, but with the same large brown eyes. "Oh, it's really you!" She nearly ran, as Braern took a step toward her, each throwing their arms around the other in obvious relief.

"I heard you were ill," Braern's voice came muffled from where his face was pressed into her shoulder. "I'm so glad you're well."

"What are you doing here?" she asked, pulling away to look up at him urgently; she only then seemed to notice Adrissu, giving a slight start as her eyes landed on him. "Oh—who's this?"

"Let's sit down," Braern said, before Adrissu could reply. So they all filed into the room that she had come from: a comfortable-looking living room with a plush couch across from a crackling fireplace and two plain chairs, one of which had a small side table next to it with a mug of tea and an open book. Braern's mother sat in that chair, lifting the mug to her lips as Aram pulled the other chair closer to hers, which left Braern and Adrissu to sit together on the couch.

"We..." Braern started as he sat, then shook his head, a resolute expression crossing his face. "Lorsan found me in Autreth a few weeks ago."

Aram and his wife, whose name Adrissu did not know, exchanged nervous, knowing looks.

"We... talked," Braern continued carefully, glancing sidelong at Adrissu. "And we decided to permanently separate. We're unbonded now."

Slowly Aram nodded, while Braern's mother visibly sighed in relief. "I'm so sorry to have put you through all this, Braern," Aram said in a low voice, brows knit as he looked down at his feet.

"Don't," Braern said quickly, shaking his head. "Don't apologize. None of us could have known what would happen."

"I'm sorry we didn't try harder to get you away from him," his mother said, her voice pained. Aram reached over and squeezed her hand: it seemed to be a conversation they'd had before.

Again, Braern shook his head. "No, I'm sorry I didn't listen to you when you did. I really thought I could... Well, I'm more sorry we parted before the business could be returned to you."

"That doesn't matter," Aram said, his wife nodding next to him. "We've made do without it for years now. You're much more important."

Their contriteness was soothing to Adrissu. Knowing his mate had been an orphan in his first lifetime and lost his parents early in his second, it was comforting to see that in this life, he had two parents who were healthy and cared for him—who could acknowledge their mistakes and work to rectify them. If they had been cruel or cold to Braern, Adrissu wasn't sure what he might have done.

Braern managed a slight smile. "When I was in Autreth, I met Adrissu," he continued, placing a hand on Adrissu's knee. "I... We... Now that Lorsan is out of the picture, we're hoping to marry."

Braern's parents glanced between themselves again, though this time Adrissu could not read their expressions. He softly cleared his throat, and they both looked back over at him.

"Aram," he said carefully, then gestured toward Braern's mother. "And, forgive me, I don't think I caught your name."

"I'm Eleen," she answered primly, her eyes searching as she looked him over.

"Eleen," he repeated, nodding. "I want to start by saying that Braern is already the most important person in the world to me. I want nothing more than to see him safe and happy for the rest of his life. I understand that the circumstances of how we met might not portray me in the most favorable light, but I have only ever had good intentions toward your son, and I will never, *ever* let anyone harm him again. I love him dearly."

For a long moment, they were both silent, looking at him with appraising expressions. Then Eleen lifted her mug of tea to her lips again, hiding a slight smile, and Aram sighed, folding his arms across his chest.

"And what is it that you do, Mr. Adrissu?" he asked. Braern smiled, his chest puffing with pride, but he gestured for Adrissu to answer.

"I am the headmaster of the second largest school of magic in Autreth, the Polimnos Academy of Magic," Adrissu said, lowering his head in an attempt to appear humble, even though his words were anything but. "I have been particularly blessed in my arcane ability, and have spent my life accruing and sharing that knowledge."

Aram nodded, looking sufficiently impressed.

"Well," he said, glancing between his wife and Adrissu. "Much as it pains me to admit, the man we picked for him wasn't exactly a great choice. So if you're who he's choosing, we won't get in your way."

"Thank you for coming to tell us all this in person," Eleen said softly, her eyes becoming watery as she looked at Braern. "If you'd written a letter, I don't know if I would have believed it. Just knowing Lorsan tracked you down... Gods, Braern, I only wish you'd left sooner."

Braern's expression became pained, and he gave a tight nod.

"It's in the past, now," Adrissu said softly, squeezing Braern's knee. He would have to be the one to nudge the conversation to safer territory. "Now that we're here, perhaps we can look into being bonded while we're in town."

All three elves looked at him in surprise, especially Braern, whose mouth dropped open in shock. His flushed cheeks and bright eyes made Adrissu want to kiss him very much, but to do so in front of his parents seemed improper, so he resisted.

"So soon?" Eleen said mildly, as Braern's mouth worked wordlessly. Adrissu shrugged, smiling first at her then back at Braern.

"Why wait?" he countered, and after a moment, Braern burst into laughter.

"That's not—I mean, I hadn't meant so *soon*," he protested, grinning, and again Adrissu shrugged. "But, well... If you're really okay with it..."

"Why wait indeed?" Aram echoed, leaning back in his chair and appraising them with a fond look. "You're welcome to stay here, of course, and tomorrow we can start the preparations."

Chapter Thirty

A week later, Adrissu and Braern were married beneath the tree temple of Menserine.

It was a small, quiet affair with only Braern's family in attendance. They wore robes that were nice, but had been quickly procured and so were not perfectly tailored; the priest that performed the rites was unfamiliar to Braern's family, and he wore the same bored expression for the entire ceremony. Although, at the end, when the priest held each of their wrists and sent his magic flowing through both of them, he gave a slight start—his eyes flew to Adrissu, widening in obvious surprise as he sensed Adrissu's overshadowing power.

The incantation that the priest muttered to link their minds sounded simple, but the heat that traveled up the length of Adrissu's arm to become a pinprick in the back of his head felt deceptively strong. It burned painfully for only an instant, then faded away, leaving behind the strange sense of something, *someone* else in his head. He could, very faintly, feel excitement and nervousness that was not his own simmering away in that spot.

A slow smile spread across his face as Braern beamed up at him, happiness bursting from what must have been their bond. Adrissu didn't hear anything the priest said, focused only on the strange, but not unwelcome awareness of their new mental link. After a moment, Braern released one of his hands and turned to face his family, still grinning, and Adrissu followed suit. The family of elves smiled back at them. Luckily, they all seemed to like Adrissu so far, despite the abruptness of his and Braern's wedding. His choice of husbands could only be an improvement, after all.

The family then gathered in Aram and Eleen's home for a celebratory dinner. Despite all the ruckus of Braern's siblings, nieces, and nephews together under one roof, Adrissu could only focus on Braern—his *husband,* now officially so. The word meant little to Adrissu—Braern's status as his mate, forever, was not at all contingent on whether or not some priest who they would never meet again clasped their hands and performed a ritual over them—but the happiness that burst from Braern at the word was completely infectious. It was strange, though, to think that all married elves had the presence of another in their heads like this.

"Not regretting your decision, are you?" Braern murmured in a teasing tone, leaning closer to him, as they sat beneath a small gazebo in the backyard and looked out on the rest of the family. "You feel... apprehensive."

"Just getting used to it, is all," Adrissu replied, shaking his head with a smirk. "Although... I've just realized it's going to be much harder to convince you I like your cooking, now."

"Adrissu!" Braern laughed, shoving his shoulder playfully. "You'd only eat bread and cheese every day if it wasn't for me. Don't try and pretend otherwise."

Amusement and affection bubbled up from the back of his head. Feeling the emotions, being able to recognize them, yet knowing they were not his own, was probably one of the most unusual sensations that he'd ever felt. He did not think he liked it, but if it would make Braern happy, it was a light burden to bear.

"It does take some getting used to," Braern said softly, his teasing smile melting to one of soft affection. "But it has its benefits."

"Is that so?"

"Oh, yes," Braern said, raising an eyebrow at him. "We can feel what the other is feeling, so..."

Desire bloomed in the back of his head; it wasn't his own, but his body responded as if it were. *That* would be... something to explore later.

"I see," he said, stifling a grin. "In that case, I'm glad we got our own villa for tonight."

"Gods, of course," Braern laughed, shaking his head. "You think I'd want to be under the same roof as my parents on our wedding night?"

"I'd certainly hope not," Adrissu replied. He draped one arm over Braern's shoulders, and the elf leaned against him, a comforting and familiar weight.

They watched in content silence as two of the small elven children, a girl of maybe ten and her younger sister, chased each other in the yard, running in tight circles until it was impossible to tell who was chasing and who was being chased. When they noticed that they were being watched, the two girls grinned over at them and waved. Braern waved readily back at them, and after a moment, Adrissu waved as well.

"Uncle Braern," the older girl asked, stepping closer to him. "Are you going to come live in Menserine again now?"

Braern's smile faltered slightly. "I don't think so, sweet one. But maybe you can visit me and your Uncle Adrissu in Autreth someday."

"Hmm," the girl said with a slight frown; Adrissu could feel the faint sense of longing tinged with sadness that came from Braern at his words, and squeezed his hand.

"Come back inside for dessert," one of Braern's brothers called from the door. The two girls went running, their conversation quickly forgotten, and Adrissu glanced down at Braern.

"Us too?" he asked, and Braern beamed up at him with a laugh.

"Us too."

When the food had all been eaten, and they were released from their familial obligation to be present for their own party, Adrissu and Braern walked back toward the center of town, where they had rented a small villa. The little two-room cottage was one of several on the same plot of land in the same style, but it was the closest thing to privacy that they were going to get without returning home. It certainly beat a room at the tavern, even if it wasn't much bigger.

"Well, husband," Braern said with a teasing tone, grinning over at Adrissu as he closed the door. Adrissu pulled the elf into his arms before he could get any further. Braern laughed, pushing against him. "Is that all it takes, then?"

"Not even that," Adrissu growled against his ear, feeling the elf's smaller form shiver against him. "I've been wanting to get you out of these robes since this morning."

"Such self-restraint," Braern murmured, a smile still spread wide across his face. His hands slipped beneath Adrissu's robe, loosening the sash that held it together as he pulled it open. "I think you've earned a reward for your patience."

"Hmm," Adrissu sighed, closing his eyes. Braern's fingers skimmed along his skin, leaving tingling trails in their wake. "What did you have in mind?"

"Come lay down with me," Braern said; and without waiting for Adrissu to answer, Braern pulled him by the waist toward the bedroom. Together they tumbled into the small bed, narrower than what Adrissu was used to, though they both managed to fit.

"My husband," Braern sighed, smiling as he said it. Adrissu leaned forward to kiss him.

"Yours," he agreed, leaning back as Braern got on top of him, pressing soft kisses along his jaw and his neck. Though the kisses were gentle and chaste, Braern wasted no time, traveling further down Adrissu's torso and pulling open more of the robe as he went, until Adrissu was finally laid bare beneath him.

"I love you," Braern murmured, glancing up at him through his eyelashes for just a moment, before taking Adrissu's cock into his mouth. Adrissu groaned, running his fingers through Braern's hair as the elf sucked up and down his length. His eyes slipped closed; he could feel Braern breathing hard around him, could feel his desire and affection coursing through the back of his head—like the feel of Braern's hands stroking his hair. It was all so *much*, a jumble of his own feelings, and Braern's, and the physical pleasure burning up his spine. He couldn't take it.

"Braern," he panted, fingers tightening around the elf's long hair. He felt Braern still against him, and when he opened his eyes, the elf was looking up at him with an expression that would have been innocent if not for the head of Adrissu's cock still between his lips. Adrissu tugged at the robe that Braern still wore. "Take this off. I want to be inside you."

Braern smiled around his cock; his tongue teased along the head for a moment, before Braern released him with a wet pop and straightened up, untying his own robe.

"You're very convincing," he said, grinning. His eyes were dark, pupils dilated, and he gave no resistance as Adrissu pushed him onto his back and started pulling his clothes off. "It's going to be different, you know."

Adrissu paused, frowning. "Different how?"

"Better, I think," Braern answered. He stretched languidly, now fully naked. "But you'll feel it."

Adrissu hesitated, considering, but whatever Braern meant, he seemed unwilling to elaborate. So instead, Adrissu tossed the robe to the floor, then descended upon him to kiss and lick his way down Braern's chest. Desire vibrated through his body as he moved, impatient, yet wanting to savor each small taste of Braern's skin and memorize the way his body shifted and moved beneath him.

"Come on," Braern urged, lightly tugging on his hair, as he kissed lower down his abdomen. "I want you in me."

Adrissu breathed in his scent deeply, before pushing himself up over the elf. He had wanted to savor this, relish in it, but the bond in the back of his head thrummed with urgent desire, pushing them forward unrelentingly.

"Who am I to tell you no?" Adrissu murmured, looking down at Braern with half-lidded eyes. The elf met his gaze, lips flushed and smiling; but his eyelids fluttered closed as Adrissu pressed his cock against him, lining himself up with his slick opening, before gliding in all the way to the hilt. Both gasped, and heat bloomed deep in the bottom of Adrissu's stomach. It took a moment for the feeling to register—Braern's pleasure echoed in his own, emanating from the back of his head, but heightening the sensations that shivered up his spine.

"Fuck," he panted, stilling almost immediately. Braern grinned, pulsating around him. "That's... different."

"I told you," Braern murmured, reaching up to run his hands up the length of Adrissu's torso. "I told you you'd feel it."

"I do feel it," Adrissu grunted, experimentally moving again and shuddering at the shocks of pleasure that burst from the bond in his head and out through the rest of him. Feeling everything Braern felt while feeling his own body's response, amazing as it was, didn't bode well for his ability to last any significant length of time.

"It's good, right?"

"I think so... It's strange."

He moved his hips in slow, lazy thrusts, closing his eyes to focus on the new source of pleasure. Beneath him Braern panted, shifting to move the angle of his hips and sending a burst of warmth that exploded through Adrissu's vision as Braern groaned, "Right there, right there."

Adrissu stilled, gasping for breath. The onslaught of sensation was driving him to the brink all too quickly. Braern groaned again, though this was now a sound of frustration, rather than pleasure. "Gods, this is too much," Adrissu panted, shaking his head.

"Don't fight it," Braern said, running his fingers through Adrissu's hair. Adrissu sighed, tilting his head to kiss Braern's palm as his hand trailed down his face. "Adrissu. My husband."

That was enough to coax him back into action. Adrissu leaned down to kiss Braern, capturing his lips as he set a quick pace. Pressure built quickly in the pit of his stomach, a different sensation than he was used to, fueled by the feedback loop the new bond created. It took only a moment for him to start coming, their lips still pressed together, stifling his cry. Braern moaned into his mouth, following him over the edge—Adrissu's vision went white with the overwhelming sensation that flooded through their connected minds.

"Adrissu," Braern gasped, shuddering around his length. "Adrissu."

The sound of his name in his mate's voice sent a softer shiver of pleasure down his spine. With one hand he stroked Braern's cock, slowly, until come covered his mate's stomach; Adrissu watched him gasp and writhe, drawing out his orgasm as a hot flood of sensation burst from the back of his head. It was utterly unlike anything Adrissu had ever felt before, so intense it was almost uncomfortable. But he could see why Braern so enjoyed it—and, he thought, he would enjoy it too, when it felt less new and strange.

Afterward, when they were clean and sated, and Braern's head lay on his chest so Adrissu could stroke his hair, Braern whispered softly into the darkness,

"Do you think it'll still be there when I come back? The bond?"

Adrissu sighed, considering. The magic connected their minds, certainly, but Braern's mind would go with him if he died. His soul would linger and find another body, but everything else would be gone.

"I don't think so," Adrissu replied softly. "When you die... *If* you die, there won't be anything for the bond to connect to anymore."

"If I die," Braern echoed. He was silent for a moment, then shifted away from Adrissu, rolling to push himself up on his elbows so he could look up into his face. The moonlight caught his eyes and cut his features in a beautiful profile, and Adrissu could see his soft expression—not quite apprehensive, but he could see the slight tension in his brow even in the darkness. "You still want me to try it. The soul transference."

"Of course I do," Adrissu said, leaning closer. He did not break their eye contact. "Why wouldn't I want you to be with me forever?"

"I *will* be with you forever, even without it," Braern protested. Adrissu sighed again.

"Yes," he said slowly. "But if you were to become immortal like me, then I wouldn't have to suffer through the time we're apart, after you die. Maybe that's selfish of me. But just knowing you'll come back doesn't make it hurt any less when you're gone."

Braern glanced away, a pained expression on his face as he laid back down, still peering over at Adrissu.

"I... I understand," he said softly. "But... I don't know if I can commit to that, Adrissu. Becoming immortal is a huge leap from being... reincarnated. We're not meant to live forever."

Adrissu bit his tongue. The argument seemed flimsy and silly, but at its core, he knew Braern resisted because the idea was too unfamiliar, and the unknown was always a source of fear. He could not blame him—the thought of having one's soul taken from the body and put into another—if someone made *him* the same offer, he would certainly resist, whatever their intentions. If Braern wasn't absolutely certain that he needed to go through such an unknown experience, then Adrissu would not attempt it.

"I cannot force you," Adrissu finally said, running his fingers through Braern's long hair once more. "It will always be on the table, though, Braern. I might ask you again periodically, and you can always tell me no, but it will always be something I want. If you ever change your mind, or just want to talk it out more... You can always come to me about it."

Braern looked up at him with his big, dark eyes for a moment longer, his expression serious and thoughtful. But then his eyes softened, and a smile settled across his features, and he leaned into the spot where Adrissu's fingernails scratched his scalp.

"I know," he replied, as he shifted to lay down on his back once again. "I'll let you know if anything changes."

If anything changes. Adrissu knew the words were only meant to placate him, but he found them unexpectedly hopeful. Their lives had changed so much from his first lifetime, but the important things had not. His mate had a different name, a different face, but was still *him*—stubborn and proud and strong, even if the personality around those core traits changed over time.

The world had changed around them, but the important things had not. His mate was here, with him. Nothing else mattered, as long as his mate was with him; what he looked like, or where they were, or how long they had together, were all of secondary importance.

So, maybe, eventually, Braern would come around, and someday he would have an immortal mate at his side. But for now, his mate was an elf, and his breathing had slowed and deepened as sleep overtook him, the bond going quiet and calm. Adrissu watched him with unbridled adoration for a moment as the moonlight gleamed across his skin, then settled down for bed alongside him. They would remain in Aefraya only another day or two, then he would fly them back to their home in Polimnos to take up their daily lives once more.

This was good, Adrissu thought. Someday it would be better, but he could wait until then.

TO BE CONTINUED

About the Author

Lionel Hart (he/him) is an indie author of MM fantasy romance and paranormal romance. Currently, he resides in north San Diego with his husband and their dog. For personal updates and new releases, follow the links below.

linktr.ee/lionelhart

Twitter: @lionelhart_

Facebook: Lionel Hart, Author

TikTok: @author.lionelhart

Also By Lionel Hart

Chronicles of the Veil
1. The Changeling Prophecy
2. The Drawn Arrow

The Orc Prince Trilogy
1. Claimed by the Orc Prince
2. Blood of the Orc Prince
3. Ascension of the Orc King

Heart of Dragons Duology
1. Beneath His Wings

Printed in Great Britain
by Amazon